# THE BLOOD STONES

## LEGENDS OF THE BRUHAI

## TORI TECKEN

*For Andrew and Tricia Meredith*
*Friends, storytellers, and mentors*

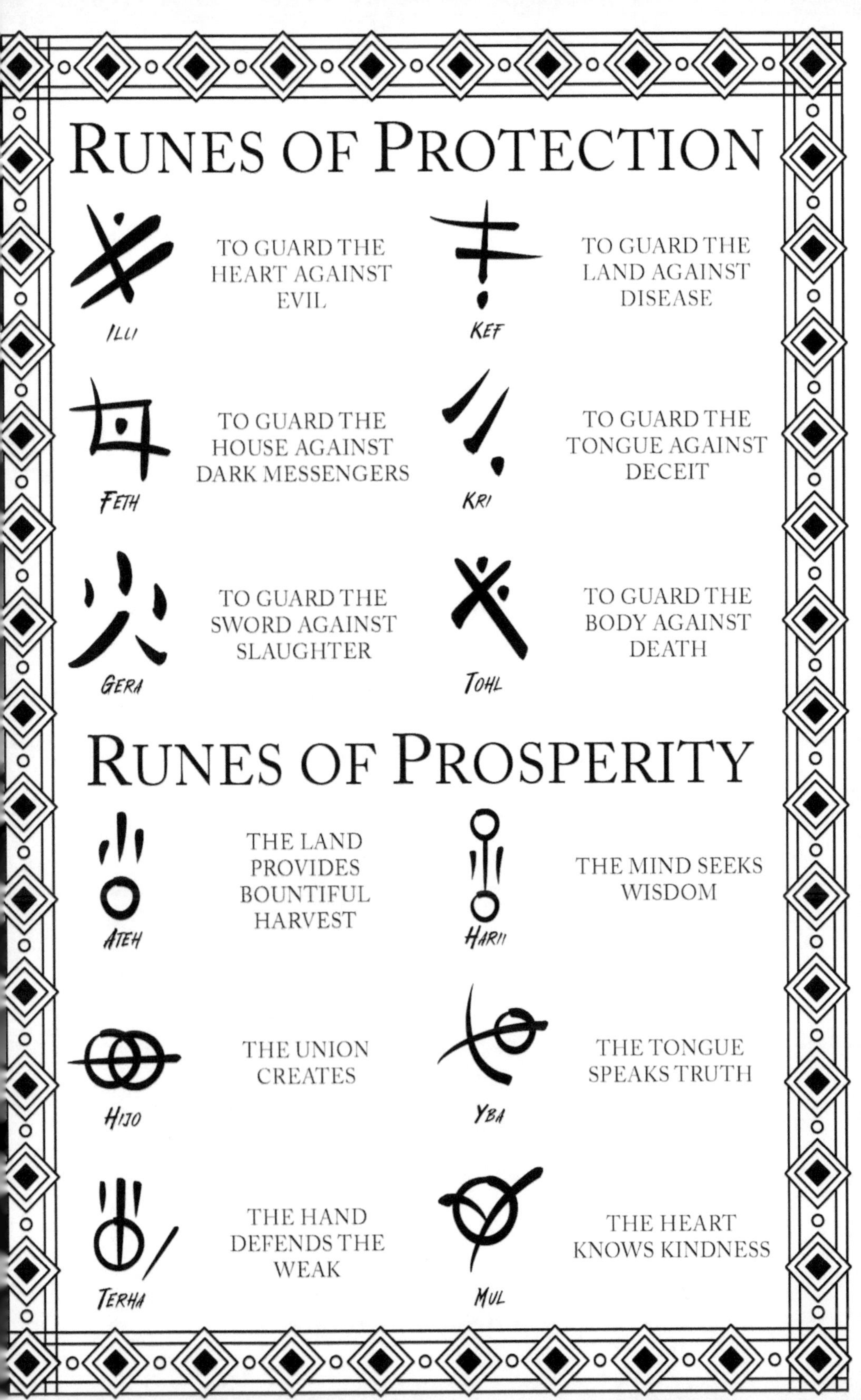

RUNES OF PROTECTION

TO GUARD THE HEART AGAINST EVIL
ILLI

TO GUARD THE LAND AGAINST DISEASE
KEF

TO GUARD THE HOUSE AGAINST DARK MESSENGERS
FETH

TO GUARD THE TONGUE AGAINST DECEIT
KRI

TO GUARD THE SWORD AGAINST SLAUGHTER
GERA

TO GUARD THE BODY AGAINST DEATH
TOHL

RUNES OF PROSPERITY

THE LAND PROVIDES BOUNTIFUL HARVEST
ATEH

THE MIND SEEKS WISDOM
HARII

THE UNION CREATES
HIJO

THE TONGUE SPEAKS TRUTH
YBA

THE HAND DEFENDS THE WEAK
TERHA

THE HEART KNOWS KINDNESS
MUL

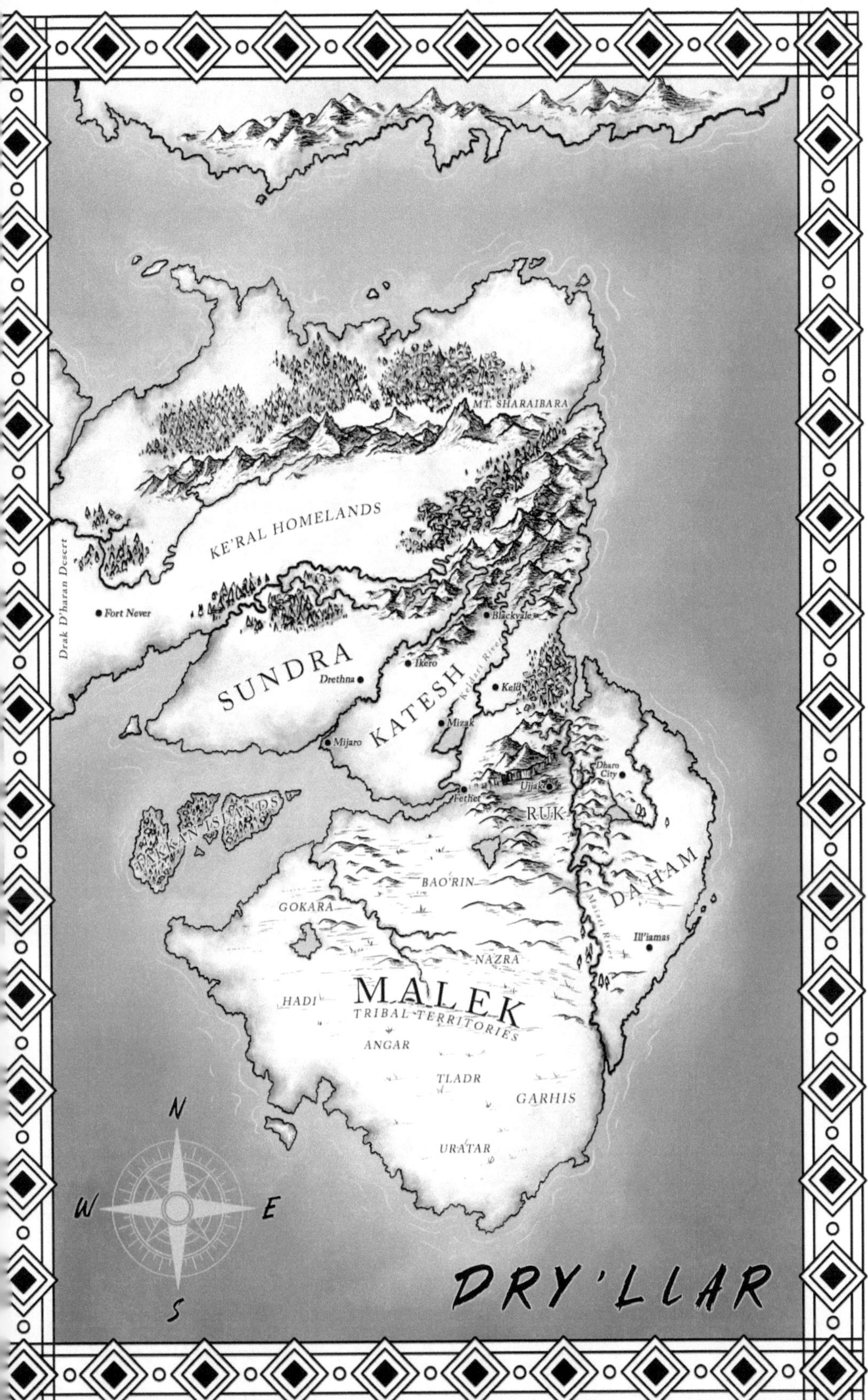

Drak D'haran Desert
MT. SHARAIBARA
KE'RAL HOMELANDS
Fort Never
Blackvale
SUNDRA
Ikero
Drethna
KATESH
Keldari River
Kelá
Mizak
Mijaro
Dharo City
Uljako
Fethet
RUK
TAKKAN ISLANDS
DA'HAM
BAO'RIN
GOKARA
Naisel River
Ill'iamas
NAZRA
MALEK
TRIBAL TERRITORIES
HADI
ANGAR
TLADR
GARHIS
URATAR
N
W        E
S
DRY'LLAR

# OTHER BOOKS BY TORI TECKEN

<u>The Phased Duology</u>

Phased

<u>Legends of the Bruhai</u>

The Blood Stones

# DRAMATIS PERSONAE

## KATESH

**Kinhariian:** the king and warlord of Katesh
**Jifra:** the queen of Katesh
**Tamarikai:** the murdered crown prince of Katesh
**Yi Jo:** a loyal palace servant
**Master Lohi:** a revered scholar and high counsellor
**Ilba Hallix:** high counsellor and close friend of Kinhariian
**Thiri Hallix:** second wife of Ilba Hallix
**Xario Hallix:** oldest son of Ilba Hallix and his first wife
**Kurin Hallix:** second son of Ilba Hallix and his first wife
**Gehrin Hallix:** third son of Ilba Hallix and his first wife
**Eiri Hallix:** youngest daughter of Ilba Hallix and Thiri Hallix
**Yuri Okujen:** a high counsellor – "the voice of the people"
**Euha Raja:** a high counsellor, representative of physicians and healers
**Bari Ujo:** a high counsellor, representative of merchants
**Itaki Ujo:** son of Bari Ujo
**Tajii:** overseer of the farmlands owned by Ilba Hallix
**Lady Suko:** wife of Tajii
**Kasaii:** daughter of Tajii and Lady Suko
**Chon:** head house servant of Tajii
**Hige:** a sweets shop owner in Keld
**Sairi:** a master craftswoman
**Bir:** a master craftsman
**Sychu:** a servant in the Hallix household
**Yrit:** an elderly *mojar* in the Hallix household
**Bithra:** a Witch of Ordrath
**Hasuya Jan:** a *garatelhai*, executed for murdering Crown Prince Jikkar

## BLACKVALE

**Tahmujin:** a *garatelhai* master
**Kirte:** the caretaker of Blackvale
**Jai:** a servant boy in Blackvale
**BOYS IN BLACKVALE (including but not limited to):**
**Nin:** son of a palace servant in Keld
**Ruh:** a Takkan Islands boy
**Hajja:** a boy who wears a mask over his face

DRAMATIS PERSONAE

**Sabba:** a Da'hamian boy
**Kajen:** a street urchin
**Tirrim/Ivveth:** a citylord's son from Fethet

## BLACK LEGION

**Jaakar:** third hand (commander of one thousand soldiers)
**Nab:** a *telhai* soldier
**Kei:** a *telhai* soldier
**Taki:** a *telhai* soldier and cook

## MALEK

**Nar Garhis:** warlord of the Garhis tribe, the Closed Fist
**Ettlan:** wife of Nar Garhis, the Open Hand of the tribe
**Syndri:** daughter of Nar Garhis
**Senna:** daughter of Nar Garhis, Syndri's twin
**Sabayaar (Baya):** younger son of Nar Garhis
**Yugha:** War Sword of Nar Garhis
**Tilis:** wife of Yugha
**Hyshir:** a Ke'ral warrior living in exile
**Malon:** a Garhis warrior
**Uhuri:** a young Garhis warrior
**Sochi:** a Garhis warrior
**Ikaio:** a Garhis warrior
**Hefiar:** a young Garhis warrior
**Durz'ekai:** a young Garhis warrior
**Ganzakh-ba:** an elderly man
**Irah:** younger sister of Tilis
**Brig:** a stallion, Syndri's horse
**Rho:** a mare, Senna's horse
**Itah:** a young mare, Sabayaar's horse

## RUK

**Xhen:** queen of Ruk
**Ona:** servant and bodyguard of Xhen
**Jime Otai:** emissary to the Maleki tribes
**Rahian:** commander of the Rukian army
**Dexa:** overseer of the Rukian mines
**Mereo:** master of merchants and trade
**Thego:** high priest of Ruk
**Kiyab:** coinmaster of Ruk

# PART ONE

# CHAPTER ONE

*21st Year of King Kinhariian's Reign*

*Any man who sheds a king's blood is great evil and must be cleansed.*
*His name must be struck from the lips of the living,*
*and his blood returned to the earth to the last of his children.*

*- Kateshi Law*

Small against the pressing tide of larger bodies behind him, Gehrin murmured words of condemnation along with the incensed crowd as they prepared to witness the death of a nameless man.

"*Aqqa!* His name is not worthy!"

Angry voices rumbled around Gehrin. He knew his father's anger, like a dark storm cloud, and the quick anger of his brothers. This was a new kind of anger that could face a man who had killed a prince with his own hands, a man so tainted by evil that his name could never again pass the lips of those who had known him. The

1

crowd had been waiting for this day. Gehrin winced as someone pushed against him and stepped on his foot. He grabbed hold of his oldest brother's sleeve to keep from falling. He didn't want to lose his place at the front of the crowd.

The man standing on the Blood Stones was bound and gagged, but he did not struggle. Naked except for the loincloth bound loosely around his hips, his skin was even darker beneath a layer of dirt and bruises. A trickle of fresh blood escaped over his swollen lips, past the gag and over his chin. Gehrin watched as it clustered into a drip, splattering against the man's foot. Despite his hunched shoulders, the man's chest and arms were strong, a witness to years of wielding spear and shield. His black hair was matted and stringy, unbound and falling to the middle of his back. He was *aqqa*. Nameless.

Gehrin let his gaze drift from the *aqqa* to the five powerful men standing guard at his side. Once *garatelhai* like them, this man would never have the honor of that title in the afterlife. *Garatelhai* were the king's oathsworn, his most trusted warriors. Gehrin's brother Xario said they were more like gods than men, each of them strong enough to fight ten enemies at once. The warriors standing silent over the battered body of the *aqqa* wore polished iron armor, the scales glittering like hundreds of tiny fans beneath the light of Aqatar's rays. The armor pieces were trimmed with blue and red colors, the gold emblem of the wolf and fox on their shoulders. They carried spears with the hafts painted black, the blades honed to a deadly edge.

Priests standing in a half circle behind the Stones beat their drums as the High Priest of Sharai stepped forward to address the crowd, his bald head shining with sweat. Gehrin thought the head and arms protruding from his too-large gray robes made him look like a turtle. The priest pursed his lips and stared out at the crowd, lifting his hands until they quieted. Then his voice boomed out over the gathered people, too loud for such a small man.

"Hasuya Jan, once *garatelhai*, has committed the gravest of all sins and brought death to the king's house. Today his blood will be spilled over the stones in payment for his heinous deeds, his life forfeit along with the lives of his wife, his son, and his daughter. Because his name is unworthy, we name him *aqqa*. Cursed is the man who speaks his name!"

"His name is not worthy!" The intensity of the crowd's voices rose like the buzzing of a disturbed beehive.

"His name is not worthy," murmured Gehrin, the words tumbling from his lips. *Father would not want me to be here.* He tugged at his brother's sleeve again, but Xario was calling out with the rest of the crowd, oblivious to the smaller boy next to him.

The drums beat louder. The *garatelhai* pushed the nameless man onto his knees. Gehrin watched as the man reached forward, resting his hands against the Stones, fingers gripping the rounded edges with white knuckles as if they could give him strength for what was to come. The dark runes carved into the Blood Stones were deep. The man's left hand covered the upward swish of one of them. Bru.

Gehrin had carefully drawn that same rune with his brush and paper hundreds of times. On the Blood Stones, the rune for bonded blood had been carved to absolve a criminal's family of his sin, but for a revered *garatelhai* warrior, the price of his crime was the blood of his family, and they would join him in paying the debt. Gehrin wondered if they were already dead. It didn't matter. The man's bloodline was tainted, and it must return to the earth root and stem to be cleansed. It was known. The greater the man, the greater his sin.

Gehrin's heart pushed up into his throat, but he could not look away. He had never seen a man executed, but he was no stranger to death. The *aqqa* lifted his head, his wild hair parting to expose his face. He did not acknowledge the crowd, but as he waited for the spears that hovered above him, his eyes rose, and found Gehrin.

For a moment, the condemned man and the boy stared at each other. When the spear blades pierced through the man's body, deep through his shoulders, chest, and back, Gehrin's breath left his body in a great rush. Moving as one, five bloodied blade points ripped holes through flesh as easily as cloth. The traitor jerked and vomited blood, shuddering. He sank, supporting himself on shaking arms for three... four drumbeats before collapsing to the Stones. As the warriors withdrew their spears, his blood pulsed from the open wounds filling the deep crevices of the runes beneath him.

Gehrin watched the way the blood ran so easily from the mutilated body, at once fascinated and repulsed by the sight. He'd never seen so much blood. Killing a man, even a *garatelhai*, was so effortless. His stomach twisted. The eyes that had stared into his own a moment before were sightless, staring out into whatever void was the final resting place for a man with no honor. A tremor found its way into his fingertips, and something pulled at his chest inside.

*Her eyes had looked like that. Like great wide empty cups, all poured out.* Gehrin dug his fingernails into the palm of his hand as hard as he could. The memory of his mother was bitter.

His brother Kurin gagged and then vomited on the ground near his feet. Xario flinched and looked away from the dead man. Around the traitor's body, the *garatelhai* warriors turned their backs on their once brother and faced away from him in a half circle. They would remain that way until nightfall, guarding the city from his spirit.

"He is *aqqa*! His name is not worthy!" cried the priests, rattling strings of bones to scare the spirit away.

"*Aqqa*! His name is not worthy!" cried the crowd, louder and more confident now that the man's death had passed.

But this time Gehrin's lips did not move. His feet were rooted to something far beneath the smooth stones, as if he were being drawn into the earth with the traitor's blood. *Hasuya Jan. His name is not worthy.* The runes ran red. Gehrin felt something rush through him from the tips of his toes to the roots of his hair, something wild and terrifying that turned his blood cold. It fled as quickly as it had come, withdrawing back down his legs and feet and into the ground beneath him. Something ached through his bones, something deep and ancient, and he trembled at its touch. He drew in a shuddering breath, staring at the body on the Stones.

Throughout the crowd ran the low hum of voices, muttering curses on the dead man and prayers to Sharai to guard them from his evil. One woman gripped the amulet around her wrist and closed her eyes, swaying as she muttered. But their feet moved, bodies shifting and pressing forward as Gehrin struggled to lift his own feet from the ground. A hand dropped onto his shoulder.

"Gehrin!" Xario pulled at him and Kurin. "Let's go."

Gehrin did not move.

"Gehrin!" His brother's voice was harsher. "We need to get back before Father finds out we left. Hurry!" Xario's fingers closed more tightly around Gehrin's shoulder.

The twist in Gehrin's belly deepened. Drawing his feet from the ground was like pulling them out of quicksand. Slowly he turned to follow his brothers out of the crowd. Near the Blood Stones, a wooden X was being erected where the dead man would hang for several days as a final punishment for his crime. Boys from the city would come during the night to stab at him with sticks and knives, adding their own blows in the hope that the vengeful spirit would flee and never return. The spirit of a traitor was a black stain on the city.

The man's empty eyes plagued Gehrin, looming in his vision as if the traitor's spirit were fixed on him, ready to drag him to the world beyond. Gehrin stumbled behind Xario, and his older brother turned, ready to scold. But instead, he frowned as Gehrin looked up at him, and pulled Gehrin's arm over toward the outside wall of the city.

Pressed against the stones, Gehrin sank into the firm support behind his back. Xario leaned down and peered into his face. "I told you not to come."

"I...I wanted to," Gehrin mumbled, blinking hard and focusing on the tips of his sandals. Scratches scuffed the tips, wearing away the leather. *Scratches on my sandals.* It was comforting, luring his mind away from the immediate memory of blood and death.

Kurin jabbed Gehrin in the side with one of his fingers. "Father's going to kill us if we bring him back like this."

Xario shook his head. "He won't find out if you don't squeal on us."

Gehrin ignored the rest, unblinking as he stared at his sandals and counted his breaths. *Nin, ruh, yan, liv…* He sighed.

"I want to go home."

Xario's face softened a little. "You gonna be alright?"

"Mhmm."

With a quick ruffle of Gehrin's hair, Xario led them away from the Blood Stones, back up the path toward the city. Gehrin looked over his shoulder, where the *garatelhai* stood in a half circle. The crowd blocked his view of the body, but the man's eyes were still clear in his mind as if they were in front of him. He knew it was a sin to repeat the dead man's name now, but Gehrin spoke it quietly in his mind. *Hasuya Jan. Aqqa. Nameless. Traitor.*

Leaving the words in the dust behind him, Gehrin shuffled his feet faster to keep up with his brothers' longer strides. Xario was a head taller than Kurin, his shoulders broad. Their father expected him to be a warrior. Already he held his spear with the balanced hand of a man born to its weight. But for all Xario's strength, Gehrin didn't think his brother would have been able to kill the man on the stones. Xario was not a killer. Not yet. Could his father have done it?

"Gehrin!"

He shuffled faster, pulling himself back to the dusty road beneath his feet. The roads into the king's city of Keld were busy with their usual wagons, carts, horsemen, and people, trickling in and out of the city like veins pumping blood from a heart. Gehrin dodged a wagon laden with branches rising high above the back of the lanky black mule that pulled it. Xario never released his wrist, and Gehrin felt as if his arm would be pulled out of its joint as his brother dragged him through the streets toward the estate district.

Single-story buildings dominated most of the wide city streets, though a few in the common districts had homes stacked on top of each other like crates of fruit, housing two or three generations. The shops and homes along the main thoroughfares were all the same, plaster and wood beams covered by black slate roofs that curved in and up into central points. The edges of the roofs hung a little way out over the street, providing small strips of shade to passersby.

It was a bit of a distance to retrace their steps back through several smaller districts into their own. By the time they reached the wide path that led toward the sprawling estates of the noble families, counsellors, and wealthier merchants, Gehrin was feeling a burn in his side. Slatted walls and gateways lined the road to either side of the boys.

Xario led them to the side gate in the wall that ran around the Hallix estate, and eased it open as quietly as he could, poking his head in and then signaling to Kurin and Gehrin that they were safe from prying eyes that might betray them to their father.

Counsellor Hallix's home was humble compared to many of the other estates, but it was maintained with pride. The smooth stone path through the gates led through several wooden archways and over a small footbridge that spanned a pond filled with golden fish. The boys ran around the main house toward the training courtyard. The wide porches of the house were empty except for one or two servants going about their daily work. They paid no attention to the boys, who were often running here and there through the estate. Counsellor Hallix was nowhere in sight.

The three brothers found their way to the training courtyard, where they collapsed on the sandy ground, their secret adventure complete. The death they had witnessed was still fresh in their minds as they looked at one another, the urgency of their return fading into the dark memory of a dying man.

"I didn't know there was that much blood in a person," said Kurin, still holding his stomach as if the queasiness hadn't quite left him. He pulled himself up to sit on an overturned bucket. "Do you think he's really dead?"

"He's dead," replied Xario confidently. "There were five spears, and *garatelhai* are as strong as ten men."

"But he was *garatelhai* too. So he is harder to kill."

Xario shook his head. "You heard the priest. Sharai's blood does not protect a traitor with no name. A man with no name is weak." Xario stood up and stripped to the waist, pulling a wooden sparring spear from the rack nearby.

Gehrin watched as his oldest brother drew back a leanly muscled arm and hurled the wooden shaft toward the bales forty paces away. The point buried itself in the dirty straw. Xario straightened again, shoulders back and boyish chest puffed out. He turned back to his brothers. "I will become *garatelhai* one day, and I will kill all traitors to the king."

Kurin scoffed from his bucket throne. "There are no other oathsworn to the king who would dare. There has not been a traitor like him as long as Father has lived."

"How do you know?"

"Father said so this morning," replied Kurin, proud of himself. "Master Lohi says you are not good at listening."

Xario darkened, retrieving his wooden spear. "And you left your breakfast on the stones at the sight of blood," he retorted. He flipped the spear around in his hand and pointed it toward the youngest. "Even Gehrin didn't do that."

While his brothers bickered at each other, Gehrin reached down and picked up a small pebble from the ground and ran it through his fingers, the smoothness soothing his skin and his mind. The faint sour of bile still lingered at the back of his throat, and he swallowed. It was strange that a person could be reduced to blood and bones and skin, their spirit captured in some other realm. It was so simple, one heartbeat between life and death. *Was he afraid? I would've been afraid. Mother was afraid.* Gehrin closed his hand around the small stone.

His brothers' argument had escalated, as it often did. Within moments, Kurin had risen and picked up his own wooden spear, and the two of them were swinging at each other. By some stroke of luck, Kurin managed to duck under a blow that would've set his ears ringing, and he brought the wooden shaft of his weapon against Xario's shin. The oldest howled in pain and grabbed for his leg. A moment later and he was in hot pursuit after Kurin, who had fled the courtyard, realizing that the tides had turned against him.

Gehrin smiled a little at his brothers' roughhousing. As their voices faded around the side of the house, Gehrin stood and walked over to Xario's abandoned spear. He curled his fingers around the shaft, lifting it from the sand. It was still too heavy for him, even though he had begun training with it on his seventh birthday. Nearly four years later, he was stronger, but the weight of the weapon still pulled against the muscles in his arms and he leaned back into his heels, adjusting to the balance. The shouts of his brothers grew close again, and Gehrin suddenly found himself knocked off his feet. Pain flashed through Gehrin's face as his chin hit the ground, Kurin's full weight knocking the wind from his lungs. The abrasive grit of the sand scraped his skin raw.

Xario dragged Kurin up from the ground, locking the younger's head in the crook of his arm. "Got you, *keht*!"

Kurin gasped. "Don't let Father hear you say that," he said through gritted teeth as he fought to free his neck from his brother's grasp. Gehrin pushed himself up. His nose and jaw throbbed, and he had a scrape across his elbow. Dizzy, he stumbled as he rose to his feet. He turned around and his brothers let go of each other. Kurin's eyes grew wide.

"Your face!"

"Let's take him to Yrit."

Reaching up to his face, Gehrin brought his fingers away slick with blood. He stared at it, the crimson stain mixing with the dust on his hands. Xario shoved a rag against Gehrin's face as he and Kurin grabbed hold of Gehrin's arms and hurried him toward the house. They half lifted him up the stone stairs and kicked off their sandals before walking inside. Gehrin's head had stopped spinning, but the pain in his face was bringing stinging tears that ran down his cheeks.

There was an interior courtyard beyond the entrance dominated by the twisted trunk of a *sabba* tree, the seven branches reaching up above the slate roof. The tree's leaves were yellowed by the sun and shaded the little garden and bench beneath them. Counsellor Hallix's study was to the left, and the boys tried to hurry past. As they reached the door, it slid open, and a man nearly ran into them. The lower half of his face was masked, and he wore a short spear at his back. A small horizontal scar arched over his left eyebrow. Gehrin blinked at the rune on the man's light armor. A *garatelhai*.

"Forgive my sons," came their father's deep voice from within the room. The masked man did not respond, simply regarded the three boys with dark eyes. His cloak curled around him as he left. Xario began to pull Gehrin forward again but was stopped in his tracks by a gruff command.

"Come."

Gehrin's brothers exchanged fearful glances over his head but didn't dare disobey. They turned into the study. Inside, Gehrin caught a glimpse of his father sitting on the cushion behind his writing table. Counsellor Ilba Hallix was a broad-shouldered man who many people would expect to be a warrior rather than a counsellor. His dark hair was streaked with gray, pulled behind his head with a leather band. His strong jawline was always set hard, as if he were angry. Now, he finished marking something on the paper in front of him before turning his stern gaze on his three sons. He gestured with his hand, and the boys tumbled into the room and stood in front of him, far enough away not to get sweat or dirt on the cushions.

The counsellor said nothing, and even though the boys wanted to fidget, they did not dare. Gehrin stood as still as a statue despite the blood running down his chin and neck. His eyes were burning, and a dull ache throbbed through his head as he pressed the rag tighter against his chin. His father's eyes stayed on him longer than his brothers, and finally the man rose from his seat, somehow filling every corner of the room despite standing behind the table.

"Xario."

The oldest dipped his head respectfully. "Yes, Father."

"You took your brothers outside the walls earlier today," Counsellor Hallix said calmly. "Where did you go?"

Xario's face grew a shade paler. It was evil to lie. "Father... we... we saw the execution."

Counsellor Hallix nodded. He reached down and picked up a wooden cup full of water. Dipping his quill into the ink bowl, he held it above the water and let five black drops fall.

Stepping around the table, he held out the cup to Xario. The oldest boy looked nervously between the cup and his father and took it in his hands. He sipped from the cup and grimaced slightly. Counsellor Hallix moved to Kurin and offered the cup again. Kurin drank and coughed.

Gehrin heard the soft rustle of his father's robe as the counsellor moved again. The wooden cup appeared in front of Gehrin. The water inside was murky black. His father said nothing. Gehrin knew it was expected of him to take the cup and drink, but the throbbing in his head and the sharp pain from his nose and jaw were blurring his mind. His lip trembled. He did not want to drink it.

"Father, I cannot."

Counsellor Hallix withdrew the cup. "You refuse a drink of water?" he asked. "Aqatar burns brightly today. Surely water will quench your thirst."

Gehrin breathed deeply, forcing himself to stay lucid as the pain began to loosen his knees. "The water is tainted."

"Ah. So it is." Counsellor Hallix placed the cup back on the table. "Xario, Kurin. Why did you drink the water if it was tainted?" His oldest sons glanced between each other awkwardly. Xario offered a small bow.

"Forgive me, Father. I deserved the punishment for deceiving you."

"I offered water. Is that a punishment?"

Xario floundered. "No, Father, but..."

"A man must use wisdom to differentiate between sustenance and poison. Water and blood are no different in this. Today you watched a man die, a man whose name is not worthy. A man who spilled the pure blood of the king's son."

Silence filled the room.

Counsellor Hallix's voice grew quiet. "By doing this, you drank poison with your eyes and opened your blood to evil. You are sons of my house and servants of the king. Would you offer the king tainted water to drink?"

"No, Father!" exclaimed Kurin.

"Then you did wrong to taint yourselves with the sight of evil blood. You did not ask my permission, and I would not have given it. A traitor must leave the earth nameless, forgotten. Yet now you will remember him."

Xario and Kurin dropped to their knees, and Gehrin followed slowly, supporting himself with one arm on the floor. Xario touched his forehead to the ground.

"Forgive us, Father."

Counsellor Hallix returned to his cushion behind the table. "Take your brother to his room and fetch the *mojar* to tend him."

Gehrin's vision swam, and his brothers gripped his arms again. He was pulled up from the floor and saw his father watching him as he was led out of the room. His feet shuffled and his shoes slid along the newly waxed floor. He tried to lift his head. The *sabba* tree in the inner courtyard seemed to be wreathed in a blurry glow, and he blinked, trying to understand the strange way the world was spinning. He passed out before they reached the door of his bedroom.

*Something fluttered across Gehrin's face as he slept. His mother's hands brushed aside his hair, passing over his temple. Her gentle gray eyes smiled along with the soft curve of her lips.* He blinked, and the room appeared in front of him as if he were being pulled through a veil. He looked up, but the face above him was not his mother's. Yrit, the counsellor's *mojar*, scowled down at him. Her leathery skin was carved through with wrinkles that sagged around her eyes. Amulets looped around her neck and wrists, runes spidering across every bit of their surfaces.

Gehrin reached up to feel his tender nose and chin. There was no pain, but a strange numbness made his cheeks feel as if they were made of air, as if his fingertips might pass right through the skin. A grainy paste came away on his fingers. Yrit slapped his hands away from his face, and her scowl deepened. Gehrin lay still. The old woman picked up a mortar and pestle that had been sitting in her lap and began grinding what looked like a black powder. When she was satisfied with it, she dipped her fingers in and then began drawing runes on Gehrin's arms and chest. He frowned but didn't dare ask. The ways of the *mojar* were their own, as his father had said more than once. As the black powder smeared into his skin, he realized what it was. He and his brothers had often used darkened cinders from the firepits as tools for practicing letters on the stones outside the house.

He watched silently as Yrit drew the last rune on the back of his right hand. *Ami.* Mother. A chill shuddered through him and pulled his hand away from Yrit's grasp. She threw up her hands and tsked at him darkly.

"Don't be a fool, boy," she rasped. "You have been marked already, long before my runes touched your skin." She picked up her mortar and pestle and stiffly rose, hobbling over to leave. Gehrin turned his face toward the wall and squeezed his eyes shut, ignoring the way it renewed the ache behind his forehead. Yrit had always eyed him with distaste, as if he were a spoiled fruit. The woman's ancient healing skills were far beyond most of the *mojars* in the city of Keld, and possibly all of Katesh. Rumors even said she had once ministered to the king himself when she was younger. Gehrin's father respected her, but Gehrin had always been uneasy beneath the old crone's gaze. It was as if she could see through him, under his skin and into the viscera beneath, like the dead animals she dissected in her hut. He shuddered, pushing the thought away. It was some time before he was able to fall asleep.

Sometime late in the night, Gehrin awoke to the cries of a small child. Pulling himself out of his bed, he padded through the darkened corridor around the inner courtyard, the wood floor cool against his feet. Reaching the final room on the right, he tapped his knuckles against the wood frame, sliding the door aside when he heard a soft voice answer from within.

His father's second wife, Thiri, paced inside. In her arms was Gehrin's little half-sister Eiri, squirming, red-faced and squalling her defiance at the thought of sleep. The tiny girl's face was glistening with tears as mucus dripped from her nose. Thiri shushed her, bouncing slightly as she walked. When Eiri saw Gehrin standing at the door, her squalling paused.

"Gah-nin," she said, holding out one chubby fist in his direction. Gehrin smiled, but it quickly turned into a grimace as it pulled at his sore chin. He reached out, and Thiri gratefully deposited the little girl in her brother's arms. Eiri leaned away from him at first, her huge brown eyes scrutinizing the difference in his familiar face. He gently pushed her hand away when she reached up to touch the wound, and she soon busied herself with the amulet around his neck.

Thiri lowered herself to a cushion on the floor, tucking her legs gracefully beneath her and smoothing her long black hair away from her eyes. "Thank you, Gehrin. I've never seen a child who could survive with so little sleep," she laughed. "I don't know where she finds the strength."

Eiri beamed up at Gehrin, babbling at him in a language all her own. She tugged at his iron amulet, pulling it into her mouth and leaving a sticky trail on his collarbone. Gehrin had been the youngest for nearly ten years before Eiri had arrived, and he had loved her from the moment Thiri had settled the newborn in his awkward arms. Her second birthday was still months away, but already she was toddling around the house, keeping everyone on the lookout so they wouldn't trip over her. Thiri spent most of her day chasing after the little girl and keeping her away from places in the estate that were still unsafe for a babe.

"Does it still hurt?" Thiri asked, motioning to his face.

"A little." Gehrin pulled at the amulet cord and chuckled when Eiri's little face scrunched up into a scowl. He let go.

"Your father said you watched the execution," Thiri said, fixing him with a discerning glance. "I am sorry that you saw it."

The man's dark eyes flickered at the edge of Gehrin's mind. *"His name is not worthy!"* The screams of the crowd had beat against him as he died. His blood poured back into the earth in great streams like water. And Gehrin had felt something, whether from the runes, the earth, or his own imagination, he did not know. It had left him with a nauseous pit in his stomach, the way he felt when he had not eaten.

"Why did he kill the prince?" Gehrin asked.

Thiri took a shallow breath, her eyes returning to her own child nestled in Gehrin's arms. "His heart was tainted with evil, like all men who take innocent life."

Gehrin didn't think that was much of an answer. "What if someone told him to do it?"

"Then your father and the king will find them, and they will meet a similar fate," replied Thiri. She pursed her lips together, the frown marring her fine features. "It is dangerous to try and understand the mind of a man like that, Gehrin."

Eiri squirmed in her brother's arms, tired of being ignored. She wiggled until he set her down on the floor, and then she toddled toward her mother, snuggling into Thiri's breast with a yawn. Thiri's arms encircled the babe, her frown softening.

"You are a good son, Gehrin. One day you and your brothers will honor your father and the memory of your mother in service to the king, and I will be glad to see it. But now you should rest, your eyes are as dark as your chin."

Back in his room, Gehrin lowered himself back down to his small wooden headrest and pulled the blanket over his chest, gripping the edges. He knew that he had disappointed his father. Someday he would serve the king as his father did. Someday he would wield a spear in battle or speak in the king's hall and wear the gold chains and winged black *heoja* hat of the counsellors. He would be a loyal servant. He would be a good son.

Gehrin's body pulled him back toward sleep. He did not want to close his eyes, afraid that the *aqqa* would be waiting for him in his dreams.

# CHAPTER TWO

*Sharai and his Oathsworn walked the stars and came to a place where the earth was barren, and into this place Sharai poured oceans and rivers. He planted the forests and carved the mountains up from the rock. And into this world he scattered the seeds of the Firstborn.*

*- Gaja Teorhei, The Memory Chant*

Gehrin squinted down the street. The sun, ancient Aqatar's bright prison, burned hotter than the day before, and the heat was stifling. He wiped away beads of sweat from his upper lip gingerly, taking care not to disturb his tender nose and chin. He had slept too long, only rising from his bed when Kurin had threatened to splash a bowl of water in his face and leave for Master Lohi's without him. The stern scholar liked Gehrin, but even that small mercy had its limits. A wounded face would not save Gehrin from the consequences of arriving late.

The scholar's home was behind the main thoroughfare of the merchant's district. It was a strange place for an esteemed keeper of knowledge, but Master Lohi liked to have, as he called it, an ear pressed to the wall of the world. The merchants and their shops were a hub of commerce and news from every corner of Katesh and beyond into the neighboring lands of Da'ham, Ruk, and Malek. The shops were already bustling by the time the three boys arrived in the district. Okija the cloth merchant was draping a deep blue fabric over a wooden rack. The silk was delicately embroidered with white doves, no doubt soon to be in the possession of a noble wife or daughter. On the other side of Okija's open shop were stacks of carefully folded woven cloths in earthy colors worn by more common folk.

Taking a short side street away from Master Lohi's house, the boys dodged through the foot traffic on their way to a smaller district lined with the houses of merchants and lesser lords. Gehrin saw the familiar gate framed by *feth* runes appear on the right side of the street, the courtyard wall showing patched cracks beneath the edge tiles. In front of the gate, a girl waited patiently for them to arrive, the green trim on her light-yellow jacket crossed neatly at the base of her neck and wrapped around under her right arm, the satin smooth and unwrinkled despite being a bit threadbare. A single black braid draped over one shoulder, bound with a matching yellow silk ribbon. She held a small cloth bundle in one hand, leaning on a walking staff with the other. When she caught sight of the three boys, she smiled and waved the cloth bundle in the air. As soon as they came closer, she pointed to Kurin.

"You have a smudge of dirt on your cheek," she said, wrinkling her nose. He awkwardly scrubbed it away on the back of his sleeve. Then she turned her scrutinizing gaze toward Gehrin, her eyes widening slightly when she saw the dark black and purple bruise around the gash on his chin.

"What happened to your face?" she asked, peering closely at it.

Gehrin shrugged. "I fell."

"You look like you fell down a cliff," she replied.

Xario broke into the conversation. "We will be late if you keep staring at his face, Kasaii. Let's go."

As Xario and Kurin set off ahead of them, Gehrin waited for

Kasaii to adjust her walking stick beneath her right arm. She limped off after his brothers, her lurching gait so familiar to Gehrin that he didn't pay it any mind. He adjusted his own pace to walk beside her and offered to carry her bundle. She refused, as she did every day.

A silk merchant was carefully draping new fabrics over the wicker racks inside his shop, the vibrant silks protected from the worst of the dust outside by the walls. Gehrin slowed as a dark blue silk with a pattern of silver wolves embroidered into it caught his eye. He was not old enough to wear such finery yet, but he imagined a *seri* like one of his father's made from the beautiful fabric.

As they returned to the eastern half of the merchant district near Master Lohi's house, they found Xario and Kurin paused in front of one of the shops. Sweet smells wafted deliciously through the air. Xario caught sight of Kasaii and Gehrin and waved a small pouch of coins in the air.

"Let's get *uban* on our way home," he said.

Gehrin and Kasaii caught up with them, staring into the open doors of the shop, which revealed all manner of mouth-watering packages. *Uban* was Xario and Kurin's favorite, soft squares of lime or lemon that melted away on the tongue. Gehrin's favorite was *kiji*, little cakes flavored with mint and jasmine leaves. His father had often brought them home for Gehrin's mother, and her eyes had always sparkled as she opened the package, sneaking a bite of the soft cake before breaking off a small piece for each of her sons.

Hige, the owner of the shop, appeared from the back room and smiled when he saw the children ogling over the sweets. "Greetings! Shall I wrap some *uban* for you this fine morning, Lord Xario? Or perhaps some *kiji*?" He offered a wink at Gehrin. His Northern Malekian accent gave his words a rough edge. "Lady Kasaii, would you like a mint *kruka*?"

Xario bowed slightly. "Many thanks, but not until after lessons."

"Ah yes, best not to have sticky fingers around Master Lohi's books," replied Hige. "But I will hold a package for you. Come back at the end of the day."

Gehrin did not want to wait for the sweets, the delicious smells were making him salivate as he ogled the small packages on the shelves. He hurried after Kasaii and his brothers with no small amount of regret.

Leaving behind the sweet smells of Hige's shop, the children turned down a small lane paved with dark slate. The front doors of Master Lohi's home were open, and inside all the partition walls had also been opened and slid to the side to make room for the small crowd of children who would soon fill the space. Master Lohi's house was one of the few on the street that had two floors, the wooden staircase at the back leading up into the scholar's private study and bedroom. None of the students were allowed upstairs.

Gehrin took off his shoes and stepped onto the smooth wooden floor. The rune *kefhrin* was painted in the doorway. The bold lines of the rune meant "strong land." Gehrin traced it with his eyes before stepping past it and into the room. Kurin and Xario began unstacking the seat cushions from the side of the room and laying them out. Within a few seconds, Kurin had smacked Xario in the back with one, and Xario was turning to him with a threat on his lips.

With a smile, Gehrin went to help them. "Master Lohi will hear you," he reminded his brothers quietly. Xario lowered his clenched fist and Kurin laid down the cushion sheepishly. After the cushions, the boys set out small writing desks in front of each student's place. Kurin leaned close to Gehrin after glancing toward the stairs.

"Do you think he will make us practice runes today?"

Gehrin offered a low hum of affirmation. Kurin sighed and set the next quill down on a writing desk with a little more force. The middle brother had never been suited for sitting long hours in Master Lohi's lessons. Kasaii lowered herself onto one of the cushions, setting her walking stick to the side and laying out parchment and ink on the small desk Gehrin set in front of her. Slowly, other students arrived and began to trickle in, taking their places around the room. Gehrin sat next to Kasaii and watched them. Most of them were the sons and daughters of lesser counsellors and nobles, a few merchants. Gehrin and his brothers were the only children of a High Counsellor except one, Itaki Ujo, the son of the Merchant High Counsellor Bari Ujo.

Itaki swept into the room in a blue silk *seri*, the long tunic nearly reaching his knees, embroidered with gold falcons and silver flowers in a statement of his father's vast wealth. His white slippers peeked out from beneath the silver hem of his trousers as he walked across the room to an open desk. He had three brushes made from soft white goat hair, laid carefully to the side of his parchment, each one a different size. Gehrin had always been impressed that no matter how long they practiced runes on a lesson day, Itaki somehow managed to keep his *seri* and hands completely clean, not a single ink drop made its way outside his parchment. Kurin's hands were always splattered with black ink after drawing runes, often accompanied by a streak across his face from brushing his hair away from his eyes.

There was a tug on Gehrin's sleeve. Kasaii leaned close to him, her breath tickling his ear. "I'm surprised that Itaki's brushes aren't made of gold too," she said. "No wonder his runes are always perfect."

"Your runes are always perfect too, Kasaii," replied Gehrin. It was true. Kasaii's family was the poorest of all the students', but she was one of Master Lohi's favorites. Her runes were always beautiful, sweeping black lines of ink that danced across the parchment.

"You're wearing a *feth* amulet again today," Gehrin observed, watching the small iron bauble dangle from Kasaii's wrist. She waved it in the air between them.

"Mother is convinced a crow will fly across my path today. She's been searching for dark messengers in her tea leaves the past two days, and today one of the leaves had a small dark spot." Kasaii grinned and shrugged. "The First Runes are the most powerful, and I am her only child. If *feth* was meant to guard a house against dark messengers, why not a human?"

Gehrin smiled back. Kasaii's mother was well known to be a devout believer in all signs, both evil and good, and was often attempting to imitate the foresight of the *mojars*. She held a near god-like reverence for Master Lohi, and asked Kasaii to repeat her lessons every evening. Gehrin had only met her once, but it had left a lasting impression as he had watched the woman's overeager solicitation for Master Lohi's opinion of something she had discovered in her morning tea leaves.

Master Lohi had often spoken of the tea leaves and bone readings that were commonplace among Katesh's healers. He maintained that understanding the Runes and the power that they bestowed on worthy scholars of their truths was a much more rewarding study. Gehrin knew that if she were allowed into these lessons, Yrit might disagree. The old *mojar*'s leather pouch of finger bones never left her belt, but he had never seen her studying tea leaves.

The stairs creaked, and Master Lohi's slippered feet came into view. His robes were the scholar white, a red belt with long tassels reaching nearly to the floor wrapped around his thin waist. His wispy hair swept loosely to the top of his head the same style as Counsellor Hallix's, but his forehead had lost much of its covering as he aged, and the thin gray strands arrived at a sharp point in the center. His beard was much whiter, neatly trimmed and ending at the center of his chest. He wore one bronze medallion around his neck, far less adornment than most of the country's famed scholars, who often preferred gaudy embellishments of gold and jewels. Master Lohi maintained the simpler attire of a man who traveled widely and often, pausing for brief periods in between to teach the youth of Keld.

In the center of Lohi's medallion was a deep carving of *harii*, the rune of wisdom. He leaned on a darkwood staff as he descended the stairs. Master Lohi surveyed his gathered students with a discerning eye, taking in the state of each of them. Not a thread of their clothing escaped his notice. Gehrin saw his brother Kurin fidget slightly in front of him, pulling hastily at his tunic.

"Kurin Hallix."

Reluctant, Kurin stood up from his desk and bowed. "Yes, Master."

The old scholar's white eyebrows furrowed in scrutiny. "If you were concerned about your state of dress, perhaps you might have fixed it prior to my entering the room."

Kurin's cheeks flushed hotly. "Yes, Master Lohi." At a wave of the scholar's hand, he sat back down on his cushion. Xario poked him in the side, and Kurin gave him a glare. Master Lohi leaned forward, supported by his staff. The old man's light frame was swathed in his light linen tunic and robes, giving him the appearance of frailty, but every student knew that a smack in the legs by his staff would bring a harsh bruise. The scholar tapped his staff against the floor.

"Let us begin our day with the First Runes. We name them, the runes of prosperity."

Gehrin recited with the others. "*Ateh, hijo, terha, yba, harii, mul.*"

"And of protection?"

"*Illi, feth, kri, kef, gera, tohl.*"

Master Lohi tapped his staff again. "Doubtless you have all heard of the execution that took place on the Blood Stones yesterday. I have been told that some of you were in attendance. The sons of Counsellor Hallix, I believe."

Hushed whispers drifted around the room, and Gehrin felt the eyes of the other students on him. While his brothers shifted uncomfortably in their seats, Gehrin met the scholar's gaze. If Master Lohi intended to scold him, it was deserved. Beside him, Kasaii touched his knee. Gehrin knew he would owe her an explanation later. She would want to know everything.

Master Lohi fixed the second brother with his whiskered gaze. "Tell us, Kurin, who was the man executed?"

"A betrayer. His name is not worthy."

"Ah, yes. A name is a terrible thing to lose. And you have given a fitting answer. Who were his executioners, Xario?"

Straightening his shoulders, Xario's voice was proud and clear. "The *garatelhai*, Master. The greatest servants of the king."

Master Lohi frowned. "The greatest servants? How is one servant greater than another?"

Xario wilted slightly. "They are the most powerful warriors who protect the king from evil."

Walking to one end of the room, Master Lohi left the students to ponder as he retrieved a small stool for himself. Placing it carefully in front of the children, he sat, arranging his robes around him. His staff leaned comfortably against his left shoulder.

"Kasaii. Are the *garatelhai* greater than the king's other servants?"

She hesitated. "They are the strongest, Master. But all who serve the king with a loyal heart are great servants in his eyes. We must all use the gifts we have to serve the best that we can."

A small smile appeared beneath Master Lohi's mustache. "As expected of you, Kasaii, a kind thought for those who have had no tales of glory told about them. Gehrin Hallix."

Gehrin looked up from where he had been writing notes on his paper. "Master."

"This nameless man betrayed his king and spilled innocent blood. Do you believe his sentence was just?"

A hushed tension fell over the room. It was a question filled with the threat of blasphemy. To question the king's judgment was unthinkable, especially against such a terrible offender. Gehrin set down his quill and ignored the stares of the students around him. He took a breath, pushing away the fluttering in his stomach. He had listened to Master Lohi's lessons, and he was prepared to answer.

"Master, the greatest sin is to give in to evil. This man did not spill blood to defend but shed it in innocence and betrayal. There can be nothing good in a man whose heart is dark. The Blood Stones will cleanse his blood in the earth because he cannot cleanse his own." Gehrin remembered the man's eyes. "He is *aqqa*. His name is not worthy."

The old scholar was nodding his approval. "To shed innocent blood and betray a master or a friend stains the earth until the stones themselves call for vengeance. It is a forsaking of loyalty and truth for deceit and evil. King Kinhariian is the father of Katesh, and our loyalty is the greatest gift we can offer to him. A king is the beating heart of his nation. The betrayal of one of his oathsworn warriors is a knife in that beating heart."

A heavy silence followed the master's words, weighted with the great evil that loomed in all their memories. A prince, murdered in the safety of the palace walls less than a year before the death of the *aqqa* who killed him. There was an awkward shuffle somewhere to Gehrin's right. On the other side of the room, Itaki's brush swept over his parchment, leaving a long stroke of black on the unsullied white.

A girl named Geohha spoke up behind Gehrin. "Master Lohi, who will the new king be? There is no prince now."

Master Lohi folded his arms, his wide sleeves coming together to hide his hands from view. "We have studied the law. What is written about the succession of kings?"

Itaki's brush clicked against the wood of his desk. "If the king cannot produce an heir from his own body, then his successor will be chosen from among the children of his counsellors. The next king must be chosen from among the people."

"The counsellors speak for the people in the hall of the king, but they are not the people," replied Kasaii. "It isn't as if the new prince can be chosen from the street corners." Her hands were tightly clasped in her lap, and Gehrin saw her absent-mindedly cleaning one of her fingernails, the way she always did when she was thinking.

Master Lohi reached for a set of small wooden tiles and placed them in his lap. He set one on the stool next to him. There was a strange feeling in the room, as if the act of speaking about a new prince profaned the memory of the first. Gehrin's own father was one of the king's most trusted counsellors, and it was no secret that Xario could be chosen. Several pairs of eyes around the room found Xario as well, no doubt coming to the same thought. Gehrin tried to imagine his brother sitting on the throne, the great spear of Katesh clasped in his boyish hands.

"Itaki's father is a high counsellor," someone said quietly. "It could be him."

The son of Bari Ujo continued his brush strokes, his face empty. Gehrin wondered if the idea of being king would please him. Surely his father would be pleased. Any of their fathers would be pleased to have a son on the throne.

"Only the king knows who he will choose," Xario said, his shoulders square. "My father will be loyal to the king, no matter what he decides."

"Loyalty is easy enough to give when you have much to gain," replied Itaki, finally lifting his gaze from the parchment. "A king who is only a wolf will lose when he cannot match the fox's cunning."

The two boys glowered at each other, and Gehrin marked the difference between them. Xario was fierce, hot fire, barely contained, the flames dancing dangerously close to the edge of a blacksmith's forge. Itaki Ujo was cold, dark ice at the edges of the ocean, a promise of winter's deadly bite.

"Only if the fox is as cunning as he believes himself to be." Kasaii smiled in Itaki's direction. He ignored her, but his jaw tightened. Gehrin poked her in the side.

"Balance."

Master Lohi's voice brought silence back to the room. Xario and Itaki settled back to their desks, angry gaze torn apart from each other. All eyes shifted back to the old man on the stool, who had stacked the wooden tiles, one atop the next, until it stood over a handspan tall. Gehrin relaxed a little now that Itaki and his brother were no longer glaring death at each other. Master Lohi placed one final tile on top of the stack.

"A king has trusted counsellors. We must seek justice, but also mercy. Balance. We have runes to protect and to prosper. The Maleki people offer their enemies a closed fist, and their friends an open hand. Balance. A kingdom cannot survive without balance, for in it there is stability. At the foundation of the kingdom lies one man, within whom lies the greatest balance of all. He must not be solely wolf or fox, but both at once. Why?" Master Lohi watched them all beneath his whiskery white eyebrows. No one answered.

"Kasaii, perhaps you would like to tell us."

Sitting up a little straighter, Kasaii seemed to be completely unfazed by the tension in the room. "Yes, Master. The wolf is fierce and bold, and the fox is cunning and crafty. The king must be both, for they temper each other."

"A warlord, and a king. On his shoulders rests the stability of our people." Master Lohi reached down to the stack next to him and placed his thumb and forefinger on the sides of the bottom tile. "But that balance can be disrupted. Without the strength and wisdom of a king, Katesh is weak." He pulled the tile, and the tower crumbled, the tiles clattering across the floor.

"The throne is a great and heavy burden, and it takes great strength to rule. Many men believe they are capable of its weight," he said, glancing toward Itaki, and then at Xario. "But only a few have proven themselves equal to the task."

Gehrin reached down and picked up a tile that had landed near his cushion. The carved rune on its face caught against the pad of his thumb. It seemed like the whole world was perched on the edge of a cliff, waiting for the king's choice. The crown prince's death hovered over the city like a dark cloud, and a new one must be chosen. Gehrin didn't want Xario to be a crown prince. He didn't want his brother to leave their house to become the son of the king. He could feel his father's stern disapproval in his mind. If the king chose Xario, it would be an honor. His brother would sit on the great throne in the palace and rule all of Katesh. *The throne is a great and heavy burden...*

It must be heavy if someone was willing to kill a prince.

The rest of the lesson passed without further incident, and Gehrin threw his full attention into his brush when Master Lohi set them to practicing runes. The old scholar was vigilant, roaming the room quiet as a cat as his students filled their parchment with the small black symbols. More than one student felt the rap of his hollow switch against their knuckles for a wayward curve or wobbly line. Gehrin finished the final stroke of *terha* and laid his brush aside, his hand tightening in a cramp. Kurin had received his second scolding from Master Lohi for the excess of ink wasted on his hands, a sharp rap of the stick against his fingers.


The wet bristles of the brushes were slippery, black ink seeping out into the small tray of water Gehrin crouched over outside. He'd brought his own and Kasaii's, taking great care to rinse them over and over until the cloudy water changed to clear. Kasaii's brush was ancient, made with a bone handle instead of wood. A tiny *harii* rune was carved in the side to bring its owner wisdom. He wondered if that was why she knew the answers to so many of Master Lohi's questions.

"Hurry up."

The boy behind him prodded Gehrin's leg with the toe of his shoe. Gehrin stood up and bobbed his head in a brief apology, shuffling back around the side of the house. Kasaii met him at the door, both of their bundles in her hand, walking staff tucked under her armpit. Xario pushed past them and dropped two coins in Gehrin's hand.

"Kurin and I are going to get *uban*. Get something for yourself and Kasaii on the way home."

Kurin jostled him, and the two older boys took off running down the street. They would spend the next two hours training with a *telhai* spear master. Gehrin would join them for the last hour. When he was twelve, he would spend two hours a day training as well. He did not wish to lose another hour of his day building calluses on his palms, but it was expected of him to learn.

As Kasaii was about to step down onto the street, Itaki moved in front of her smoothly, his brushes tucked away in a leather satchel at his belt. Kasaii nearly stumbled as she tried to stop her forward momentum, her weak leg buckling slightly. Itaki's cold fox-like eyes flickered over the walking staff.

"You were right. The fox must be careful he does not overestimate his cunning."

Gehrin's own surprise matched the expression on Kasaii's face.

She opened her mouth to answer, but Itaki waved his hand to stop her from speaking, the fox eyes scrutinizing her, narrowing. "The most dangerous game of all is played by the flea behind the wolf's ear, imagining itself powerful because it sucks at powerful blood." He glanced at Gehrin, then back at Kasaii. "Be careful, little flea."

He spoke with the same venom Gehrin had seen other nobles use in conversation with his father. His father was right. The nobles were not wolves or foxes, but snakes, hidden in the brush to strike at unwary hands that wandered too close. Itaki turned to leave, but Gehrin reached out and caught the blue silk sleeve of his *seri*, stopping the older boy in his tracks.

"You will remove your hand," Itaki said.

Gehrin straightened his shoulders and squeezed his eyebrows together the way Xario did when he was angry. "You will not speak to her in that way."

"I will speak in whatever way I please. That is the privilege of my birth." Itaki pulled his arm free. "She would do well to remember her place, as I remember mine."

"She is under my father's protection, and she is a student of Master Lohi," replied Gehrin, anger coiling in the pit of his stomach and through his arms. "And she is my friend."

Itaki brushed his sleeve. "Your father is generous with his patronage. I wonder what profit it will bring him?"

The tension in Gehrin's hands curled his fists, but a soft touch from Kasaii on his arm stopped him as Itaki walked away. The walking staff tapped against the stone path as Kasaii entered the street, heading in opposite direction to the rude Ujo boy.

Gehrin hurried to catch up with her. The moment of tension faded from his limbs, leaving behind a strange tingling of unspent energy. He glanced at Kasaii from the corner of his eye. Her eyes glimmered. Fishing the two coins out of a fold in his belt, Gehrin held them up.

"Hige was saving sweets for us," he said. Kasaii nodded, lifting her chin as they headed toward the delicious-smelling shop on the end of the street. As soon as they came within sight, the big man inside smiled, his eyes twinkling.

"Master Gehrin! Lady Kasaii!"

Cradled in his huge hands, Hige held a small package tied with blue string, waiting for his young customers. Gehrin accepted the package from Hige and opened it to find three little *kiji* cakes and four squares of *uban* nestled inside. The sweet smell wrapped him in familiar comfort, and Gehrin reached for his coins.

"None of that, young master. That's a gift."

Gehrin smiled. "Many thanks, Master Hige."

The man scoffed, pleased. "I am no such thing, and I'm pleased to do what little I can in memory of your honored Mother. You both enjoy your sweets, now."

The two children left the shop and found a quiet street corner where they could eat beneath the tiled eaves of a shop. On the street, a man hurried past toward the noble district, pulling a small wheeled cart, its load of wood tied down tightly with rope. Gehrin opened the paper package and tucked the string away in his belt. Later he would use it to play with Eiri and the kittens that lived in the corner of the stable. He dug a square of the sticky *uban* out and handed it to Kasaii, who took a nibble and sucked her cheeks together at the tartness. The tangy lemon scent wafted between them. Gehrin inhaled a deep whiff of the *kiji* before biting into the soft, chewy rice cake. Mint and jasmine swirled together on his tongue, familiar and comforting. Kasaii licked her fingers.

"Itaki would not be a good king."

Gehrin reached for a second cake, considering. "No, I don't think so," he agreed. The king was father to all, from the highest counsellor to the lowest child in the gutter. Itaki would not want to be that kind of king. Kasaii reached into the package in Gehrin's hand and pulled out another *uban* square, the yellow sweet clinging to her fingers as she lifted it to her lips.

"What if the king chooses you?"

A pause, and Gehrin slowly stopped chewing. "I will not be chosen. Xario is the eldest, and Kurin only a year younger." The thought of the king choosing him almost made him laugh. "Xario is going to be a warrior."

Kasaii nodded. "Yes, but a king is more than a warrior. If you were king, I think you would be a good one. You are strong and kind." She laughed. "And I could be a counsellor."

"You draw an empty bucket," Gehrin said, smiling despite himself. It was true. Kasaii's imaginings were just that... empty. And he was glad. He didn't want to sit on a throne in the palace. Kasaii looked down the street, her eyes locked on something far away, as if she were still imagining the older version of herself dressed in a counsellor's robe, the silver tassels hung about her waist. But her dreaming did not keep her tongue still for long. She pulled the last *uban* from the paper.

"I can't believe you watched the execution. What was it like? Was your father terribly angry?"

Gehrin's hand froze. *The traitor's dark eyes fixed him to the ground, and something pulled at Gehrin's feet from beneath...* He shivered involuntarily. "I... I don't want to speak of it today."

Hiding her disappointment behind a carefree grin, Kasaii flipped her braid over her shoulder. "Yes, I suppose it would draw an evil spirit. But you must promise to tell me soon. Tomorrow."

"I will."

Kasaii rose, using her walking staff and the wall behind her to lever her weight upright. She fixed Gehrin with a pointed stare. "Promise."

Humoring her, Gehrin lifted two fingers to his forehead and then touched hers. "I swear it. Tomorrow?"

Satisfied by the promise sealed with Gehrin's life at stake, Kasaii set off down the street with a wave, her *feth* amulet swinging around her neck. Gehrin watched until she disappeared into the long alleyway that ran past her house. She was a strange force of nature in herself, as if Sharai had formed a tiny whirlwind over the sea and fashioned it into a girl.

Despite their differences, Kasaii had never questioned Gehrin's quiet observance of the world. She had simply inserted herself into his life and took on the mantle of friend without demanding anything of him except the same loyalty in return. A fierce protector of the simple and beautiful things in the world, she had opened Gehrin's eyes to many things that before had gone unnoticed. Colors were brighter around Kasaii, as if her presence sparked in them a greater vibrance. No one could hide even the smallest wound from her searching gaze. He had once seen her stop to bind the knee of a young street urchin who had fallen in his haste to escape the wheels of a merchant's wagon.

The bright glow of Aqatar had dimmed a little by the time Gehrin stood up, the package empty in his hand. He tucked it into his belt and walked down the street away from the market district. His sandals made soft indents in the dirt. A woman veiled in red passed him, and he carefully stepped out of her way. The tiny bells strapped around her ankles and wrists chimed musically as she walked. Gehrin noted the red-inked claw tattoos over her delicate hands. Witches of Ordrath were not uncommon in the city, he had seen them before, and they always fascinated him. He saw her black lined eyes lower to look at him as she stepped past, beautiful even through the light veil. No doubt she was on her way to a noble house to bring pleasure or read bones. Gehrin wondered if Yrit had been veiled and beautiful like that once, when she was younger.

He continued down the street, but he passed by the road that led to his home district, drawn back closer to the city gates. When the darkness grew heavier, they would close, opening again at the day's first light. The city gates were massive things made of wood and iron, as tall as five men standing on each other's shoulders. The iron bands running the width of the doors were spiked on the outside with great iron teeth. No army would be able to breach them.

Gehrin walked past the watchmen, who paid him no mind, and stopped just outside the gate. He crouched down, squatting on his heels and leaning his elbows on his knees. He had gone as far as he dared. A hundred paces or more away from him, the wooden X still bore its gruesome burden. The man's body was a strange shade of gray, littered with bruises. The deep red that had poured from the spear wounds the day before had darkened to a blackish stain. The man's head hung down, his chin touching his chest and veiled by stringy black hair. Tiny black flies buzzed incessantly around the body, intoxicated by the smell and taste of death. Gehrin pulled his tunic up to cover his nose, but he could not look away, annoyed with himself for returning, and yet inexplicably fascinated by the grotesque view.

Hugging his arms to his chest, Gehrin shivered as the first echoes of the night's coming chill reached his small body. *Aqqa.* He spoke the word in his mind. Then a darker one. *Hasuya.* A name that was no more. The earth had taken it back with the man's blood. A name that was forbidden to pass the lips of any man, woman or child who had known him.

Had this man once dreamed of becoming a *garatelhai*? Had he thrown his spear into a bale of hay? Had his father been proud of him? To kill the son of his king, what dark evil had taken hold of him? Had he known that by the blood staining his hands, he had condemned his wife and children to death as well? Their bodies were no doubt buried in some unmarked grave beyond the city walls, exiled for eternity. No one would visit them and place an offering of remembrance on the stone the way Gehrin often did for his mother.

He should not have come here. Another shiver, and Gehrin reached forward and drew a rune in the soft ground. *Illi.* To guard the heart against evil. A First Rune was powerful. Surely it would protect him. Gehrin pushed himself up on stiff legs and turned away from the dead man. He did not slow his steps again until he had reached his father's house.

*Shadows curled around the path like writhing snakes, and the deep blackness of the world closed in on Gehrin as he was drawn forward. His feet moved without command, and he held out his hands like a blind man groping in*

*eternal darkness. Whispers surrounded him, but he could make out no words. He heard the flapping of wings behind him, but when he turned to look, he saw nothing but the shadows. On the path ahead of him, dark streams of water trickled across the smooth stone, and he knelt, thirsty.*

*His fingers touched the water, but when he drew it close, they were stained red. Horrified, he stared down at the water that was not water. The stain spread across his hands.*

*Gehrin stood up and searched the darkness but saw no one. He opened his mouth to speak, but his tongue felt strange. He touched it and felt only empty space. A scream tore from him, and he backed away from the rivers of blood at his feet. He choked and coughed, and blood splattered his hands. Turning to run, he froze in terror.*

*The wooden X stood close enough to touch, and on it the dead man hung, his body marred by the bruises and wounds from rocks and spears. Blood poured from him down onto the stones beneath, running back to the path Gehrin had just left. Gehrin could not breathe. His lungs refused the air. A raven flew across his vision, an ink splotch in the darker night.*

*"His name is not worthy!" it crowed. Gehrin's lips moved in response, even though no sound came from his empty mouth.*

*"His name... is not worthy..."*

*The dead man's eyes opened.*

*The ropes binding him to the wooden beams fell away like ash. Gehrin couldn't breathe, and the shadows swirled around him, filling his nose and mouth as the man reached for his throat.*

Gehrin surged awake, trying to drag as much air into his constricted lungs as he could. The room was black, and someone's hand covered his face. He tried to push it away, opening his mouth to call for help. He thrashed, his arms knocking a bowl off the table beside his bed. It clattered to the floor as a wad of cloth was shoved in between Gehrin's teeth and strong hands pinned his arms to his chest. Something rough was pulled over his head, and he was lifted from the bed and slung over a broad shoulder. Gehrin struggled to free his arms and kicked, crying out around the gag. He heard a grunt from the man carrying him, and then something hard connected with his face. The pain welled up fresh and sharp, and Gehrin was sick to his stomach. Still, he struggled, even as the soft breeze touched his exposed legs and he realized they were outside the house. He lurched backwards as he dropped from the man's shoulder. Rough wood beneath him prickled against his skin. Rope was looped around his hands and feet and pulled tight. Something closed above him, and the little light filtering through the sack disappeared. Once more, Gehrin found himself in utter darkness.

# CHAPTER THREE

The ropes had begun to chafe against Gehrin's wrists hours ago. He curled into himself as much as the small space would allow. The box was still as dark as it had been when he'd been shut inside, and no daylight filtered through the tiny cracks. He could hear the clatter of hooves and the box shook slightly, sometimes lurching to one side or the other. He heard nothing from his captors. The last voice that he had heard was Thiri's, bidding him goodnight as he fell asleep. He tried to imagine the sound, soft and soothing. Familiar. The string he'd saved for Eiri was still nestled in his pocket.

His father must have enemies, although Gehrin could hardly imagine anyone daring to kidnap one of his sons. His father was a favored advisor to the king of Katesh and would be a powerful adversary for anyone who was foolish enough to cross him. Slavery did not make sense to Gehrin either, who would steal a noble son from his bed to be a slave?

Gehrin had considered the possibility that he was not the only member of his family to be in this situation. But he quickly banished the thought. Surely he would have heard a struggle if someone had tried to take Xario. His brother was much stronger than he was and slept with a wooden spear by his side. He was almost a man, and he would not have gone so easily into the night.

The sharp bite of shame filled Gehrin. He should have fought harder to free himself, instead of bringing dishonor to his father's house, trapped in a wooden box, bound hand and foot like a thief. What would his family say when they awoke to find him missing from his bed? No doubt his father would question everyone in the household. Thiri would cry for him. That much he knew, and the thought gave him a small amount of comfort. Perhaps even Kurin would cry. Eiri would look for him in his room, her dark eyes wide and confused. Xario would not cry, because he was almost a man. And in the darkness of the little box bumping along some unknown road, Gehrin had never felt more like a small boy. Tears squeezed out of his eyes and dripped down his cheeks. He impatiently tried to sweep them away, but his bound hands bumped against his still tender face, and he winced. He choked back a sob, the fear and the slow torture of the lurching movements driving him further away from his determination to stay strong.

Shame retreated in the face of self-pity. Gehrin whimpered softly, nursing his bruised face in his hands as best he could. He even longed for the gruff familiarity of Yrit's ministrations. As the hours passed, he began to drift in and out of the tiny space his world had been reduced to. He reached up and tried stroking his own hair. It was a poor substitute for the memory of his mother's gentle caress, but if he squeezed his eyes tightly shut, he could imagine her long hair combed into silky waves, her smile tinted with the deep red color she always tapped against her lips from the little clay pot on her table. He remembered how soft her hands were. He remembered watching her die.

He slammed his bound fists against the side of the box. His muscles seized and his chest closed beneath the grip of some invisible terror. He hit the wooden walls of his prison again and again, shrieking past the gag in his mouth and the horrid thick dryness of his tongue. The dirty cloth tasted like sweat and dust, and the stale flavor had crept down the back of his throat. As he cried out, he choked in disgust on his own spit and phlegm.

The sound of hoofbeats clopped on. The box lurched, and light filtered through the cracks, then faded. And Gehrin cried. He slammed against the wood until blood ran down his wrists from both the chafing rope and the slivers embedded in his hands. He raged until exhaustion wore him down to a limp defeat, sinking back against the boards beneath his head. He heard the soft snort of a horse. He shivered, the last reserves of his terror pulling at his body. Was he going to die?

The dead man's eyes bored into the back of his memory like spears. The man's wife and children were dead for his treachery. Gehrin shook his head wildly. His father was one of the king's most loyal counsellors. He could not even imagine a world where his father was executed for treason. And yet, he wondered if the *aqqa*'s children had believed the same. Perhaps they had been carted away in the dead of night, ripped from their warm beds and locked inside wooden boxes just like he was.

Death seemed to be chasing him, but he could make no sense of it. Try as he might, it was too vast for his young mind to understand. The priests had said his mother had been lifted to the stars. Master Lohi talked about death as though it were a passage between one life and another, a dark channel into some higher realm. To Gehrin, it was only a disappearance.

His teeth had worn grooves in the wad of cloth, and the last tears dried into caked trails on his cheeks. He was spent, and the aches and bruises that made up most of his body began to protest in earnest. Gehrin uncurled one finger from his fists and reached out to the wall of his box, drawing a square with a dot in the center.

*Feth.*

Two diagonal lines with a dot below.

*Kri.*

A long line with two others crossing its center. A dot below.

*Kef.*

He continued, drawing each rune against the dim wooden boards.

*Gera. Tohl...*

His finger paused, and he tried to swallow past the horrible desert that was his throat. He had gone back to see the *aqqa*'s dead body. He had looked upon evil, not once, but twice. He remembered the tainted water in his father's cup. And in the fresh memory of his father's lesson, he had walked back to the city gate and opened himself to be tainted. Gehrin pressed his finger against the wood.

*Illi.*

How foolish he had been to ward himself against evil as if it would protect him from the darkness he invited into himself. He imagined Master Lohi's disappointed frown. *Runes are powerful, they are not meant for trivial use. Misusing them invites evil as easily as using them in good faith repels it.*

Gehrin's body lurched along with the movement of the wagon now, as if he were becoming one with his tiny prison. Time had slowed to something indistinguishable, weighed down by his guilt. He reached out his finger to the wall again. If he did not understand the lesson, he must repeat it until it was written in his mind. Master Lohi would have given him paper and quill and instructed him to list the runes until he dreamed them.

Runes of protection. *Feth. Kri. Kef. Gera. Tohl. Illi.*

Runes of prosperity. *Ateh. Hijo. Terha. Yba. Harii. Mul.*

*Feth. Kri. Kef. Gera. Tohl. Illi.*

*Ateh. Hijo. Terha. Yba. Harii. Mul.*

*Feth.*

*Kri.*

*Kef.*

*Gera.*

*Tohl.*

*Illi.*

When sleep claimed him, Gehrin's dreams were filled with runes. When he woke again, he set his finger to the wood, drawing the first line of *feth*.

At some point in the endless night of the box, Gehrin finally lost the tight control of his bladder. His legs were sticky with dried urine.

He buried his face behind his hands the moment the lurching movement stopped and the lid above him was lifted. The light blinded him as large hands closed around his arms and lifted him from the box. A sack was pulled over his head once again, giving his eyes welcome relief. He nestled into the shoulder of whoever was carrying him, but that small comfort was quickly denied him as he was passed down to someone else. He heard a sniff and a sharp intake of breath. A woman's voice, brisk and sharp.

"*Aisht*! The smell of these boys. Take him to the third cell."

Gehrin was dropped to his feet and half-dragged across a cold stone floor. His body could not uncurl itself from the position he had held for so long, and his knees and hips groaned under the forgotten effort of supporting his body. He gasped as fiery needles raced up and down his legs. He stumbled as the ground disappeared beneath his foot and he was hauled backwards. He quickly realized that he was going down steps. Gehrin was unable to tentatively feel his way forward, and his body reacted with a faint surge of adrenaline as he was hurried down the broad stairs. Their footsteps echoed faintly as they reached the bottom and were once again on flat stone. The hand on Gehrin's shoulder hauled him sharply to the left, and there was a brief pause. The scrape of a key, and then a door somewhere near Gehrin's feet creaking as it opened.

He was shoved forward, his hands guided to a wooden stick. He felt around and realized that another wooden stick was placed below it. A ladder. On shaking limbs, Gehrin descended, and eight steps later, his foot struck the ground. The sound of wood scraping and then the door closed above him. He reached out, but his fingers only found empty air. The ladder was gone. Inside the dark sack, Gehrin could hear nothing but the sound of his breathing, quick and shallow from the exertion of moving his stiff body. He stood quietly waiting. He didn't know what for. The world above him was silent. There were clearly no answers to be found there. Not yet.

He pulled at the sack over his head and dropped it to the floor. Down below his feet was a scattering of fresh straw. He spread out his toes over the stalks, relishing the feel of something other than rough wood. Beneath the straw was dark gray stone, which ran in every direction. Large stone blocks formed four walls around him. The only light allowed into the cell was from the iron grate in the door that had closed above him in the ceiling. Another prison, but this one was large enough for him to move in.

Gehrin moved to the farthest wall and sank down against the cool blocks. He pulled at the gag. It was knotted tightly at the back of his head, but he was determined. He bit back a yelp as his finger-tips sent sharp lances of pain through his hands. The ends of his fingers were raw and scraped, evidence of the hours he had spent tracing runes in the wood. He shook his head, clearing his mind of the runes for the moment. He was finally able to see, and he was determined to use that to his advantage. Taking stock of the condi-tion of his body, he discovered that except for his fingertips and the bruises still covering his face from his previous injury, he was unharmed.

When he was finally able to work the gag free, he was more concerned with the state of his parched throat and swollen tongue. There was no source of water in the cell. An empty bucket sat in one corner, but he gathered that it was most likely there for human waste. Which brought him back to the unpleasant state of his breeches. He reached for the laces at the front, which was more difficult with his hands still bound. After a brief struggle and falling sideways into the straw, Gehrin managed to work his legs free and kick the offensive item of clothing away from him. He lay in the straw, panting with the effort, left in his loincloth and long tunic, which at least covered half of his legs.

He tried to wet his lips with his spit, but there was very little. His mind wandered to the barrel of rainwater in the corner of his father's courtyard and how he and his brothers would drink so greedily that water spilled down over their tunics. Were they searching for him? He had no understanding of the time that had passed between his capture and his arrival in the new cell. Perhaps a day. Perhaps two. It seemed only a few heartbeats since he had sat down under the eaves to eat *kiji* cakes. And yet it could also have been an age ago. Gehrin frowned down at his hands.

Kasaii had made him promise. Would he ever be able to tell her about what he'd seen that day on the Blood Stones? It was the origin of the evil that had befallen him since. It must be.

Huddling against the wall, Gehrin pulled his mind away from the unclean memories that plagued him and focused on the stone blocks that made up his cell. Without anything else to occupy his time, he began to count them.

*Nin, ruh, yan, liv, yul, hajja.* Six stone blocks high. He counted again. *Nin, ruh, yan, liv, yul, hajja, sabba, kajen.* Eight blocks wide. It was not a small cell. It was almost half the size of his own room. Gehrin frowned, a soft sound reaching his ears. It was a tapping noise from somewhere beyond the trapdoor. It was so quiet it might have been a drip of water. The tapping noise stopped. He held his breath, waiting.

*Tap, tap, tap.*

Gehrin managed to lift himself off the floor and walked over to stand beneath the iron grate of the trapdoor. The tapping stopped again after a few heartbeats, and then resumed. It was not above him.

"Is someone there?"

He cast his voice into the space above his cell as loudly as he dared, unwilling to call down the wrath of whoever might be guarding him. The tapping stopped. Gehrin waited, but it did not start again. He called out once more, but there was still no answer. A strange emptiness filled him. For a moment he had almost believed himself not alone. He returned to his place along the far wall, gathering the straw into a little pile and curling up like a mouse in a nest, tucking his bound hands beneath his head. He bit his lip against the sting as the cords rubbed against his raw wrists, and tears burned the edges of his eyes. But there was so little water left in his body, none would fall. He stared across the cell at the wall. Slowly, the light from the trapdoor dimmed, and Gehrin watched the still darkness.

The sound of creaking hinges woke Gehrin so suddenly that he scrambled to the corner, scattering his bed of straw in every direction. Chest heaving, he watched as the ladder descended into the cell, thunking against the stone. He waited for some monster to appear to drag him out onto the Blood Stones or back into the wooden box.

A small, sandaled foot stepped tentatively down to the first rung of the ladder, followed by another. Gehrin sat frozen in shock as a boy's head appeared at the top of the body that lowered into his cell. He gaped, mouth open, as the other child turned to face him. A boy. A boy like him? He choked back a sob, unsure how to react. The boy's face melted into an expression of grave concern. Stepping forward slowly, he held out his hand and set down a small bucket that sloshed when it reached the floor.

"I have brought water for you," the boy said softly. He dipped a small ladle into the bucket and held it toward Gehrin. Terrified, Gehrin stared at the clear liquid, then back at the boy. Seeming to understand his distress, the boy lifted the dipper to his own lips and sipped. Once again, he held it out to Gehrin. The fear began to crumble as Gehrin's weak and parched body sensed the closeness of relief. He wanted to grab the dipper out of the boy's hand, to drink like a ravenous beast.

He reached out slowly, fingers brushing over the other boy's as he took the ladle. The water touched his lips, and he nearly cried. The rush of cool liquid over his lips, tongue, and throat had never tasted so sweet, so full of life and magic, as that drink did. When he finished what was in the ladle, the boy immediately offered him another, and he drank his fill again. He would have asked for more, but the boy put the ladle back into the bucket.

"Slowly," he said with a generous smile. "I will return with more soon."

Gehrin found his voice somewhere in the sated desert of his mouth. "Are you a prisoner too?" he asked, his voice cracking beneath its unfamiliar use.

The boy stood, lifting the bucket. "I am Jai. I will come back with water again."

As he turned to go back to the ladder, Gehrin leaned forward and grasped hold of the edge of the boy's long tunic, desperation driving his weak body. "Please," he whispered. "Don't leave."

With a smooth motion, the boy turned and knelt, placing a hand on Gehrin's shoulder. "I will return." He held two fingers to his forehead, and then to Gehrin's. "I swear it."

Releasing the tunic, Gehrin leaned onto the cold floor as the boy ascended the ladder, clutching the promise to himself. He had failed to keep a promise, but he was weak and evil. The boy had brought him water and life. He was good. *Jai.*

The door slammed shut.


Jai kept his promise, and before long he descended the ladder again with the bucket and a ladle, and this time he also carried a small bundle that Gehrin could smell as soon as the other boy stepped onto the floor. The bundle was opened to reveal a small leg of meat, three luscious grapes, and a piece of bread. It was a humble meal, but to Gehrin's eyes, not even the king of Katesh could have enjoyed a better feast.

He waited for Jai to hand him the food, and then ate slowly, his jaw stiff and aching. He was also slowed by his bound hands. He drank from the ladle of water several times, and with sustenance, the foreign vessel he had inhabited began to feel like a body of his own again. Jai watched him quietly, sitting cross-legged on the floor. With the water and food, Gehrin's mind had sharpened past the dull blur it had been since the ill-omened night, and he looked at the boy across from him more closely.

Jai was no older than Gehrin himself, and he held his thin frame straight and proud. His dark eyes were set above prominent cheekbones. His black hair hung down to his shoulders, slightly wavy but combed. This boy was not a prisoner, or perhaps if he was, he had been released from his cell and given better treatment. A thousand questions raced through Gehrin's mind, but he forced himself to choose one.

"Am..." his voice trailed off, and he took a breath to pluck his courage back from the corner where it was attempting to retreat. "Am I going to die?"

"You are not here to die."

Gehrin struggled with his next words. "Is... is my father... a traitor?"

Jai picked up the empty food cloth and water bucket. "We are all sons of Katesh, and Sharai is our father."

Confused, Gehrin opened his mouth again, but Jai shook his head.

"No more questions. I have to leave you, but I will return."

And then he was gone, and Gehrin was sitting alone in a stone cell with only one true answer. He was not going to die. No one meant to kill him, at least not yet. But what, then, was the reason for his imprisonment? Was his family alive? Would he ever see Aqatar's burning light again? The questions would drive him mad, and so he put them away into a room at the back of his mind, imagined closing them in wooden boxes and storing them away in dark corners.

Some time later, he heard a faint scream. The sound startled him back into his corner. He cowered as the sound of running boots thudded above his cell. Then all was quiet. Curiosity pulled Gehrin toward the trapdoor, but it was not strong enough to break through the fear that rooted him to the floor. The sounds he heard were too muffled to understand, but he knew something was wrong. He hoped that Jai was not the source of them. What if the other boy never returned?

When all was silent again, Gehrin decided not to retreat to his straw pile. The weakness in his body pulled his mind toward a defeated despair. The water and food were not enough. He needed to move, to run. He tried running from one end of his cell to the other, but it was too short a distance to truly stretch his legs. He relieved himself in the empty bucket in the corner, wrinkling his nose at the stale smell of the breeches still wadded up next to it. He disliked the endless quiet, the nothingness of waiting. His brothers had often tried to teach him to enjoy doing nothing. It might have been a lesson worth learning. But there were others that might occupy his time.

Moving to the center of the room, he drew in his breath, letting it fill his chest and lungs. He sank into one of the forms his training master had begun to teach him a few months before. Knees slightly bent, his core level with his hips. His hands were not free to follow the forms as he had been taught, but he still attempted to punch forward with his fists balled within the confines of the rope. He moved through the forms, focusing on pushing strength through his core and out into his arms and hands. Once he tried punching against the stone wall, but the rock easily defeated his fists, and he shook his bruising knuckles.

The trapdoor opened.

Expecting to see Jai, Gehrin turned around with a word of greeting on his lips, which died as soon as he saw a tall man wearing light armor and a black cloth masking his face. Fear gripped Gehrin. He lunged backwards as the man stepped forward, reaching for his arms. He battled his fear, sucking in a deep breath and thrusting it through to his fists, punching into the man's chest.

The hit barely slowed the man at all, who snatched Gehrin up over his shoulder and carried him up the ladder. In the compromised position of staring at the man's armored back, Gehrin was once again forced to accept defeat. But this time, he was not blind inside a cloth sack, and he swiveled his head from side to side, trying to make sense of the world turned upside down. A stone hallway appeared at the top of his cell. Other trapdoors lined the floor on both sides. Gehrin heard a shout from one of them, a stream of words he could not understand, but he grasped the anger in them.

At the far end of the hallway Gehrin's captor turned left and entered a wide room, closing the door and setting Gehrin down on the floor. Once again, Gehrin found himself in a slightly larger prison. There were no doors other than the one blocked by the armored guard. The walls were all stone, and there were no windows. What surprised him was the stone bath pool in the floor. Next to it stood a tall woman who appeared to be near Yrit's age. Her mouth was downturned in a scowl, and she whisked toward Gehrin, knife in hand.

He hadn't expected to be executed by an old woman, but Gehrin supposed old women could kill another person as well as anyone else. He backed up a step, but it wasn't fast enough to save himself. His hands were yanked upwards, and she began sawing through the ropes binding his wrists. Gehrin blinked.

The cords fell away, and the cool air met his raw skin with a painful bite. The woman pulled at his tunic, attempting to lift it over his head. Gehrin shrank back, locking his arms at his sides. He'd only ever bathed with his brothers since his mother had died, and the thought of this strange old woman removing his clothes was an affront to his modesty.

She clucked at him, irritated, and bent to look him in the eyes. "Nobleborn or no, you're going to take off those clothes and get into that water and scrub yourself until you squeak, you hear?"

*Nobleborn.* Gehrin was confused. Did she know he was the son of a counsellor? "Do you know who I am?" he managed to say.

She glowered at him from wrinkle-lined eyes. "You are nothing you are not told to be."

"I am Gehrin Hallix. My father..."

The slap resounded through the room, and the force of it staggered Gehrin. He clasped his hands to his face, doubly bruised, and stared at the old woman as old and new pain coursed through him.

"You are no one." She pressed a small pot of soap into his hand and shoved him toward the pool. "Wash."

Under her watchful eye, Gehrin removed his tunic and loincloth, trembling more from shame than the cool air. The old woman pointed at the water, and he stepped down into the shallow pool. It was warm. Small channels ran across the floor of the room between the pool and the walls, disappearing beneath the stone blocks. Gehrin eased his sore body into the water, grateful for the warmth and the small amount of privacy away from the old woman's prying gaze. He found a rag folded at the side of the pool. With shaking hands, he opened the lid of the small soap pot and dipped his fingers into the grainy paste inside. It smelled of lemon and herbs, and the smell brought the memory of Hige's *uban* squares back with a bitter-sweet tang. He could almost taste them as the smell invaded his mouth and nose.

He scrubbed his body with the soap, noticing how the water emptying into the pool from the small floor channels was hot. The warm water was even more comforting than the food Jai had brought for him, and he could feel his stiff muscles relaxing. He turned his back to the old woman and the guard, washing himself with as much discretion as he could muster. Even as a prisoner, he was still the son of Ilba Hallix, and he would not shame his father by forgetting his family's pride, despite the old woman's ignorance.

As the layers of sweat, urine, and dirt were scraped away beneath the rough soap, Gehrin began to breathe calmly, his shoulders relaxing into the water. The familiar comfort of the bath brought him bittersweet memories of home. His brothers tumbling around the courtyard, scrabbling at each other like a pair of wildcats. Kasaii's endless but comforting chatter. His father's strength and wisdom. He clung to these memories, gentle as they brushed against his awareness like paint strokes. He gripped them tightly in his mind, tears stinging the back of his eyes.

"Boy!"

The woman's sharp voice sliced through his memories, an unwelcome knife. Turning, he saw her gesture toward a pile of clothing near the wall.

"Take one tunic and one pair of trousers, put them on."

Gehrin's skin crawled with the sudden chill as he stepped free of the pool's embrace, trying to hide his nakedness with his hands as he crossed the room. He reached for a tunic from the pile by the wall. A stack of trousers sat next to them. He pulled the tunic over his head and tugged the pants up to his thin hips. The cloth nearly fell back around his ankles, and he hurriedly tied the laces to tighten the waist. The clothing was made of rough linen, far humbler spun than what Gehrin was used to. Even his tattered and stinking tunic from home was still softer than what he wore. But the old woman had thrown it aside, and for the first time Gehrin saw the pile of clothing beneath it, all dirty, ripped rags. Brown, gray, and some that might have once been a color he would have recognized, but the world had faded them to an indistinguishable hue.

He was not alone.

When the guard took him back to his cell, Gehrin climbed down the ladder quietly. He didn't want to fight again until he was sure he could win. He stepped onto the stone with his bare toes and realized that the horrible smell was gone. His waste bucket was empty, and his soiled pants were nowhere to be seen. A small wooden table had appeared against one wall with a water jar and dipper, and more food. In the corner where Gehrin had slept, Jai sat back on his heels, a dripping brush in his hands. Next to him, a bucket of soapy water. The floor around him was spotless, the stone scrubbed clean just as Gehrin was. Jai smiled.

"Better?"

Gehrin tugged at his hair, loose and damp against his shoulders. He had never been a prisoner before. But the stories he had heard were nothing like this. He glanced down at the soapy bucket of water beside Jai's knees.

"I don't understand," whispered Gehrin. "What are you doing?"

Jai stood up slowly, drying his hands on the front of his clothes. "I was brought to serve, like you. Soon you will understand."

Gehrin shook his head. "I'm not a servant. I am the son of Counsellor Hallix. My father will be angry if I do not return home."

Facing the ladder, Jai placed his hand on the wood. "No. You are no one." He climbed up slowly, taking his bucket with him. Even after the door closed, Gehrin stood, silent and lost.

# CHAPTER FOUR

*The ancient texts acknowledge the presence of great power drawn from the earth as if it were as natural as eating and drinking. But there are gaps in the history, long centuries of silence, until at last we reach the days at hand, where magic is bound to nothing more than superstition and the prophecies of old women.*

*- Master Lohi*

Lohi had never been fond of adornments. The bleak, ancient simplicity of Blackvale's forgotten fortress suited him perhaps more than any other place he had ever been, its stone walls guarding the ancestors of Katesh long before the gold-tiled palace in Keld had appeared. Many of Katesh's more superstitious citizenry thought it was haunted by the spirits of warriors long dead, a place where evil could snatch any unwary passersby. But it was exactly that promise of power and strength that Lohi was counting on.

The old man drew his staff across the ground in a sweeping arc. The runes were speaking to him, he could hear the whispers from the ground beneath his feet and the earth's strange music running in rivers through the stone and the rock. Two small dashes with the staff in the arc's center. The bones of the world were listening, waiting for him to find the truth. He'd spent his earlier years in lustful pursuit of the power that had lain freely at the hands of the Firstborn. He had learned every line and curve of the runes so intimately they were written in his dreams. He had devoted a life to uncovering their secrets and the hidden knowledge buried with the slow decay of time.

In the frailty of his age, they were less like lovers and more like old friends. The vigorous desire to consume the secrets of the ancient runes had dimmed to a stalwart purpose: to rebuild the Oathsworn as they had once been. A new order, one of his own making, fashioned by hands that had served their king without evil.

Loyalty demanded a high price from some, and Lohi had paid it with a clear conscience. To the eyes of his people, he was loremaster, a teacher of young minds, keeper of ancient knowledge. To his king, he was much more.

He was not alone in the courtyard.

The man striding toward him was younger than he was, but still old enough that the hair gathered behind his head was a deep gray. He still wore the armor and sigil of the *garatelhai*, though he was past the days of battle. His stern brow was marred by a long scar that ran from his hairline to his chin. His grizzled beard was cropped short against his face, uneven. An iron *terha* amulet hung from his wrist.

"Welcome, Tahmujin, my friend," Lohi greeted him warmly. "It has been too many years."

The old spearmaster bowed. "Too many years? One long, restless night, perhaps."

"The night is forever restless. It is the way of the world and old men," replied Master Lohi with a smile. "What news of the *garatelhai*? I fear the treachery of one of their own could prove poisonous to the rest."

"They are loyal," Tahmujin replied. "Many curse the spirit of the *aqqa*. But a *garatelhai* turning against the king has dealt a far worse blow to the people. Their trust has been shaken, there are murmurs that others may prove disloyal. I have advised our king to keep only his most trusted warriors near him." There was much he did not say, and Lohi knew that the unshakable battle lord had his own doubts. None of them had expected such a betrayal, least of all from a *garatelhai* who had proved himself such a faithful servant. His blood stained the Stones outside of Keld, scorned by his brothers and his king.

A gentle wind blew leaves across the courtyard's expanse toward the whipping posts. The rest of the space was bare, soon to become a place of rebirth for the boys huddled in their stone cells below. One of them had already been marked by the harsh bite of the prisonmaster's switch. A street boy dragged from the gutters of Mizak, dirty and feral. But Lohi had his reasons for choosing him. As he had for choosing them all. Only time could prove the sacrifice worthy.

Tahmujin folded his arms. "Is the boy here?"

The boy. Lohi leaned on his staff. He could feel the same animosity in Tahmujin as he had felt from the king. He had gambled his life against the request, and the king's fury had burned deep, but the weight of Lohi's long years of loyalty had tipped the scales.

"He will be reforged with the others."

Tahmujin spat in the dirt. "You cannot reforge evil. He will taint the others."

"That remains to be seen." The scholar reached out and put a hand on Tahmujin's shoulder. "You have known me through all the seasons of your life. You have trusted me on fields of battle and in the hall of the king. I know of no man more loyal than you. I ask much of you now, my friend, to trust me in this final war we must fight. There is no one better able to forge these weapons than you. Will you trust me once again?"

The fiercest battle men must fight is the one inside themselves, and Lohi saw that battle in Tahmujin's eyes as the old *garatelhai* studied the courtyard. The death of the prince was still seared into both of them like a brand, for it had been their failure to foresee the imminent danger that had cost the king his most priceless treasure. Without a child, his throne would sit empty, prey for the ravenous wolves who circled it from the shadows. Without a child, the kingdom of Katesh would be thrown into chaos and bloodshed.

Tahmujin returned Lohi's gaze, hard as iron. "If he proves evil, I will kill him with my own hands."

"You will have no reason to stain your hands with his blood," promised Lohi. It was a gamble, true. A gamble that could cost Lohi his own life if time proved him wrong. But living as long as he had, Lohi was confident that he could take a measure of the boy and see the man he could become.

The spearmaster regarded him for a moment, held in the momentary grip of indecision. "We are one blood in this," he finally said. "I will forge these *bruhai* for the king."

"Your loyalty will be remembered," replied Lohi. "You will begin tomorrow?"

"At Aqatar's first light."

"The runes will guide us, as they once guided the ancestors. Have faith."

The *garatelhai* left Lohi and returned to his rooms, and the old scholar knew that Tahmujin would not waver again. The reign of King Kinhariian had tested them all, forged them into something strong, bendable. A weapon that did not ease when it was bent would break too easily. It was natural to question your path. Even the strongest men bore that weakness.

A small shadow crossed the courtyard and stood with his head bowed a few feet away from the scholar. Lohi regarded the servant boy with interest. His left forearm was wrapped with a bandage, and he looked as if he might fall asleep on his feet waiting for Lohi's acknowledgement. The tasks he'd been given could have been divided amongst three or four servants, but he had said no word of complaint, not even when he'd dragged the buckets of urine and dung out of the cells and out behind the wall.

"Jai." Lohi acknowledged the boy so he could speak.

Jai bowed deeply. "Master. Everything is finished as you instructed."

"You spoke to all of them?"

"Yes, and I only said what you told me to." The boy stared at his feet, shifting his weight from one to the other. His scant nine years were shown in the wide-eyed youthfulness of his face, his bare toes wiggling into the courtyard dirt.

Lohi tapped his staff against the ground. "It has been some time since I was last here. Do you remember the runes?"

Jai closed his eyes and diligently recited, "Runes of protection. *Feth, kri, kef, gera, tohl, illi.* And the runes of prosperity. *Ateh, hijo, terha, yba, harii, mul.* Master, I drew runes over the cell doors so my brothers would be protected. I know you did not instruct it, but..." he looked up. "Have I done wrong?"

"The runes are meant for these pure purposes," replied Lohi. "And you must learn to listen when they guide you. You have done well, Jai."

The boy looked up, barely containing the beaming pleasure that radiated from his face. "You will begin training us soon? I saw Master Tahmujin when I left the kitchens. Kirte told me not to bother him."

Lohi had no doubt that the old housekeeper would have liked to be less bothered herself. She put up with Jai's enthusiastic questions simply because Lohi had placed him in her care, but these days she was overseeing more than her fair share of young boys, not all of whom shared Jai's obedient nature.

"Are you injured?" asked Lohi, drawn once again to the bandage over Jai's arm.

The boy tried to hide it behind his back. "No, Master!"

Over the years, Lohi had learned that the best way to discover the truth of a thing from young children was to simply wait patiently and stare at them, and the words would soon spill over. Jai's eyes diverted back to his feet.

"Well, only a little. One of my brothers was angry when I went into his cell with food. He... he bit me, Master."

Lohi's wispy white eyebrows lifted. "Bit you?"

"Yes Master. With his teeth." Jai fidgeted. "The guards beat him.

I tried to make them stop but they did not listen. I think he was just afraid."

The genuine compassion in the boy's voice brought a smile to the corners of Lohi's mouth. It was only further proof that he had made the right choice in bringing them here. Jai's gentle acceptance of his "brothers" would soften what was to come. Lohi leaned more heavily on his staff, his old joints beginning to complain that he'd stood outside for too long and should seek the comfort of his cushions.

"Jai, what would happen if you harmed one of your brothers?"

The boy's head shot up, bewilderment written across his features. "Master, I would never harm them."

"That was not the question you were asked."

Jai bowed slightly. "Forgive me, Master. If I harmed one of my brothers, I would deserve to be punished. Harming a brother invites evil."

"Mmmmm. And if evil is invited in?"

"The blood is tainted," replied Jai quietly. "I understand, Master."

"There are many things that you and your brothers must learn, Jai. Remember the story of the first Oathsworn. Sharai was betrayed because Aqatar strayed from his brothers and his loyalty. You must be strong, just as your brothers must learn to be strong."

"Stronger than the *garatelhai*," the boy whispered. "That's what Kirte said."

"Yes, now go rest. I'm an old man, and I have been too long from my bed."

The boy bobbed in a hasty bow and raced away into the dark corridors. He had always been one of Lohi's best students, but he was not the only one beneath Blackvale's sloping roofs. Somewhere in a cell beneath his feet was another, a scared boy who had been ripped away from his family. A regrettable sacrifice, but one that would be honored in the years to come. And still another whose life would be forever weighed against the sins of a traitor. Lohi sighed, feeling the faint pull at his lungs. The air no longer strengthened him the way it once had, and sleep beckoned him back to its blissful arms.

And yet, one worry taunted him.

He had not known true fear for many years. But now, on the cusp of seeing everything he had planned come to fruition, his death was a black shadow on the horizon. Whatever years he had left, they were not as many as he would need. Tahmujin was a good man, a strong leader who was respected by the *garatelhai* and even much of the divided Counsel. But he would not be able to weather the coming storm alone. Even the small unit of warriors guarding Blackvale concerned him. Tahmujin had chosen from the most loyal, and yet... there was another who had been thought loyal, given charge over the prince, and had brought the soul of the kingdom crashing to its knees. Even now, the king held onto his throne by threads, weakened by the absence of an heir from his own body. The Council would expect him to choose from among their children, as was the ancient law. Such a succession would shift the power of a dynasty that had been ruling Katesh for twelve generations. A blade was hovering above the heart of King Kinhariian.

And two old men were the only ones standing in its way.

Master Lohi tapped his staff against the earth. Two old men and sixteen boys who were locked away beneath the stone. It was time to begin.

# CHAPTER FIVE

*I began to forget the sound of the trees, of the wind.*
*I knew stone, blood, and the horrible truths I carried with me.*
*In the windless silence of that stone, I was bound to them forever.*


*- Sonho*

"Ay, wake up, *keht*."

Gehrin's eyes flew open. Someone was speaking to him, *touching him*. Hands digging through the pockets of his linen pants. As his eyes sharply came into focus, he found himself face to face with a boy. It was not Jai. Gehrin drew back, away from the invasive touch.

"What – who are you?"

The boy hissed at him and jerked his chin forward, his nose only inches away from Gehrin's. "Yah, you a real fancy one, guess so." He looked Gehrin up and down and wrinkled his nose as if he smelled something unpleasant. "You got any food?"

*Food?* Gehrin's sleep-addled mind struggled. He looked up and realized that the trapdoor to his cell was wide open, the ladder resting against the opening. His eyes swerved back to the boy in

61

front of him, and he was keenly aware of the sharp scent of sweat and dirt. The boy's teeth were jagged, and his wild hair looked as if it hadn't seen a brush in weeks. Or ever.

"You hiding food?" the boy asked again, reaching for Gehrin's pocket. Gehrin shoved his hands away. He wanted this boy out of his cell. But the boy let out a wildcat's growl and shoved back, knocking Gehrin against the wall. Gehrin's head hit the stone, sending a rattling ache through his teeth. Then the boy's hands were at the front of his tunic, dragging him up to his feet.

"We gonna fight, *icha*?" he spat in Gehrin's face.

Gehrin jerked away. "No!" he wiped the spittle from his cheek and stepped back. The boy followed him, not letting him retreat. He leaned forward with his fists still balled up in Gehrin's tunic.

"I don't... I don't want to fight!" Gehrin said. He wanted to go home. His hands curled into themselves, ready in case the wildcat boy jumped him.

"Hey, street rat," came a voice from above. "Let him be. He didn't put us here."

The wildcat boy tightened his grip on Gehrin's tunic, then scoffed and pushed him away. When the boy disappeared up the ladder, Gehrin sagged against the wall. A new face peered down into the cell. "You're the last one, then. Come up here."

Gehrin hesitated, his hand scraping against the rough stone as he pushed himself upright. Nothing had made sense since the moment he was snatched from his bed in the dark. He wanted to go home. He wanted his brothers. He wanted Jai. At least Jai had been kind to him. The small cell had provided its own kind of strange safety, but the door was open. It pulled him, promising answers. He thought of Xario. His oldest brother would climb the ladder without hesitation. He would have fought the wildcat.

Gehrin climbed the ladder.

When he reached the top, the boy who had peered down at him pulled him up by his arm, helping him through the opening. He was in the middle of a solid stone room, this time viewing it right-side up. Six trapdoors lined the floor, four of them open, including his.

On the far side of the room, two armored guards stood by the large wooden door. They wore no sigils, no markings to show their oaths to a master Gehrin might have recognized. The hafts of spears were visible behind their backs.

"You're not another street rat, are you?" asked the boy who had pulled him up. He was taller than Gehrin by half a head, and his body was stronger, thicker. His hair was not as long, grown shaggy around his ears. He wore the same clothing that Gehrin did, loose tunic and pants. Across the room, the wildcat was fiddling with the lock on one of the closed trapdoors.

Gehrin hugged his arms to his chest, keeping one eye on the more threatening of the two boys. He didn't understand what was happening, or why the doors were open, but the guards didn't move a muscle despite the boys being loose in the chamber. Gehrin arranged his face into a scowl. Maybe if he looked angry, the other boys wouldn't try to hurt him.

"Can you speak?" Taller Boy said again. "Who are you?"

His dialect was different, rougher than Gehrin's, but the way he spoke sounded noble. He carried himself proudly, regarding Gehrin with the bearing of someone used to being above others. The wildcat was not to be trusted, but this boy was different.

Gehrin straightened his shoulders and puffed out his chest as much as he could beneath the light tunic. "I am Gehrin, third son of Counsellor Hallix," he said, keeping his voice steady.

Taller Boy's eyebrows rose. "A counsellor's son? Sharai's blood..." he breathed out. "My name is Tirrim. My father is the citymaster of Fethet."

Fethet! Gehrin was equally surprised. A small city near their neighboring country of Malek, on the southernmost border of Katesh. He had never traveled so far away from his home, but his father had visited the city. His head swam, and he resisted the urge to sit down. If a boy from the Northern capital city of Keld and a boy from the southernmost city of Fethet were both held prisoner here...

"Where are we?" Gehrin asked.

Tirrim shrugged. "I don't know. They put me in a box, and when they took me out of it again, I was here. We're still in Katesh, I think." He glanced toward the wildcat, who was crouched over one of the other open trapdoors. "The street rat won't tell me anything. I don't even know his name."

The boy in question glared up at them from beneath his tangled hair and scoffed. "You care too much about names, *icha*. Like your name mean something here." He made a rude gesture at them and looked down into the cell below him again. "Ay, you coming up here, *keht?*"

There was no response from whoever he was speaking to in the cell, so the wildcat began descending the ladder. Four. There were four of them in the chamber. Gehrin eyed the closed trapdoors. Were there others?

"Why are we here?" he asked.

Tirrim folded his arms and scowled at the guards. For a moment, his expression made him look so much like Xario that a fresh wave of homesickness washed over Gehrin, bitter and desperate.

"I asked the old woman in the bath, but she wouldn't tell me anything. The guards haven't said a word. Whoever brought us here is twelve kinds of a fool if he's kidnapped a counsellor's son."

Gehrin found a small comfort in the boy's confident words. His father would find him, it was only a matter of time. His father had allies and servants in every corner of the country, and even beyond. And he was a loyal advisor to the king. The king himself would surely aid Counsellor Hallix in finding a treasured son. And when he was found, those responsible would be executed on the Blood Stones, their evil blood cleansed by the earth. And this time, Gehrin would not watch. He would not be tainted by their evil.

A curse exploded from the cell where the wildcat had disappeared. Gehrin scrambled over to peer inside, followed by Tirrim. Below, two boys were locked in a scuffle, the wildcat gripping fistfuls of the fourth boy's hair. They spun, and Gehrin caught a glimpse of the cell occupant's face. The lower half of his face was completely encased in a mask. Wildcat let loose a string of curses as he grabbed for the mask and received a knee to the stomach in return. The street boy wrapped his hands around the smaller boy's neck, pressing him down against the stone floor. The masked boy fought against the chokehold, but he wasn't as strong.

Gehrin moved for the ladder. He had to stop it. The boy was going to die. Iron fingers grasped hold of his shoulder and flung him to the side. He slid to a stop on the stone floor and watched as a guard descended into the cell. The scuffling sounds stopped, and a moment later the guard reappeared, dragging Wildcat by the back of his tunic. The boy was scratching and pummeling the guard's armor with his fists like a thing gone mad. More guards came through the door, and Gehrin was herded from the cell block with Tirrim. He stumbled over a raised stone block in the floor, and Tirrim's hand steadied him from behind.

Emerging from the dark corridors, Gehrin shielded his eyes with his hand as the light seared them. He blinked, trying to adjust his vision, and would've stopped in his tracks if the guards beside him hadn't pushed him forward.

There was a small crowd of boys.

Guards were pushing them all from separate doorways into a massive central courtyard. Gehrin could see nothing past the high walls, but this was like no building he had ever seen before. A tower rose into the sky across from him, built with stone blocks that must have taken a giant's hand to move.

There were new faces everywhere, and Gehrin found himself searching among them for someone he recognized, but there were none. They were all roughly pushed into a line, one shoulder width between each boy as they nearly spanned the width of the courtyard. They all appeared to be roughly the same age, some faces a little younger or a little older than Gehrin's nearly eleven years. Gehrin was separated from Tirrim, who was herded toward the other end of the line. The masked boy appeared two lengths away, still struggling to regulate his breathing. Most of the boys looked Kateshi, but along the line was a boy with skin darker than Gehrin's, standing at least a head taller than the rest. Da'hamian. The neighboring country was known for men who towered over their Kateshi brothers, and this boy was no different. Gehrin had seen Da'hamians many times in Keld, all of them giants.

Two lengths to Gehrin's left was a smaller boy with bone white hair and skin. The mysterious Takkan Islanders were rare in Katesh, and this was Gehrin's first time being so close to one. The boy looked over and saw Gehrin staring. He smiled, but something seemed strange about it, as if some wild beast was attempting to look less intimidating. Gehrin looked away.

He jumped as the guards ringing the perimeter of the courtyard shouted, "*Garatelhai!*"

A man strode onto the dirt, his breastplate marked with the sigil of the *garatelhai*. He was older than Gehrin's father, his sparse beard gray. A scar marred his face. He wore boots and armguards made of dark leather, and two spears were sheathed at his back. Gehrin stared in disbelief. He'd been taken by *garatelhai*. An oathsworn warrior of King Kinhariian.

The *garatelhai* stopped before the line of boys and looked at each of them. He stared longer at Wildcat, who was being restrained by a guard, his arms tied with rope. Gehrin dreaded that strong, stern gaze being turned on him, but it came, and it was as if the *garatelhai* could see inside him, down to his guts. The man moved on to the next boy, and Gehrin felt weak in the knees.

The old warrior spoke. "Whatever home, whatever family, whatever name you bore, it is gone. Here, you are no one, and you serve only Katesh and her king. You will make this sacrifice, and you will prove your loyalty and your strength. You are no one. Say it."

Confused, the line of boys looked at each other, and a handful of them murmured a response. The *garatelhai's* voice grew dark.

"Say it."

"I am no one." The words burned in Gehrin's throat, and anger churned in his chest. He was Gehrin Hallix, son of Counsellor Ilba Hallix. That was his name.

"From this day forward, you have no family save the one that kneels here in this courtyard with you. These are your brothers.

Harm your brothers, and the price will be taken from your flesh." The warrior flicked his wrist, and the guard holding Wildcat marched him forward toward three posts driven into the ground at the far end of the courtyard. The boy struggled, but his hands were looped into the iron rings on one of the posts and tied. The guard ripped open his tunic, baring the boy's back, and withdrew a thin wooden staff from his belt.

The sound of wood striking flesh rang through the courtyard, and Wildcat gripped the sides of the post, a strangled cry tearing free from him. The *garatelhai* master stepped back.

"You will run from one end of this courtyard to the other. Twenty times. The longer you take to run, the more lashes your brother will receive."

To the far left of Gehrin, one of the boys crawled forward. "Please, I want to go home!" he cried piteously. "Please let me go."

In three giant strides, the warrior had crossed the space between them and lifted the boy off the ground by the front of his tunic. The boy screamed, tears rolling down his grubby cheeks.

"You will run, or you will join him at the post," said the *garatelhai*, his voice low and calm. He dropped the boy to the ground in a small heap and waved them all toward the far end of the courtyard. Gehrin heard the staff crack against Wildcat's back again. From the line of boys, one small figure stepped over to the edge of the dirt. The masked boy.

Gehrin followed. Friend or foe, Gehrin would not leave the wildcat to such punishment. He walked forward to the edge of the dirt, standing next to the boy in the mask, who did not look at him. It did not take long for the rest of the boys to make their way to the line, and they began to run. Gehrin ran toward the whipping post, fixing his eyes on the red welts spreading across Wildcat's skin. He stopped a few feet away, turned, and began running back the other way.

*CRACK.*

Gehrin forced himself to ignore the sound, the angry strike of the staff, and the horrible cries coming from Wildcat's mouth. The other boys ran with him, even the small boy who had begged to go home. The Takkan boy streaked ahead of the others, his bone white hair whipping back behind him. He was still smiling.

*CRACK.*

Gehrin pushed himself faster, his feet skimming over the dirt just as they had on his many races with his brothers, the three of them feeling the rush of the wind across their cheeks in their father's fields. He imagined Kurin tied to the wooden post. He imagined Xario locked in a small stone cell. He remembered his father's wisdom. He turned for another length of the courtyard. The small boy who had begged for home stumbled ahead of him, falling to the ground. Gehrin paused, reaching down to pull the boy to his feet.

"Go."

The boy nodded, dripping sweat and blowing air hard through his mouth. Whoever he was, his body was soft, his lungs foreign to the strain of running so far. Behind him, the Da'hamian boy lumbered forward, his steps heavy but steady, eyes fixed ahead.

*CRACK.*

Faster. He could run faster. The fear, anger, and confusion of the past days lent their speed to Gehrin's body. There was purpose here. A simple command. Run. *Run, Gehrin.*

*CRACK.*

Sweat began to drip down the back of Gehrin's neck, his long hair sticking to his face and shoulders as the exertion began to overtake him. He had run ten lengths, and he felt a strange stillness as he ran. There was nothing but the dirt beneath his feet, the sweat, the air against his face, and the edges of the courtyard. Eleven lengths. Twelve.

*CRACK.*

Several boys began to slow, dragging huge heaving breaths in as their bodies grew weak. The Takkan boy was still in front, running with a lightness to his step as if he would never grow tired. The Da'hamian's stride never faltered, never slowed, one step after another, eyes still fixed ahead. A glance over his shoulder showed Gehrin a glimpse of Tirrim close behind. Thirteen, fourteen, fifteen.

In the overhang at the edge of the courtyard, the *garatelhai* watched, silent.

Gehrin's side burned, and his legs began to feel like stretched *uban*. He tried to breathe slowly through his nose and mouth, but his lungs refused to cooperate. He drove himself onward through pure force of will. He would not stop. His bare feet dug into the dirt, propelling his raw muscles despite the harsh complaints.

He began to slow, dropping farther back. Ahead of him, the Takkan boy finished his final length. Gehrin turned for the eighteenth length. He was little more than jogging now, swinging his arms for momentum. Several boys passed him, but they looked as ragged as he was.

*CRACK.*

Nineteen. Gehrin glanced up at the wildcat, who was clutching the sides of the post, knuckles white around the iron rings. Was his punishment wrong? He had tried to harm one of the other boys, and he must pay the price, just as the *garatelhai* master had said. Master Lohi would have said the same. Shedding innocent blood was a grave sin. But Gehrin wasn't sure if he was running because the master had commanded them to run, or because he could feel some pity for the other boy's pain.

No matter how fast they ran, the wildcat had been marked. This was right.

Gehrin stumbled across the line of dirt, finishing his final length. His legs wobbled and he collapsed to the ground. Breath was an elusive indulgence to his burning lungs. The Da'hamian boy crossed the line, his steady march finally coming to an end. His loud breathing reminded Gehrin of a forge bellows.

The last few boys dragged themselves the final length. The Takkan boy's eyes, on the other hand, were still wild and energetic as he stood a little way apart from the others. Once again, he saw Gehrin watching him and offered a jagged grin.

The *garatelhai* stepped onto the dirt. "Back into line where you were before."

The boys moved slowly back, arranging themselves in the same order. One of the guards dragged the wildcat boy back over to the line and dropped him back into his place. He could not stand, and crumpled to his knees, chest heaving. He did not raise his head.

"I am Master Tahmujin of the *garatelhai*," said the warrior. "You will obey me without question. Your life belongs to the king, and your only purpose is to serve him and learn strength and obedience. If you disobey the king, you will die."

He took a pouch from his belt and opened it. He dangled a wooden medallion from his fingertips, letting the boys see the rune inscribed on the flat disc. *Nin.* "I will give you new names, and you will leave the old names behind. They have no place in these halls, and you will not use them or speak of them from this day forward. Do you understand?"

Murmurs of affirmation rippled softly through the line. Gehrin was numb, his body and spirit melted somewhere in the trail of steps he'd run through the dirt.

Tahmujin stepped forward, his voice booming. "When I speak to you, you will respond 'yes Master'. Do you understand!"

"Yes, Master!" the voices raised as one, tired but fearful of the man who held them all in his iron grip. He tossed the pouch to a guard. One by one, a medallion was pulled free and hung around the neck of a boy. Gehrin reached down and looked at his rune.

*Liv.* The number four. He looked down the line and read the medallions. All of them were numbers. *Nin. Ruh. Yan. Liv. Yul. Hajja. Sabba. Kajen. Yelba. Deth. Niveth. Rudeth. Ahdeth. Ivveth. Ulveth. Haveth.*

Gehrin swallowed. These were not names. They were as good as nameless. And a nameless man was a weak man. Gehrin looked up at the grizzled warrior in front of him. Why would the king take his name? The king honored the names of those who were loyal to him. Counsellor Hallix's name was known throughout the kingdom as belonging to a man who had earned the king's great favor. Gehrin's name had honor because it bound him to his father's.

He closed his fingers around as much of the medallion as he could. They could not take his name. *Gehrin.* He whispered it in his mind. *I am not Liv, I am Gehrin.*

Master Tahmujin pointed toward wildcat, then to the building on the left side of the courtyard. "Take your brother and tend to him. I will send for you again soon."

At first, none of the boys knew what to do. Gehrin approached Wildcat slowly, meaning to help him walk inside. But the Da'hamian boy reached down and scooped the smaller boy up, lifting him to his feet with a gentleness that seemed strange for such a large frame. Sabba. The Da'hamian boy's new name was all Gehrin knew, the name he had been given by his parents was forbidden by their stern master.

The building's interior was the same dull stone blocks and floor that the cells were, but the large, open room was lined with beds. No, they were not truly beds, Gehrin decided. More like cots covered with straw. The wooden headrests near the top of the beds were cruder than the smooth one Gehrin slept on at home but looked luxurious in comparison to the hard stone he had slept on in the cell. On one side of the room was a long table with loaves of bread and jars of water. Another table had several small jars and a collection of plants and herbs. The horde of ravenous boys fell on the food like a pack of feral dogs, shoveling the bread into their mouths. Gehrin followed Sabba and the wildcat boy to a bed on the far side of the room.

Wildcat pulled his arm free of the bigger boy with a jerk and eased himself down on the straw mat. Gehrin read the rune on his medallion. *Kajen.* Number eight. Gehrin looked up at the Da'hamian, who was standing above the injured boy like a hulking statue. None of the other boys seemed particularly concerned with the little party in the corner of the room. Gehrin rose and made his way to the table of food. He poured a small cup of water and looked briefly over the small jars and herbs that had been left out. The smell of several of them reminded him of things he had seen Yrit use. They must be for healing, but he knew too little of them to know what might help. He dipped his finger experimentally into a small jar of paste that looked like the one Yrit had smeared over his chin only days before. It had the same consistency, but he couldn't be sure.

"I can help."

The small voice behind Gehrin belonged to Nin, the boy who had begged Master Tahmujin to let them go home. His short hair reminded Gehrin of Eiri's tousled dark curls. He was skinny and small and had dark circles beneath his eyes. Gehrin looked down at the jars.

"Do you... know about them?"

The boy nodded. "Some of them. My mother..." he paused and glanced back toward the doorway. "I know some of them."

Gehrin watched, fascinated, as the boy pulled leaves from each of the different stems, sniffing them. He pulled the lids off each pot, touching and smelling the different oils, pastes and creams. He finally decided on three herbs. Combining them in a small mortar bowl, he ground them together with a pestle, his small hands moving deftly, clearly accustomed to this work. Once the herbs were ground into tiny powdery flakes, he added a grayish paste and mixed it. Holding his creation in both hands, he headed toward the wildcat's... Gehrin shook his head. *Kajen's* bed. He had to remember.

Nin approached the bed, and Gehrin did not miss the way the street boy's gaze narrowed into a dark distrust. The giant Da'hamian had finally left to join the others, leaving his slightly feral charge alone in the corner.

"I made something to help your bruises," said Nin, his hands shaking slightly as he dipped his fingers into the mixture and reached out toward Kajen's battered back. Despite his pain, Kajen slapped his hands away with a growl.

"Touch me and I bleed you, *keht!*" he spat toward the small boy. "Yah, you some kind of twelve fool."

Gehrin found himself stepping in front of Nin as the boy hurried backwards. He took the mortar bowl from Nin's hands and set it on the floor next to the street boy's bed. "He's trying to help. Put it on yourself, then."

They retreated, leaving the wounded boy to himself. Gehrin chose a place in the opposite corner. The straw was familiar, though he was unused to having a real bed beneath it. From this vantage point, things would be quieter. He settled down to watch. The other boys were still squabbling over the food, the last crumbs doled out between the louder and stronger. Gehrin was surprised to see that Sabba did not take advantage of his size to intimidate the other boys into giving him any of the food. He stood near the back of the group, saying nothing.

The masked boy, Hajja, was given space. None of the others wanted to get close to him. He still had not removed his thin iron mask. Gehrin wondered why he wore it. None of them would've known who he was, and even if they did, who would they tell? Perhaps he was disfigured. Gehrin had seen a beggar boy once in the marketplace whose lips and nose were strangely deformed. It would make the boy an outcast, for in Katesh such things were a sign of ill fortune. But Gehrin only wondered if the boy was lonely sitting by himself.

Tirrim broke away from the group of boys and jogged over. He held out a crust of bread. "Here, I saved you some."

Realizing how hungry he was, Gehrin took the bread and chewed gratefully. It was good, dense bread filled with dates. The sweetness of the fruit was like a little taste of home. Gehrin had often climbed the date palms in his father's fields with his brothers.

Claiming the free bed next to Gehrin, Tirrim held out his medallion and looked at it. "Ivveth. This is a whole wagon full of dung. They can't just change our names and keep us here."

There was precious little a group of boys could do to change what the *garatelhai* did or did not do with them. In the presence of these new masters, their names were Liv and Ivveth. The old warrior had spoken with the authority of the king. For now, Gehrin decided, it was better to do as he was told. If it kept him from the whipping posts, he could say the names out loud.

"The master said it was the king's command," said Gehrin quietly. "Disobeying your king and shedding innocent blood are the greatest of all sins."

Leaning in closer, Tirrim fixed Gehrin with a dark glare. "But if he makes us *nameless*? All of us? I'm going to wait until they give us more freedom, and then I'm going to run. They can't keep us in this place forever. They can't."

"Maybe they will." Gehrin pulled a piece of straw between his fingers. "If we run, then we disobey the king."

"You want to stay here with criminals and thieves?" asked Tirrim. He gestured back toward the rest of the room with a sweep of his hand. "Look at them? Beggars and street rats. They're nothing. I don't think any of them are from noble families. You're a counsellor's son!"

Gehrin pulled the straw apart. He thought of the *illi* rune and the body of the dead *aqqa*. How far would the evil take its revenge for his weakness? Outside these walls, a counsellor's son was protected by the power in his father's name. But here, the wildcat had not cared who he was, and he might easily have been the one choked on the floor of his cell. The *garatelhai* master had not cared who he was and had given him a medallion with a different name.

*My father will find me.* Gehrin would hold onto that belief like a drowning man to a rope. "Maybe they will still let us go home."

Irritated, Tirrim flopped back onto the straw. A slight figure approached and sat down on the bed next to his. For the first time, Gehrin got a closer look at the strange, masked boy. Gehrin couldn't look away from the mask. It was made of iron so thin it molded over the bridge of the boy's nose, leaving two holes for the nostrils, but none for the mouth. The iron was smooth beneath the bend for the nose, as if the rest of his face had been erased. Tight leather straps ran around the back of his head and over his ears to hold the mask in place. The boy looked up at Gehrin.

His eyes were blue.

Gehrin had only ever seen one other person with blue eyes. Shortly after his mother died, he had seen a traveling troupe of acrobats in the marketplace of Keld. One of the young men had flipped high in the air, tumbling down and rolling smoothly up to his feet again right in front of Gehrin and his brothers. He had given Gehrin a wink, his blue eyes sparkling, before jumping away. Gehrin had asked his father about blue eyes, and was told that they were rare, colored like precious stones.

The boy's hair tumbled down to his shoulders, but it was not tangled like the wildcat's. His tunic was baggy over thin shoulders, but his eyes were piercing, sharp as blades. Gehrin felt uncomfortable looking at them. While the acrobat's eyes had sparkled and danced and were full of warmth, these were cold and hollow, unblinking. Those disturbing eyes placed so near the blankness of the iron mask made Gehrin uncomfortable, and he averted his gaze.

"What is your name?" asked Tirrim. "Can you speak?"

The boy did not answer, did not blink, just stared at them with his horrible, empty eyes. Gehrin wished that Tirrim would leave the boy alone. Despite the new freedom of being released from the cells, he didn't know if he liked it. He lay down in the straw and rolled over to face the wall, trying to hide the fresh stem of burning tears that gathered at the back of his eyes. With one finger, he drew a rune against one of the bed's wooden slats.

*Father please. Come find me.*

# CHAPTER SIX

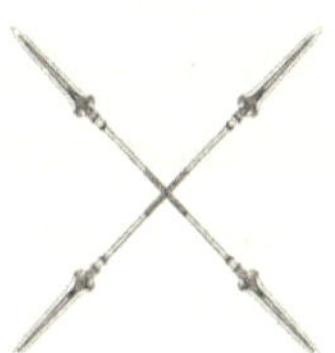

*Little is known about the origins of the Witches of Ordrath. They keep the secrets of countless lives, but their own are most closely guarded. As the highest order of courtesans, they are afforded only by the noblest patrons and highly valued for the information they buy and sell. In the streets they are known as the red women. These are women who know secrets whispered in the darkest, highest corridors of Katesh, knowledge passed from noble lips loosened by plea-sure and candlelight.*

*- A History of the Orders of Aqatar*

"**F**ather, please, let me look for him!"

"*You will not disobey me in this, Xario. If your brother can be found, the men I have sent will find him.*"

Xario gritted his teeth and wiped the sweat away from his eyes. His arm muscles ached from throwing the wooden spear. The years of training and building strength meant so little now that Gehrin was gone, and Xario was stuck like tree roots to this small training court-yard. His father had forbidden him from searching. He and Kurin were not even allowed to walk out into the city without an armed guard.

And worst of all, Gehrin had vanished without a single trace. It was as if he'd been spirited away by a shadow. There had been signs of a possible struggle in his room, things strewn on the floor as they'd been knocked from a table or his bed. But that was where the trail ended. Xario gripped the spear haft until his knuckles turned white. Then he gripped it harder, his hand turning painfully numb.

Xario tried to imagine his brother's fear, and the fresh wave of loss swept over him. Quiet, thoughtful Gehrin, who had always tried to soothe the ruffled feathers between his brothers.

Gehrin, who had watched their mother die, and then been the first to offer Thiri a kind smile when she arrived in their house. Xario kicked the sand. Gehrin didn't deserve any of this. And their father's search had turned up nothing, not a single footprint. He had questioned all the servants, even old Yrit. The *mojar* had drawn runes on the floor of Gehrin's room and claimed that the earth had told her he was still alive. At Counsellor Hallix's request, she had also drawn runes over the older two boys' rooms for protection.

Xario had had enough of runes. He wanted his brother back.

He threw the spear.

He needed the purpose, something to release the taut muscles that had seized up inside him the moment he'd awoken to find the house in disarray at his brother's disappearance. Dark tension hovered over the estate like a storm cloud, leaving everyone inside on edge. Even Eiri had been more irritable, her normally sunny disposition sullied by the mood of the house.

Xario jerked the spear from the bale of straw. His father kept telling him that he was almost a man. But being almost a man was the same as still being mostly a child. He turned and threw the spear. It buried itself in the same spot in the straw.

"A fine throw, young master," said a smooth voice. A woman stood at the edge of the courtyard, veiled in red fabric sheer enough to show her darkly lined eyes. Tiny charms dangled from the silver coronet around her forehead. Through the veil, Xario could see the wry curve of her lips and the shine of a jewel nestled above her right nostril. He recognized her immediately. She came to visit his father often with information. Xario knew little about this mysterious, beautiful guest, but he knew that she was called Bithra.

She took several steps toward him, the trail of her red gown slithering across the sand like a brush viper. "Strong arms for strong deeds," she said. The perfume she wore made Xario's head swim, her eyes pulling him into their depths like a black whirlpool in the sea, weakening his knees. His tongue was trapped behind his lips. Her nearness to him sent a rush down to his toes. She leaned down to him, her fingers tracing a feather-soft line across his arm.

"Where is your father?" she asked.

His tongue struggled to free itself from his lips. Xario swallowed and pointed toward the house. Bithra's veil did not hide her smile.

"Perhaps you could escort me to him?"

Xario nearly tripped over his own feet as he led the way into the house. He slipped off his shoes and hurried across the smooth wood floor to his father's room. Behind him, Bithra's small ankle bracelets chimed softly. Xario rapped against the door's thin frame.

"Father."

His father's deep voice drifted through the door. "Come."

Xario slid the door open, pushing it wide enough that Bithra could step through without getting too close to him. As she passed him, she bowed her head to the man sitting behind the writing table. Counsellor Hallix eyed her and then the boy standing outside the door.

"You are here to give me your report, not weave your spells over my son."

Bithra swept her arms in a deeper bow, her voice a low murmur of reassurance. "I merely respect the strong son of a greater father."

Ignoring her, Counsellor Hallix waved his hand impatiently toward Xario. "Leave us."

Turning away from the alluring woman in red, Xario's earlier anger resurfaced. His father's best efforts to find Gehrin had come to nothing. Several days ago, he had asked Xario and Kurin to tell him of any places the boys had gone in the past few months, any hideaway that might be a place of refuge for Gehrin. Xario had wanted to explore those places himself, but his father had said no.

Xario stalked through the house and somehow his feet led him once again to Gehrin's room. Inside, he caught sight of a smaller figure huddled near the bed. It was Kurin, a bowl of coal ash next to him. He had drawn runes all over the floor, the new, darker black mixing with the fading lines Yrit had drawn days before.

Kurin looked up when he heard the footsteps. "I thought the runes should be drawn fresh." His fingers were covered in the black soot, staining his tunic. He had a smudge of it across his cheek. Xario looked down at him and at the scraggled lines of the runes, drawn in haste as they always were when Kurin held the brush. Some of them were barely recognizable. The burnt smell of the ash hung in the room's stale air.

"You think drawing some black lines on the floor is going to do anything to help bring Gehrin back?" asked Xario. "You, who scoffed behind Master Lohi's back when he made us practice runes?"

Hurt flashed across Kurin's face, but it quickly hardened to anger. "And you think throwing your spear into the straw bale does a lot of good? You've been doing nothing but sulking about like an owl since Father told us to stay here."

Xario jabbed the sharper end of his wooden spear into one of the blurry runes. "Father can't find him. None of it has done any good. None of it! Gehrin's gone, and no one wants to admit that he might be dead somewhere. I'm throwing my spear so when we find whoever took him, I can kill them."

"You're going to kill them with a wooden spear?" Kurin's laugh lacked any true mirth. "You're not a *garatelhai*, no matter how highly you think of yourself. Even a simple *gerhai* swordsman could best you."

"And I would last longer than you," spat Xario. He jerked his spear away from the rune, letting it swing dangerously close to Kurin's face. "Better than scribbling in the dirt." His conscience warned him that he was being harsh, but he swept it away. Whatever

Kurin was about to say in response died on his lips as loud shouts erupted somewhere outside the house walls.

*They found him.* The thought was an outburst in Xario's mind, flooded with wild hope. Their feud momentarily stilled by the sound, the two brothers fled the room and tumbled from the main entrance nearly on top of each other.

A young man stood on the path, twisting the woven ends of his tunic belt around in his hands. A worker from his father's fields. A strong hand descended on Xario's shoulder, and he was moved aside. His father descended the steps as the young worker managed a hasty bow.

"Master! We found a boy drowned in one of the wells on your south farmlands. The body soured the water..." he trailed off. "Please, Master, the overseer sent me to fetch you."

*The body.*

Xario's stomach dropped into the soles of his feet. He turned, not waiting to hear the next words spoken between his father and the messenger. Kurin let out a soundless sob and sank to the steps. But Xario did not stop his headlong rush through the house until he had burst from the back door toward the stables. Thiri called to him from where she sat with Eiri playing with a kitten, but he did not answer. He ran into the small stable and threw a rope bridle over the head of his black pony, Kaii. The pony whickered softly as Xario pulled himself up and threw a leg over the animal's warm back. Setting his heels to the surprised pony's sides, Xario urged him out of the stable and toward the back gate. The guards had just opened the gate to allow a wagon through, and Xario sent Kaii barreling out, ignoring the shouts of the guard behind him.

A pull to the left, and the pony and the boy were on the road leading away from the estate at a fast-paced trot, Kaii's hooves beating a drumbeat against the dirt.

*A body.*

Xario leaned forward toward his pony's ears, which were flicking backwards for his command. He clicked his tongue and squeezed his heels, and Kaii's quick trot lengthened into a gallop, his mane sweeping back into Xario's face as the wind began to rush past them. The road straightened and led away past the city's main gates. The southern farmlands that Counsellor Hallix owned were on the other side of the city, but with Kaii in full gallop the ride would take far less time than the usual leisurely pace.

Xario banished everything from his mind except the dirt road between Kaii's ears. The pony's nostrils flared, and he let out soft snorts with each thundering stride. By the time they reached the farmlands, Xario's legs were slathered with sweat and thick flecks of white foam, the pony's chest heaving. It didn't take long to find the small crowd of workers clustered near one of the stone wells. Xario flung himself from his pony's back and ran through the rows of barley. As soon as the overseer saw him and recognized the son of Counsellor Hallix, he bowed quickly. The workers bobbed their heads, murmuring awkward respect.

"Young master," the overseer said gravely. "We were expecting Counsellor Hallix."

Xario did not care who they were expecting. "Where is he?"

With a jerk of his finger, the overseer motioned to a dark form on the ground beside the well. "We found him this morning. Haven't tended this field for days."

The body was lying on a tattered robe. Xario gagged at the stench that pierced through his nose and mouth as he got close. The skin was mottled, a grotesque canvas of red, black, and yellow. The body had bloated to such a horrific size that it was nearly larger than Xario, and sheets of skin were peeling from the arms, hands and feet. Strings of black hair were plastered to the face and neck, and a cloud of flies buzzed around the face and extended belly. Xario covered his nose and mouth with his hand and stepped back.

*No. This monster cannot be my brother.* The body was unrecognizable. It was a boy who might have been Gehrin, but there was nothing familiar about him. The puffy lips, cheeks and eyelids obscured any features that might have looked like someone Xario knew. He didn't even look human anymore. It *wasn't* human.

"That's not my brother."

"A drowned body doesn't much look like anyone," offered one of the workers quietly. He held something out to Xario, a silver chain. Xario felt himself recoil from it even before his brain truly understood what it was.

"Found this around the neck."

Dangling from the end of the chain was an iron amulet, its shape instantly familiar. The lies that Xario had told himself after seeing the bloated carcass crumbled. *Blood and earth.* Gehrin was dead. Xario's breath fled, and he sank to his knees, the amulet clutched between his fingers.

The rocks around Gehrin's cairn were still strewn with a scattering of petals his father's household had left two days before, when they'd erected the small shrine to his memory. The horrible body was buried deep beneath the rocks, hidden forever from view. Of the family, only Xario and his father had seen it. Counsellor Hallix had warned them all that his spirit could be fearful and angry. They had left all the appropriate offerings at the shrine to appease it, but Xario knew it wasn't enough. Counsellor Hallix seemed to believe the lie that Gehrin could have fallen into the well. There was no proof that he'd been murdered. There were no marks on the body that could be distinguished as weapon wounds, despite the numerous cuts and splits in the skin. It was a tragic accident. Gehrin wasn't the first boy who had met an untimely end through some unfortunate adventurous mishap. Those were the words others had used to try and soothe the grief. Well-meaning friends and family came to the Hallix estate, leaving gifts and sharing sorrow. Xario made himself scarce. He couldn't manage to look one more person in the eyes and murmur thanks for their intended solace. There was no peace to be found in words.

His brother had been murdered. Xario knew it in his heart.

There was no chance that Gehrin had simply stumbled into a well. His brother haunted his dreams, begging Xario to come and find him. In the room next to his, Kurin cried out in the night, and Xario wondered if he, too, was plagued by Gehrin's memory in the dark clutches of sleep. Thiri spent most of her day in her rooms, her eyes red-rimmed as she went through the motions of caring for Eiri, who often called out for "Gah-nin?"

If their father grieved, it was hidden behind the stony silence he kept in his rooms, visited by strange messengers night and day. Xario had seen Bithra again just that morning, her dark eyes sweeping over him as she passed through the inner courtyard. Her gaze made him feel as if he had no secrets, as if she could see his thoughts as easily as she could see his face.

As he stood before the small shrine, the winds over the rocky plains blew Xario's cloak around his shoulders, pulling at him. In the distance, a pony approached with a small rider clinging to its back. As the figures drew closer, Xario recognized Kasaii, her cheeks red and hair windblown around her face. She pulled her pony to a halt a few feet away. She dropped the reins, and the animal contentedly began cropping at the scrub grass patchworked across the rocky ground. Xario approached them and reached up to help her down, taking the brunt of her weight as she lowered herself out of the saddle. She limped toward the shrine.

She gripped a few stone lily flowers in her hand. The ride had not been kind to them, several stems were broken and hanging at odd angles. She placed them in a crevice of the pile of rocks where they would not be blown away by the wind. Xario watched her quietly as she closed her eyes, no doubt offering prayers, though what good it would do, he did not know. Gehrin was dead. Stone lilies and prayers would not bring him back.

Kasaii's eyes were red rimmed when she opened them, unshed tears glimmering. The two of them stood looking at the pile of stones for a long moment, each of them lost in their own remembrance of the boy who lay beneath.

"They say he was so full of water you could not recognize his face," Kasaii said, her voice breaking softly. "Do you think it took a long time?"

Xario frowned. "A long time?"

Her voice lowered even more. "For him to die."

The image that her words conjured in Xario's thoughts was too much to bear. He wiped his tunic sleeve across his nose. "There's too much we don't know," he said, echoing his father's words.

"My father said that when he was young, he knew a boy who fell down a well pit and broke his leg. But the men digging the well came back the next day and pulled him out. He didn't die." She paused. "Gehrin would never fall into a well."

She returned to her patient pony, and he followed her, giving her a boost to mount up behind its thin withers. Her eyes lingered on the shrine briefly, and then swept down to him before she turned the pony away. Xario watched her disappear down the dirt path toward the city, her hair flowing like a black flag. She'd been a good friend to Gehrin, and it gave Xario some small comfort that she didn't believe the story either.

He pulled the small tool knife from his tunic belt and knelt before his brother's shrine. He traced the runes of Gehrin's name in the smooth upright stone at the shrine's center.

Then he drew the tool knife across his palm, wincing at the sharp sting. He watched the blood well to the surface of his hand. He stared at it, watching the thin line of crimson lazily flow off the edge of his palm and drip down over the stone. Xario swallowed, hoping that the words he chose were the right ones.

"I send my blood into the earth," he whispered to the stones, "and swear by it. As sure as I live, I will find the one who killed you, brother. I will find them, and then I will kill them."

He laid his hand against his brother's name, leaving a dark stain over the runes.

# CHAPTER SEVEN

*Aqatar the Oathsworn betrayed Sharai and killed his master, and Sharai's blood flowed in rivers into the earth, and the earth drank his power. But Sharai, the immortal walker of the stars, stood up on his feet and cursed Aqatar in the presence of the Oathsworn, and sealed him into a great fire, where his hatred burns still.*

*- The Firstborn and the Weaving of the World*

The wooden staff drove Gehrin's breath from his body as it punched into his stomach, knocking him off his feet. The ground welcomed him with its unforgiving resistance, and he slid across the gritty sand. He lay there, staring up at the cloudless blue sky, his body aching in every possible place. The *telhai* guard who had delivered the blow stepped back, silent, waiting for him to rise. If he waited too long, the staff would crack across his shins in punishment. Master Tahmujin did not let fallen boys rest. He expected them to be back on their feet, ready for the next round, as if they were made of iron. Gehrin was not made of iron, he was made of bruises and bumps.

A few feet away, the Da'hamian boy Sabba was taking his own

beating, grunting as the wooden staff of the guard rapped against his shoulders and hands. His raised arms were thick enough to shield much of his face and chest, but the dark skin was still slightly discolored by a patchwork of bruises that matched Gehrin's.

Gehrin rolled to his side, pushing himself up slowly to stall for time. The past few weeks had passed in a blur of training, scrubbing floors, running the courtyard, and falling into his bed so exhausted that he was asleep nearly before his head reached the straw. Tahmujin and the gruff housekeeper Kirte oversaw their every waking moment. Gehrin's hands were red and raw from the soap and water he used to scrub the stone, and the rest of him bore the marks of the wooden staff. Every day he faced a guard with the blunt weapon and was told to avoid being hit. Every day he managed to twist out of the way of a few blows, but many more landed. The guards were *telhai*, after all. Trained warriors against clumsy and unpracticed boys.

A few of the boys managed to fare better than the others. The boy who always smiled, Ruh, seemed to be made of some kind of smoke and mist. His ghostly white skin starkly contrasted the dark purples and blues of the bruises, but there were far fewer of them. He seemed to bend around the staff, boneless. One of the boys had claimed that the Takkan people were half-spirit, one foot in the world beyond.

Kajen the wildcat had tried to fight back once. He'd leapt for the guard with his teeth bared, only to be tied once more to the whipping post. The boys had run for him again under Tahmujin's critical eye, but there were two layers of red welts laced across his back now. And still he spat on the ground behind Tahmujin's back and made crude signs at the guards. It seemed as if the punishment had only fueled his arrogance instead of taming it.

Gehrin faced the guard, closing his hands into tight fists. His fingers had been on the receiving end of the staff before, and he'd quickly learned to keep them protected. And despite the pain in his body suggesting otherwise, he knew that he was getting faster. Perhaps only a little, but it was something.

He dodged the first swing of the staff, and it whistled past his left ear. Without hesitation the guard changed direction and swept the wooden weapon toward Gehrin's shins. Gehrin managed to hop high enough to avoid the blow, but he didn't miss the next. The staff connected with his right shoulder, knocking him face first onto the ground. He spat sand out of his mouth, feeling the sting of a fresh abrasion across his chin and cheek.

Angry, he glanced toward the rack of staffs next to Tahmujin. The old warrior watched over the field of boys with displeasure. Gehrin wanted a weapon of his own, wanted to defend himself with more than just his body. He was exposed, helpless. What good were hands and feet against solid wood? Even when he had trained in this type of combat with his brothers, they had both been weaponless. Hands against hands. It seemed that Master Tahmujin wanted to make battered and bloody heaps of them all. Gehrin wondered if he enjoyed watching their struggle.

He pushed himself to his feet again.

The midday meal was long overdue by the time Tahmujin finally called for them to stop. Kirte and Jai brought out plates of bread and dried meat. The boys had begun to clump together in small groups, finding familiarities in each other. Gehrin sat down next to Tirrim and Nin and a stout boy who had been named Deth. The wildcat sat by himself more often than not, but every once in a while, he would choose to sit at the outskirts of one of the groups. Today he sat near Gehrin.

"My bones feel as if they're broken in a hundred places," said Tirrim as he stiffly lifted a strip of dried boar meat to his lips. "I think the master is trying to kill us."

"No, he tryna break us, maybe then kill us," replied Deth. "Not the first time I felt wood against my back. My da..." He glanced up at the guards, standing silent around the edge of the courtyard, and said nothing more. The boys had learned to be careful which words they used when speaking to each other. Speaking of their past lives was strictly forbidden, and more than one of them had received a sharp blow after forgetting that rule. Gehrin and Tirrim sometimes whispered to each other at night in their beds, telling each other stories of home. But here in the courtyard, they were Liv and Ivveth, boys who had no other names.

Nin, who usually only spoke when someone asked him a question, chewed his bread slowly around a split lip. He'd become Gehrin and Tirrim's shadow, following them everywhere like a loyal dog. He was the only one who had some skill with healing and he had been forced to put his knowledge to the test with the assortment of new cuts, bruises and scrapes that appeared on the boys every day. Despite this, some of the bigger boys pushed him around when the guards weren't looking. Gehrin and Tirrim at least offered him a respite from that.

"Do you think someday he'll teach us how to fight with a real weapon?" Tirrim asked, glancing over at Tahmujin. "If he does, I'm going to fight my way out of here."

"And do what, *icha*?" Kajen's mocking tone drifted over.

"Go home," replied Tirrim, his voice low, watching the guards.

The wildcat wrestled a gristly bit of meat between his jaws, ripping a piece free. "Yah, and then? They gonna find you and stab you full of holes until you die, guess so."

Tirrim grumbled under his breath, but Gehrin watched the street boy curiously. He swallowed his bite of bread. "Kajen, what does *icha* mean?"

Kajen glared at him for a moment, as if he were trying to understand why Gehrin would ask. Then he shrugged and spoke around his food. "You a noble blood, yah? Live in a house. Wear nice silks and piss silver. *Icha*."

Although he wasn't sure he really understood, Gehrin returned to his food, unwilling to test his fortune by asking the wildcat another question. He had seen Kajen start fights over less. For the most part, the boys had learned to leave him be.

"Is Ruh really a half-spirit?" asked Nin. He was looking across the courtyard at the ghost-colored boy, eating a safe distance from the others. The two closest to him were Hajja, the masked boy, and Sabba. The three of them made a strange trio. Sabba's hulking frame was too large for his age, and he spoke only a little Kateshi, but he was friendly enough despite his lack of understanding. Hajja had never spoken a word, and none of the boys had seen his face absent the iron mask. There had been whispers amongst one of the groups that they would try to take it off him to see what lay underneath, but in truth, his hollow gaze frightened them.

Ruh's constant smile made everyone uneasy. At first, Gehrin didn't understand where the boy's happiness could come from in such a place. But he wasn't convinced it was happiness. There was something threatening always beneath the surface of the curved lips, a distance that he kept between himself and the other boys.

"Spirits don't have bodies," replied Tirrim. "Everyone knows that."

Nin wasn't convinced. "But what if he's only part of a spirit?"

"That means his ma humped a spirit. Makes no sense," retorted Deth.

Gehrin frowned at Deth. The other boys were foreign to him, as if they'd been plucked from another world. His father would have had them beaten for speaking the way they did. Besides Gehrin, Tirrim was the only noble blood among them. Ahdeth was half-noble, a bastard from the port city of Mijaro, but he had joined a group of the rougher boys.

Kajen leaned back, rolling his eyes and finishing the last mouthful of his bread crust. "Spirits got no shaft to stick 'em with, *keht*. Ruh just the same meat and blood as you."

The boys fell silent, finishing their food and leaving the subject of Ruh's lineage alone for the moment. A whip cracked, and Tahmujin was among them, driving them from their rest on the ground back up to their feet. Back to running, and then lifting the logs stacked at the end of the courtyard. Gehrin let his mind slip into the familiar haze, removing himself from the monotony of the work. Pushing his legs forward into a run, he kept pace with Tirrim, his calloused feet digging into the gritty sand. The air was warm in his lungs, and his body had begun to accept the rigorous days. Running. Rolling, pushing, lifting the small logs. Back and forth. All under Tahmujin's dark, watchful gaze, a ready stick against the legs or back of whoever fell behind.

Gehrin found his gaze wander to the blue sky above the edge of the old fortress' walls. The wind whispered against his ear, and he imagined that he could hear prayers for his safe return. His brothers' voices urging him to come home. His father's calm promise that they were searching for him. He pushed his legs faster.

The creak of the wooden bed was music to Gehrin's ears as he fell onto the straw. He embraced the wooden headrest, leaning his forehead against its firm curve. Exhaustion dragged him toward the blissful darkness of sleep. Next to him, he heard Tirrim fall onto his own bed, breathing heavy after their last run. Tahmujin had pushed them harder today, and at the end, the small log might have been solid iron as Gehrin had lifted it above his head. Up, then down to the ground, then back up. Twenty times. Then running. Then the logs again. Relief in the small spaces of time when Tahmujin allowed them to rest and breathe, but that relief was all too short lived. The boys who struggled were refused even that small respite. Nin had fainted twice in the last few days, his weaker frame succumbing to the demands of the merciless *garatelhai* master. Gehrin had attempted at first to help him back to his feet, but he was driven off by the guards.

*You must make your own strength,* Tahmujin had said. *In battle, if you fall, you die.*

They were training for battle. What good a ragtag bunch of boys could do against warriors, Gehrin did not know. He heard Tirrim rustle next to him as he turned to face Gehrin's bed.

"I want a fig."

Gehrin shifted stiffly to face his friend, despite his body pleading for sleep. Tirrim stared up at the ceiling, hands folded across his bare chest. Most of the boys had discarded their tunics days before.

"Have you ever had Malekian figs?" asked Tirrim.

"No," Gehrin responded. Malek was known for its many war tribes, and his father had once said that they were the finest horsemen he had ever seen. Gehrin didn't know anything about their figs.

"The most delicious thing I've ever eaten. The warlords would bring baskets of them for us when they came to visit my father." Tirrim kept his voice low, but his eyes were fixed on some place far away from the stone walls that surrounded them. "The tribes have orchards, trees full of figs as far as you can see. The branches are bursting with them, as purple as a bruise and sweet. My father told me he would take me to see them someday."

Gehrin's mouth watered at the thought. "What are they like? The warlords, I mean."

"They have tattoos on their faces and ride the strongest horses you ever saw. My father says that they bred the ancestors to the horses that the Black Legion rides. They bring gifts to my father and come to eat with us often. But only the warlords from the tribes who are friendly with us. Some of them aren't."

The black warhorses ridden by Katesh's Black Legion were famed throughout the land. The elite cavalry of the *garatelhai* numbered nearly a thousand strong, and they were unmatched in battle. Gehrin remembered when his father had bought ponies for his sons, and Xario had refused any color but black for his mount. He had been determined to look like a *garatelhai* horse warrior, even then. A smile touched Gehrin's lips. He missed his own little gray pony, missed the feeling of the wind against his face as he and his brothers rode across their father's fields.

"... and my father says we must keep good blood between us. The Malekian warlords are great fighters."

Gehrin blinked at the stone walls around him, the barley fields fading from his vision. Tirrim sighed, lost in his own memories of home. Across from them, Nin was already asleep, his body completely still on the straw. But on the other side of Tirrim, a small, masked face watched them intently, sitting with his arms around his knees. The blank blue eyes did not make Gehrin as uncomfortable as they once had, it was one more thing he had learned to accept. Many of the boys still gave him a wide berth, distrustful. Hajja stayed mostly to himself, an eerie shadow at the edge of the strange life they all lived now.

Gehrin wondered if Hajja had ever had a fig. He had still never seen the boy eat anything. Hajja always ate away from the others, his back turned. The guards even allowed him to eat inside. But Gehrin had seen the way that Tahmujin's eyes narrowed whenever Hajja was near him. Their master was freer with his staff around the masked boy, the strikes finding Hajja's back and legs more than any of the rest of them. But Hajja had seemed to hover near Gehrin and Tirrim's small group more often lately.

"... and you'll come to visit me in Fethet, and we will eat figs together." Tirrim finished. Gehrin nodded absent-mindedly. His eyes were fluttering closed, an unseen weight pulling them down despite his best efforts to stay awake and listen to what Tirrim was saying. His thoughts swirled into nothingness as he drifted away.

*Someone was yelling. Xario, trying to wake him up, they would be late to Master Lohi's house, he would be angry with them.*

"LIV!"

"LIV!"

Gehrin jolted awake, disoriented by the still unfamiliar name being shouted in his face. Small hands shook his bare shoulders. Nin's face was directly in front of his own, eyes wide and scared. Sounds of a scuffle somewhere in the room. Gehrin pushed himself up off his bed, sweeping a hand across his blurry eyes. It was still dark.

He saw the dim shapes gathered around the bed past Tirrim. A group of boys, struggling with something. Tirrim was shouting, angry, trying to pull at them. Beneath the struggle, Gehrin caught sight of something that brought a rush of sudden, angry heat to his chest.

Gehrin stood up and had launched himself across Tirrim's bed and into the knot of bodies before he fully realized what he was doing. Faces turned toward him in surprise. Deth. A street boy with a hawk nose named Niveth. Three others. The strong smell of sweat filled Gehrin's nose.

They had ripped the mask off Hajja's face.

There was a strange awkwardness as the boys stared down at him. A deep scar cut a groove in the left side of his upper lip all the way to his cheekbone, missed his eye - which was staring, terrified - and then finished with a light line up to his hair. A piece of his lip was gone, pulled up into the scar like a jackal that had begun to raise its hackles. White teeth flashed in the open space.

Two of the boys were trying to hold Hajja's arms down against the straw, but he had fought one hand free, desperately holding it over his face, legs kicking and body thrashing to try and drive them away. He reached out for the mask at the edge of the bed, and Niveth tried to pull it away from him. Gehrin grabbed Niveth's arms to stop him. Hajja jerked the mask up to his face, shaking as the other boys finally let go of him.

"Get your hands off me," Niveth hissed, turning to face Gehrin. He stood a half head taller, all lean muscle and sharp angles. "Wanted to see what was under that mask." He leaned closer, his sour breath washing over Gehrin's face. "And I know I'm not the only one."

The other boys stood behind him, a heavy threat. Gehrin knew Tirrim was there, but two of them against five? He glanced down at Hajja.

Still shaking, Hajja had pulled himself into a small curl, hands fumbling with the leather straps that held the mask against his head. His chest heaved in an irregular pattern, as if he couldn't breathe.

Gehrin looked up at Niveth, his hands closing into tight fists. He remembered what Xario had taught him and tucked his thumb down against his curled fingers.

"We cannot hurt a brother," he said, trying to make his voice lower and stern, the way his father had spoken to his brothers when they were arguing.

Niveth sneered. "Not hurting him. Just wanted to see under that mask. He's real ugly, doesn't even have much of a face at all."

Gehrin didn't move. "We cannot hurt a brother."

The taller boy's face darkened, even in the dim light. "And you're gonna tell on me, *keht*? You think you still some noble blood here?" He jabbed his finger against the wooden medallion on Gehrin's chest. "You're no one just like the rest of us."

Gehrin said nothing, waiting for the boy's anger to bubble over, knowing at any moment a blow might come swinging for his face. But they were all facing him, and leaving Hajja alone. Gehrin didn't know if that would be much comfort when he nursed a bruised cheek later, but he stood rooted to the ground. He knew he could not stand to watch what might happen if he didn't. Niveth's eyes glittered.

"Yah you some kind of fool," he said. He reached out and pushed Gehrin back a few steps. Gehrin braced himself and returned to his place. That was the final straw. Niveth jumped forward, but his fist swung for Gehrin's abdomen, not his face. The breath *whooshed* out of Gehrin's mouth as pain blossomed in his stomach. He tried to grab Niveth's hands. The other boys jumped into the scuffle, and Tirrim swung at one of them, yelling.

Niveth's weight pushed Gehrin off balance, and they fell to the floor together. Trapped between the hard stone and the heavier boy, Gehrin pushed upwards with his arms and knees, managing to roll Niveth off him. A blurry white flash shot past him and leapt into the fray.

Everyone was yelling. Niveth got his hands on Gehrin's shoulders and was pushing him back against the stone, trying to keep him pinned against the ground and helpless. But Gehrin had wrestled with Xario and Kurin many times. He twisted his shoulder, bringing his elbow free and aiming for Niveth's face. He missed, but the point of his elbow drove hard into the boy's neck. With a low cry of pain,

Niveth's weight shifted, and Gehrin scrambled away and up to his feet. Niveth advanced on him, eyes alight with fury.

A huge form stepped in between them, holding his big hand out, palm up toward Niveth. Sabba shook his head. "No."

Gehrin nearly sagged with relief. He looked toward the rest of the boys and was surprised to see Ruh helping Tirrim up to his feet. One of the boys with Niveth was lying on the floor, groaning, blood gushing from his nose. Nin was next to Hajja's bed, his small fists clenched, but still staying a safe distance from the bigger boys.

The door to the room flew open, crashing against the wall as they separated, and Tahmujin himself strode into the room between them, his face darker than a thundercloud. His voice boomed through the space, echoing off the stone walls.

"Which one of you started this?"

The boys scrambled away from him, standing submissively in a row, heads bowed. The boy on the ground, Ahdeth, tried to sniffle through his bleeding nose, but it sounded more like a bubbling wheeze. Niveth lifted his hand and pointed at Hajja, who was still curled in the same position.

"Master, he did."

Tahmujin's eyes narrowed at the small boy on the bed and flicked his hand. One of the guards grabbed Hajja by the back of his tunic and dragged him off the straw. Hajja went limp in his grasp, still silent. Hot rage boiled in Gehrin's chest. *It's not right.* He stepped forward.

"Forgive me, Master, but Niveth attacked Hajja. He began the fight."

Tahmujin's gaze flickered to Niveth. "Is this true?"

His face eerily calm, the street boy shook his head. "No Master. He lies."

"I will not waste time on deciding the truth and lies. Take all three." The old warrior glared around the room. "The rest of you will be silent. If I find any one of you has left your cot, you will run until your feet bleed."

Gehrin was marched out of the room and back into the courtyard, Niveth behind him. The wooden posts drew nearer, and a nervous fluttering in his stomach made Gehrin feel sick. Ahead of him, Hajja was tied to the farthest post, sagged against the wood. Cold iron scraped against his hands as they were drawn through the post rings. The chill of the night sent gooseflesh rising across his back and arms.

"I have no use for boys who cannot follow rules," said Tahmujin gruffly. He turned to one of the guards. "Leave them there through the day. No food or water."

As the guards returned to their posts and Tahmujin disappeared into the fortress, Niveth leaned toward Gehrin as far as his captive wrists would allow.

"There is blood between us now, *keht*."

Turning his face away, Gehrin looked at the boy to his left. Hajja gripped the rings, his knuckles white. His chest was no longer heaving with strained breath, but the movement was still jerky, irregular, as if his lungs had forgotten the rhythm, eyes tightly closed.

"Are you alright?" Gehrin whispered.

Blue eyes opened and turned to meet his. The mask was still, frozen in its blank expression. But the eyes stared back at Gehrin, and Hajja nodded, his shaggy hair bobbing. Gehrin leaned his forehead against the wood.

The night wore on like a slow trickle of water. Once or twice Niveth tried to bait Gehrin with an insult, but Gehrin kept his face turned toward Hajja's side. When morning dawned, Gehrin had lost feeling in his arms, blessedly fading the sensation of sharp needles beneath his skin. The rest of the boys appeared in the courtyard and began their run. Gehrin felt strange watching them. He should be running too. His legs itched to move.

The hot sun beat down on their backs, and Gehrin found himself wishing he hadn't been so quick to discard his tunic. Hajja still wore one but sweat ran down his face and neck. Gehrin could feel his body drying out like a salted fish. His mouth became sticky, and he eyed the bucket of drinking water enviously when the other boys drank from it. Several times he caught sight of Tirrim watching them. The other boy looked concerned, but no one dared say a word for fear of the stony *garatelhai* master watching over them. During one of the runs, Ruh had made a point to smile at Gehrin every time he approached, a wide grin that lifted his eyes into little crescent shapes. Gehrin found himself smiling back despite his cracked lips.

Watching the others distracted Gehrin from Aqatar's heat and the ache in his body. Ahdeth's face was swollen from his broken nose, eyes puffy and bruised like two plums. Ruh and Sabba ran near each other, a strange pairing of dark and light, Ruh slowing his pace to match Sabba's steady rhythm. Deth ran alone, eyes trained on the ground and his shoulders hunched forward. A bruise colored his cheek that hadn't been there the night before.

Running. Lifting the logs. Pushing them end over end across the courtyard. It was the same as the day before. And the day before. Gehrin wanted to run, to stretch his arms. Pain lanced through his shoulders and back every time he shifted his weight. Even Niveth was silent, too consumed by his own discomfort to add to Gehrin's. It wasn't until night fell again and the others had disappeared back to their beds that Gehrin began to wonder if they would ever be untied. Tears ran down his face. His body hurt. He couldn't feel his arms. He wanted water. He wanted food, his belly growled in displeasure at its emptiness. His lips were cracked and sore, and his tongue felt thick. Memories of the horrible dark box threatened the edges of his mind. He squeezed his eyes shut and recited the runes.

Someone said his name softly. He forced his blurry eyes open and saw a familiar face near his own. Jai was untying his hands from the rings. When the rope released him, Gehrin crumpled to the dirt, his arms heavier than bars of iron. Jai supported his shoulders and helped him sit against the wood post. Then he turned to Hajja and did the same, followed by Niveth.

He had a bucket of water with him and held the dipper to each of their lips. "Drink slowly," he reminded them. Niveth ignored him and managed to grasp the dipper, guzzling the cool liquid down his throat. Jai pulled the dipper from his hand and dropped it back into the bucket. He took Hajja first, helping him walk across the courtyard and into the barracks room where the boys slept. Then he returned for Niveth, who angrily shrugged his arm away when Jai tried to put it over his shoulder. Despite the other boy's hostility, Jai still walked beside him back inside the stone walls.

Gehrin waited against the post, biting his lip as the first painful hints of feeling returned to his fingers and arms. Soon Jai was crouching beside him again, a gentle hand on his shoulder.

"Come."

Jai was stronger than he appeared, and the smaller boy did most of the work lifting Gehrin back to his feet. Gehrin accepted the support gladly, unsure that he would stay standing without it. Leaning onto Jai's shoulder, he shuffled through the dirt. Exhausted tears spilled over his eyelids, but when he tried to lift his hand to wipe them away, he found that the movement took more effort than he was expecting.

"You were strong today, my brother. Do not cry."

Jai's gentle voice only brought more tears. Burned by Aqatar's angry light, sore and aching, Gehrin had felt despair. Escape was useless. He would be hunted down and Tahmujin would kill him. Jai's promise that he was not meant to die was only a promise so long as he did everything they told him to do. Even if his father did find him, would Tahmujin let him go so easily? He was beginning to believe that he might never see the world outside the stone walls again.

As he passed Kajen's bed, the street rat looked up at him with a smirk. "You soft in your brain, *icha*. Have plenty fights of your own without sticking your fool nose into everyone else's, yah?"

Gehrin ignored him and Tirrim, who was sitting on the edge of his bed, waiting to talk. Gehrin didn't want to talk. He wanted to sleep, and he wasn't sure he wanted to wake up.

# CHAPTER EIGHT

*You draw an empty bucket.*

*- Kateshi saying*

The discordant sound of voices rising from the Council chamber reached Master Lohi's ears not long after he stepped beneath the sloping golden roofs of King Kinharian's palace. He had arrived late, the journey on the long road from Blackvale still aching in his old bones despite the softer saddle he'd had made. He leaned heavily on his staff as he made his way through the open stone courtyard toward the inner chambers of the palace. *We will see what mischief has been going on in my absence.*

A servant hurried past him, carrying a tray of wine and cups. No doubt the Council required a good deal of the drink. They needed their heads swimming if they were to make any decisions. Master Lohi reached the chamber and the guards bowed, sliding the large doors to the side to let him in. Immediately he was greeted by a small crowd of faces as the men and women of the Council turned to watch him enter. Some were pleased by his presence. Others were not. Lohi ignored them all, his gaze fixed on the man at the far end of the chamber, perched on his uncomfortable throne.

The king's sharply featured face and embroidered robes belied his true power. Lohi knew it well. Beneath the red silk and jewels beat the heart of a warlord, a man imprisoned far too long by the stifling air of a Council chamber and the babbling voices of lesser men. Above him, the golden faces of the wolf and the fox swirled in their eternal circle of balance, red gems glimmering from their eye sockets. Their fur looked almost like scaled armor as they guarded the throne of the man who sat beneath them. Master Lohi walked through the center of the chamber and paused at the foot of the raised dais.

"*Nyheli garhai*," he said, bowing low. "Forgive me, I am late to this chamber."

"Forever sworn," echoed several voices around the chamber, repeating the traditional blessing. Shallow, meaningless oaths, most of them. Master Lohi had spent years measuring the worth of each one, he knew how the scales tipped.

Kinhariian nodded to him. "Welcome back from your travels, my friend. Perhaps you can bring some of your famed wisdom to this chamber of fools."

"There is wisdom to be found even in the voices of those we do not understand, great one," replied Master Lohi. He met the king's gaze, saw the darkness around Kinhariian's eyes that had plagued his handsome face long before the Crown Prince's death. But he would not speak to soothe his king's heart with news of Blackvale. They would speak of such things later, when self-interested ears were not present. Lohi drifted back away from the throne and took his place in a cushioned chair to the king's left. One high counsellor on the right and one to the left, as it always had been. Master Lohi's attention drifted to the man sitting across from him.

Counsellor Hallix was proud, built on generations of men sitting beside the throne of their king. Living in the shadow of the throne for so long could make a man covet its power. Master Lohi had never wished to cage himself between the arms of carved wood. He was a man unblemished by such lofty desires. His knowledge and talents were more useful where they were, serving a great king. Counsellor Hallix had proved himself loyal without fault. But a man without faults was the most dangerous of all.

The dark visage of the father was so like that of his son, and Gehrin had even inherited his father's stony thoughtfulness, only the eyes betraying the depth of their nature. As Counsellor Hallix and Master Lohi exchanged respectful nods to acknowledge each other, the old scholar smiled to himself. *Yes, the son will be a powerful servant.*

The Council resumed its discussion, which devolved quickly into argument. Rain had been scarce this growing season, and the farmers and landowners were struggling to produce the quotas that were required to feed the people of Keld, and therefore the outer cities would suffer as well.

Counsellor Ujo, representing the merchants, held out his hands gracefully, his rich blue robes fluttering about him. "Great king, if we cannot grow enough food for our people, we will need to purchase more from our neighbors. Our trade profits are still high, but I fear such a great need will deplete more gold than we can afford to lose."

"The Maleks have had good prosperity in their fields and orchards. But they will charge more than their crops are worth, take advantage of our misfortune," replied Counsellor Murii. He spoke for the tradesmen of Katesh, his thick neck bearing the weight of an iron chain carved with runes.

"Malek is not our only ally," cut in Counsellor Hallix, one hand smoothing the dark beard around his chin. "Our ambassador from Da'ham has reported that they may also have an excess harvest. If Malek will not honor fair price, there are others."

Scowling, Counsellor Ujo folded his silken sleeves against his chest. "And how do you propose we pay for this excess harvest that our allies will so graciously share with us? Will you dip into your own great stores of gold, Master Hallix?"

"If my king commands, I will give the last piece of gold in my treasury to feed our people," replied Counsellor Hallix, his eyes boring into Ujo's. The merchant counsellor's face grew red.

"You insult my honor."

Counsellor Hallix did not move. "How so?"

With a wide, sweeping gesture to the gathered counsellors, Ujo attempted to defend himself. "Sharai witness! Which one of us here would not give our own wealth for our great people? Honor is a virtue, Counsellor Hallix, but do you believe yourself greater than the rest of this respected counsel?"

If he does, it is true, thought Master Lohi with a bit of mirth. Great men need not defend their honor, their actions speak for them. Loud in the lips, weak of honor.

Before Hallix was required to give a response to Ujo's accusation, King Kinhariian slammed his hand down on the arm of his throne. Silence fell over the room immediately. Fatherly pride filled Master Lohi. Even if they despised him, Kinhariian demanded their respect.

"A room full of bickering children? Yet again, you prove your breath in this chamber is a waste of air, Counsellor Ujo. Hallix, say your piece," said the king. Master Lohi saw Ujo's face ripple in anger before smoothing into a mask of indifference as he stepped back into his place amongst the thirty-odd counsellors with an exaggerated bow.

"You honor me." Counsellor Hallix stood and descended the single step to the floor, looking around the room as he spoke. "Our kingdoms have grown and stretched farther than ever before, and it is likely that Sundra will soon be waging war against the Northern peoples at the edge of their lands. We do not know when that blade will fall but they will no doubt ask for our help. King Markolian wishes to destroy the plague on their border once and for all. That is an inevitable truth that we must prepare ourselves for."

"So, you would decrease yet more of our gold stores, and yet I have not heard how you plan to increase them again," complained Counsellor Okujen. His long black beard was braided, and small charms looped through the strands. He was dressed moderately compared to his peers, but Lohi knew it was all a matter of theatrics, an effort to represent the common people of Katesh by appearing like them, priding himself on his humility. Lohi regarded the willowy man with displeasure. Okujen enjoyed the sound of his own voice far better than the clamoring cries of the people he served.

"The tribute we receive from the mines of Ruk has not been increased in nearly ten years," said Counsellor Hallix. "I propose we raise it." A hum broke out in the chamber as the counsellors and their lesser advisors broke out in heated discussion.

Master Lohi nodded. It was a good plan, one that he would have suggested himself had the king called on him. The small country of Ruk had been conquered ages past by the greater forces of Katesh and her warlord kings, and its most recent rebellion quelled nine years ago. Despite its size, the wealth of Ruk was undeniable. Deep craters and canyons ran for miles down, dipping tunnels and channels like long fingers into the earth. And cradled in those caverns and hidden passages far below the surface was vein upon vein of gold and jewels. In the lifetimes that it had taken for the vast system of mines to be dug down into the caverns below, they'd only seen a small portion of what waited in the darkness.

Ruk was still ruled by one of its own, Queen Xhen, but the golden tribute she paid to King Kinhariian filled the coffers of Katesh's royal palace. It was a vassal state, bound to a greater country. Master Lohi glanced toward Ujo again, who looked furious. The merchant counsellor was half-Rukian, and Lohi was well aware of his divided loyalties.

"Great one! It would risk Queen Xhen's great anger, and she has been a valuable ally to our people. We could offer to borrow the extra gold we need. A promise of repayment would be a symbol of our good will, and you cannot-"

Kinhariian was up out of his throne, face mottled with fury. "How dare you seek to lecture me, Ujo. Repayment?" he spat. "Ruk is mine, as Katesh is mine. If I raise the tribute, Queen Xhen will pay it. She sits upon her piles of gold like a raven while our fields wither beneath Aqatar's fire. I have sat on this throne for too long, perhaps you have all forgotten that I am warlord *and* king of Katesh! You have all grown soft in your easy lives, soothed like suckling babes with your honeyed wine and silks. You would destroy the power and honor of this nation while you squabble over the refuse like dogs in the street! Get out of my sight!"

Stunned into silence, the room was frozen. Kinhariian glowered down at them like a great bear until they began to bow and shuffle hesitantly from the room. The doors slid shut with a clack, and suddenly the room was too quiet and too large.

Kinhariian strode down the dais and disappeared into an open door behind the throne. Master Lohi stood slowly from his chair, making no rush to follow his irate king. The space between the throne and the wine cup in his chambers would do much to cool Kinhariian's temper.

The king's chambers were simple. Lavish furs were draped over the edges of the raised bed, and firelight glinted off the golden lamps, but there were few other signs of the vast riches due a king who towered over all the countries in Dry'llar. Two of the king's *garatelhai* guard stood motionless in the corner of the room, iron and leather armor gleaming. Kinhariian drank from his cup noisily, then poured himself another.

Counsellor Hallix entered the room behind Master Lohi, sliding the door shut behind him. Neither of the king's high counsellors spoke. Finally, Kinhariian set down his drink and reached up to tear the gold chain from around his neck. He tossed it to the floor, and then placed his palms flat against the table.

"The world was simpler when I had a spear in my hand."

Master Lohi lowered himself into another chair near the fire that was crackling from its square pit in the floor. "Perhaps not the world, but the man."

A slight scoff at that, but Kinhariian would not disagree. Above the bed, the king's great carved spear hung on two pegs, a strip of red silk tied beneath the spearhead. Master Lohi had seen Kinhariian the warlord, strong as an ox, wielding his spear against the horse lords of Malek when several of the tribes had plagued their southern border. The tribes had been beaten back soundly, as they always were when they grew too restless to fight against their own kind. It was their stubborn pride and blood feuds that kept them from uniting under a single warlord king, the way their brothers in Katesh had done well over a century ago.

Counsellor Hallix's voice rumbled from beside the door. "Forgive me if I was too forward, my king. We knew this would not be an easy path."

"Ilba, you have been at my side since we traded our wooden sticks for sharp blades. The Council chamber is yours as much as it is mine. Ujo does not know his place."

"Still, speaking with Queen Xhen's emissary to discuss the tribute before we revealed it to the Council might have served us better," replied Hallix. "She is growing reluctant to send any tribute at all, I think." He was staring into the fire, still smoothing a hand over his beard. Kinhariian shook his head, pouring another cup of wine and holding it out to the counsellor.

"Here. Drink. It would not have mattered when we told them about the tribute, and this way they cannot accuse me of keeping them ignorant. The counsellors already wish me off my throne. Speaking with them is like putting my hand into a basket of adders, and I have felt the bite of their fangs too deeply." Another cup of wine disappeared down the king's throat. He dropped the cup on the table. "Arrange for a meeting with Xhen's emissary. I will speak with him tomorrow."

Counsellor Hallix bowed deeply, and as he left, Kinhariian waved a hand at his guards. Only the king and the old man were left in the warmth of the fire. Kinhariian sat down across from Master Lohi.

"You wear the weariness of your travels on your face, Master."

The old scholar smiled. Kinhariian had never outgrown the habit of calling Master Lohi by the title he had used as a young boy. Lohi had spent many days patiently teaching the prince his runes when he would have rather hunted and swung a spear. And beneath the king's crown, Lohi still saw the eyes of that young prince. And those of his son.

"I am getting too old for a saddle," Lohi admitted. "The road seems longer every time I travel upon it."

The king leaned back in his chair, curled fist against his mouth as he stared thoughtfully into the fire. "Tell me of your travels."

*Tell me of the Bruhai. Those are the words you wish to say.* "I believe that we will be successful, my king. Your servants are strong, and we will strengthen them far beyond their limits. Everything I have promised you will be yours." *The boy is strong, my king. You will be proud of him.*

"I will avenge my son. Even if I have rooted out those who took his life, the others stood by and rejoiced in it." The king's eyes were trained on the flames, dark promises swirling beneath the calm surface. "I will bleed them dry. They grow bold because they believe me weak. Every moment in that Council chamber they circle my throne like jackals. Eight years has given them much time to work their tricks."

"You must keep them at bay a little longer," replied Master Lohi. "Prince Tamarikai's death is a dark cloud over this palace, but it blinds them. We must keep them blind."

"They expect me to choose an heir. I cannot make another son, despite trying. Jifra cannot keep a child in her womb, and the others will not conceive at all." The king leaned forward, resting chin in his hands, deep sadness curled around him like a dark spirit.

Master Lohi tapped his staff against the wooden floor. "You are still in the strength of your life. There is no need for an heir now. And when there is, you will choose."

Kinhariian's eyes flickered away from the fire and settled on the old man's face. "The one I choose must be stronger than all others."

"He will be, my king. He will be strong enough to defend your throne."

The main gate of the Hallix estate opened, allowing the old man and his walking staff to pass through. The guards bowed, recognizing him. He had not walked this path for many months, not since the Crown Prince's death when he had come demanding answers to questions that Counsellor Hallix did not know. The world had been chaos, then, a dark maelstrom of death and betrayal. The king still expected a knife around every corner. Master Lohi knew that after the executions of everyone who had played a part in the prince's death, a knife would be too loud a weapon. No one would dare risk such open violence again. The Council was dangerous, and not all of them were fools. Power was dangling just beyond their fingertips, and Lohi could see them all licking their lips, slavering like dogs over bone marrow.

Master Lohi pulled himself up the steps into the house, carefully slipping off his shoes. Moments later, the servant who had come to greet him let him into Counsellor Hallix's rooms. The soft scent of incense burned in one corner, and the stone-faced counsellor regarded him from behind his table. There were no cushioned chairs in the room, and Lohi's joints creaked as he lowered himself to the pillows on the floor.

"Welcome, Master Lohi."

"Thank you for your hospitality."

Quiet settled, both men waiting for the other to make the first move in a game that they had been playing opposite one another for many years. Master Lohi chose to move the first piece.

"When I returned, I was told your son had been found. May his spirit walk among the stars." Master Lohi touched two fingers to his lips and then twisted them out and away from himself, a sign of respect for the dead. "My spirit weighs heavy with this news."

"As does mine," responded Counsellor Hallix quietly, his expression carefully crafted into an unreadable mask. Nothing out of place. "I will not rest until I know whose hands were responsible."

*Ah. Yes, the story of a young boy falling into a field well. Tragic, and perhaps enough to feed a lesser mind. A story for the mourners and priests. I have taken a son from you, and the boy in the well was simply a necessary sacrifice to maintain the appearance of innocence. He was no one of conse-*

*quence.* Master Lohi smoothed his thumb over the runes in his staff. "You do not believe it was an accident, then?"

"Do not play your games here, scholar." The mask cracked ever so slightly, a displeased tilt appearing on Counsellor Hallix's lips. "As his respected teacher, you were close to my son. Can you believe him capable of such stupidity?"

"I cannot."

"Then I invite you to imagine the truth. My son, taken from his bed in the darkness, and robbed of his life. The earth weeps for innocent blood spilled. But what could be gained by such a vile act?"

*And so it begins,* Master Lohi thought to himself. *The intricate dance of pieces across the board.* A simple question asked by a father bereaved of his young son, seeking answers. A man with power shown to be powerless in the face of pointless tragedy. To all other eyes, this was the truth. Master Lohi tugged at his beard thoughtfully.

"In order to answer this question, we would need to understand the mind who designed the act," he replied. "It would seem that our kingdom is besieged by evil. Two great sons lost, taken before their time. A prince and a boy who could have stepped into his place." Master Lohi was pleased to notice that Counsellor Hallix's eyebrows lifted. He continued. "It is doubtful that our prince was killed by the design of one man alone. A trusted warrior thrust the knife, true. But perhaps servants turned their faces, or even a counsellor whispered in the right ear. There is an order to these things. Perhaps we pulled the stem and not the root."

Counsellor Hallix's face darkened. "Speak plainly, if you can."

"My dear counsellor, do you truly believe there is no one left who would do harm? Do you believe that our king is safe? And if our king is not safe, then the man standing in his shadow cannot be safe. You are close to King Kinhariian's heart. If he must choose a son from among his counsellors, who else would he look to?"

A muscle twitched in the side of Hallix's jaw. "I will not be threatened."

Master Lohi nodded. "You have power. The rest of the Council holds only the illusion of power. Our laws would give them that power, if only our king did not stand in their way. Or you, Counsellor Hallix. If the son of a lesser counsellor were to sit on the throne, our nation would not stand. Katesh would become a coliseum, animals tearing each other apart over pieces of the throne's power. Counsellor Ujo is deep within the clutches of Queen Xhen. Ruk would rise against us, and with them, others."

"You say I hold power, but I am not the only one in the king's trust," replied Counsellor Hallix. He sat still, not even a tapped finger betraying him. "You have been busy of late, Master Lohi. Riding to the far edges of the kingdom in search of ancient knowledge, hidden in your rooms with your brittle books. Tell me, have you discovered a rune to expose the king's enemies and save his throne?"

*You cannot imagine all that I have discovered, young pup.* "I have discovered things that may prove useful."

Counsellor Hallix made no effort to hide his distaste then, and his voice carried an edge of mockery. "No doubt. And yet you keep your secrets like a *mojar*. I have grown distrustful of secrets."

"That will serve you well." Master Lohi pushed himself up to his feet, his staff anchored to the floor. "*Aisht*, to feel strength in my limbs once again. May Sharai grant me enough to see these dark days through. Yes, he will give me enough, I think. I will take my offering to the shrine and write runes for your son."

"I will send a servant with you."

"I thank you, but it is unnecessary. I will keep one ear to the wall of the world, and I may hear something of worth. I will send you word," Master Lohi promised.

Counsellor Hallix stood and offered a curt bow. "If I can discover the whereabouts of my son's murderer, I will bring him to justice."

"*Illa*. May the heart resist evil. And may you find the justice you seek." Master Lohi gathered the front of his robe. He shuffled to the door, then paused to look back at the man behind him. Counsellor Hallix stood solemn, a pillar of his own secrets.

"These days are full of darkness, Counsellor Hallix. Guard your sons. And guard your king."

The audience was over, and Master Lohi left the house, finding his traveling slippers where he had left them on the step. The air was too cold, and he drew his robes closer around his shoulders. The front gate seemed farther from the house than when he had arrived. When he returned to his own home, he would tell a servant to fetch a basin of warm water for his feet.

"Master!"

Brisk footsteps approached him, youthful in their urgency. Master Lohi smiled as Xario came from the training courtyard. The boy's face had grown harder lines since Master Lohi had last seen him. His eyes were shadowed with a new and terrible maturity, a thing that could only be found in the eyes of someone who had seen death. The bright light of innocence had fled, leaving gruesome knowledge in its wake. It came to all sons and daughters, some sooner than others.

Master Lohi traced a rune on Xario's forehead. "Sharai guard you."

"Master..." Xario looked unsure, eyes darting between the scholar and the house. "Please help me."

"What help would you ask of me?"

Xario's arms and hands were taut, nervous energy bubbling up through his body. "Master, I don't believe that Gehrin fell into the well. I know that you see many things, and many people. Please, help me find out who killed him."

*This one is made of something strong, but different than his brother. One smooth stone, one sharp rock.* Regarding the boy kindly, Master Lohi put a hand on his shoulder. "Trust your father in this. Anything you suspect, surely he must already be aware of. If something else must be known about Gehrin, he will find it."

Xario's face fell. "But–"

"Tend to your brother's spirit. Bring your offerings." Master Lohi tightened his grip on the boy's shoulder, watching the dark spheres of his eyes struggling against an onslaught of tears. "Look."

Master Lohi took the end of his staff and drew runes in the dirt. "Do you see?"

Xario wiped a hand under his nose. "Gehrin."

With the tip of his sandal, Master Lohi swept the runes away, returning the dirt to its unmarred state. "And now what do you see?"

"Nothing."

"But do you remember the rune?"

"Yes."

The scholar nodded. "You have seen it and carry it with you as if written in a book. Just as you remember your brother. Your blood and your brother's blood are the same. We carry those we have lost in us and draw strength from them. That is a thing more powerful than spear or sword."

Xario's shoulders drooped as he stared at the space where Gehrin's name had been written, and one tear managed to break free of his grip and wander down his dirt-smudged cheek. "So, I must do nothing?"

Master Lohi leaned forward until his face was close to Xario's. "You ask the wrong question. A better question is: what must I do? Learn and listen. Train and grow strong. Do not dull your spear with grief. Sharpen it with purpose."

Shoulders shaking, Xario's tears spilled over onto his cheeks. Master Lohi gently wrapped his arm around the boy, letting Xario cry against the wide sleeves of his robe.

"You will do great things, my boy. Let those great things speak of your brother and carry him with you. Bring honor to your king. That is how you can honor your brother's memory."

# PART TWO

## THREE YEARS LATER

# CHAPTER NINE

*The closed fist must find its balance in an open hand.*

*- Maleki proverb*

A satisfied smile curved across Syndri's lips. Overlooking the little ravine that ran like a groove through the cracked skin of the earth, she could see the small figures in the distance. Warriors and horses, six of them, a small raiding party. No doubt they had seen her and the nine other Garhis clan warriors when they crested the ridge. Fate was set, there would be a fight. Syndri's fingers twitched, yearning for the smooth grip of her swords. Soon enough. It had been over a moon since she'd spilled blood with them, and she was tired of riding out to the edges of the tribe's land with no one to challenge. The other tribes had grown soft, too scared to challenge her father's warriors. As they should be. Stepping onto Garhis lands was death.

The heavy hooves of her black warhorse, Brig, stomped impatiently beneath her. She could feel his heavy muscles bunched, gathering power. His nostrils flared; ears pricked forward in the direction of their prey. Syndri stroked his neck.

"He's as bloodthirsty as you are."

Syndri turned in her saddle to see her twin sister, Senna, eyeing the pair of them from atop her own warhorse. Her twin was the opposite side of her coin, lithe and curved in the places she was supposed to be, whereas Syndri was built with their father's massive frame. Unlike Syndri's partly braided wild mane, Senna's gleaming dark hair was gathered into twists that ran from the top of her head down her back in one long braid, red yarn woven through the plaits. It was simple, but Senna had never been drawn to the extravagant style that most Maleki warriors favored. She wore no charms in her hair, no rings on her hands, and only a simple woven necklace made by their grandmother. Even Senna's tattoos were simpler, light lines snaking up her arms and curling around her neck down to her collar-bone. Syndri's own dark red tattoos banded in rings around her arms, spiked across her upper chest and neck, and came to sharp points atop her cheeks.

Impatience bubbled through Syndri's gut as she fixed her eyes on the warriors across the ravine. Their foreheads were brown, even darker than their skin, the color of the Tladr tribe. Her father's oldest rival. It didn't surprise her that they stubbornly insisted on continuing their raids on Garhis lands while the other tribes withdrew. She wanted nothing more than to send their heads spinning from their shoulders, but Yugha, her father's War Sword, had not given them the signal. Instead, they waited on the little hill above the ravine, giving their enemy the chance to run with their tails tucked between their legs like curs. But the Tladr warriors clustered their horses together, making no move to run, hefting tall spears into the air in challenge. Spears. Such weapons were most likely gifts from a Katesh trading caravan, and disgust curled like a worm through Syndri's gut. Spears were no match for the swords of true Malek warriors.

Several horse lengths ahead of Syndri, Yugha sat on his bay mare, his permanently frowning face marred by an old scar running the length of his right cheek and chin. Yugha was Nar Garhis' second in command, and he had led the warband to many victories.

But now, scowling across the ravine at the Tladr riders, he sat still as a grassmouth lizard, waiting for the right moment to swallow his prey. Syndri fidgeted atop Brig. She was ready to taste blood, to send her enemies down to the Nameless Lands, where they would be forced to tell the tale of their defeat.

After what felt like an age to Syndri, Yugha barked a command, closed fist raised in the air, his bay warhorse turning to lunge toward the stone bridge that spanned the ravine. Syndri let out a blood-curdling screech and urged Brig after him, hearing the pounding hooves of her sister's mount and the other seven warriors following behind her down the hill.

The familiar tendrils of battle tightened around her body, an enticing mixture of rage and joy. As the warhorses thundered across the bridge and out onto the flat plain beyond, she reached over her shoulder to slide one of her swords free from its sheath. The blade snaked out of the leather with a *whsst* and tickled her ear as it swung past.

Ahead of them, the Tladr warriors sent their horses forward in a gallop to meet Yugha. His swords were drawn, the naked blades flashing in the sun. Syndri balanced in the saddle, imagining a strong thread connecting her through Brig's broad back and into the ground. Letting go of the reins, she reached up for her second sword. The blades swung in a wide loop on either side of her stallion.

She caught the glint of Senna's blades beside her, her sister leaning forward over the neck of her roan mare, Rho. Syndri let out a wild yell, baring her teeth as the Tladr warriors hurtled toward them, screaming their last war cries. She chose her opponent, a man with his hair shaved into black tufts on either side of his head, tattoos nearly obscuring his dark brown Tladr forehead. Syndri curled her lips into a feral grin at the sight of the spear he carried. The mistake would cost him. Spears were the weapons of Katesh, not Malek.

The two horses passed each other so closely that Syndri could have reached out and grabbed the Tladr horse's bridle. She bent backwards as the spearpoint hissed over her, slicing her sword up and out in a sharp jab, the edge of her blade carving across the man's hip. Brig galloped on, and she turned him with pressure from her legs. The stallion slid and swung in a perfect circle; nostrils flared as his powerful muscles bunched beneath Syndri's thighs. The Tladr was spinning around to face her again, a red stain spreading down his leg. He howled at her, his horse charging slower this time. Syndri tightened her grip on the hilt of her sword. Brig's black ears swept flat against his head, neck extending as he sank his teeth into the other horse's shoulder. A jolt shuddered through them both at the impact, unseating the Tladr warrior as his horse lunged to the side. He fell to the grassy plain in a tumble of leather and furs, rolling to his feet.

Leaning back, Syndri slowed Brig and threw her leg over his neck. She raised one sword in the air toward the Sky Clans, whispering the names of her ancestors to witness this death. Their eyes were on her, she knew, and she would shed blood in their stead. The Tladr spat at her, his forehead tightened with pain as he favored his injured leg. Syndri wasted no time closing the distance between them, facing the man with a devilish snarl on her lips. She dodged his first spear thrust, dancing around the sharp edges and bringing her own sword down overhand into his shoulder. As he fell to his knees, sudden pain shot through her, and her leg nearly buckled. The hilt of his short hunting knife protruded from the meat of her thigh.

Pure battle rage coursed through Syndri, keeping her on her feet as she grabbed him by the front of his tunic, dragging him close to her face as she plunged her second sword through his belly.

"The ancestors will not be there to welcome you, cur," she hissed. "You are too weak to join the Sky Clans. Tell those in the Nameless Lands that the daughter of Nar Garhis sent you."

He spat blood in her face, the warmth staining her cheeks. But his defiance faded as life flowed from him, and he fell to the ground, staring up at the sky he would never reach. Exultant, Syndri reached her bloodied swords over her head in salute to those who were watching her from above. She glanced over her shoulder to see her tribesmen dispatching the other Tladr. One or two bodies already lay on the ground. Senna's swords were locked against the spear haft of a woman wearing more furs than leather. Syndri's heart lurched as she saw Senna's sword slip to the side, giving the other woman space to swing the end of her spear up to crack against Senna's head.

As always, Syndri underestimated her sister's agility. Senna twisted back and under the spear, driving the point of her left sword up into the Tladr's throat. Syndri made a small grunt of approval and relief as Senna ripped her blade free, kicking the woman's body away.

Steeling herself against the pain in her thigh, Syndri stiffly knelt and pulled the small bag of gold from the Tladr's belt. Taking the carved totem from around his neck, she smashed it beneath the pommel of one of her swords.

Lurching awkwardly to her feet with a wave of nausea sweeping over her, Syndri ripped her belt free and tied it tightly around her upper leg above the buried knife. The light of battle was waning, and Syndri's ears buzzed and muffled sound as she looked at her wound. She looked away, swallowing down the bile that rose in her throat.

Senna saw her from across the field and headed toward her, stepping over a body in her way. Yugha was forcing the last two Tladr to their knees. They would be nailed to posts on either side of the bridge as a warning to any of their kin who might venture this close to Nar Garhis lands. Syndri didn't need to watch. She had other things on her mind.

Senna knelt in front of her, inspecting the wound. "Breathe deep or you'll faint," she said, reaching into a bag at her side and handing Syndri a strip of leather. "Better if you sit down."

Carefully lowering herself back to the ground, Syndri lodged the leather between her teeth and closed her eyes, trying to control the way the inside of her brain was whirling like a sand dervish.

Senna closed her fingers around the knife handle, and Syndri ground her teeth together at the agony of that simple touch. Senna glanced at her.

"Ready?"

Syndri took a breath and gave a curt nod. The knife slid free, and the white-hot pain that flooded through Syndri's leg and up into her body was colder than the Nameless Lands. She spat the leather out onto the grass and would've punched her fist into anything solid she could reach, but since only Senna was available, she slammed it into her other thigh instead. Senna gripped Syndri's arm to steady her as she swayed, light-headed. She cursed the man lying dead beside her with ill luck even in the cold silence of the afterlife.

"It's a clean wound," Senna said, her quiet voice taking on the soothing cadence it often did when she was tending the horses. "The ancestors show you an open hand."

Still reeling from the knife being pulled free from her body, Syndri looked away as Senna rinsed the wound with her water skin and pulled a pinch of salt from her bag. Dark spots danced in front of Syndri's vision and she let out a guttural scream as Senna packed the salt into the cut and bound a wad of clean cloth tightly against it to staunch the gush of blood.

Senna pulled the cloth tight around Syndri's leg, and then stood, offering her hand. "Come. Yugha will be ready to leave soon."

"He was not in such a hurry to ride down here," muttered Syndri, accepting her sister's help to lurch to her feet. She was still faint, but she wasn't weak enough to say so. She drew deep, cleansing breaths of the grassland air through her nostrils. The tang of death curled inside her nose and mouth alongside it. Her gut churned.

The body of the Tladr warrior lay at her feet. The rush of battle faded, but the thrill of yet another enemy falling to her swords remained. She resisted the urge to kick at the body. Cur. She spat, the glob of bubbling saliva splattering against his blood-stained cheek.

When Senna retrieved both her own and Syndri's swords, Syndri noticed a rip in her sleeve beneath the shoulder, the faint stain of red around the edges.

"She cut you," said Syndri, reaching out and ripping the cloth open further to expose a thin line left behind by a glancing blade. Senna shrugged away, glaring.

"And you ruined my tunic," she retorted, pulling at the scraps of fabric. "Here, you can carry your own blades."

Toward the bridge, a man screamed, the shrill, unfettered shriek of a man beyond the limits of pain. The sound echoed over the grasslands. Yugha was making swift work of them. Syndri reached out and grasped Senna's neck, pulling her sister's forehead to her own.

"Closed fist," she murmured. They would live on to fight again, their enemies would rot and sink down through the earth into the Nameless Lands, where there was no light to recognize the faces of warriors.

"Come," Senna said, softer. "You will need help to ride."

Setting her teeth hard against each other, Syndri whistled for Brig. The black stallion perked up his head from where he'd been cropping at grass a short distance from them. He trotted toward her, and shoved his head against her chest, lips teasing at her wild hair. She limped to his side, ignoring the pain from her leg as it threatened to buckle under her weight. When she tapped at his chest and behind his shoulder, the stallion lurched toward the ground and folded his legs beneath him so she could mount easily. Lifting her leg even that far was still agonizing. Senna saw her settled and then walked off to find her own mount as Brig heaved back up to his feet.

Near the bridge, the wooden beams that marked the entrance to Garhis lands had become warning pillars, the fluttering tunics of the Tladr warriors their flags. Both men hung against the wood, broken and quivering masses of flesh, iron spikes driven through their limbs, sentenced to a slow and agonizing end.

Syndri rode past them with her head held high, and the warriors of the mighty warlord Nar Garhis galloped back over the plains, leaving the bodies of their enemies behind them.

Red flags whipped in the wind above the low stone wall surrounding the Garhis village. The wall was a perfect square guarding the hide-and-wood-frame houses, workshops, and storerooms of the rapidly growing tribe. Syndri's chest swelled at the sight of her father's *gat*

rising from the center of the village, the felted hides stretched tight over a wooden framework beneath. Someday she hoped to see the stone walls rise higher than the height of two men, the proud red flags visible for a much further distance. Nar Garhis was already one of the three most powerful warlords in Malek, and one day every tribal knee would bend to him alone. It was written in the stars, as Syndri's grandfather had said on the day of his son's birth.

Syndri curled her lip, feeling the wound in her leg, the face of the man who had inflicted it still fresh in her mind. The Tladr tribe would be the first, and their bowed heads would be a sight that filled her with pleasure for a lifetime. She urged Brig into a trot toward the opening in the wall, steeling herself against the jolting pain in her leg. Senna rode to her left, and Yugha just ahead of them, holding his deserved place as the Sword. As soon as they passed through the gateway, the other seven riders broke away to return to their homes and tend to their horses.

The village was bustling with activity, most of the *gats* had thin fingers of smoke reaching toward the sky from the hole in the center of their domed roofs. The well near Nar Garhis' *gat* was a hub of activity as men, women, and children filled an assortment of containers. To the right, a small clearing was full of hides stretched over frames, the women laughing and singing work songs as they rolled felt and tanned leather from the herds of kehroxen grazing just beyond the wall. Syndri's father's herds were fat and healthy. It had been a good year for calves. The year was flowing with milk and meat, as her grandfather often said. Interspersed with the kehroxen were the horses, bred for war and strength for generations. A fresh crop of young colts and fillies were already beginning their training with the Garhis youths who would one day become warriors.

Nar Garhis and his wife Ettlan stepped out of the *gat*'s doorway to greet the returning warriors. His eyes met Syndri's, and while he did not grace her with a smile, she caught the glint of pride in his eyes, a look he reserved for her and her siblings. The warlord of the Garhis tribe was larger than life itself, something sky-touched in the way he led his people, commanded their respect. Syndri's mother often said he was as much kehrox as the creatures grazing the land, big-boned and stubborn and as vital to his people as the air.

Syndri had inherited those heavy bones. As she dismounted, pulling her injured leg over Brig once again, she felt the weight of them as she landed on the ground, clenching her jaw. Ahead of her, Yugha pulled up his mare, his blood-spattered scale armor telling the story of their victory before it came from his lips. Her father clasped arms with his War Sword, and the two men pressed their foreheads together.

"The blood of the Tladr runs back into the earth," Yugha said, his voice gruff. "It was a small raiding party."

With a pleased grunt, Nar Garhis gripped Yugha's shoulder. "It was well done. I will give you a skin of *hiffe* to take back to your *gat*. Share it with your wife and daughters." Behind him, Ettlan had disappeared into the *gat* and returned with a heavy skin of the Malekian fermented mare's milk and fig wine. Yugha accepted it, slinging it over his shoulder, pushing back through the small crowd that had gathered to celebrate the victory with his family. Syndri caught sight of Yugha's wife, Tilis, waiting outside their *gat*, her thin frame hidden beneath a thick hide robe that bulged over her belly, heavy with child. Her face showed no sign that her husband's return gave her joy, but when he approached her, she reached up and gently touched his cheek. Syndri looked away. Whatever happened in Yugha's *gat* was no concern of hers.

Senna stepped forward to the carved post in front of the warlord's doorway and pulled a small skin from her belt. She held it up over the post and let the blood of a Tladr warrior drip over the stained wood. The tribe shouted their approval with whoops and the name of their warlord. The Sky Clans would be pleased. Syndri smiled.

Then her father was in front of her, his huge hand cupping the back of her skull and cracking their foreheads together so hard Syndri's teeth rattled. A cold sweat had broken out on her forehead, and she knew she was going to have to sit down soon or she would fall on her rear in front of her tribe.

She smiled. "Greetings, warlord. We have sent more of our enemies to the darkness. The only name they will carry is that of Nar Garhis, whose warriors were the last thing they saw under the sky."

Her father's dark eyes sparkled as he drew away from her, and the thick brown hair around his lips twitched. He reached for Senna next, repeating the same greeting. Hands brushed against Syndri's shoulders, her scale armor clattering as the men and women of her tribe touched her in passing, sharing the remnants of the blood stains to gain strength from the victory.

Ettlan gestured her daughter toward the *gat*. "Come."

"I must tend to Brig," Syndri said, attempting to turn back toward her horse. Senna put a hand on her arm, shaking her head.

"Go with Ettlan. If you have not finished by the time I am done with Rho, I will come back for him."

The wound burned in Syndri's thigh, icy tendrils creeping up and down her leg. Too tired to argue, Syndri followed Ettlan into the *gat*.

Wooden latticework ringed the lower half of the tent-like structure, supporting long beams that reached up into a central ring. Nar Garhis' *gat* was the largest in the village, much larger than anything their ancestors had built. But their ancestors had been nomads, moving from place to place, driving their herds. The Garhis tribe had chosen this land, a place to rest from the wandering of their ancestors.

The comforting scent of cookfire smoke and the slight heaviness of damp hides from last night's rain reached Syndri as she took her first breath inside. She and her sister had moved into their own *gat* when they'd reached the age of adulthood several years past. But she still spent as much time as she could gathered with her family around her mother's cookfire. Senna's cooking didn't compare, and Syndri had been forbidden from it long ago after proving she could ruin meat and vegetables as easily as she could a Tladr warrior.

Syndri sat down on a small stool near the firepit, pulling at the shoulder laces of her armor, and then the laces beneath her armpits. Her body felt lighter as the armor fell away, but she missed the weight, feeling naked without it. As with all Garhis tribe children, both Syndri and Senna had trained day and night in scale armor until it was a second skin, inhibiting their movement no more than a woven tunic. As she drew her trousers cautiously away from her bandaged leg, she wrinkled her nose and sucked air through her teeth. Blood had seeped through the cloth.

Her mother sat beside her, a small clay pot in her hands. Ettlan wrinkled her nose as the removal of the armor revealed the smells beneath.

"You reek," she said. "Come, let me see."

She pulled away the pot's cloth covering to reveal a pungent paste of green leaves. Syndri slowly unwound the bandage to let her mother finish dressing the wound. Ettlan poured salted water over the wound, flushing away the previously packed salt so it would not dry out the skin more than it already had on the ride back to the village. Then she laid out her small leather bag of needles and horsehair thread for stitching wounds.

Syndri looked straight across the *gat*, fixing her eyes on the wooden lattice and chewing a hole in the side of her cheek to keep herself from focusing on the needle puncturing the skin of her leg. Ettlan stitched the skin back together, leaving a slight gap at the end to let the fluids drain. At least the herbs Ettlan used had begun to numb the area, giving it a strangely detached lightness. Syndri distracted herself with thoughts of the battle.

Not that it had been much of a battle.

It was the fourth raid in less than a full moon cycle. The Tladr didn't seem to take their losses seriously, and Syndri was surprised they had enough grown warriors to send out against the Garhis anymore. The Tladr had not faced her tribe with any large force since she'd been small enough to ride in a sling on her mother's back. They were cowards, nipping at the heels of the greater tribe just enough to be a nuisance. Perhaps one day her father would send Yugha and the full strength of the Garhis warband out to destroy them forever. Syndri flexed her hands, feeling the phantom grip of the swords she'd laid aside with her armor. The Tladr had used spears this time, weapons of the soft lords of Katesh whose heritage on the prairie and horseback was nothing but a memory as they draped themselves with lavish silks. Some said that the king of Katesh was a great warlord. Syndri scoffed at the idea. No doubt he was some fat fool who couldn't remember the sharp end of his spear from the haft.

Her mother pulled the cloth bandage tight around her leg. "Too much blood will sour the milk," she said quietly. "Do not forget that the Sky watches more than your sword. I do not want your hands to be forever bound to your blades."

Syndri pulled her mind away from her thoughts. Her mother's eyes were fixed on her as they often had been when she was young and had just done something worthy of disapproval. She frowned. Her mother had always been proud of her kills, just as her father was. Ettlan's womb had been blessed with two daughters and a son, two of them born with closed fists. And yet, something strange was in her gaze now, something that Syndri didn't want to see.

"Have you said the same to Senna?" she asked.

"Your sister does not yearn for her swords when it is time to put her hands to the earth instead," replied Ettlan sternly. "There is no spirit of peace in you."

Syndri reached for her pants, pulling them gingerly over her wrapped leg. "The battle spirit has made us strong."

"Iron must be cooled in water after heating in the flames, Syndri. You are more than a blade to this tribe."

There was always wisdom in her mother's words. Nar Garhis was not the only leader of the tribe, his wife ruled the herds and the orchards, watching over the tribe's daily life and days of peace. A warlord was only one side of the blade, a protector in times of war. Syndri swallowed down any dissent. Her mother would not allow her an argument.

"I hear your words."

"Good. A closed fist..."

"And an open hand," finished Syndri. Her mother gripped her

shoulder and then placed a hand on Syndri's cheek. Her touch was warm, but Syndri pulled away.

"Syndri!" cried a young voice from the doorway. A flurry of lean arms and legs and the flash of an impish grin barreled into the *gat*. Ettlan intervened before the small figure could tackle Syndri off her feet.

"*Ayyah*! Fool boy, would you reopen your sister's wound?" Ettlan scolded.

Despite the cooler weather, Syndri's younger brother was stripped down to nothing but his pants, feet bare and the tell-tale scrapes and scratches along his ankles and calves exposing that he had been up in one of the trees around the village watching for the raiding party's return.

As Syndri gripped his neck to press their foreheads together, Sabayaar managed to catch his breath a bit, still fidgeting. He had never been able to control his energy, always moving with his feet and his mind.

"Senna said they're all dead. Did you kill some?" he asked, glancing toward the scale armor on the floor. Syndri ruffled the scruffy black hair on the top of his head, more bird's nest than human hair, and tugged at the skinny black braid that protruded from the back of his skull like a tail.

"All of them," she replied, leaning down to look him in the eye. "There were none left by the time Yugha and Senna came. And I only needed one of my swords."

He laughed. "When I go on a raid, I'll only use my bare hands. I will leave my swords in the *gat*. I'll fight a hundred warriors by myself."

Syndri held out her hands, palm open. "And all the tribes will fear the name of the mighty Baya," she said, using the pet name she and Senna had given him when he was a baby. He wrinkled his nose at it but danced around her to pick up her blades from the ground, giving one of them a swing.

"Sabayaar."

Ettlan never had to raise her voice above the gentle hum it

usually made, but her children knew when they were being warned. The twelve-year-old boy reverently put the swords back down next to the armor.

"Enough play now," Ettlan said. "Go help Okta with the hides as you promised."

As quickly as he had arrived, Sabayaar disappeared out the doorway, racing off to help scrape the hides strung on frames out at the edge of the village. Syndri nodded to her mother and followed, ready to tend to Brig and see him back to the herd.

The black stallion's ears perked forward when he saw her, blowing a low whicker out of his nose in greeting. Senna had already taken Rho out to the field, the mare's bright roan coat visible just beyond the south wall. Brig followed Syndri like a big dog, nudging against her shoulder as they walked through the village. Syndri limped, shifting her weight just enough to take pressure off the wound. At least her mother's herbs were doing their work, the pain was a dull throb now.

Her mother was right, despite the immediate rush of indignation Syndri felt at the idea that she was more than a blade. Her grandfather had built his tribe on the edge of a blade. He'd fought for his territory, driving back the Tladr and the Uratar tribes when his children were babes in arms. The Garhis tribe had grown from a small tangle of ragged warriors to a powerful warband loyal to Syndri's father. They'd built a wall, and someday it would be a wall that rivaled those in the Northern kingdoms. Her father would be a warlord king, and the tribes of Malek would touch their knees to the ground before him. Syndri could see it in her mind's eye, close enough to touch. Her father's kingdom would be built on the edge of her blade, just as the tribe had been built on his and his father's.

Brig nudged her a little harder, and she nearly missed her next step. Realizing they'd made it out of the village wall and to the grazing herds beyond, she smiled and turned to the stallion, rubbing the little swirl of hairs in the center of his forehead.

"Have my head in the sky again, don't I?" she murmured to him, running her hand down the smooth side of his face to his nose. The fine layer of hair around his nostrils was as soft as a hare's downy hide. She'd walked out into the herd to choose her warhorse, and he had chosen her. As a foal, he'd trotted up to her and shoved his tiny head against her chest. Now, she leaned her forehead against his, and he blew out a huff of hot air, content.

Pulling the saddle from his back and the bridle from his head, Syndri took a rag from her belt and began to rub him down, scrubbing the dried dirt, sweat, and blood from his coat. He relaxed further and further as she worked, eventually closing his eyelids, his lower lip drooping. Syndri leaned against him, feeling his warmth as the day began to grow cool.

Finishing with him, she slapped his rump as he ambled off lazily to join the herds. The tribes grazed their kehroxen and horses together. Although warriors watched over the herds, the horses were an extra safeguard against packs of wild dogs that dared come close enough to try their luck. The spotted leopards were less brazen, but a cat well hidden in the prairie brush or in one of the twisted trees could easily pick off a straggling calf.

The kehroxen were calm, steady beasts, content to graze the stalky grass of the plains, their content lowing a familiar background to the land. Their stony back scales gave way to thick outercoats of long hair. Hidden beneath the outer was an inner coat of soft, downy fiber that spun soft and smooth through the fingers of the tribeswomen, weaving the story of their people into every tunic and blanket. Emissaries from the other lands came to the tribes to trade for kehrox fiber and for the tribes' unmatched quality in leather. Although sacks of barley flour, spices, and iron for forging were the primary focus of trade, sometimes the tribe haggled for curiosities of fine fabrics and colorful jewels. Once the merchant had tried to trade them something called *paper*, on which he had made small black marks with a feather, but Nar Garhis had seen little use for it and had claimed the man was trying to trade worthless goods for his leather.

Syndri glanced up at the sky. It was as gray as a kehrox, dark wisps of cloud threatening rain. The water was welcome in the hot summer, but soon the days would grow a bitter chill and the rain would turn to ice and snow. It was cold, hard work, fighting in the winters. The raiding parties would be smaller and fewer. Nearly all the tribes would hunker down like moles into their *gats*, reluctant to leave the warmth of their fires. Out on the plains, their breath would freeze into clouds, frost lining the men's beards. The grips of her swords would feel like cold stone in Syndri's hands when she pulled them from their sheaths. But men still died in the winter, and it was easier for the Sky Clans to see their blood against the white snow. *More than a blade...* Syndri wrinkled her nose and looked out over the herd. The light was fading quickly into the horizon, but she could still see the shapes of the animals. The smell of them was dark and earthy, comforting, and their deep bellows and hums wrapped around her in the gloom. She could make out several silhouettes in the distance, guarding the edges of the herd. One silhouette was larger than the rest, strange and inhuman.

Hyshir had come to them when Syndri was ten or eleven summers old, a great beast half-starved by the plains of Malek, rejected by the tribes, even hunted by the Uratar. He had spoken no language known to her people, the sounds he made were harsh, guttural, and broken. His back and shoulders were laced with horrible, angry wounds cut deep into his hide. They couldn't pronounce the name he called himself, so her father had named him Hyshir, *strong horn*. Yugha had wanted to put a sword through the giant creature's throat, said the danger was too great to leave him alive. But Nar Garhis had seen something in Hyshir that he trusted, and he had stayed Yugha's hand.

Syndri had watched her mother and the other healers tend to the beast, her childhood curiosity brimming over. She and Senna had peered at him through the doorway of the *gat* her father had built for him, sometimes leaving him small offerings of food. It was always gone the next time they came. And when he was strong again, Hyshir had stepped from the *gat*, his huge shoulders stooping beneath the doorway that was much too low for him.

He was at least two heads taller than Nar Garhis himself. The bones in his face were heavy around deep black eyes that seemed to see all things in every direction. One large, twisted horn protruded above those eyes, sweeping back over his skull. The other was broken a handspan above his brow, jagged edged. His scarred skin was hidden beneath a thick layer of hair so dark brown it was nearly black. He stood on legs like tree trunks, thick with muscle and sloped backwards into cloven hooves instead of feet. Senna had said he looked like a kehrox standing up, but her father had cuffed her on the ears, and she had never said so again. The one word they had been able to understand from his language was *ke'ral*, the name of his people. But he would not say where they were from.

The first time the Uratar had come raiding, Hyshir had paid back Syndri's father tenfold for his mercy, killing four of the blue-tattooed warriors with a massive club he'd fashioned from a kehrox leg bone, breaking their skulls and ribs with a single blow. Syndri had watched her father gift Hyshir a woven red cloth to tie around his forehead, and from that moment on, the great horned creature had been one of the tribe. After the many years he had been with them, he had learned to speak enough of their language to tell them that he was from a land far away, across the water. He told them he had walked for many days, but gave them no more of the story. When her mother had asked him how he had received his old wounds, he said nothing. Ettlan had not asked him again, and when Syndri had shown disappointment in not knowing the rest of his adventurous tale, her mother had simply told her that some stories were for telling and others were not meant to be told. Syndri had been dissatisfied with that, and resolved to ask Hyshir questions until he gave her the rest of his story.

It had been nearly ten years since he had arrived, and Syndri still did not know it. She had spent many days alongside him, watching over the kehroxen and horses. He was never gruff with her when she spoke to him. In fact, he seemed to enjoy the company. He taught her to close her eyes and listen to a different story, the secrets beyond her vision in the smells and sounds of the world. He was a gifted killer, but in all other ways he was gentle. Warriors in the

Garhis tribe often came to blows over some insult, often bloodying each other as much the Tladr or Uratar tribes ever did. But Hyshir never took part in it, never used his strength against anyone in the tribe. Syndri scoffed at the thought. Not even her father would best that incredible strength. Hyshir could probably lift her father over his head without a bead of sweat.

The horned giant caught sight of her watching him and raised one thick-fingered hand in greeting. Syndri nodded and raised hers in return. She stifled a yawn against the leather sleeve of her tunic, the blankets in her *gat* calling her to their comfort. No doubt Senna would be there already, an early sleeper and awake before the first light of the morning crept back over the line between sky and earth. Syndri frowned at the thought. Today had been for the blade. Tomorrow the earth. Closed fist, open hand.

She limped back toward the village wall, easing her clenched fingers apart.

# CHAPTER TEN

Gehrin was going to die. The murky water curled its fingers around him like a predator, clawing his breath out of his lungs and sucking it into the depths beneath his feet. His heartbeat filled his ears, rising with the panic bubbling up through his body, dulling his brain as he fought to focus, resisting the urge to gasp for air. The rope tying him was stuck on the joint of his thumb. He squeezed his hands tighter, tighter. In his head, Master Tahmujin's voice broke through the panic.

*Control it.* You are not going to die unless you choose to.

*Control it.*

*Control it.*

He had done this before. He could do it again. Gehrin blew the last of his air out between his lips, a thin strand connecting him to life evaporating in bubbles somewhere in the dark water. He turned his wrist, pulling his thumb as far in against his palm as he could, and pulling the fear in at the same time. The rope scraped as it edged over his hand. And then he was free, reaching down to the rope binding his bare ankles together. A tug, and that rope fell away, sinking to the bottom of the well. His lungs screamed with want for air, and he knew he was a hair's breadth away from opening his mouth and sucking in water.

Kicking hard against the stone side of the old well, Gehrin launched himself upwards through the cold, desperation driving him to the surface. His burning lungs twisted, and he drew a gasping breath seconds before breaking past the water. The air hit his face as he exploded into a fit of coughing, scrambling around in the water to find a place for his hands to cling. He locked his fingers on the stones, his wet hands slipping against the treacherous slime coating the walls. His hand was lanced with a sharp stabbing pain as it sliced across a sharp edge. The water closed over his head for one... two... three terrifying heartbeats.

He couldn't breathe. He needed to breathe. He wanted his mother. He imagined her soft hand reaching down to him through the depths, her rouged cheeks full of life, black hair draped like silk over her shoulders.

He surged up through the water and back into the blissful air, coughing and heaving the unwanted water out of his lungs. He dragged himself around the stones until he found the rope hanging down against the stone three arm lengths away. The muscles in his back and shoulders strained as he pulled his body weight up and out of the water. One hand over the next, his bare skin chafing against the rock as he scrambled up to leave the water behind.

*Control it.*

After an eternity of climbing, Gehrin's hands touched the ring of stones at the top of the old well, and he used the last reserves of his strength to tumble over onto the sand. Water trickled from his ears and nose as he gagged, his throat bubbling. He felt the approach of the wooden stave a heartbeat before it connected with the side of his head and knocked him off his feet. Still heaving water from his lungs, he brought his hands up to protect his head, blinking quickly to clear the stars from his vision. Dropping his crossed fists, he was rewarded for his reflexes by knocking down a hit that would have connected with his exposed belly. He blinked again, this time the blurry form of the *telhai* guard in front of him coming more into focus.

Gehrin shook his head. Focus. Watch the muscles in his arm, the step of his leading foot. The man was going to swing from the left. Dancing back a step, Gehrin avoided the staff and twisted, darting forward into the man's reach and slamming the heel of his palm against the hard jaw. There was not enough power behind his fist to do any real damage, but the man's head snapped upwards with a satisfying clack, and he stepped back to regain his balance.

With a cough, Gehrin waited, his hands up in front of his face again. His breath still sounded like strangled bubbles were trapped in his throat, but to relax too soon would result in another painful blow. The *telhai* warrior gave a sharp nod and dropped his weapon down by his side, jerking his chin to dismiss Gehrin.

Finally dropping his guard, Gehrin retreated to the line of boys standing still as statues a few steps away. He stood in his place between Sabba and Nin, one giant, one slight as a brown weaverbird. Sabba handed him his tunic, which he pulled gratefully over his shivering shoulders. As the adrenaline wore away, his body began to express its displeasure. His wrists ached, the skin raw from the scratch of ropes, fresh injuries layered over those from previous days. This was the fourth day in a row Tahmujin had taken them to the old well at the back of the fortress. One by one, they were bound hand and foot and lowered down into the dark water. To survive, they had to work themselves free.

The first day, one of the boys, Kajrith, had drowned before they could pull him back to safety. Tahmujin had told them the boy was too weak to serve a king if he could be defeated by water. By the next morning, even his body had disappeared, as if he'd never existed. Gehrin had felt a profound sense of relief that it had not been his own body floating lifeless in the well.

Gehrin heard a splash. One more of his brothers had dropped into the well, but he didn't want to watch. He was safe, he had defeated the fear and the water, and Tahmujin said that made him strong. Every day he survived made him stronger. He sniffed and spat a wad of mucus out onto the sand, careful to miss the bare feet standing around him.

"It's Kajen. Kajen is in the water now," said Nin, his voice plagued by the faint tremor that always made him sound nervous.

Nin was still damp from his own turn in the well water, his scrawny chest bare above the waist of his pants. His hair had dried stiffly, plastered like dark mud against his cheeks and forehead. He watched the mouth of the well, a nervous sentinel. There was a splash from below, a shout from one of the boys standing closer, and soon the Wildcat's strong hands appeared on the rope. He pulled himself over the edge and swung lithely down to the dirt in a perfect imitation of the creature that shared his name. The *telhai's* staff swept in a wide arc over his head, but Kajen ducked and let his fist fly into the man's hand. The staff dropped to the ground. The *telhai* silently nodded, sending Kajen to his place in the line. The Wildcat sauntered over and pushed his way in between Nin and Gehrin, forcing the smaller boy to shuffle aside.

He sent a wink and a grin toward Gehrin. "Not so hard, eh, *icha*? What were you doing down there, scratching your ass?"

Gehrin grinned despite himself and continued to relax the muscles in his arms and hands. Next to him, Sabba spoke in a low voice, his Da'hamian accent weighing his words with a layer of thick honey.

"You just missing view of my face."

Kajen puckered his lips at Sabba and threaded his hands through his long hair, pushing it back over his head. Sabba snorted. Somehow, Kajen and Sabba had both seemed to miss the skinny lankiness most of the boys wore, filling out and already looking more like men than boys even at the age of fourteen, the way Xario had. Gehrin counted in his mind. His oldest brother was seventeen, Kurin sixteen. No doubt if he had stood between them, he would've been just as much of a scrawny sight as he was dividing the Wildcat and the giant. He'd grown, but mostly just up, the rest of him still caught in awkward boyhood.

Eiri would be so changed. Little Eiri with her chubby hands and rose-tinted cheeks. She'd be four now, running around the estate with her black hair flying loose, throwing little pebbles into the fish pool. Gehrin's eyes burned, and he focused on the well. That was not his family anymore. They were just faces and names in a distant world. A world far away from the stone walls and high cliffs of Blackvale. He'd begun to force himself to imagine what it would be like to walk past them on a street in Keld, stepping past with a brief nod to respectfully acknowledge a stranger.

"Yah, *icha*, you got your head up in the sky, guess so." Kajen was leaning close to Gehrin's shoulder, eyes twinkling with mischief. "Thinking about that pretty friend?"

Gehrin pushed Kajen away, shaking his head. "Thinking about your dung breath," he retorted. Only once Gehrin had mentioned Kasaii, not long after they had first come to Blackvale. Kajen had never forgotten, and frequently teased him about her. Gehrin pressed his thumb against the scrape on his upper palm, the bite of the cut sending a pleasant thrill through his mind as it pulled him away from the fading memories of the faces of the people he had loved. He pressed harder.

Night's faint chill had spread its fingers through the air as Gehrin trudged out to the center of the courtyard, his shadow barely visible in the sand. Every night Tahmujin chose two boys to stand watch. How they chose to break up the long dark hours was their own choice, but if both fell asleep at once, they were rewarded with a day tied to the posts. Gehrin was alone for the moment, and he took the opportunity to fill his lungs with a deep breath, pulling in the familiar scents of sand, dust, and the earthy green of the trees beyond the walls of the fortress. He sat down cross-legged, performing his routine of scanning each side of the courtyard, and the tall black cliff face beyond the farthest wall. The rough rock of the mountain rose like a looming tower over Blackvale's western side. Gehrin knew nothing of what lay outside the gates, but it was easy to guess that the fortress had been built in a location that would prevent any attackers from gaining easy access.

Another boy appeared in the dim glow from the barracks room doorway, and Tirrim soon dropped down to the sand. Reaching into his tunic, the city lord's son withdrew a small clump of sticky rice and handed it to Gehrin.

"Here. Nin saved some for us."

Gehrin frowned around his first bite. No wonder Nin was so skinny, always giving away his food. He would have to make a point to return the favor tomorrow. The soft grains of rice stuck to his teeth and the roof of his mouth as he chewed. Although there was no sign of anyone else in the courtyard, Gehrin knew that even now they were being watched. But compared to the rest of the day, it was the closest they came to privacy and speaking without fear of being overheard.

"I found something."

Again, Tirrim's hand disappeared into his tunic, his fist reappearing with something hidden between his fingers. He reached out and pressed a round object into Gehrin's palm. Gehrin squinted at it. It was a small purplish fruit.

His eyes widened. "Where did you find figs?"

"*Aish*! Lower your voice or we will not have them for long," replied Tirrim, swatting Gehrin's head. "Mistress Kirte sent me down to the storeroom with Jai to help him fetch up two bags of rice. I saw a basket of figs and stashed two away in my tunic before anyone saw."

"You *stole* them?"

Tirrim rolled his eyes. "No one saw me."

"Sharai's blessing! Master Tahmujin will strip your skin from your back."

"The only way he'll find out is if you loosen your tongue." Tirrim glared at him and reached out to snatch the fruit away. "Give it back then, if you're so afraid."

Gehrin pulled his fist tighter toward his stomach. "No, I want it." He lifted the treasure to his lips and sank his teeth into the flesh of the fruit. It was overripe and mushed quickly in his mouth, but the sugary juices dribbled down his chin and fingers. He struggled to keep himself from slurping the messy fruit. It would make too much noise. He held his hands against his mouth and quickly swallowed down the last of it, licking the remnants from his lips and chin.

The luxury of fruit was one he had nearly forgotten, but the sweet taste brought memories of far grander meals back to his mind, of savory delights he'd once taken for granted. His mouth watered around the lingering hint of fig as he remembered smoked pork, fresh vegetables glazed with a thin layer of honey, and the *kiji* cakes he had eaten so many times with his mother. Kirte fed the boys well, but their meals were simple, meant to keep their bodies strong. There were no added luxuries.

Gehrin's stomach growled at the memory of such rich foods, and he placed his palm against his flat belly. Tirrim finished his fig, taking more time with the treat than Gehrin had. "Are you tired?"

"No."

Tirrim shuffled around and leaned back onto the sand, sliding his sandals off his feet and pulling the leather string out of his messy top knot of hair. "I thought you might die in the water today. You came up out of the well like a gasping fish."

Gehrin twisted a string from the hem of his tunic around his finger. "I don't want to die." It was a simple enough thing, wanting to survive. When he had first arrived at Blackvale he had thought that dying might be better than living, stuck in the straw in the stone cell. He'd wanted to die because he was too afraid of what would come next. He had watched his mother die, her body withering away until half of her face had melted down like water. Everyone said she'd gone to the stars, as if she were visiting a city across the sea.

"I don't think anyone wants to die. I'm going to live so I can go home to Fethet."

Gehrin broke the string around his finger. "You draw an empty bucket. We can't leave, Master Tahmujin-"

"Is teaching us how to be strong. Someday we'll be so strong that we can leave, and Master Tahmujin won't be able to stop us."

Gehrin couldn't imagine being stronger than the mighty *garatelhai* warrior. Tahmujin seemed as if he were carved from stone and sharp iron instead of skin and bones. "We are warriors for the king now. My father said the greatest honor a man has is his loyalty."

Even as he said the words, they tasted thin and brittle on his tongue. He wanted to return to life under his father's roof, the bitter coil of homesickness had still not relented from its place in the space between his ribs.

"My father often talked of honor," replied Tirrim, his expression fixed in a dark glower. "Honor for your family. How can we be honor-able if we leave them behind?"

"We protect them by protecting the king. My father is a loyal advisor, and we have always been in the king's favor."

"The king's favor leaves more bruises than Master Tahmujin's staff. I never asked to be brought here, and neither did you. Kajrith died in the well, and Master Tahmujin threw his body over the walls and down the cliffside for wild animals to eat. There was no priest to send him to the stars, and if he had a family, they probably already think he is dead. No one will pray at his shrine."

Gehrin placed his hand warningly against his lips. "It is treason to speak against the king."

"What if it was you? It could be any of us lying at the bottom of the mountain. What if you were a rotten corpse, eaten by wolves and foxes? Where is the honor in that?"

Uncomfortable, Gehrin fidgeted with his hands as his friend's gaze burned into him. Was it not enough to want not to die? To serve the king as his father would want him to? He was angry at

Tirrim for pushing at him, and he didn't want to talk about it anymore.

Tirrim scoffed and looked away, but his voice finally grew softer. "It's different for some of the others. They don't have families to go back to. Kajen says he wouldn't leave even if they opened the doors and let him walk free. Sabba's father sold him for five silvers. Ruh was a slave. But you and I are different."

Gehrin didn't feel different. He was tired. And the sugary juice of the fig was making his stomach feel faintly uneasy. *You are a son of Katesh, as are we all,* his father had often said. Gehrin looked up at the great dark sky, stretching far away into the distance and disappearing down the side of the world. Tiny specks of light scattered across it, each one sending its meager light out over the land below. He wondered which star his mother had found.

Tirrim watched him for a while, and Gehrin could tell that his friend was angry with him. The other boy turned onto his side, facing away. "Wake me after a while."

It wasn't long until Tirrim's breathing grew deep and slow, broken intermittently by a breathy snore. Without Tirrim's company, Gehrin found his own eyelids growing heavy with the promise of sleep. He shook himself, sitting up straighter and peering into the darkness, following a zig-zag pattern through the cracks between the stones of the fortress walls. During the day, the greens of the outside forest that had crept in through the years were brushed like an artist's paint over the stone walls. At night, they just looked like dust. The stones were piled in impossible stacks, filling every possible nook and cranny and somehow creating an impenetrable wall.

At the far left, a stone tower jutted up somewhere beyond the courtyard, a dark stain against the darker night. The four corners of the roof angled into a sharp point like a flat spearhead. In days long past when the fortress had been built, there might have been a signal fire lit at the tower's peak, drawing the eyes below to its sanctuary.

But there was no warm fire aglow atop the tower. The secrecy to which the boys were sworn seemed to permeate the entire fortress. In the three years since Gehrin had found himself in the stone cell for the first time, he had never seen anyone enter or exit except Master Tahmujin, the twenty or so guards that rotated through the courtyard during the day, Jai, and Kirte. Gehrin had often wondered why the king would keep them hidden. Why they'd been taken like slaves in the dead of night. But they were questions to which he would find no easy answer.

He squinted at a dark shadow that pulled his gaze away from the tower and back down to the edge of the courtyard. The light from the boys' barracks room had been snuffed out, and the half moon and stars were the only source of sight. Hugging the wall of the courtyard across from Gehrin, the shadow slid noiselessly along the stone. It might be Jai, the servant boy came and went where he pleased during all hours of the day and night, doing Kirte and Tahmujin's bidding. But whoever the shadow was, they were not moving with confidence. Every few steps, they paused. Gehrin swallowed, a sudden unease gripping him. He rose to his feet, wishing he had one of the wooden staves in his hand. He had nothing but his fists if the shadow meant him harm.

The shadow crept to the edge of the corridor and disappeared into a small doorway. Gehrin took a step forward, unsure of himself. He had been assigned a night watch, but was it safe to leave the courtyard? Was it a test? He walked forward, gathering his courage around him in shreds as he took each step. As his feet left the sand and found the stone floor, the hairs on the back of his neck prickled. Someone or something was behind him. His shoulders tensed and he turned, bringing his right arm up to protect his face at the same time he swung out with his left.

A familiar white face shrouded in a hood bent back to avoid his fist with inhuman speed, a blur in the dark air. Gehrin's swing carried him forward, the surprise sending him off balance. His left foot slid forward to stop his momentum, but his shoulder collided with the smaller boy's chest. He grabbed hold of Ruh's arm to steady himself, and the Takkan boy's eyes flashed as he shoved Gehrin away. His constant smile had wavered, and the corners of his lips were drawn strangely down. He took a step away from Gehrin and raised one finger to his mouth, stopping Gehrin's questions before they left his lips.

He pointed to the shadowy doorway where the first figure had disappeared and crept around Gehrin to follow it. Forcing his feet to lift from the stone, Gehrin followed, his body taut. He'd barely taken three steps through the doorway when he heard a shout ahead in the corridor. Another shout, and the sounds of a scuffle, and then a piercing scream echoed around Gehrin's ears, followed by begging and blubbering as the guards restrained whoever had tried to sneak past them.

Ruh pushed at him, propelling them both back through the corridor. Gehrin hesitated as the begging intensified, followed by a loud thud. Ruh's grip was surprisingly strong, and he managed to pull Gehrin away. They nearly stumbled over each other in the rush to return to the courtyard, and when they reached it, Ruh sank down against the wall, pushing his hood back. His bone-white hair stuck out in all directions.

"It's Deth," he muttered.

Shocked, Gehrin glanced back toward the doorway, where all the horrible sounds had stopped. "What do you mean?"

Ruh leaned his head back against the stone. "I tried to stop him when he ran. I told him he was a fool. I guess I was right," he said, his strange smile returning to his lips. "He'll just die sooner than the rest of us."

Trying to calm the racing beats of his heart, Gehrin placed his hands flat on the ground, feeling the grit beneath his fingers as he had in the cell years ago. The roughness over the stone that somehow brought his whirling thoughts circling back down to the present. Across the courtyard, Tirrim lay asleep, a small lump in the sand.

"Do you think... think he's dead?" asked Gehrin quietly.

Ruh shrugged. "Maybe. Maybe not. But he's a fool either way." Despite the half-smile that still lingered on his lips, the Takkan boy's dark eyes were troubled, and he pressed two fingers to his right eye. "Jasha's Eye will judge him, as she judges all."

Invoking the goddess of the Takkan islands was blasphemy in Katesh, but Gehrin held his tongue. The cold presence of death prickled at his shoulder, and the silence in the courtyard was as heavy as the crushing water in the well. He dug his fingers into the grit.

The wind was bitter as it swirled around the line of boys. Each of them stood rigid at the edge of the sand, tunics hanging on their wiry frames like tapestry rods. Gehrin clenched his hands tight to the sides of his thighs, his eyes set on the boy kneeling in the court-yard in front of him. Three *telhai* stood around Deth, who was whim-pering around the gag in his mouth, struggling to free his hands from the ropes.

Gehrin let himself unfocus, the courtyard blurring into a wash of tan and gray and the faint glow of Master Tahmujin's armor. He could hear Tirrim's controlled breaths next to him. At his left, Hajja kept his gaze trained on the ground, the mask hiding the strange grimace of his broken mouth. The sky was blue and cloudless, broken only by Aqatar's fiery light. Master Tahmujin's voice boomed through the stones.

"Which of you wishes to leave?"

Not a single set of lips moved in the line of boys, but Tirrim tensed ever so slightly. Master Tahmujin came close, peering into their faces. His short spear balanced dangerously in his hand, hovering near chests and throats. He swung the spearhead toward Deth.

"One of you has chosen to abandon the king and this brother-hood. He has left behind the name he was given. He is now..."

*Aqqa.* Gehrin closed his eyes and drifted back into the memory of that day near the Blood Stones, heard the shift of armor as the *telhai* brought their spears down. Saw the eyes of the traitor fade into the world beyond. He remembered the tiny river of blood reaching the tip of his sandal. Angry voices around his head, the press of bodies as the crowd leaned toward the condemned man to send him to his death with their hatred ringing in his ears. And once again, the man's name whispered through Gehrin's ears. *Hasuya Jan. Aqqa. Deth. Aqqa. Traitors both.*

Something beneath him churned, gripped him from shoulder to foot as if his legs were made of iron. His stomach twisted. Several boys to his left, he saw Hajja drop to his knees, hands spread on the sand. Hajja's eyes were tightly closed, all other expression hidden behind the mask. One of the *telhai* shouted at him, tried to pull him to his feet, but Hajja's knees buckled beneath him, and he would've fallen again if the guard had not lifted him bodily and held him by the back of his tunic.

Deth's body lay in the sand, and two of the *telhai* picked him up like a sack of barley and carried him out of the courtyard. Master Tahmujin swept the red stain into the sand with his foot.

"Some of you may find the spirit of the wolf and fox. But some of you are weak," the *garatelhai* said, looking directly at Hajja and standing over the spot where Deth's body had crumpled only moments before. "And if you are weak, better that you die here on this sand today to save us the rice and barley it takes to keep you alive."

Gooseflesh shivered up Gehrin's arms as the wind curled around him again, bringing the faint hint of winter that had begun to creep over the fortress. Tirrim's words from the night before plagued him, creeping around his mind like vipers. *Someday we'll be strong...* but what would that strength be for? Gehrin watched the powerful warrior leaning against the haft of his spear and imagined that someday he would be the one standing over blood in the sand.

# CHAPTER ELEVEN

*Idle hands are as dangerous as those with a sword.*

*- Maleki saying*

Syndri pushed sweat-soaked hair out of her face and scraped her tanning blade down the flesh side of the kehrox hide, separating the fur and skin from the greasy tissue still clinging to it. A few flies buzzed around the long tanning boards that she and several others worked, but far less than the hot summer would have brought. They were tanning the last hides before winter, and already the insects flying around Syndri's greasy hands were sluggish. She worked the blade down in short, controlled sweeps, careful not to dig too deeply and ruin the hide. Even a single cut would render it far less valuable. She worked the last threads of tissue away from the bottom edge, and then straightened up with a groan. She'd been so intent on her task that she hadn't stretched her back or arms for a good long while, and her body protested with creaks and pops as she swung her arm in a circle to loosen her shoulder.

Despite the early winter air, Syndri's sleeves were scrunched up past her elbows to stay free of the globby bits of fat still clinging to the hides. The work had kept her warm, and now that she was still, the cold began to make its presence known. She shivered and rolled her head from side to side, releasing the tension in her neck. Eight boards and hides clustered together in the area reserved for such work at the edge of the village, within easy reach of the herds outside and the slaughter field. Large tubs behind the boards sat full of soaking hides and dirty water. A strong smell of animal fat and blood permeated the air, but Syndri was used to it. The closest *gats* were far enough away to avoid most of the rank scent.

Her sister appeared, walking toward her from the center of the village. Syndri leaned the tanning blade against the board, relaxing her grip around the bone handle. She reached for a small bucket of clean water and washed the worst of the grime from her hands as she waited for Senna to come closer. Several calls of greeting came from around the tanning circle as Senna made her way toward them. She greeted them back, and then turned to Syndri.

"The emissary from Queen Xhen will be here soon. Yugha went to escort him to the village. You need to wash up," Senna said, crossing her arms over her leather-clad chest. She glanced down at the hide on Syndri's board. "How many did you finish?"

Digging a bit of fat from beneath a fingernail, Syndri smiled. "Three."

"Good." Mischief twinkled in Senna's eyes. "You need a wash in the river."

Syndri leaned her head to the side and sniffed at her tunic. She grimaced. It was true, she stank like a dead kehrox. She pulled her sleeves back down around her wrists. "First one to the river is war chief for the day."

An arched eyebrow from Senna. "Your leg is not strong enough."

As if aware of her plans, the wound in Syndri's thigh ached dully. Ignoring it, Syndri launched herself into a run and made a dash for the space in the outer wall. She soon slowed to a limping run as her leg sent stronger signals that she was overworking it.

Frustrated, Syndri kept at the dogged pace. A gust of wind fluttered around her as Senna streaked past at a full run. A few kehrox stragglers at the edge of the herd lowed in concern and lifted their heads to watch the two women, one running, one limping over the grassy field toward the copse of trees near the river.

Legs burning, Syndri pushed herself faster until she knew any misstep would have her sprawling on her face. Senna stayed far ahead, her leaner form gliding along the ground like the shadow of a kestrel in flight. A pang of jealousy flashed through Syndri as she strained her body and the healing wound. But even if she had been in full form, it wouldn't have been enough. They hadn't raced to the river like this in years, and in that time, her girlish frame had given way to stocky muscle. She was strong, not swift.

The ground broke away in a soft and shallow canyon down to the river that ran alongside the Garhis village. It was only twelve or fourteen horse lengths across, but it was the lifeblood of the Garhis herds and therefore its people. The grassy dirt grew sandier near the edge, and Syndri's hide boots left heavier footprints as she awkwardly plunged down the bank after her sister. Senna was already stripping her boots and leathers off, flinging them to the side in a messy pile. Syndri lurched to a stop at the edge of the water and yanked her shirt over her head, dropping it as she kicked her boots from her feet. The bitterness of the air made her suck in a breath as her skin was laid bare to the elements, but the first bite of the water against her feet and legs pulled a gasp from her mouth as she waded in.

Senna stood in the water up to her neck, teeth chattering, with a victorious smile on her face. "You're getting slow, *teitei*," the words quivered over the glassy surface between them, her gloating softened by the childhood pet name.

Syndri took a deep breath and slipped farther into the water, letting the icy surface rise to her neck. Her body fought against the cold, shivering and pushing her back toward the warmer bank and her clothes and boots. But Syndri forced her muscles to relax, sweeping her arms in half-circles to stay afloat. Her leg grew blessedly numb.

A hideous shriek sounded from the riverbank, and Syndri spun around to see what wild animal was bold enough to approach them. Long limbs and wild hair filled her vision as a body hurtled into the water less than two armspans away from her, sending a huge splash into her face.

"Baya!" she sputtered around the water streaming from her hair and nose. Her little brother's head appeared, his gleeful grin separated in two by the gap between his front teeth. Syndri reached out and hooked her arm around his neck. With a swift pull, she sent him beneath the icy water.

He bubbled and spat as soon as he resurfaced and sent another splash of water up into Syndri's face. Senna waded over to the two of them and the fight rose to a fever pitch until all three had grown used to the cold. Syndri scrubbed at her body with a handful of the sand beneath her feet, washing the last traces of the kehrox hides away. She let herself sink and slowly her hair condensed down from its usual wild mane into thick ropes.

Sabayaar had climbed out of the water and shaken his hair like a wet dog before pulling his pants back on and heading over to the nearest tree, swinging up into the lowest branches. Syndri watched him with an affectionate shake of her head. Twelve years old and as flighty as the wind itself, as her mother would often say.

She and Senna waded back to shore, trading the numbness of the water for the sharp and cold air. One cold pool for another. She retrieved her clothes and shook the sandy dirt out of them. One of her boots had been flung nearly to the top of the bank's edge in her rush to follow Senna. Her clothing still smelled, and she regretted not bringing fresh pants and tunic along with her to the river, but the walk back to the village would be short.

The run to the river had left a grumbling ache in Syndri's thigh despite the cooling relief of the water. She pulled her second boot on stiffly.

"It is healing well," said Senna. "It is a wonder that Father has been able to keep you from the raids this past moon."

Syndri curled her lip. "I feel useless."

"Just today you helped Baya train with his swords, you dried herbs with Mother, restacked our wood pile, and tanned three hides. Every task is important."

"You sound just like Mother."

"An open hand," replied Senna, softening her tone in a mischievous imitation of Ettlan and keeping pace with Syndri's slower walk. "Perhaps you should listen to her more often. If Father ever becomes chieftain of the Maleki, there will be no more raids."

The thought of such a widespread peace filled Syndri with pleasure... and dread. She had often tried to imagine her place in such a world, but she could not. If there were a great city in Malek where her father ruled like the warlord kings of Katesh, it would give him great power and unite the tribes for the first time in centuries. But Syndri knew such power would not be won easily. More than just raids, a great war would be fought. The other tribes would resist her father's rule and try to put their own chieftains on that seat. A great closed fist, the greatest the Maleki had ever seen, would sweep across the land.

"Father will have to fight for that peace. A closed fist is still needed."

Senna narrowed her eyes. "You are still needed, you mean."

Their minds had been one since birth, and Syndri knew better than to hide her feelings from her sister. Twins were a rare gift in the Maleki tribes, a great sign of favor. When twin calves were born to a kehrox, the Sky Clans were extending a blessing. When twin sons or daughters were born to the tribes, it was a portent of great destiny.

"I feel restless," admitted Syndri. "I can feel blood on the winds. My skin tingles as it does before a storm, but this storm will be Father's war."

Senna stopped and looked out to the darkening sky beyond the village. Oncoming night had chased all the sky's blue into the west, streaking the great roof of the world with silver, purple, and orange. It was magnificent, colors bleeding into the tops of the grassy bluffs far to the south.

"To meet the storm, we will need our balance, or we will be swept off our feet."

Syndri noted how much her sister had taken Ettlan's features as she grew older. They had the same warmth, the same softly defined beauty in their faces, the same faithful perseverance. The same stubbornness.

"Be careful, or you may be named our tribe's next wise woman," Syndri teased. But Senna did not respond with her usual smile. She stopped suddenly to pick snowberries off a small bush hiding in the long grasses. The tiny golden orbs glistened in her cupped hand, a first harvest from the winter-loving bushes that dotted the plains. They would be more tart during the early winter, but they were Baya's favorite that way.

Senna hissed as one of the thorns caught her thumb, slicing a thin red line across the skin. She sucked the finger, tucking the berries into a pouch at her belt. "I've been dreaming."

"Oh?"

"The same dream. Over and over. And when I wake up, I remember it. All of it."

Syndri grew still. "A vision?"

Her sister's voice dropped to a whisper. "I think so." Senna looked out over the grasslands, out to the soft swells of the hills to the south. "In the vision, there is a shadow over this land, a shadow with great black wings that follows after you as you ride through a great river of blood." Senna turned, her gaze boring into Syndri's with an intensity that was frightening. Her voice rose. "At your side run a wolf and a fox. They both will claim you, and the wolf will take your place in death."

Syndri stared at her sister, a chill seeping into her bones. *A vision. The Sky Clans have given her a vision.* Senna blinked, sweeping a hand across her eyes before leaning her head against Syndri's shoulder.

"I'm sorry, *teitei*. I'm sorry..." she murmured. Syndri stroked her hair, shushing her. There was nothing they could do about it now. The Sky Clans had spoken, and what the vision meant could only become clear with time. The sounds of the village in the distance broke the eerie silence as the two Garhis warriors held each other under a flame-colored sky.

There had not been visions in the Garhis tribe for a generation. Ettlan's mother had been given visions, she had even predicted Syndri and Senna's birth thirty years before they had come squalling into the world. But Senna's vision had not been one of birth, but of death. It was troubling, and Syndri could not strike the unsettling words from her mind as she stood at her father's side to receive the Rukian emissary. Her father was dressed in his best hides, a mountain of a man in black at the front of his *gat*. Ettlan stood on his left, his open hand, smooth river stones shivering across her forehead from a silver chain and deep red boots beneath her warm leathers and furs. Senna had dyed the boots herself with crushed beetles and berries, working the crimson stain into the leather. Her hands had been red for days after that.

Syndri's twin swords stood like sentinels at her back, sharp blades encased in leather. After her sister's vision, the nearness of the bone hilts was strangely comforting. Senna had told her not to say a word to anyone about the vision yet, but the secret burned behind Syndri's lips. Ettlan would know what to do, how to interpret the dark words. But Senna was afraid of what it could mean. If the vision marked Syndri as a symbol of danger, there was no telling how the tribe might react.

*A river of blood.* Syndri was bladeborn, emerging from her mother's womb with a closed fist. She would fight her father's war and see his enemies slain in great droves across Malek. She had always known this, and she had clung to that purpose. A great river of blood must be spilled for such a war. She was not afraid of it.

She lifted her chin to face the North. She was not afraid.

Queen Xhen's emissary Jime Otai rode through the gate ahead of several wagons loaded with trade and gifts, his dapple-gray horse splattered with mud. He was a tall, thin man with hands that looked like bat claws beneath the wings of his long black robes. The blue trim around the neck and sleeves signified his elevated position as a servant in the queen's house. The hem of the silk clothing was filthy, and Syndri held back a smirk. His finery marked him as a stranger to their harsh lands. There were no polished stone floors in Malek. At least he had worn furs over the silk.

Nar Garhis lumbered forward and held out his hands, palms level with the ground and open to the sky. "Welcome to the Garhis lands, Emissary Otai. I offer you my open hand in a symbol of our peace."

The emissary swung his leg over his horse and handed the reins to one of his escort riders. "Nar Garhis, I honor that peace." His Maleki was flawless, only a slight accent betraying his foreign heritage. He bowed stiffly, back straight as if he were strapped to a tanning board. To Syndri's eyes he was a strangely built man, with a narrower waist than shoulders, but as tall as her father. His gaze was sharp and pointed above an even sharper nose. His shoulders hunched ever so slightly forward, giving him the appearance of always leaning over the person he was speaking to.

Otai's eyes swept briefly over Syndri and Senna before settling on their mother. He gave a short bow to her. "An honor to see you in good health, Open Hand."

The Northerners used strange words to speak to one another, and they were constantly bobbing their heads like submissive curs in the jackal packs. It was bold to trust a man from another tribe enough to lower your eyes to the ground. Syndri shifted, uncomfortable in her stiff new leathers. She had nearly worn her old ones until she'd seen the look on her mother's face. The heavier weight of her scale armor would've been a welcome comfort compared to the finely tooled tunic and trousers. But it was important for Queen Xhen to hear of the wealth and prosperity of the Garhis tribe. It was important that the North knew their strength. Syndri's fingers itched toward the bone hilts.

Nar Garhis led the emissary into his *gat* while several tribesmen and the Rukian guards took the horses away. Already tired of the long-winded talk that was coming, Syndri gave Senna a look before following her father and mother inside.

Ettlan had spared no luxury within. Thick hide rugs and furs were stacked around the low table. Silver cups filled with Da'hamian wine sat at each place. The former were gifts from the emissary's previous visit, and the latter recently acquired from a trading caravan. The central firepit sent a thin plume of smoke slithering through the opening at the top of the *gat*, and the scent of seasoned kehrox meat made Syndri's mouth water as she sat down at the far end of the table. The emissary removed his sullied cloak and sank down to the pile of hides with a practiced fluidity. Silver rings glistened on his fingers, and a medallion with a single blue jewel rested against his chest. The wealth of Ruk was famous through the lands for good reason. Syndri found her eyes drawn to the glittering gem in the medallion, a far deeper blue than the clearest water she'd ever seen.

Nar Garhis eased his bulky frame down to the head of the table and took a long drink from his silver cup. Once he had drunk his fill, the others at the table lifted their own cups to their lips. Syndri let the smooth, spiced wine spill down her throat, draining the cup's contents. Beside her, Senna did the same. It was good wine, far better than the watery ale they drank most days.

Baya sat in the far corner of the room, unable to join the table until he was of warrior age, but he watched the emissary with grave interest. Syndri gave him a wink, and he grinned.

"My queen sends her greetings, Nar Garhis," Otai began as Ettlan refilled the cups with more wine. "I have brought more gifts for your tribe, and it is my queen's desire that they are received in good faith."

Nar Garhis took another drink, letting a short silence settle over the *gat* before responding. "And you must take your gifts back to your queen. We have no need of anything but the gifts the earth gives us."

Syndri pulled apart the steaming meat on the platter in front of her. Her father must refuse the gifts, for to accept them would show weakness. The goodwill of a tribal chieftain of the Maleki could not be bought with silver. But the gifts could be left even after they were refused. It was a ritual that had gone on for years. Emissary Otai would return to his queen without the gifts. Syndri sipped her second cup of wine slowly, swirling the spices around on her tongue.

Otai withdrew several items from a bag at his side, handing a pair of golden earrings to Ettlan first. "For the beautiful Open Hand of the Garhis tribe, a token of my queen's favor."

Ettlan smiled as she took the earrings, the gold stark against her brown hands. "And I will send a roll of our finest white calf hides in return."

The neckline of her tunic rubbed at Syndri's skin every time she moved. It would take time before the leathers were broken in, and she hated it. She chewed another piece of meat, the tender flesh melting into the taste of the earthy herbs.

"Your daughters are of particular interest to my queen," Emissary Otai was saying. He set two golden torcs in front of Syndri and Senna. "Yours is a tribe of great warriors. It is no great surprise that your tribe holds a position of strength in the southern lands of Malek."

Senna slipped the torc around her neck, the gold ring perched atop her sharp collarbones. Two wolf heads snarled at the ends, guarding her throat. Syndri left hers on the table and offered a half-smile to the emissary. She had a knotted strand of leather cord around her neck with her wolf totem, smoothly carved and unbroken. She would not hide it beneath Rukian gold. Emissary Otai watched her, his shrewd eyes trying to take her measure, no doubt.

Syndri let him. *If the silk-clad queen of Ruk wants to know the measure of the daughters of Nar Garhis, let him tell her what he has seen.*

The meat disappeared quickly as they all ate, their fingers greasy and covered in flecks of the herbs. Syndri reached for a fig from the bowl in the center of the table, breaking the fruit open and scraping the inside out with her teeth. She tossed another one to Baya's corner where he sat with his own platter of food. He tore at his meat like a thing half starved, which boys his age often were, despite how frequently they were fed.

The emissary told her father again of the great mines of Ruk, the veins of silver and gold that ran through the deep rock beneath their lands. He said that Queen Xhen was much beloved by her people, a mother to all. Syndri glanced at her own mother. Ettlan sat with the dignity of a queen, her strong shoulders covered by a thick gray jackal pelt. Her new golden earrings hung from her ears, smooth river stones sparkling in the silver band around her forehead. Her black hair was swept back in braids and thick loops, soft strands framing her face. The mother of the Garhis tribe was second to none, no Northern queen could ever match her. No doubt if Queen Xhen ever deigned to make the long trek to the Garhis lands herself, she would arrive with fine silks soiled and shivering in the cold. Syndri nearly leaned over to say so in Senna's ear but thought better of it. Her father would not be pleased by an insult to the queen who called herself their friend.

Emissary Otai leaned back, his silver cup still half full of wine. "You are a man with great ambitions, Nar Garhis. You would see the Malek clans united beneath one king. Such a task must be daunting even to you."

A low rumble came from Nar Garhis' barreled chest as he laughed. "You are not a warrior, Emissary Otai. Such things are not daunting to me. The Sky Clans have shown many blessings to our tribe, and our warriors are the strongest in Malek."

"I would stand against any warrior from the North," Syndri said quietly. "As would any of our tribe."

"Bold words from a bold warrior," replied the emissary. Syndri didn't like the way he smiled at her, the way his eyes betrayed his words. "No doubt you have heard of Katesh's *garatelhai*. They are the finest warriors I have ever seen. The armies of Katesh are strong."

Syndri set her cup down on the table. "And that is why your queen pays them tribute."

"Indeed, but perhaps one day that will no longer be true."

*Ah yes, no doubt these 'bold warriors' would be of great help to you.* Syndri bit back a grumble. Ruk had an army, but it was much smaller than the great legions of Katesh. If Queen Xhen was helpless to remove the chains of her overlords, it was her own affair. The thought that Nar Garhis would even consider fighting against

Katesh for such a weak queen made Syndri clench her fist beneath the table.

Baya finished his platter of food, finally sated. He rose and skipped out of the hut without sparing a second glance for their guest. Syndri envied him.

When the rest of the food had all been eaten, and the wine had disappeared in enough quantity to satisfy Nar Garhis' hospitality, the chieftain promised Emissary Otai that they would talk again tomorrow, and he would hear what new proposition Queen Xhen had sent.

"Syndri, escort our guest to his *gat* and see that he is settled," Ettlan said, placing a steadying hand on Syndri as she rose and swayed a little. Syndri gestured to the doorway and led the way outside. The dark village was quieter now, the distant lowing of the herds comforting as they settled down to sleep. Syndri led Emissary Otai to a small *gat* near her father's, reserved for the use of guests. His men would be housed with different families throughout the tribe. They walked in silence, and Syndri lifted the hide doorway. A fire had already been lit, and a raised bed arranged with furs.

"Is there anything else you need?" she asked. Her words slurred with too much wine, and she kept steady feet through sheer willpower. Emissary Otai gave a brisk shake of his head, sitting down on the furs. Syndri turned to leave.

"Your father is a great man," he said suddenly. "And I believe that you and my queen share a common vision."

Syndri paused at the door. "And what vision is that?" *A great river of blood.*

"The tribes united under a great man."

"A great man? Or a great queen?"

Emissary Otai's eyes glittered in the firelight. "A closed fist, and an open hand. Your people have a great belief in this balance, and I believe it will take both to achieve your father's rule."

"Do all Northerners add so much honey to their words?" The wine was making Syndri's head swim, and she did not want to talk to this man from Ruk. She wanted to go fall on top of her own furs and sleep.

To her surprise, the emissary laughed. "Nar Garhis is fortunate to have you by his side."

"If my father is to rule the tribes, the Sky Clans will bless our blades. What strength can your queen give him that he does not already have?"

"It is true that alliances must benefit both sides. That is what I have come to discuss." He pulled his leather boots from his feet and threw them to the side, finished with the conversation. "It has been a long way to travel. I thank you for your hospitality."

Syndri let the flap fall as she left the *gat*, grinding her molars together, the stale taste of wine souring her mouth. Her own *gat* was not far, and she stumbled inside. Her furs welcomed her as she curled on top of them.

# CHAPTER TWELVE

*Death might have been a kindness. I was marked for it; I could not escape it. And while I still live, it is as the dead. Nameless, and unknown. But perhaps that is the true kindness.*

*- Sonho*

The boys moved through the spear forms as one, their lean shapes caught in a strange dance between awkwardness and grace as they maneuvered the long wooden staves that Tahmujin had finally given them. Master Lohi watched them from the small window in his room, a small cup of warmed rice wine bringing a bit of life back into his old fingers. Down on the table beside him were an assortment of rocks, bits of iron, papers of varying ages. Not a single used cup or bowl littered the room. Kirte frequently expressed her displeasure at him for his mess, but he didn't allow her to remove anything but the dishes, which she did almost before he was finished with them, clucking her tongue like a mother hen at her wayward chicks.

Master Lohi sipped the wine, feeling its warmth flooding through his ribs and into his belly. Pulling back his long sleeve with his off hand, he set the cup on the edge of the table and returned to the view outside the window. Master Tahmujin stalked across the stone corridor under the curved overhang along the side of the courtyard, his gnarled hands clasped behind his back as he scrutinized his young charges. The *telhai* guards were quick to snap their switches across the backs, knuckles, and shoulders of the boys at any misplaced step or overextended swing.

Between the ages of thirteen and fifteen, they were all the same, and yet each of them had begun to take steps onto his own path, showing glimpses of the man he might become. Some of them would already be working long hours in their fathers' trades or joining the ranks of the warlord's *telhai*-in-training. Others, like Kajen, would've found their way to a dark prison cell or a swift death by an executioner's blade. Others would have already been long dead by other means. Master Lohi's eyes found Ruh as the ghost-like boy flowed through the forms like water. A true Takkan Islander, born of the sea. It would've been a waste, truly, to see such talent struck from the earth so young. A boy who had already stained his hands with death before reaching Blackvale's ancient walls, a rarity among the innocents surrounding him.

Master Lohi remembered the small face peering up at him from the dirty straw far below in the muck of a pit in Mizak, the strange smile on an eerily calm face. The son of a common whore, awaiting his execution for murdering one of his mother's patrons. Eight stab wounds, the man's face and neck ravaged as if by an animal. His mother had wept and begged for her son's life outside the barracks, her dirt-smudged face even more ghostly than the boy's as she clawed at her breast in grief.

Outside in the courtyard, the little murderer stabbed through the air with his staff, feet dancing through the sand weightlessly. There were many in Katesh who believed the white skin and hair of the Takkan to be proof of some kind of half-spirit nature. It was a childish superstition, but this small boy certainly played the part.

What Master Lohi recalled most about the Islands was the green. It was visible from the boat miles away, the trees thick and vibrant, rising from the water like an earthborn fortress. He had seen that breathtaking view three times in his much younger years. Peace had been forged between the two nations, but it had been a slow and delicate process. Men loved to make war, they reveled in the glory of it, committing their names to be carved into the killing fields for all eternity.

Peace was the work of a scholar, the dream of old men who wished to wash the blood from their tunics. Men whose hips groaned with a dull ache after a few moments of standing at a window. Master Lohi retreated to his cushions behind the low table, sinking down onto the softness of them with a sigh. He pulled and fussed with them for a moment until they were in just the right place.

One of the room's panels slid open and Kirte appeared, a tray in her hands. The old woman bowed briefly, then shuffled forward, her mouth set in the prim line that had appeared with age. The memory of her thick black hair and sparkling eyes still hung like a tapestry in the back of Lohi's mind. They had both grown old, somehow.

"I've brought your tea."

The tray was set down atop the mess on the table, the sharp aroma of peppermint doing little to hide the bitter, cloying scent of the fennel beneath. Kirte knelt across from him and poured the tea into a cup, holding her sleeve daintily back from the liquid. Master Lohi took the cup when she offered it to him and watched her a moment before sipping the bitter herbs.

"Will you see him today?" she asked.

Master Lohi sipped, only years of practice preventing a grimace at the taste. "Yes. Ahhh, as always, your brews are the nectar of the stars."

"And as always, you are a master of empty flattery. Drink the rest or your bowels will grow stones again."

He watched her rearrange the tray when he finished, her simple gray tunic and skirt clean despite the dirt, sand, and dust that pervaded every inch of the castle. She kept the old fortress with the pride of a queen.

"Tahmujin has sent for Bithra," Kirte said standing, tray in hand. "I told him he best keep her out of sight."

"Bithra?" The name of the woman tasted sourer than the tea Master Lohi had just finished. A scowl darkened his features. "Tahmujin is a great man, but his blind affection for that veiled serpent will be the ruin of us all if he does not give her up. A soft pair of thighs bewitches him as easily as a sand viper's venom."

"You were so easily bewitched once. Or have you forgotten?"

Master Lohi leaned back on his cushions. "You would have made a powerful queen. You told me once that you had no regrets. Has that changed?"

Kirte met his eyes with a firmness. "We are too old for such games. It does not matter now."

"You could've been a mother."

That pain had been so long buried that her expression did not change. She glanced toward the window. "I am mother to many, now."

A soft voice came from the other side of the panel door. "Master, may I enter?"

Kirte bowed and slid the panel aside to admit Jai as she left. The boy rose from where he had knelt to wait by the door and came to the center of the room. His hair had grown long enough to be gathered up at the top of his head, held with a leather band. He bowed deeply, bent far enough that his face was parallel to the floor. When he rose again, Master Lohi did not miss the way his eyes flickered toward the runes on the desk. Though he did not move, the inside of him fidgeted.

"You have a question, Jai?"

"Do you think we will ever know the secret?"

"There are many secrets in the world, Jai. It is not possible for one man to discover them all, and even many men over many ages can only gather enough to take glimpses."

There was a hunger in the boy's eyes, a deep yearning for understanding what was still hidden. Since he had learned how to hold a brush, he had carefully traced the lines of the runes alongside Master

Lohi whenever the old scholar had visited Blackvale. Jai had memorized their names when his words were still the babbling of a toddler. What a scholar he would have made.

"Bring me Liv. Let us see what other secrets we can bring to light."

Jai bowed and hurried from the room. It was a matter of moments before he returned, a soft knock at the wood panel. It was not Jai who stepped into Master Lohi's room, but a boy whose face held only the passing glimmer of the soft youth he had once been. The resemblance to Counsellor Hallix was striking. *All fathers leave a mark on their sons,* Master Lohi thought. *If not on their face, within their spirit.*

Liv stopped short just inside the doorway, frozen like prey as he stared at the old scholar seated comfortably behind the table. He dropped to his knees, his forehead touching the rush mats on the floor as a guttural sound escaped his lips. The tail of black hair bound up at the back of his head had grown much longer, sweeping the ground beside the boy's cheek. Bruises littered his forearms and shoulders, green and purple brush strokes over the sun-darkened canvas of skin. But he was strong.

"Master." The word was choked out, and the forehead stayed pressed tightly to the floor. "Master, you found me."

And Master Lohi waited, letting the wild storm of emotions run through the boy's mind. This was not the first test, and it would not be the last. "Welcome, Liv. Please, be comfortable."

The forehead left the mat, dark eyebrows knit tightly together in confusion beneath as the boy leaned back on his haunches. "Master, it is Gehrin Hallix. Do you not recognize me?"

Anyone who had known the boy of eleven would recognize the boy of fourteen. Hidden beneath the sharper jaw and broader shoulders was the little boy who had so carefully drawn the brush over parchment in Master Lohi's house in Keld. He'd been dressed in silks then, not these simple woven trousers. It was a pleasant memory. In time he would learn to cherish it as it was meant to be, a stepping stone across the river of his life.

"Whoever you have been before is no longer who you are, Liv."

The boy's throat apple rose and fell as he swallowed around a dry mouth. He opened his lips to speak, but they closed again with a nearly imperceptible tremor as he began to understand. Master Lohi said nothing, waiting. Curling his hands into fists on his knees, Liv finally managed to loosen his tongue.

"You are not... you have not come to take me home?"

"You are home."

"This is not my home!" The boy's face flushed red, his fists clenched tightly against his knees. "Please, Master. I want to go home."

"You have no other home."

"No..." the protest died away into nothing. Master Lohi watched the war waging in the young face, the push of anger and the pull of fear locked behind those inquisitive eyes, now so dark and fixed on the rush mats in front of his hands. He saw the questions brought to the surface, hastily scrutinized, and returned to the tightly bound chest, locked away behind the heart. If Liv did not speak them now, they would remain there with the boy that had been.

"Would you leave your brothers?" Master Lohi prodded gently, watching the boy's eyes glance toward the window. *Yes, you have already begun to think of them so... the wolf is strong in your blood, boy. I was not wrong to choose you.*

Out of the many, one question was given voice. "Master Lohi... why was I taken?"

"Ah, but you were not."

The youthful eyes filled with the swell of injustice, his protestations kept at bay only by the strict training of Master Tahmujin and his own prudent nature. Master Lohi explained.

"You were not taken. You were given. Chosen."

"Taken from my family-"

"Given to your brothers."

Again, the push of anger. Master Lohi could see it writhing along the lines of Liv's face, burning in his eyes, a desperate wanting of something he could not have. But he would not break. Master Lohi had no time for weak spirits.

"And to your brothers you are bound, body, soul, and strength. Without them, you are nameless. *Aqqa.* You are no one."

Something dark settled over Liv's face, something older and more sinister than the boy himself, as if the word conjured some evil within him. The warmth of anger flushing his cheeks slowly cooled, leaving behind an icy stillness. Good, Master Lohi thought to himself. It was a step to the next stone.

"Starting today, you will resume your lessons with me after training with Master Tahmujin. I have many things to teach you, Liv. You still know little of the world, and you will need to know much more if you are to become *bruhai.*"

Again, a moment of silence as the boy's face betrayed the many thoughts beneath the surface. "Master Tahmujin has called us *bruhai* many times. What does it mean?"

Once again, Master Lohi was pleased with his young protégé. How quickly he could bury his more volatile emotions in favor of gaining new information, asking questions to determine his next course of action. One of the few remaining sources of deep pleasure left to a man who had seen his fair share of the world was the gift of youthful discovery. The old scholar settled a little deeper into his cushions, tapping his fingers against his thigh.

"You and your new brothers are the first *bruhai.* The *garatelhai* warriors are the king's greatest protectors, like Sharai and his first Oathsworn who came with him from the stars. But you are *bruhai,* leaving behind your name and the life you knew before. The oaths you take will bind your blood to the service of Katesh and protecting the one who sits on her throne. You will be above all others, bound to your king."

Liv's gaze remained fixed on the rush mats. "You chose me. Why?"

*Why you and not your brother? Why the scholar and not the warrior?* Master Lohi reached for his cup again, refilled it with rice wine. "Why do we need both the wolf and the fox?"

The answer came quickly. Every child of Katesh could answer such a simple question. "The wolf is fierce and bold; the fox is cautious and cunning."

"What good is great strength if it cannot be tamed by a thoughtful mind? I am no great warrior, and yet our king favors me with his trust. Enough trust to train the minds of his *bruhai*. It is why Master Tahmujin and I have come to teach you as one. You ask me these questions to understand, to learn, to discover what sort of world you find yourself in. A man who asks many questions of the world will find himself privy to its secrets."

"Yes, Master."

"You and your brothers are one, now. One purpose. I chose you because I believe I can trust you to protect them. Each of you holds the lives of the others in your hands. That is what it means to be *bruhai*. Do you understand?"

Liv bowed his head slightly. His obeisance was pleasing, and despite Tahmujin's concerns, he did not need a strong hand to be guided into his role. Time would prove Master Lohi's predictions correct, as it always did.

"Good. Tomorrow I will send for you again, and you will recite your runes."

Surprise flickered over Liv's face. "Yes, Master."

"And then you will tell me what you have learned about your brothers. If you are to lead them, then you must know them as dearly as yourself. Now go back to your training."

Rising from the floor, Liv bowed. He said nothing, lips pinched tightly together as he turned to leave, every muscle taut as he fought to master himself in front of Jai, who appeared behind the door panel and stepped in as soon as Liv had disappeared into the hallway.


Master Lohi pushed away from the comforting support of the cushions and pillows and rose to his feet with the help of his staff, which bore his weight like an old friend. He waited a moment for his knees to settle their creaking as the young servant boy waited for his command.

"Jai, take Hajja to the east barracks. Be sure no one else follows you."

Inside the empty east barracks, the dim light from an open door to the courtyard shone over a haze of dust floating in the air. At the far end of the room stood the solitary occupant, thin frame and knobby shoulders hunched forward as if to make himself smaller.

Master Lohi shuffled into the room, his staff tapping softly against the floor to announce him. Hajja managed to lift his head when Master Lohi approached, but his blue eyes darted quickly away from the old man's gaze. To the boy's credit, he no longer trembled when the scholar came near. Master Lohi reached up and pulled the leather string at the back of Hajja's head, and the mask came free, clattering down to the stone floor.

"Lift your head," Master Lohi commanded.

Thick black hair hid much of that empty gaze, deep wells of haunted misery contained within eyes that fixed on some point beyond Master Lohi. But it did not hide the ravaged face beneath. The scar began at the ruined left side of his mouth, cutting away enough of the upper lip to bare white teeth in a permanent snarl. The puckered red wound continued up along the cheek, narrowly leaving the eye intact, and ended a half finger-span above the eyebrow.

The scar hid further devastation within and the reason for his silence.

It was a hideous sight, the beauty of youth destroyed forever. But life remained, mercy afforded to a condemned soul. Mercy that had come from Master Lohi's own hand to the great disapproval of Tahmujin and even the king. But now, gazing at the gruesome mask of the boy's face, the sickly pallor turning his skin nearly as white as the Takkan boy, Master Lohi knew that his insistence on that mercy was rewarded.

"Look at me, boy."

There was a faint tremble in the boy's hands. Master Lohi reached out with the tip of his staff and lifted Hajja's chin, but the eyes still did not meet his.

"You are not as broken as you would have me believe," Master Lohi said quietly. "I gave you mercy when others would have taken your life. I wonder if I should have let them. After months in this room, you have nothing to show me but failure."

The eyes flickered in his direction.

"I once saw you wield power great enough to render seasoned *garatelhai* as useless as small children." Master Lohi pressed the staff against Hajja's scar. "If you can only draw power in great pain, remember your mother and your sister. You live while they rot away in the earth. You are the last of your family, and you draw breath only to pay for the sins of a traitor."

The side of Hajja's jaw clenched, and his blue eyes filled with a thin line of tears. He swallowed hard, and not a single tear spilled over the dam. Lohi withdrew a piece of iron from his robes and placed it on the stones near the boy's feet.

"Show me."

Hajja knelt on the stones. The deep lines of *tohl* in the iron square seemed to draw the boy in like a web. His fingers reached for it, smoothing across the cool metal until his palm covered the rune. For a moment, nothing happened. The sound of wooden practice staves cracking against each other out in the courtyard came faintly through the closed door.

A thin tendril of what appeared to be hazy smoke materialized in the space between Hajja's hand and the iron. Barely visible, but it was there. The boy's hand shook with effort, and his face paled further.

Withdrawing a knife from his belt, Master Lohi jabbed toward the boy's upper arm. The blade was pushed to the side by some invisible force, skimming away from the skin by a hair's breadth. Hajja's hand flew away from the rune. Leaning forward onto his arms, he vomited watery bile onto the stones.

*Tohl. Guard the body against death.* Master Lohi clutched his staff. Satisfaction eased his tightly drawn face.

A lifetime of work, of study, of traveling to the far reaches of the empire to discover the secrets written about the runes in every language, every myth and legend told, separating the truth from the imaginary. The truth was in front of him. Years ago, the boy who was Hajja had fought against the justice being served to him, and Lohi had watched in awe as power had exploded from him, wrenching away the blade that had taken his tongue and sending five grown men toppling to the stones.

And Hajja was not the only one. Liv also possessed some strand of whatever gift led to the untapped rivers below. Power streamed through the earth, just as Sharai had left it.

Legends told of great warriors who could reach into that power as if it were a stream of water, wreaking death and destruction, but also life and prosperity. There had been no such power since the ages long past, thousands of years... but the earth had begun to speak again. And if Hajja and Liv could hear its voice, there would be others.

"Sharai's blood." Master Lohi's eyes burned and reveled in the pleasure of a life's work coming to fruition. The boy finished his retching and sank back. He would learn to control it. His body would acclimate to the presence of power.

The throne would be safe.

Master Lohi pushed himself upright, returning the small knife to its sheath at his belt. "You will come to me every day and together we will master this gift. And then we will teach the others, if they can learn. You cannot erase the stains of your old life, but as *bruhai* you may yet atone."

Tears streamed down the boy's face, and he curled his hands

tightly over his knees. Master Lohi left him, his old limbs filled with renewed vigor as he returned to his study. The power of the runes was within his grasp.

# CHAPTER THIRTEEN

"**W**hat in eternal darkness is that?"

The round wooden object hooked onto her sister's right arm looked every kind of ridiculous. Syndri laughed, clapping her hands against her thighs. A slight twitch below Senna's eye was the only betrayal of her annoyance. She lifted the wood up, partially covering her face, only her red forehead and brown eyes visible over the rim.

"It is called a shield," Senna responded curtly. "Emissary Otai tells me that there are warriors across the sea who fight with them. The Islanders."

Syndri scoffed. "You'll do little fighting with one sword arm trapped behind that thing. Come now, put it away and get your sword."

"I will try like this."

Sky and stars, but Senna was stubborn when she wanted to be. Syndri reached back over her shoulder to draw her twin blades, the familiar rasp whispering in her ears as they swung free. She shrugged. "I'll be gentle."

Bending her knees slightly, Senna hid behind the shield, her single sword out to the side like a thornbush spine. Syndri grinned at her and took a solid grip of her sword hilts, glad for her sister's sake that they were sparring near the river and no one from the village was watching. The grass bent and swished around their knees. Syndri lunged, her left sword flicking forward, snakelike, toward her sister's thigh. The shield dipped down, and blade bit into the wood as Syndri brought her right sword around toward her sister's now exposed neck. Senna jerked to the side, her sword blocking Syndri's in a sharp clang of metal. Syndri pulled her left sword free, flipped it in her hand, and used the hard bone pommel to smash against the shield.

Senna took a step back, unbalanced for a brief second. Syndri pushed forward, another swing blocked by Senna's blade. The shield shook on Senna's arm as Syndri's second sword slammed against the wood, sending several slivers flying. Senna skipped back several steps, frowning at the shield. Syndri chuckled.

"Ready to pick up a real weapon now, *teitei?*"

Senna shifted the shield on her arm, taking a better grip of the straps inside. Stubborn, thought Syndri again.

This time, Senna did not wait for Syndri. She charged forward like a bull kehrox, shield out in front of her as she yelled, bringing her sword up in a wide underhanded arc. Syndri blocked it with her left sword, knocking the blade away from her knee. She stabbed forward with her right sword, taking advantage of Senna's high guard. But as her blade disappeared beneath the lower rim, Senna dropped the shield down quickly, trapping Syndri's blade beneath it and stepping down on it with her foot.

Taken by surprise, Syndri stumbled forward, letting go of the hilt before she was pulled completely off balance. She was down to one sword against Senna's sword and shield. The swords met again above the shield, and Syndri reached out with her free hand and grasped the edge of the wood. Before she could pull it away, Senna shoved the shield forward, hard.

There was a crunch as the rough wood slammed into Syndri's nose, knocking her backwards. She staggered, blinking as stars flashed through her eyes. Something warm and wet dripped down over her lips and she tasted the blood on her tongue. She shook her head, trying to clear the tears brought to her eyes by the stabbing pain in her face. The kiss of cold metal touched her neck, and she saw the blurred form of Senna smiling at the other end of the sword.

"I like it."

Syndri spat blood out over the grass and muttered several offensive names for her sister under her breath, one of which included a comparison to a pile of kehrox dung. Senna laughed, and Syndri shook her head one more time, feeling gingerly along the bridge of her nose. A cut across the top still bled profusely, staining her lips and chin a darker red than her forehead. Senna put the shield down and reached her hands out, swatting away Syndri's.

"Let me see."

Syndri hissed through her teeth as Senna prodded and shifted. With a quick push of her fingers, Senna moved the broken bone back into place with a crackling snap. Syndri growled and pulled away from her sister. A rustling sound behind them heralded the appearance of Baya as he shimmied down the tree he'd been perched in. He grinned broadly at Syndri, squinting at her bruised face. She shoved at him.

"*Aich*, you're going to sprout wings and feathers if you stay up in the trees all day," she scolded him half-heartedly. Her voice came out with a strange nasal tone, and Baya chortled. He bounded through the grass and snatched up the sword that Syndri had dropped earlier. Flipping it easily around in his hand, he advanced toward his sisters.

Senna crouched, holding her sword out to him in a mock challenge. "What a fearsome warrior this is!" she teased.

Baya attacked, swinging his blade with all the might his twelve-year-old arms could muster. Syndri watched him with a smile, the throbbing in her nose forgotten momentarily as she watched her brother and sister spar. Senna had always known the right intensity to use, enough strength and speed to push Baya, but not so much that he gave up. She was a patient teacher.

As she watched Baya swing and barrage the shield, Syndri narrowed her eyes, watching the moments where Senna was leaving herself open, what weaknesses the shield opened but also how it provided Senna with a larger area of protection than a simple blade.

Syndri couldn't imagine letting go of one of her swords in favor of some unwieldy block of wood strapped to her arm, even if Senna had managed to break her face with it.

Ducking away from Senna's exaggerated swing, Baya charged across the grass toward Syndri, his face alight with laughter. He yelled out a boyish war cry, his voice cracking between the shrill notes. Syndri let him swing at her, taking one step to the side as the blade whistled past her ear. On the next attempt, she reached under and grabbed hold of his wrist, twisting just enough for the wild grin to shift into a slight grimace. He refused to drop the sword.

"Submit, little brother," Syndri said, leaning toward him and donning a fearsome expression, baring her teeth against the pain in her nose. It was a game they had played since he was old enough to drag around a practice blade.

"A warrior must not submit," Baya retorted, his body contorting as he tried to free himself from her grasp. "The Sky Clans will see my courage and I will defeat you."

Senna walked up behind them. "The Sky Clans witness! Surely you tremble with fear, my sister. This warrior is too great and powerful for us alone."

Dropping the sword from his right hand, Baya snatched the hilt with his left and flipped the weapon, driving the hard pommel toward Syndri's belly. She jumped back, barely escaping what would have been a certain bruise to her lower ribs. She let go of Baya's wrist, and he shook a fist in the air triumphantly.

"A neat trick, little brother. Well done."

He glowed with the praise. "Hyshir taught me! I practiced with him yesterday."

Syndri's forehead tightened as her eyebrows lifted in surprise. The huge beast rarely touched the great bone club that her father had allowed him to make years ago. She'd never even seen him touch a bladed weapon. The bone club was nearly as big as Baya, and paid homage to the immense strength of the creature who wielded it. Syndri had tried to lift it from its place on the ground once, and could not imagine having the power to swing it in a fight.

"Hyshir taught you this?"

Baya nodded, pushing a wayward shock of hair away from his eyes. "I asked him to teach me how to use the bone club, and he said he would not. He said a club is not the weapon for a warrior like me." Syndri watched her brother's chest puff out at the memory of being called a warrior by the Ke'ral. Baya turned the sword around in his hand and pretended to jab some imaginary foe with the hilt.

"So instead, he showed me this. Like you say, *teitei*, a sword is more than a blade, yes?"

"Mmm." Syndri watched him hack at the grass. "You must use whatever you can to win. The Sky Clans honor those who live. *Aich*, give me that, you thief."

Baya handed the sword back to her. "Only four years and I can go with you. I'll kill as many Tladr as you have in my first season."

"You'll have to get a bit taller first, or they won't be able to see you." Syndri reached out and pulled the long tail of hair at the back of his head. He pushed back at her, and they wrestled across the grass, Syndri letting him gain the upper hand just long enough to boost his confidence before she lifted him off his feet and dropped him to his back in the grass. He scrambled up, hissed at her, and took off running for the trees along the river.

"Come. Mother will want us to help prepare. We've been gone too long already," Senna said.

The sounds of voices rising above the usual volume already drifted across the plains from the village. There would be a great feast tomorrow, the dances and songs of the Garhis tribe would fill the air in honor of the Clans who watched them from their cloudy plains above. Before the cold winds of winter gave way to snow and ice, one last celebration would send the warmth of summer on its way. Emissary Otai had not been with them for any such rituals before, and Syndri knew her father was extending a great honor to the foreigner by allowing him to observe it.

"It will be a good sign to have a birth during the songs," mused Senna as they began to walk back. Yugha's wife, Tilis, had begun her labors early in the morning before the light had risen. Even now, she paced the birthing *gat* alone, with Ettlan and the other midwives waiting outside for her to bid them enter. She had borne four children before this one, three strong and full of life, and one she had sent to the Sky Clans, born too early. Her oldest would turn into his sixteenth year and become a warrior in the coming spring. Like Ettlan, she was one of the revered mothers of the Garhis. Yugha, as the child's father, had gone into their family *gat* to prepare the food and bedding for his wife and their new child, and to call on the Sky Clan mothers for their blessing on the birth.

A child born during the songs of winter would be lit with their own fire, as the elders said, burning hot and fierce to drive away the cold of death. Yet another sign that the Garhis tribe was growing in its power. The Sky Clans were showing their favor. The child would be blessed.

The days were growing shorter, and already the light had dimmed far further into the south than it would have a season past. Syndri was glad that the winter songs would be sung tomorrow, two days of dance and revelry before Emissary Otai returned back to his mistress' rocky lair to the North. And then the warband would return to the borders to drive back any Tladr or Uratar who had chosen to wander too close to the border. Ettlan was right. Syndri yearned for the thrill of the hunt. The days of peace she spent in the village tanning hides and sparring with Baya were not enough to keep her restless spirit at bay. But tomorrow she would drink and she would dance.

Syndri left her swords in her *gat*. This day was a day for her hands to be filled with wine and ale. The scent of roasting kehrox spitted over the massive fire built in the center of the village filled the air with an intoxicating aroma of meat and spices as it crackled and split over the flames. Nar Garhis himself turned the spit, red-faced and sweating and stripped down to his trousers, his great hairy chest and belly bared to the chilled air as he laughed and drank, surrounded by a crowd of similarly undressed warriors. In contrast, Emissary Otai stood near enough to join the conversation, yet far enough that he would not roast alongside the meat, swathed in his blue and black silks. A new black kehrox hide was draped over his shoulders, a gift from Nar Garhis.

With the great fire and laughter lighting the center of the village, Syndri barely noticed the chill as she found her sister helping drag the huge, tanned hide drums out into a semi-circle. Syndri pulled at Senna's arm and shoved a horn of wine into her hand.

"Drink, *teitei*! Your cheeks are still pale, you've not had enough wine!"

Behind her, Baya took a sip from his own horn of wine, face already flushed. Syndri threw her arm around his thin shoulders. "Come, little brother!"

Leaving Senna to tend to her own drink, Syndri dragged Baya over to Ganzakh-ba, an elderly tribesman who was painting the faces of the men and women with marks of the Sky Clan, his fingers stained in shades of black and red from the bowls of dye at his knees. Syndri pushed Baya down on the stump, feeling generous and full of wine and the strength of the tribe.

"Revered One, today let my brother be one of us. Paint him with the mark of our warriors."

Ganzakh-ba smiled his mostly toothless smile and dipped his fingers into the red ochre, smearing the paste over the boy's forehead and eyebrows until Baya's face matched Syndri's, his Garhis tribe heritage emblazoned on his skin.

"Four years, little brother!" said Syndri, clapping him on the back and sending him stumbling forward a pace. "Four years and then you will ride with us."

Baya touched his fingers to his forehead, a wide grin splitting his face, an extra tooth on the left side of his mouth layering over the one beneath it like a scale. He jumped and whooped, his rolling yell boyish and thin, but fierce. Syndri laughed as he ran for the open gate toward the herds, no doubt heading for his young mount Itah. He had recently gentled her to ride and had nearly burst with pride when he had showed his older sisters how the little chestnut filly already responded well to his soft touches to turn this way and that way. Even Ettlan had said they made a fine pair.

Syndri raised the horn after him and drank, the tang of the wine hitting the back of her throat. She'd already finished two horns full, and her body was pleasantly warm, her fingers and gut tingling. A group of young girls danced through the crowd, playing small hand drums and pipe flutes in the imitation of one of the winter songs that would be sung soon when the sun reached the highest point in the sky above them. When the Sky Clans were looking down over the village with bright eyes from astride their windblown warhorses.

It would be soon.

Syndri could feel the excitement in the air like the tension before a great storm. Senna and the other drummers had set up their massive hide drums in a semi-circle around the flat space for the dancers. Senna's smoothly muscled arms were bare, long straps of dyed cloth tied around her biceps and wrists, and she tapped her drum with one of her sticks, the end wrapped into a ball of hide. The straps around her arms quivered as the drum's hollow boom shook through the air. Syndri caught her sister's gaze and smiled, sauntering over to the drum.

"Don't miss a beat," teased Syndri.

"You're more likely to trip on your own feet," replied Senna, taking a long gulp from her own wine horn. "You and our father have wasted no time on your wine."

"More wine would do you a world of good," Syndri clapped her sister on the shoulder. She glanced toward her father, who had left the turning of the spit to someone else and was gripping Emissary Otai's shoulder as the two spoke together. Nar Garhis' long braid tumbled freely down the middle of his back, coming loose from the tie. Soot stained his trousers and arms, and his skin was reddened from standing so near the fire. Behind him, like the great shadow of some otherworldly demon, stood Hyshir. The massive beast hovered at the edge of the crowd, towering over even the tallest Garhis warrior. Syndri noticed that Hyshir had tied the colorful strips of cloth around his wrists. Despite his appearance, he was a Garhis.

Emissary Otai's contrast to the creature and even Nar Garhis was nearly humorous. Syndri snorted into her newly refilled wine. Ettlan had cautioned her to be more hospitable to their Northern guests, but as Syndri scornfully scrutinized the little group of them gathered behind the emissary, she curled her lip. The Rukians looked over her people with disdain, sipping their wine out of cups instead of horns. To Syndri's mind, the sooner they returned to their own lands, the better. Emissary Otai's silver tongued words dripped like honey over her father's ears, spinning grand tales of the battles they would win for the Garhis tribe and the greatness her father could achieve with Queen Xhen at his side.

It was a pretty tale. But there was no honor in begging help from those stronger than you. If it was within the favor of the Sky Clans to bring her father to glory, he would do so by the strength of his warriors and not the soft soldiers of a Northern queen.

A commotion around the edge of the crowd brought Syndri away from her wine-soaked reflections. There were cries and shouts as her mother broke through into the clearing, a joyful smile on her beautiful face. Ettlan raised her hands to the sky and let out a high-pitched rolling cry that was immediately taken up by every other Garhis voice in the village.

A healthy child. A favored birth.

Syndri shook her fist in the air. A child born with fire in their veins to keep out the cold of winter. No doubt a great warrior had been brought into the world. And now Ettlan could resume her duties as the Open Hand, the ruler of peace, and the songs could be sung.

Ettlan stepped into the middle of the open space; hands still raised. "Garhis! I call you!"

Syndri and a thousand other voices cried out as one. "GARHIS!"

"The Sky watches over us with favor. The cold winds will blow over us, but they will not bite. The ice will not douse our fires. We welcome winter without fear!"

Ettlan walked to the drummers, her back straight despite her tiredness after assisting the birth. Syndri felt a rush of pride as her mother walked with an uncanny grace alone across the clearing. She looked across at Emissary Otai. He was watching her mother. Now you have truly seen a queen, Syndri mused. Ettlan took one of the wrapped sticks from Senna and held it out toward her gathered people.

"Hyshir! I call you!"

Murmurs of surprise floated through the people as a small path opened to the giant Ke'ral. Each year Ettlan chose someone from the tribe to strike the first drum beat. It was a great honor and a show of strength by whoever was chosen.

The massive beast walked to Ettlan on his strange legs, his cloven hooves leaving marks despite the hard packed ground. The hide clothing he wore would have drowned any of the human warriors around him. He reached out and took the stick from Ettlan in his four-fingered hand. He approached Senna's drum, the center of the semi-circle, and lifted the stick high in the air. He bellowed, his breath freezing in the air as he dropped his arm.

*BOOM.*

The drum's voice rolled out over the village and the songs of winter began. Syndri walked out into the clearing alongside several others. They'd all strung horn beads into their braids, and each movement set them clattering like a shower of rain. Horn bangles were stacked on their forearms and ankles, carved with symbols for each season. Each of them carried two ceremonial wooden swords. Syndri lifted hers above her head and clacked them together, matching the drum beats. She swung one in a wide arc before bringing it back against its twin with another sharp crack. She crouched, stomping one foot and then the other as she moved toward her sister and the other drummers, swords clattering together.

The earth and the sky pulled together like a taut string, the sound of the swords and the drums and the stomp of dozens of feet over the ground reverberating through the bones of the village. The cold wind curled around Syndri's face, lifting her, tempting her from the warmth of the dance. Her breath burned in her lungs, the taste of the coming winter ice creeping in through her nostrils. Her bare toes twisted and dug at the hard earth, tingles of pain shooting through them as the blood rushed into cold skin.

The drums shook, dyed cloth fluttering around the arms of the dancers and drummers. A low hum began around the crowd, rising and falling like a gale of wind. Ettlan began the first song alone, her voice cutting above the cacophony of sound.

*Great winter, ice and wind*
*Snow covers grass and tree and herd*
*Burn with fire*
*Heart and blade and horse*
*Burn with honor*
*The Sky Clans watch and send the wind*
*Place coals beneath our feet*

The Garhis tribe answered Ettlan's call, clapping hands above their heads while the dancers stomped the hard ground. Sweat dripped down the back of Syndri's neck despite her wearing only thin cloth bands wrapped around her chest. The chill of the wind broke against the warmth within her as she danced. Across from her, Senna's braids tumbled around her shoulders as she struck the drum.

Syndri threw back her head and howled, shaking her wooden bangles above her head. Burn with fire. Heart and blade and horse. The words tumbled around her from hundreds of throats. Her feet burned, her hair stuck to her forehead and neck in damp sweat-soaked strings.

*Burn.*

*Burn with fire.*

Ettlan walked out to the center of the dancers, her open palms still facing the sky. Someone had placed a braided grass crown over her braids, and the last whispers of green from warmer days wove through the deep brown hair.

She ruled in times of peace, her graceful wisdom shepherding the tribe. Every man, woman, and child in the village watched her hands sweep through the air, hardly daring to breathe, to disrupt her quiet dance. The wildness and noise of Syndri and the others had disappeared, leaving only the swaying, softly humming figure of her mother.

Finishing her dance, Ettlan brought her hands together above her head in a sharp clap. In response, Senna and the other drummers brought their sticks down one last time. The sound swelled and faded across the plain.

The moment of silence was quickly broken as the tribe began drinking and celebrating. Syndri stumbled back to her *gat*, full of wine and tottering on feet that were finally beginning to feel the cold. She pushed aside the door flap and reached for her furred boots, sliding her toes into the soft warmth of them. Her hand ruffled through the hides and furs of her bed, instinctively reaching for her sword sheaths. There was nothing there. Frowning, she pulled aside the blankets and looked on the other side of the low wooden cot. Her initial confusion quickly dwindled to cold anger as she realized Baya must have taken them. He had done it once, many seasons before, and she had cuffed him soundly around the ears for it.

There was no one else. The brief idea that Emissary Otai's men could have come into her *gat* and stolen her swords was nothing less than ludicrous. They wouldn't dare. She pushed her way back outside and headed for the herds, her anger fueled by the wine in her gut. When she found him, she would tan his hide alongside the kehroxen skins stretched over the wooden frames.

The kehroxen huddled together, their breath steaming the air as they grunted and gave soft lows as she approached them. Syndri looked out over the horses, intermingled with the other beasts, searching for the bright chestnut hide of Itah. The little filly usually stood out from the others, but Syndri didn't see her.

She walked over to Uhuri, one of the young warriors guarding the edge of the herd. "Have you seen Sabayaar?"

Uhuri picked something out of his teeth with the corner of a fingernail. "Not since he rode off a while ago. He went that way." He pointed over the herd to the west. The wide plains were empty beyond the herds.

"*Aich*... little fool." Syndri swore under her breath and made her way through the beasts until she reached Brig. He whuffed through his nose, ears snapping up as she pulled herself onto his back. Setting her heels to his sides, they wove through the horses and kehroxen until they emerged out onto open grass. Brig's ears flickered back, and he jumped into a gallop as Syndri leaned low over his neck.

She'd coddled her brother too much, and he was growing too big for his trousers. Ettlan had been right to scold her for letting Baya handle her blades. He was not ready.

The wind flung Syndri's hair away from her face, and she nestled down against Brig's mane, letting his big head and neck give her a small shelter from the cold. Brig slowed to an easy lope, his hooves bouncing smoothly over the ground as he gave little snorts with each stride. Syndri knew the route that Baya usually rode with Itah, but there was no sign of her brother or his mount.

A flash of chestnut pulled her attention to the left, and she leaned back, Brig slowing immediately to a walk. She lifted her arm to call out, but Brig laced back his ears and stomped, fidgeting to the side.

The chestnut filly was not alone.

A strange rider rode toward her on a stocky gray horse, leading Itah by her rope reins. His tribal tattoo was covered by white paste that had been slathered over his face, giving Syndri no chance to see which enemy tribe he hailed from. A body was draped over the withers of his horse.

Syndri's blood ran colder than the icy wind, and her stomach fell to somewhere in the soles of her feet. A long black rat tail bobbed over the head of the body. The breath left her, and she pressed one fist against her chest. Her heart pounded against her ribs.

The enemy warrior pulled his mount to a halt about ten horse lengths away from her, and held up his right hand, palm open. *Open hand...* the absurdity of it broke through the fog in Syndri's mind. The man swung off his horse, and pulled Baya's body down, laying it on the ground between them. Syndri pushed herself off Brig's back, her limbs numb. She didn't even feel the jolt when her feet hit the ground. She approached her little brother's body like a ghost, feeling nothing as the wind whipped her hair around her face.

Baya's face was smudged with blood from a cut across his forehead that added its own stain to the red ochre dye, but his chest was ruined by a deep wound that had cleaved the skin from his ribs and his soul from his body. His face was ashen gray, and the breath had long since fled from his lungs. Syndri held a trembling finger beneath his nostrils, but any hope of finding life was a faint echo.

The warrior pulled the sheaths with her swords off his back and laid them down beside Baya. When he spoke, his voice was hushed, as if he was afraid to disturb the dormant fire between them.

"I did not know he was a child until the killing blow had been struck. He came close to our border."

Syndri smoothed her hand over her brother's forehead, wiping away the blood and the ochre paint left a stain on her fingers as she revealed the untainted skin beneath. Her brother had died with the color of warriors painted on his face. The Sky Clans' judgment could not be known, there was no telling what they might do with him. Her fingers found the wolf totem around his neck, unbroken.

She looked up at the warrior, and slowly rose to her feet. The white paste used by messengers hurriedly painted over his face revealed a few light patches of the dark tattoo beneath. Tladr. A Tladr had killed her brother. Covering his tattoo would not save him. Open Hand would not save him.

"I have brought him back to his people. I have left his totem unbroken for the Sky Clans."

Words. Empty words to cover the cowardice of a warrior who had murdered a child. A warrior who hid his face in hopes of peace. A warrior who was no warrior at all. She looked into his eyes.

"But yours will be broken."

Pulling one of her swords from its sheath, she stabbed him through the heart.

# CHAPTER FOURTEEN

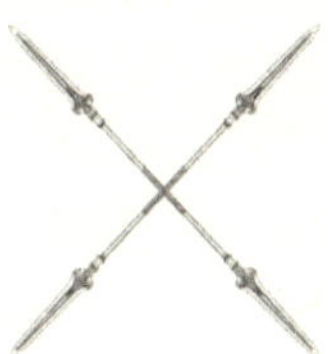

*To Xario, Tenth Leader of the Third Hand of the Black Legion under
Garatelhai Jaakar*

*I have sent instructions to your unit commander that you are to return to Keld
for a time. Your commander will allow a respite from your duties in the
Legion as long as I have need of you here. Return as soon as this letter arrives
to you.*

*- Counsellor Ilba Hallix*

The gates of Keld stood open like great jaws yawning out into the farmlands. Guarded by *gerhai* on either side with long spears, the open doors to the city offered a glimpse into the busy streets beyond, and the curved roofs of the buildings that lined them. Xario sat tall astride his black mare, his own spear held easily and supported by the leather cup attached to his stirrup. Behind him rode three other Black Legion *telhai* who had ridden back to the city with him, each given their own short respite from the barracks in Mizak. The *gerhai* nodded respectfully to the black-armored riders as they passed under the shadow of the gates.

It was not out of respect for his status as the son of Counsellor Hallix. He was returning to the city as a *telhai* leader in the Black Legion, and his black armor and fanged half-mask gave him an authority he would never have earned by his father's name alone. His mare's hooves clopped against the swept streets. A street merchant rushed to pull his wagon out of Xario's way, and people on foot scurried away to the sides of the buildings like mice as the riders passed. Xario kept his eyes fixed ahead. The Black Legion *telhai* rarely rode into the city alone, his presence was an oddity. No doubt there were whispers spreading already. Within an hour, no doubt it would be known that Counsellor Hallix's son had returned home.

As the four men rode inside the gates, one of them called ahead. "Will you come drink with us tonight, Xario? It will be good to see the women of Keld again!"

Xario twisted in his saddle. "I will join you if I can. Ride on."

The other black horses trotted past him, each rider moving on to his own house within the city. The heads of the short spears strapped to their backs glinted in Aqatar's light, sharpened to razor edges.

On a whim, Xario kept his mare walking past the street toward his father's estate, and instead headed down the familiar path he had once taken as a boy nearly every day. He stopped in front of the small sweet shop on the corner, the same delicious smells wafting out as they always had. Though the mask on his face hid his smile, he allowed himself the small moment of nostalgia as he dismounted, carrying his spear with him inside.

Hige turned and saw him, and the man's eyes quickly grew as wide as the puffy rice balls he was placing on a tray. He bowed low, bending nearly in half at the waist. "My lord *telhai*! An honor to have you within the walls of my shop. How can I serve you?"

Lifting the mask from his face, Xario smiled. "A package of your best *uban*, Master Hige. Many thanks."

The older man's eyes crinkled up in joy. "Young Lord Xario!" he exclaimed. "Ah, forgive me, not young lord now." He held out his hands, gesturing to the black armor. "And returned as a warrior of the Black Legion, as you said you would. You've grown into it well."

He reached back to a table and produced two small packages. "Take two. One for your family."

Xario took the two packages and pulled two copper coins out of his belt purse. But Hige waved him off.

"No need, Young Master."

"Hige, you will let me pay you for your work," Xario took a third copper coin out and pressed them all into the older man's hand. "It has been far too long since I've tasted your *uban*."

Pleased, the shopkeeper relented. Xario returned the mask to his face, covering his easy smile with the menacing fangs of the Black Legion, the leather smile carved into something ghoulish and dark. His black cloak brushed the doorframe as he stepped back outside, and after removing one of the squares, the packages of *uban* were placed carefully inside a bag behind his saddle. Xario sucked the lemon candy into his mouth. It was still the perfect blend of tartness and sweetness. He pulled himself back into the saddle and turned his mare toward his father's estate.

Two years had changed nothing about the walled courtyard or the slated triangular roofs rising above the sprawling house. Xario rode to the stable and dismounted. His father's stable servant bowed and reached for the mare's reins.

"I'll see to her," Xario said. "No oats until tomorrow morning. She rode fast."

The man bobbed his head again. "Yes, my lord."

When the mare was contentedly munching a bit of hay in the stable, rubbed down and dry, Xario left his spear and cloak with her saddle and hefted the leather supply bags over his shoulder. He scratched at his short beard as he crossed over the small pond, a new generation of colorful fish gracefully swimming beneath the bridge. Beneath the front entrance, he slid off his boots and pushed aside the door panel to the inner courtyard.

"*Yabo!*"

A little girl rose from where she had been crouched in the court-yard playing with several small dolls. Her black hair was tangled and hung low to the middle of her back, her eyes sparkling as her rosy cheeks erupted into a wide smile.

Xario put down his bags and opened his arms, kneeling down so he was the same height. "I've come home, Eiri!" She leapt into his embrace and nestled her face against him, her arms flung around his neck. She leaned back and frowned, poking at the patchy black stubble around his jaw.

"It's scratchy."

Xario laughed. "Shall I shave it all off?"

She considered and scrutinized him for a few heartbeats. "You look like *abi*."

*I am the son of Counsellor Hallix, no matter where I go,* Xario thought grimly. He lifted his little sister high into the air, and she giggled, holding her arms out like a bird's wings. Xario set her down carefully, and she ran back to her dolls. Grabbing them up, she brought them closer, holding them up proudly. They were made of cloth, little mouths and eyes stitched on their linen faces, red dots on their cheeks for blush. One of them was dressed in black, two in brown house garments, and one wore a pretty blue dress.

"*Ama* made them for me. This one is you!" she held up the doll dressed in black. "And this one is Kurin, and this one is me. And this one is Gehrin."

A lump rose in Xario's throat, but he took the doll in the blue dress and pretended to study it carefully. "This one cannot be you."

Her little eyebrows scrunched together. "Why not?"

"It's not pretty enough."

She giggled and took it from his hand, flitting back into the courtyard and setting the dolls back around the little meal of pulled apart leaves and twigs she'd made for them. Xario rose from his knees and handed the bags to a servant nearby. It was time for a less pleasant reunion.

He walked the familiar tread of the wooden floor around the courtyard to his father's room. Apprehension filled him, and he wondered if he would ever stand in front of this door without it. His father's presence radiated from the room.

"Father."

"Come in."

Xario gently slid the door to the side and stepped into the room. Incense burned on a table in the corner, filling the room with a heady spiced aroma. Xario faced his father's low table and knelt, bowing his head to the mats on the floor, his hands flat on either side of his face. The leather armor dug into the front of his neck. The armor of the Black Legion was not made for bowing.

"Rise."

Xario pushed back, kneeling comfortably and placing his hands against his knees, finally lifting his gaze to the man sitting behind the table. Counsellor Hallix was writing something, the quill scratching softly across the paper. Xario remained silent, taking deep breaths of the incense-infused air. He was tired from riding, his eyes dry from the winter breeze. His mind wandered to thoughts of a warm bath and a night in his old bed. But here he would sit until his father allowed otherwise.

The quill stopped.

"You wear the armor of the Legion well."

"Thank you, Father. It is an honor to wear it."

Counsellor Hallix poured two cups of wine, and Xario accepted his gratefully. He waited until his father had taken a sip, and then drank from his own cup. The wine was overly spiced, the way his father preferred it. Xario could feel his father's eyes on him, studying him, looking for cracks or defects. He kept his back straight and his eyes fixed forward.

"You have made a good impression on your commanders. Two years in the Legion and already a Tenth Leader, that is impressive progress."

*Are you proud, Father? Proud of these accomplishments?* "I seek only to bring honor to your name and to the king."

Counsellor Hallix scoffed and flicked his hand dismissively. "I believe it is time that you and I spoke plainly to one another. You are my eldest son and heir. You are a Tenth Leader in the Black Legion, and you are a man. It is time you stopped speaking like a boy."

"How would you have me speak, Father?"

"Tell me of your *ambitions*."

Surprised, Xario cleared his throat. "My ambitions?"

"Yes. You must have ambitions of some kind. You have become a leader in the Black Legion. You command one hundred men. Is that the furthest your path leads you?"

"I... one day will become Hand of the Legion, if I am chosen."

Counsellor Hallix frowned. "That's the boy talking. Will you let others choose your ambitions for you?"

"No, Father."

"Then what are your ambitions?"

Xario curled his fingers into his sweating palms. "I will become Hand of the Legion. And then, if I can, I will become High General."

There was no change in his father's expression, no easing of the shoulders looming toward Xario. The brooding dark cloud that hovered over him spread its tension into Xario's arms and hands, and the muscles in his limbs grew tight. He knew that his father desired something more of him, and he dreaded the words that he knew would come from Counsellor Hallix's lips. But still they came.

"I will make you king."

It was not treachery, though every word dripped with the promise of it. Xario felt the weight of his armor, the stiff leather pressing against his inner tunic. Outside the walls of his father's house, it was a second skin. Here he felt as if he might be suffocated by it. His father set down his cup.

"The king refuses to give in to the Council's demands for an answer. He must choose a successor by his fortieth year if he cannot produce an heir of his own. There are those in the Council who would like to see that law eradicated, to force the king's hand sooner. But I am content to wait. Queen Xhen is waiting for any sign of weakness, and if this choice shifts power from a monarchy that has lasted generations to the wrong family's power and interest? Katesh is not strong enough for that. The council would tear itself apart. King Kinhariian has never been a man who could be forced to do anything. I believe the Council has created their own demise, trying to push a boulder uphill. But he will have to choose, and we must be ready. You are the closest thing he has to an heir of his own blood."

Xario knew that his father believed him the most likely choice as the king's heir. It was no secret. It had been spoken in every circle of the city since the Crown Prince had been murdered. Itaki Ujo and Xario had been pitted against each other as rivals for the throne, but Counsellor Ujo was not nearly as close to the king's favor as Counsellor Hallix. And while the Ujo house was wealthy enough to buy the throne, they were not beloved enough to keep it. For Xario's part, he would have just as readily stayed behind in the military camp outside Mizak and left the succession of the throne to more interested people.

His father was watching him. "You keep your thoughts hidden behind your filial respect. Speak."

Xario had only seen the king's great Council Hall a handful of times when his father had brought him to the palace as a boy. He had seen the carved wooden throne settled beneath the watchful gemstone eyes of the fox and the wolf above. He imagined sitting on the hard wood, looking out in disdain over the squabbling counsellors below. He imagined the eyes of Katesh looking to him, worshipping him as the father of a nation.

"I do not believe I would be a good king. My place is with the Legion."

"Your place is where you can best serve your country."

Xario pulled his courage together. "Or where I can best serve you?"

After a moment of silence, Counsellor Hallix's stern face softened. "Good. A strong man does not simply go where he is directed. He must know his purpose. You already serve this house by your presence in the Black Legion. Tell me, what have you observed of your commanders?"

"You want me to be your spy?"

"I wish you to tell me things of interest. Do not forget that as the king's advisor, I already have far more capable informants in place in the Black Legion than you. But I wish to know what you have learned of those above you."

Xario shifted slightly. Sweat ran down the back of his neck, and his armor was beginning to chafe at him. He'd hoped to have already slipped into the warmth of the bathhouse and a clean set of clothing, but the conversation made him sweat far more than the hot sun outside. "Third Hand Jaakar is a good man, a good teacher. He is the oldest of the Hands. He is brother to Tahmujin, one of the king's most trusted *garatelhai*. He is strict but respected."

"Any one of your Legion brothers could have told me as much. Is that all you have learned?"

"Jaakar is stronger with short weapons. He trains us with the long spear, but he prefers short spears and the swords that the Maleki warriors use. He has a young granddaughter that he is fond of in Mijaro, she will be of marriageable age in two years. He will hear nothing said against the king or the other Hands, even in jest. And he has a weakness for spiced lamb. He has a birthmark in the shape of the *yba* rune on his left side, so his men believe that he cannot lie. The other Hands look up to him, and even the High General gives more weight to his advice than the others." Xario paused, wondering if he'd finally said enough. "Do you wish me to go further?"

"That was better. Jaakar is a well-respected man, and his favor would be of great benefit to you. There is no better teacher in the Black Legion. You have done well to study him. I want you to tell me if he receives a visit from his brother."

"Lord Tahmujin? He has only come to the barracks once, and it was some time ago."

Counsellor Hallix tapped his finger against the table. "Tahmujin is at this moment in Blackvale."

"Blackvale?" Xario knew little of the abandoned fortress tucked into the Northern mountains of Katesh. It had been an outpost long ago when King Kinhariian's ancestors were first building the skeleton of the great city of Keld. It was easily defensible, the front gate approached only by a stone bridge hovering over a chasm that cut away into the forested cliffs below. Guarded by a few *telhai* and *gerhai*, it was hardly a place of note.

"Tahmujin has been the commander of Blackvale for nearly four years, in secret. He is training soldiers."

"Why?"

"I can only imagine that the king has some use for them. Perhaps some new fighting unit. Master Lohi has also traveled there frequently. But whatever purpose they serve, the king has not seen fit to inform me of it," said Counsellor Hallix. Despite the calm tone, Xario could tell that his father was displeased.

"And you have a spy there."

"Yes. You have met her before. Her name is Bithra. She sends me a report whenever she is summoned there to serve Tahmujin."

The faint memory of the red-garbed woman floated past Xario's consciousness pleasantly. She had haunted his thoughts more than once since he had seen her as a much younger boy. He could still remember the smell of her, the way the charms on her wrists and ankles had softly jingled as she walked.

"I remember."

"No doubt. She has been a particular favorite of Tahmujin's for some time, at my behest. This is why it pays to know the weaknesses of those around you. Bithra has loosened Tahmujin's tongue enough to give me some knowledge of his purpose at Blackvale."

Xario chewed the inside of his lip, slowly pushing the pieces of what his father was telling him into place. "Do you wish me to go to Blackvale?"

"No. I already have enough presence there to bide my time. I want you to become invaluable to Jaakar. You will need the support of the Legion if the Council turns against you when you are chosen."

*If I am chosen.* But his father's confidence forged his doubt into a dreadful expectation. If his father had chosen him to be king, it was only a matter of time before the king did the same. He would be marched into the Council Hall and the counsellors would chafe at his presence the way his armor chafed at his skin. They would hate him for being Counsellor Hallix'ss son.

"Father, if the counsellors turn against us-"

"Then you will have the Black Legion at your back. And they will be powerless to stop you."

The light over the city had finally dimmed as Aqatar sank behind the mountains to the west. The whitish walls of the buildings were cast with an orange glow. The hustle and noise were quieter now, but not less. Some merchants closed their shops, while others prepared for their evening of work. Xario walked out into the streets, passing by a man carefully moving racks of colorful silks together in his small corner shop. Finally free of his armor, Xario felt light as a feather in his green *seri* and soft sandals. His hair had grown too long. All but a small section of it was free of the usual tie on top of his head, and it hung freely down his back. It had been a long time since he had worn the everyday clothing of a noble.

He slowed his pace, allowing his feet to meander him through the city, taking in the smells and sights he had missed in Mizak. Dominated by the presence of the Black Legion, Mizak was a much less vibrant city, bleak in its utilitarian style. The city merchants revolved around the needs of the soldiers, far less colorful. There were only one or two silk merchants there, compared with the dozens that occupied the shops of Keld. The daughters of the few nobles who resided in Mizak were adorned far less grandly than the daughters of Keld's wealthy houses.

Xario stopped in front of a jeweler's table, picking up a small hair comb. The wings of a delicate dove spread over strings of tiny blue gems that matched the bird's sapphire eye. He lifted it from the silk cushion, turning the beautiful piece over in his hand. It was a masterful design.

"A truly rare piece, my lord!" said the jeweler. "I have only made one like it."

"It is a fine piece," replied Xario. "A credit to your craft."

The man bowed, pleased by the compliment. "It would make a fine gift for a beautiful woman. Perhaps a wife?"

Xario smiled. "I have no wife. But it deserves to be worn by a beauty to match it."

Eiri was too young for such a precious piece of finery. Thiri preferred simpler clothing and adornments. Xario had only seen her wear hair combs this fine before Eiri was born. He placed it back on the silk. He chose a small pair of red gemstone earrings for Thiri and a matching necklace for his little sister. As the jeweler packaged them carefully, Xario looked back at the hair comb. On a whim, he picked it up and handed it to the craftsman.

"It is too fine a jewel to leave behind."

The jeweler accepted the bag of coins with a bow. It was an exorbitant sum to spend, even on something so fine as the comb. His fellow *telhai* would tease him relentlessly if they had seen him spend his soldier's pay on such a bauble. He tucked the comb carefully into the inside of his tunic above his belt with the silk-wrapped earrings and necklace.

His wanderings took him past the blacksmith at the end of the merchant's row, where he left instructions for a new spearhead and haft to be made for the Third Hand. He would take it to a woodcarver when it was finished. It would be a fine gift, his father's idea. Perhaps he would take it to a *mojar* to inscribe it with the *yba* rune in honor of Jaakar's reputation.

And then, his errands done, his wanderings took him down another street he had walked many times in his childhood. He stopped in front of a gate lined with *feth* runes. The crumbling tiles around the top of the wall had seen no improvement in the past years, and the humble, weatherworn roof over the gates was in a similar condition, the wood cracked and warped.

Xario knocked on the gate.

It was quickly opened by an elderly manservant, who bobbed in several bows. "Lord Xario! Please let me announce the honor of your visit to my master."

"No need, Chon. My father is away but I believe I can manage entertaining Lord Xario."

Stepping carefully off the steps of the porch, Kasaii maneuvered down to the clean-swept yard, leaning on a carved staff. Xario watched her with a strange tightness in his chest. Her bright eyes sparkled above the curve of her lips, which had been painted with the barest touch of red. The healthy glow in her cheeks warmed her smile. She was sixteen, and any traces of the awkward girl had vanished with the promise of womanhood. But she still carried a touch of the wild spirit she had always been. It glimmered in her eyes and the way her eyebrow tilted teasingly as she looked at him.

"Your visit is unexpected, Lord Xario."

"I apologize, I should have sent a servant ahead of me. I will not intrude on you - I can return tomorrow or... the day after." Xario suddenly felt foolish for turning up unannounced. But Kasaii just laughed. "We are still friends, aren't we? Come in and have some tea."

She gestured back to the main room of the house on the right, and Xario followed her up the steps. Despite her weak leg, she seemed to have grown more graceful over time. She floated up the steps, only the slightest lurch giving away her condition. She pushed a second panel of the room open, leaving them open to the front courtyard and the eyes of the servants.

Once inside, she indicated a place for Xario to sit on the mats in front of a low table. A simple teapot and cups already waited for them. Kasaii fetched a third cup and set it on the table, and at the same time, her mother appeared from another room, her cheeks freshly brushed with rouge to cover the pale pallor of her skin. She bowed deeply when she saw Xario.

"Young Lord Hallix!" she exclaimed. "What an honor to have you visit us. I heard that you had returned to Keld. Your father must be pleased to have you back."

"Thank you for your hospitality, Lady Suka. I do not know how long I will be staying before duty calls me back to Mizak. I did not want to leave again without a visit to old friends." He glanced at Kasaii. Lady Suka looked pleased.

"You are welcome in our home whenever you have need of it," she replied, settling down on a cushion between him and Kasaii, who pulled her right sleeve away from her hand and carefully poured the tea into each cup. Then she handed the first to Xario. He breathed in the tang of the ginger and the earthy turmeric. He sipped gratefully. Kasaii and her mother waited until he had finished his first cup before refilling it and taking small sips of their own. He was being treated as an honored guest, the way his father would be. It was a strange thing to be suddenly viewed as a man when he had only memories of boyhood in this house.

"Is your father in good health?" Lady Suka asked.

"He is."

There was a long, strange pause during which Xario waited for either of the women to speak about something else. But suddenly he realized that they were waiting for him. He sipped.

"And your husband, he is in good health? My father relies on him, he is an invaluable overseer. Our fields would not yield half without his managing them."

Lady Suka inclined her head. "You honor us. My husband is strong and well. He says that the barley fields will have low yield this year, though not as low as the year before."

There were no more words spoken after that for a long time. Xario grew frustrated with himself. He had never been good at discussing small matters. The floor was hard beneath his knees, and he smelled the faint musty scent of the room's wooden beams. He should have gone home. He was *telhai* now, and he'd been with the rough company of soldiers for too long. Kasaii watched him across the table, and he was uncomfortable under her gaze. He did not know why.

"What is it like?" Kasaii asked gently. "Tell me about the Black Legion."

Xario smoothed his thumb over the glazed teacup and let his mind sift through the things he could tell her. "We train every day. In that it is much the same as when we were children. I have learned to use knives and swords, and Lord Jaakar makes us spar without weapons. He says a man must know how to use his fists as well as a blade, because either one could save his life."

"The Third Hand is a man who has earned much respect in Katesh," breathed Lady Suka. "He is a great warrior."

Xario nodded, imagining his father asking Lady Suka if that was all she had learned about the man. "He has taught me a great deal in my time there. The king offered him a comfortable retirement, and he refused. He requested that the king allow him to continue training the Black Legion, for he knew no other task he would be fit for."

"What of your soldiers?" asked Kasaii. "You command one hundred *telhai* and *gerhai*, do you not?"

Xario knew each one of the hundred by name. He knew which of them had left families behind in their cities, which of them had the vices of drink or gambling, and which he would trust with his life if they ever saw battle. He knew which of them were fathers and mothers, which of them spent their pay in the pleasure houses of Mizak, and which of them came from other lands, leaving behind their birth country to fight for the warlord's army. Wryly, Xario realized that he would have had much more to tell his father if Counsellor Hallix had asked about the men under him instead of those above.

"They are strong, and train well. Lord Jaakar does not suffer laziness among his soldiers."

"And neither do you, I would think," replied Kasaii, fixing him with a curious look. "You were always destined to be a leader in your father's estimation. He must be proud."

A show of pride was a frivolity Counsellor Hallix would not have had time to spare on his eldest son. Xario knew what his father expected of him. He always had, ever since he first gripped the small practice spear at the age of four. Each son had a role to play, even Gehrin's death had served to prove their father's resilience to the other counsellors.

As Xario finished the last sip of his tea, he noticed Lady Suka watching him closely. He set the cup down in front of him to inquire if something was wrong, but she spoke before he had even managed to open his mouth.

"Forgive me, Master Xario, would you mind if I read your tea leaves?"

She reached for his cup, and he hesitantly handed it to her. She set it down and peered into the saturated bits of leaf at the bottom. Xario glanced at Kasaii, whose mouth quirked ever so slightly in a barely concealed smile. Waving her hand over the cup, Lady Suka handed it back to Xario.

"Do you often observe the *hijo* rune in your daily life, Master Xario?"

Xario swallowed carefully. "I can't say that I have."

"The runes of prosperity are a sign of good health and favor from Sharai. There is a *hijo* rune in the leaves. A sign, perhaps, to seek a beneficial union. I am only a simple student of such things, but perhaps the priests can give you greater insight."

Color rose in Xario's cheeks, and he realized he was crushing the cup in his hand. He placed it down gently and rose, unfolding his legs from the cushion. "My gratitude for your wise words. I thank you for opening your home and your table, Lady Suka."

He bowed, and Lady Suka quickly shook her head. "You honor us with your presence, Lord Xario. We will continue to entreat Sharai and his Oathsworn for your good health."

Kasaii walked with him to the gate, her steps delicate on the sandy ground. The servant opened the worn wooden door and bowed. Xario turned to Kasaii, unsure what it was he wanted to say, only that he wanted to say something before leaving her.

"I am glad you came," she said. "It is good to see you."

"And you."

"Don't mind Mother. Sometimes I think she has spent too long squinting at teacups and only sees what she wishes to," she said, her voice tinged with amusement. Xario chuckled.

Her smile drew out some part of him that longed for the days of boyhood, the memory of small feet running through the streets of

Keld, hurrying to Master Lohi's classes with flushed faces and bundles of brushes and paper and rune squares. His heart ached for those days when he and his brothers had just been simple boys. He also knew it was not something he could ever return to. Even if he could, he had come this far, and now it was time to forge ahead on the path that had been laid out for him.

He looked away from her and studied the worn wood frame over the gate. A small spider's web glimmered faintly in the top right corner. "I saw fresh stone lilies on Gehrin's shrine this morning. Was it you?"

She nodded silently. Her expression of compassion and sympathy tugged at his heart. He had no words to express his gratitude at her simple way of honoring his brother's memory. Impulsively, he reached into the fold of his tunic and withdrew the comb. He took her hand and pressed the jewel into her palm. She stared down at it, and then looked up at him with some faint confusion on her face.

"Please accept it. I..." Xario paused. The words didn't seem right on his tongue, only in his mind. *I would like to know that you are wearing it when I am gone.* The thought of the bright silver gracing her smooth hair, gathered perfectly on the top of her head in a soft circle, brought him somehow closer to those warm memories of days past.

She smiled and gently touched the little gemstone beads. "Thank you."

She tucked it into the coil at the top of her head, and the dove's wings spread vibrantly against the black of her hair. Xario swallowed the desire to stay, to ask if he could take one more cup of the ginger tea beneath the creaking eaves of the old house. But instead, he bowed his head once more and left. He did not look back, but imagined her standing at the gate watching him, the silver comb shining in her hair.

# CHAPTER FIFTEEN

*The child born with a closed fist is full of fire many waters will not put out.*

*- Maleki Saying*

Syndri dragged the headless body behind her horse. The head knocked against Brig's shoulder, the strings of long hair loose over the sightless eyes, blood dripping over the stallion's leg. The brown of the Tladr tribe on the forehead had begun to show through as the white paste that had once hidden it cracked and flaked.

Brig had seen plenty of bloodshed in his years, but the big warhorse still snorted and sidestepped, as if he could somehow run away from the mangled flesh hanging from Syndri's saddle. Syndri drove him on with her heels, one hand on the reins of her own mount, the other leading the skittish chestnut filly behind. Itah was wild-eyed, kicking out at the body dragging behind her. Baya's body was carefully tied to her back, his arms wrapped around her neck. Death hovered over them all like a grim cloud, the smell of blood and urine and shit strong enough that it cut through the fresh winter air. The body of the young Tladr warrior tumbled over the ground, covered in mud and dirt.

It was a slow ride back to the village. Syndri's eyes never wavered from the blurry line between earth and sky in front of her. Itah resisted, pulling at the reins in an attempt to flee. The little horse was still young, her rider's youth mirrored in her own skittish fear near the smell of death.

Numbness crept through Syndri's limbs, and her hands clenched around reins she could not feel. The air was neither warm nor cold, finding no cracks in the armor of grief Syndri wore around her like a cloak. The thickness in her throat threatened to choke her, but she embraced the discomfort. Her hands still held the sensation of her blade punching through the young warrior's chest. Muscle, sinew, and bone had given way beneath the force of her killing blow, draining his life so quickly that his eyes had stayed open in shock as he fell, already dead as the blade pierced his heart. She'd stared at the two bodies lying side by side. The Tladr warrior looked nearly as boyish as her brother, lying crumpled on the ground, limbs splayed at strange angles. After the trembling in her hands had lessened, Syndri had reached out and yanked the carved totem from around his neck. She'd chased his horse away toward the border. Let the Tladr weep and wail for a son as the Garhis tribe would weep for theirs.

As the village slowly came into view over the last small hill, the weight of the Tladr totem was heavy against Syndri's neck. She'd placed it there next to her own so that the Sky Clans would have no trouble finding the face of the young warrior's killer. And when she reached the village, she would crush it into the dust.

She circled wide around the herds. The bodies might disturb the kehroxen, and she would allow this Tladr no further chance to cause harm. When the tribesmen and women guarding the herds saw the strange little traveling party, several of them shouted in confusion or alarm. In front of the gate, Syndri dismounted from Brig and untied the rope dragging the Tladr from around her belly. She fastened the severed head to her belt.

Uhuri came running up to her, his shocked face filling with

horror as he quickly looked at the bodies. "Syndri, what in the sky and stars..."

"Take Brig."

"What is this?"

"Take Brig."

He did not press her again, but took the black stallion away toward the herds, glancing over his shoulder. Syndri pulled Itah along behind her with one hand, the other dragging the mangled body of the Tladr. She brought her brother home through the gate of the village.

She did not look to the right or left. She walked through the gate of the village and into the crowds of Garhis still drinking, dancing, and singing. As she strode through, the sounds changed. Joy and revelry gave way to the first wails of grief and despair as Baya's body was recognized. Syndri pushed on, her body exhausted, the muscles in her arms and legs beginning to ache beneath the strain.

The crowds opened to let her through as she reached the center of the village. She stopped as she caught sight of Nar Garhis and Ettlan. Dropping Itah's reins, she untied her brother from his horse and caught his body as it fell to the side. Her eyes stung as she lifted Baya in her arms, realizing how much heavier he'd grown in the past few seasons. She took him to his mother, and nearly lost the strength in her knees as she saw Ettlan's face turn toward them.

The Open Hand of the Garhis tribe reached out for him, her face draining of its color. She pulled him from Syndri's arms and sank to the dirt, holding her son in her arms. She touched his face, felt his chest for the heartbeat that had long since fled into darkness. The world around them grew still and silent. Senna appeared, dropped to her knees beside Ettlan, and gripped the shoulder of their mother's cloak.

Ettlan turned tear-filled eyes to Syndri, her lips open in a silent question that could not be uttered. Syndri found her own voice caught behind the grief lodged in her throat.

"He was killed. By a Tladr."

Gasps of shock and anger erupted from the rows of Garhis who were close enough to hear her quiet words. Syndri went back to Itah, who skittered sideways as Syndri grabbed the rope by the filly's hooves. Hefting it over her shoulder, she dragged the Tladr's body into the center of the Garhis village. It was the first time anyone from the enemy tribe had entered the gates of the city. She untied the head from her belt and tossed it with a heavy thump near the body.

"I have brought you the body of the man who killed him."

Ettlan did not look at the Tladr. She continued stroking her son's face, her tears running through the blood and dirt on his cheeks. A low keening sound came from her lips, trembling in the air. The grassy crown in her hair shivered.

Nar Garhis strode forward, his huge frame shadowing his wife and son on the ground. "A Tladr on our lands?" His voice was dark, the rumble of a great bear. Syndri had no words to answer him. Not yet. She would tell the story in the quiet of her father and mother's *gat*.

"Are there others?" her father asked, his eyes searching the western wall of the village, as if expecting his enemies to appear over the stacked stones. Syndri shook her head.

"No."

Nar Garhis crouched next to the body, pulling at the shredded armor that still clung to the torso. The man's belt and small pouches that were tied to it had only partially survived, most of the leather had been scraped away over the grasslands. Nar Garhis gripped the head by its torn and tangled hair, lifting up the face of the man who had killed his son, as if seeking answers within the sagging mouth and eyes.

The wails that had broken out when Syndri had first walked through the village had tapered away into the mournful silence required to respect the dead. The Death Songs would be sung, but in this moment, the low, broken hum stumbling from Ettlan's lips was the only voice allowed. Those closest to the dead must mourn first. And Syndri was not ready to add her voice to her mother's. Senna's tears were flowing freely down her face into the back of their mother's cloak as she gripped Ettlan's shoulders.

Nar Garhis tossed the head aside, and turned to Syndri, his dark eyes flashing in anger. "This man bears the white face of a messenger."

Anger boiled in the pit of Syndri's stomach. If the Sky Clans protected such a man, they were fools and cowards. "He killed Baya."

"Did he wear the messenger's face?" demanded her father.

"He killed Sabayaar."

Her father's face contorted, and he reached out and pulled Syndri to him, dragging her by the front of her tunic. "Did you kill a man wearing the messenger's face?"

"He killed... *Sabayaar*."

Nar Garhis growled in fury and threw Syndri aside as if she weighed less than a child. She hit the ground, a flash of pain through her hip and elbow. Hands gripped her shoulders and arms as she pushed herself to her feet. Sochi and Ikaio, two of her fellow warriors, held her firmly to face Nar Garhis' judgment. Syndri stood steady. The weight of what she had done was nothing beneath the weight of her brother's still body cradled in their mother's arms. Ettlan's guttural moans of agony sent fresh stabs of pain through Syndri's chest, her own grief locked away before the faces of her tribe. Her father could not be merciful. Messengers were protected by the Sky Clans. To cover a tribal tattoo was a decision the Tladr warrior would not have made lightly.

He had invoked the ancient protection of the Sky Clans to bring her brother back to his people. And she had driven a blade through his heart. And she would do it again.

Nar Garhis lifted two closed fists up into the air. "A warrior of our tribe has broken the ancient laws of Malek and drawn the anger of the Sky Clans on her brothers and sisters. Take her outside the village to the post. She will draw the anger of our ancestors away from our tribe. She is Silent and Bladeless."

The two warriors at her sides pulled Syndri roughly away from the village center, brushing through the crowd as they began to murmur amongst themselves, shock and horror coloring every face. Some of them dared a sympathetic glance toward Syndri, but many were already pressing closer to the Nar's *gat* and the anguished scene, sharing in the grief pouring from Ettlan. Several mothers clutched boys of Baya's age tightly against them.

Then Syndri was led out the village gate into the frosted plains beyond. The grass bent under her boots, and she looked up at the gray sky. The clouds were dark and loomed low over the hills, as if the Sky Clans were already turning toward her in displeasure.

A lone wooden post stood at a distance from the village, a cross-beam across the top. It had been years since Syndri had seen it used. Her back pressed against the hard wood as Sochi and Ikaio tied rough ropes around her wrists and arms and strapped them tightly to the crossbeam. Neither of them looked at her, and she did not acknowledge them. She would adhere to the Maleki laws in that, at least. She saw Sochi's eyes flicker toward her briefly, and then he disappeared behind her. The two warriors' footsteps were silent in the long grass, so she could not listen to them retreat.

Syndri lifted her face to the looming clouds. She imagined the faces of her ancestors turning toward her in anger, striking her with the elements until she hung from the post like the Tladr warriors that Yugha had left behind at the crossing in the border raid a season ago. And suddenly, she realized how tired she was. The cold broke past the numbness of grief and curled icy fingers around her limbs. Strength drained from her, and she sagged against the wood, letting the tight ropes hold her up.

She searched every corner of her soul for some shred of remorse, some acknowledgement that the death of the Tladr warrior had been done with regret. The sight of her brother's small, lifeless body drowned her, stole the breath from her lungs and crushed it against her chest like a hammer.

"Forgive me, Baya..." she whispered, the tears finally breaking past the edges of her burning eyes to fall unimpeded down her cheeks.

Night fell, morning followed, and the second day passed at a slow crawl. Syndri had long since lost feeling in her arms, and despite the warmth of her hide cloak and heavy winter tunic, the chill had seeped so far into her bones that they felt brittle. The dried trails of snot and tears had frozen on her face as the wind mercilessly flogged her skin. Her lips were numb, and her hands had turned a purplish shade that threatened to steal the blood from her fingers forever.

The sun had just begun to set when they came for her again. This time, it wasn't Sochi's and Ikaio's faces that greeted her, but Yugha's. Her father's War Sword wore the same stoic expression that often darkened his features. He yanked the ropes free from her arms and caught her when she fell forward from the beam. He waited until she had her feet under her again.

The first pang of shame found her then. Yugha should be in his *gat*, surrounded by the warmth of a fire and caring for his wife and newborn child. She did not even know if it was a son or a daughter. No duty should be enough to call him away from them.

*Forgive me.* She could not speak to him, the silence imposed on her by her father had not been lifted. He would not meet her eyes, but he kept his hand on her shoulder as they moved slowly toward the village.

The joy of the winter songs had seeped out of the village. Here and there a grass crown lay trampled into the dirt, but all other traces of the celebration had disappeared. Not one person looked up when Syndri and Yugha walked past, going about their tasks with a dull familiarity, as if the events of the day before had sucked away the tribe's life and left behind husks.

Her father's *gat* was warm with the fire crackling in the center pit. Yugha opened the flap and followed Syndri inside. Nar Garhis sat in a chair covered in hides, propping up his head on one hand, his face troubled. Ettlan sat on her bed, her eyes trained on some distant place beyond the walls of the *gat*, deep red splotches betraying the tears she had shed. Behind her, laid in a peaceful repose as if only asleep, Baya was cradled in the furs. His hair had been carefully rebraided and laid over one shoulder, and his face and body had been washed.

Near his feet sat Senna. When Syndri walked through the door, the two sisters met each other's gaze briefly. Senna did not look away.

Syndri lowered herself stiffly to her knees. She was Silent and Bladeless, her warrior's pride stripped from her until her father gave it back to her. If he chose to. Yugha remained behind her, his presence somehow comforting despite the knowledge that he would draw his sword and cleave her head from her neck if her father ordered him to do it.

Nar Garhis drew in a deep breath and settled himself straighter in his chair. "Do you understand the laws you have broken?"

"I have shed the blood of a man under the protection of the Sky Clans."

"And do you take responsibility for the blood on your hands?"

"Yes."

The huge man sighed, a flicker of his age showing through the hard lines of his face. "So be it. You have used your blades without honor. Your actions were for yourself, not for your tribe."

Syndri looked at her mother, but Ettlan still stared at the hide wall, her hands resting limply on her lap. Perhaps she'd been right. A closed fist needed an open hand for balance and honor. But no matter how hard she tried to feel remorse for what she'd done, she could find nothing but the hollow emptiness of her brother's death.

"A Closed Fist demands your death to appease the Sky Clans. But your mother brings the balance of an Open Hand. You will be exiled to a place outside the village, where you will live and serve as a guardian of the herds. You will leave your armor and your blades behind, for you are not worthy to wield them. You will learn to find balance, and when you have, we will discuss whether you are welcome in the tribe."

"I will obey," Syndri whispered.

Her father may as well have ordered her death. Syndri closed her eyes and felt Yugha's presence behind her. Could she reach for his sword and fall on the blade before she was stopped? The promise of darkness, her face Bladeless, seemed to lose its edge of horror as she knelt on the floor of her father's *gat*. Her body felt numb and weightless, as if that darkness was already pulling her away from her bruised body and into the ground beneath. She could fade away, become nothing.

Soft hands cupped Syndri's face.

Ettlan knelt in front of her, eyes shimmering in the red, puffy flesh of her face. "I will not lose two of my children. You will live, and you will honor us."

The warmth of her mother's hands on her cheeks stayed with Syndri even as Yugha led her out of the *gat* and toward her new life of exile.

The pyre they built for Sabayaar was taller than a man's height. His body was wrapped in white hides to show the Sky Clans his innocence, that despite his manner of death, he was still a child. The flames rose twice as high as the pyre, eagerly consuming the dried wood and roaring into the overcast sky. The gray clouds had not cleared since Baya's death. A light sprinkle of rain fell but did nothing to discourage the pyre's rage.

Syndri stood beside her small travel *gat*, hastily erected close enough to the village that she could bear witness to her brother's final journey into the sky, but far enough away that she could not make out more than the blurry forms of the tribe surrounding the pyre. She felt naked in her simple trousers and tunic, an old hide cloak wrapped around her shoulders. The weight of her armor and the leather straps of her sword sheaths had become a second skin, as natural to her as drawing breath.

She stood watching until the fire had reduced the pyre to a great pile of ash. One lone figure walked toward her, her hair pulled free from its usual braids and flowing around her shoulders. The women of the village would not braid their hair for twelve days, one for each year of Sabayaar's life.

Senna carried a small bundle with her, her face drawn and lacking its usual inquisitive brightness. Syndri said nothing as her sister disappeared into the *gat* and returned a moment later without the bundle.

"I brought you an extra blanket and some food. Father knew, but he did not say anything to stop me. He does not show it to the others, but his heart aches."

"Our laws cannot be broken. He had no choice."

Senna shook her head and looked out to the smoking remnants of the pyre. "Would any of us have the strength to see what you saw and keep our blades sheathed?"

"Our mother would have."

"Our mother is blessed with the heart of peace. It was she who stayed our father's hand against you. He believed the Sky Clans would demand your life in payment. Ettlan reminded him that there are more ways to pay with a life than by death."

Syndri folded her arms beneath her cloak. "The Sky Clans may rot in their own cloudy *gats* if they refuse Sabayaar."

"Even your tongue is a blade, *teitei*." Senna put her hand on Syndri's shoulder. "You already have the death of our brother's killer at your feet. You seek vengeance but you will find none."

Syndri faced her. "I am outcast, and our brother's bones cool in a pile of ash," she said, pointing toward the pyre. "And yet with a few fingers of white paste, this Tladr dog is protected by the Sky Clans. And Baya's death is worth less than his."

"The Sky Clans have seen far more of this world than we have in our years, *teitei*. The laws we have help us keep balance and-"

"Stop," snapped Syndri. "It is easy to speak words that mean nothing."

Senna reached out and gripped her shoulders, fingers digging into flesh. "I believe that our brother is riding through the clouds with our ancestors. I have to believe it. I have to trust that the Sky Clans would not turn my little brother away because of a mistake. And I will continue to believe it until I am dead."

"And if you're wrong?"

Syndri's question hung in the air between them, darker than the smoke of Baya's pyre. Senna's fingers loosened and fell away. Whatever answers she considered behind her worried brow did not reach her lips, but her eyes filled with a thin line of tears.

"I don't know, Syndri. Today I don't know."

The anger that coiled through Syndri withdrew at the sight of her broken sister. She was not angry at Senna. She was not even angry at her father. It burned so fiercely in the pit of her stomach, deep and raw, with nowhere to go. Even if she held her blades in her hands, whose blood would satiate the desire for vengeance now? The Tladr warrior's body would be returned to his own tribe. Her father had left his totem unbroken as a truce. And so, the cycle repeated itself. A dead son returned to his mother, killed without honor.

Even if she were given her swords and raged through the Tladr villages until every last one of them lay unblinking at the sky, their blood would not be sacrifice enough. When she reached the day of her own death, her sins would be weighed against theirs, and the Sky Clans would judge the worthiness of her choice.

She reached out to draw her sister close and gently rested her forehead against Senna's. "Forgive me. What I have done has brought you more pain, and for that at least I am sorry."

"The blade could've been mine as easily as it was yours," replied Senna softly. "As you feel my pain, so I share your anger. The Sky must witness, I will rise or fall with you."

"And I with you."

# CHAPTER SIXTEEN

*Master Lohi once told me that the runes connected us to the earth's blood, veins pulsing through the dirt beneath our feet. But what he did not know, I knew. The runes connected me to the earth's pain, and memories as countless as the stars.*

*- Sonho*

The forest was quiet. The presence of the *telhai* and the line of silent boys was enough of a disturbance that the birds had retreated to their safe treetops. It was the second time that Master Tahmujin had allowed them outside the walls of the fortress and down into the trees below. The sight of the wide world beyond the stone had filled Gehrin with a fearful thrill. It had been nearly four years since he had seen anything outside the courtyard and surrounding rooms.

The trees rose like wooden spears up into the sky, endless rows of them, clutching their last remaining leaves above the light cover of snow that hid the forest floor from view. Gehrin nearly collided with Sabba's massive back as he tried to take in every sight and sound.

Even the air was fresher and lighter here, free from the oppressive staleness of Blackvale.

Nin shuffled behind him, shivering. He was still the smallest of the boys, his wider eyes and scrawny frame giving him the appearance that he was much younger than his fourteen years. To Gehrin, the air was not cold enough to bother him, but Nin had worn a cloak over his tunic and trousers and was pulling the edges close around his shoulders. When they stopped, he huddled close behind Gehrin for warmth.

Master Tahmujin brought them to a place at the foot of the mountain where a small shrine was carved into the rocks, its red triangular roof a sharp contrast to the thin layer of snow clinging to the scalloped ridges. Inside, a stone face with a circlet of stars stared out over the forest. Shrines were less common in the rest of Katesh, but here, the ancient founders of Katesh had worshipped stone reliefs like this one, their own crude imitation of the face of Sharai and his Oathsworn. Gehrin had never seen one this old before. But as Sabba shifted to the side, Gehrin caught sight of what lay beyond the shrine.

Twenty lengths away huddled a small group of people, dressed in rags and a layer of grime. Iron chains bound their wrists together, and their feet were bound with rope. Gehrin stared at them, his shock at seeing anyone outside of the usual inhabitants of the fortress overtaking him. He searched their faces, momentarily fearful that he would recognize the features.

But he did not know any of them. One man spat in their direction, his wild hair matted and snarled around his shoulders. A thickly muscled *telhai* with a broken nose kicked him sprawling into the snow, the chains clanking and pulling at the wrists of the others.

One of the prisoners was a woman, her ragged dress torn so badly that she was clinging to the last shreds of it to cover herself. Gehrin's stomach twisted at the sight of her left hand. All her fingers were broken. A thief.

Several of the *telhai* guards walked away from the boys into the trees, their boots crunching softly until they faded from earshot.

Master Tahmujin stepped over to the prisoners and reached down, unlocking one of them from the others. The man he dragged out to the edge of the trees was young, perhaps a few years older than Gehrin. The *garatelhai* warrior gripped the prisoner by the back of his hair, lifting his chin up.

"This man is a criminal. Our king has given us the task of executing him and the others who have broken his laws and lost their honor. Niveth, Sabba."

The two boys stepped forward without hesitation at his command. Master Tahmujin pulled two short knives from his belt and handed them each one of the sharp weapons. It was the first time either of them had been given anything beyond a wooden staff. Gehrin watched as Niveth gripped the bone handle and flipped the blade around in his hand. Sabba took his with a steady calm, his eyes never wavering from the prisoner at Master Tahmujin's feet.

A sinking feeling crept into Gehrin's gut, but he pushed it away. Master Tahmujin had told them many times that they were being trained as *bruhai*, a bloodsworn warrior to protect the throne. This would not be the last time they killed in the king's name. And yet Gehrin struggled to swallow around his suddenly dry mouth.

Master Tahmujin pulled the rope away from the young man's feet and shoved him forward toward the trees. The prisoner tripped, and painfully pushed himself up from the snow, festering wounds visible around his bared ankles.

"He will be given fifty lengths to flee. Then you will follow him, and you will kill him. If you fail in this task, you will take his place. Am I understood?"

"Yes, Master." There was no hesitation.

Niveth and Sabba spoke in unison. Niveth's eyes trailed after the prisoner, a nearly feral look entering his eyes as if he were a wolf hunting its prey. The prisoner fell to his knees, hands clasped together, babbling pleas for mercy, that he could not feed his family, that he would serve the king as a slave for the rest of his days if only he could be spared.

There was no honor in his words. Gehrin frowned, willing the man to be silent in the face of his death. Dying without honor was worse than any pain or suffering. Master Tahmujin kicked the man aside with a curse. Seeing that his plight was in vain, the prisoner scrambled to his feet and began to limp away into the forest.

Niveth stood coiled like a serpent, every muscle taut for the inevitable spring. Sabba stood strong and silent, the knife too small in his huge hand. Gehrin wondered which of them would reach the man first. He prayed it would be Sabba, because he knew that the Da'hamian boy would send the prisoner quickly to his end. Niveth, like a cat, would no doubt choose to play with his prey before death. There was no honor in that, either.

The limping man disappeared into the endless line of trees. At a word from Master Tahmujin, the two boys leapt forward, running after him. Niveth was fast, one of the fastest runners of any of them, but Sabba's long strides kept pace. Then they too, disappeared.

The thought of running to freedom flickered and died in the back of Gehrin's thoughts. The *telhai* hidden amongst the trees would not hesitate to kill either prisoner or *bruhai* boy. He settled into the heels of his feet, relaxing his body, and breathed out little clouds through his nose.

It was not long before the other two boys reappeared. Niveth looked angry, his face mottled red from more than just the colder air. Gehrin felt a slight twinge of relief. Sabba's knife was still in his hand, blood darkening the blade.

Tahmujin took the knives and wiped the blood clean on a cloth. Sabba returned to stand quietly next to Gehrin, hands limp at his sides. His chest heaved slightly from the exertion of chasing down his quarry, but the irregularity was something more. He stared down at the ground.

The man who had spat at them was dragged forward, fighting and scratching at the *telhai* like a wild animal. The *telhai* with the broken nose pummeled him across the head and neck with his fists until he sullenly gave up.

"Ruh, Nin."

The white-haired Takkan boy stepped forward, but Nin hesitated. Gehrin could feel the other boy's fear seeping through his cloak. He gave Nin a nudge forward from behind.

"Follow Ruh," he muttered under his breath. The thought of a blade in the Takkan's hand was more than enough to suppress his fear for Nin's ability to fight and kill a man like that. Small and trembling, Nin stepped forward next to Ruh, his head of hair dark next to Ruh's white. Tahmujin eyed him with open disapproval before untying the man's feet. With a curse, the prisoner took off running into the snow.

Ruh turned his blade, testing the grip. Nin looked as if the hilt of his knife was burning into his hand, twisting his expression into some form of dread. At the signal from Master Tahmujin, Ruh grabbed the back of Nin's cloak and pulled him along into the trees, and the two of them sped through the snow together, knives flashing.

One or two of the other prisoners had begun pleading with the *telhai* guards. One offered to pay in coppers that Gehrin doubted he even had. As Gehrin watched them, he began to study each gaunt face, wondering which of them he would be told to kill. He wondered how fast they would run, if they would fight back, or if he would even have to kill them at all. If the other boy Tahmujin chose reached them first, he might still end the day not knowing what it felt like to kill.

He'd butchered pigs and chickens before. Kirte saw to it that each of the boys took turns helping prepare their own meals. Three days ago, Kajen had burned the meat nearly to char and Kirte had made them all eat it. Gehrin could still taste the ash on his tongue.

Pigs and chickens bled red, the same as the blood that coated the knives Ruh and Nin now carried through the trees. And yet, somehow, the thought of human eyes staring up at him in fear broke any fragile belief he could muster that it would be the same.

Something stirred in the trees, and Gehrin saw Ruh's white hair bob into view amongst the dark red-brown wood. Three heartbeats later, Nin followed. As they grew closer, Gehrin realized that both of their blades were red.

If Tahmujin was surprised by Nin's blade, he did not show it. He wiped them clean and sent the boys back to their places. Sweat beads lined Nin's forehead, the odor of exertion wafting from him, and he shivered as if the cold was still seeping through his cloak. He clasped his hands together, trying to stop the shaking. He looked up at Gehrin, eyes red-rimmed.

"Liv! Haveth!"

In a daze, Gehrin responded, his feet carrying him forward over the snow to stand before Master Tahmujin. The prisoner thrown to the ground gave a soft gasp as she landed. The woman held her injured hand against her chest, the fingers grossly misshapen and purpled.

*Please, do not make me do this...*

The smooth handle of the knife pressed against Gehrin's palm. He didn't remember stretching out his hand. Haveth's tall, thin form next to him felt threatening, the shining blade in his hand strange after the years of wooden practice weapons. Tahmujin kicked the woman away, and she struggled to her feet, stumbling away along the path that the others had left before her. A path that led to her death somewhere in the trees, and a blood covered blade.

The heartbeats slowed. Gehrin fixed his eyes on the woman's back until she was gone. He heard Master Tahmujin's command faintly, as if there was a great rushing waterfall roaring in his ears. His feet moved, and then he was running, the wind whipping past his cheeks like tiny blades.

Haveth was taller, but his lankier legs did not keep pace with Gehrin's. Pushing himself faster, faster, Gehrin hurtled toward the inevitable horror ahead. He saw a dark flash behind a tree to his left, the telltale black of the *telhai*'s cloak in the snow. The trees flew past him, and he followed the tracks away from the main path. They were smaller, lighter than the ones before. She could not have gotten far.

He crested a small rise near a stream trickling down and away from the mountain. The tracks slid over the rocks to the other side, and he saw movement about twenty lengths ahead of him where the tree trunks disappeared into a copse of tall brush. He jumped the stream, his blood on fire as he controlled his breaths with each stride. The familiar tension of adrenaline tightened his arms, and his grip on the dagger would've taken the strength of Master Tahmujin himself to break.

He came upon her in the brush. She'd given up, pulled herself and the remnants of her clothing against the thorns, curling in on herself as if she could disappear into the dried leaves.

Gehrin reached forward and took hold of her good arm, dragging her away from the thorns. His master's voice echoed through his ears. *Between the ribs, into the heart. Back of the neck, into the spinal cord. In the throat, across the jugular. Up into the armpit, near the heart.* It was a monotony of killing. The fastest way to ensure death. An assassin needed nothing but a sharp blade and a sure sense of the deadliest mark. He could end it with one blow.

She looked at him then, her dull eyes fixing on his face. And he saw his mother. He saw her gaunt cheeks and her drooping eye and lip, the way she still tried to smile at him in those last moments before her death. He saw Kasaii, staring up at him with disappointment and fear.

This woman was evil, she had broken the laws of the king. Gehrin held her life in his hands, a fragile thing that could be crushed like glass in an instant. It was a kind of power he had never known, and it spread, icy and nauseous, through his gut. He stood over her, staring into eyes that had already accepted the death he held. Haveth appeared over the stream, dirt and snow covering the front of his tunic, knife in hand.

Gehrin heard a step behind him and turned to see a *telhai* step from behind a tree, waiting. Gehrin's own death was written on the head of the spear he carried.

The woman touched his hand with her mangled fingers. Her cracked and bleeding lips moved, but the words were too quiet for Gehrin to hear. Behind them, the *telhai* took another step. Haveth slowed to a walk as he approached them. The air was thick with waiting.

Gehrin dropped to his knees and stabbed. She gasped, and the horrible sounds from her mouth that followed soon faded as she went limp against him. The chains around her wrists were cold fire against Gehrin's arms as he carefully let her fall to the snow. Her black hair tumbled around her, blood spreading from the wound below her breast.

The *telhai* did not move. Haveth did not move. Gehrin gagged and staggered over to the brush and vomited, heaving until there was nothing left in his belly.

Gehrin took his bowl of rice and soup to the edge of the courtyard, pressing his back against the post where he'd spent the night tethered as punishment soon after arriving at Blackvale. The food tasted like water, the flavors lost on his tongue. The atmosphere in the courtyard had been bleak, most of the boys still walking under a hovering cloud of the death they'd left behind in the forest. Niveth had expressed his anger that Sabba had stolen the kill from him, but no one listened.

It was another test that Gehrin had passed. One more step toward whatever end he was pursuing at Master Lohi's hand. He ground the rice between his teeth, the thought of the elderly scholar driving a sharp twist through his chest. He felt broken inside, as if the pieces of him had been removed, picked apart and put back inside in the wrong place. Sometimes he tried to understand, tried to force his mind to work through what happened and what was coming. But he was in a world where his life belonged to someone else. Whatever he understood didn't matter, as long as he obeyed. If he obeyed, he would survive.

Gehrin swallowed the tasteless rice, a sticky lump catching in his thick throat. He blinked down at his bowl, tears running down his cheeks that he could not feel. They dropped onto his hand, and he watched them run down the side of his thumb. They were so clear.

"*Yah*, Liv!"

Kajen dropped down cross-legged beside him, a bowl in each hand. He always managed to swindle more food than he was supposed to from Kirte. How he ate as much as he did without growing a great belly that hung over his trousers was a mystery to Gehrin. The boy was still a wildcat, unpredictable and sharp, but he had settled into his role in Blackvale with ease once he'd accepted it. Gehrin envied him in a way, having no family to return to, nothing that beckoned to him outside the stone walls.

"You missed the figs!" Kajen dropped one of the purple fruits into Gehrin's bowl of soupy rice. A few drops splattered onto Gehrin's hand over the fading tear trails. Kajen bit into his own, his cheeky grin completely out of place in the somber courtyard.

"Thank you."

"*Aich*-ah! Your face will stay that ugly forever if you scowl so hard," Kajen said. "Then the girls won't think you're pretty, guess so."

A faint memory of Kasaii rose to Gehrin's mind, her carefree smile as she turned back to look at him. He let it stay, sinking into the warmth of the days when he had walked with her to their classes with Master Lohi. He wondered if he would ever see her again.

"The only girl here is Kirte," he answered. The old woman was practically their grandmother, her sharp words and thin switch softened by the occasional extra bowl of rice.

Kajen shook his head around a full bite. "Nah. Master Tahmujin has a red woman here. An Ordrath."

"What?"

"I seen her leaving when I took a piss a few nights ago. Pulled up my trousers real quick, wouldn't want to offend an Ordrath woman! Even gave her a bow, and she smiled at me."

"Don't they wear veils?"

Kajen's smile disappeared. "*Yah*, she smiled at me, alright?"

"Alright."

"You're an empty bucket, Kajen," said Tirrim as he sat down across from them. "There was no red woman here in Blackvale. You're dreaming with your little spear again."

Kajen scoffed. "Ten kinds of fool. You're just jealous."

Letting them bicker over the red woman, Gehrin scooped another bite of rice into his mouth with the flat spoon. Tirrim knew he didn't want to talk, and Gehrin was grateful that he was keeping Kajen busy.

Several of the boys sat listless with their bowls around the courtyard, stirring the food without eating. Sabba ate heartily, but the usual jovial light had not returned to his eyes. Hajja sat near him, sneaking bites behind his mask. He still wore it like a second skin, but Gehrin had seen the horrible scars that lay beneath, and he had not soon forgotten the sight. The boy Yul had once remarked that Hajja's face looked like a fish that had gotten a hook through its lip. Ruh had punched him in the mouth when the *telhai* weren't looking, and Yul had sullenly nursed a split lip of his own for several days.

Ruh was not in his usual place near Sabba now, and it took Gehrin a moment to find him. At the far end of the courtyard, Ruh sat under the tiled overhang on the stone corridor with Nin. While Ruh held a bowl, Nin had none.

Gehrin stood up and walked toward them, leaving Kajen and Tirrim still exchanging insults behind him. He sat down on the cold stone, a shiver running through him as he settled in. Nin's face was a strange pale shade of its usual brown, and he looked as if he might throw up what little food remained in his stomach. Gehrin exchanged a glance with Ruh, who shrugged and grinned like he always did. Whatever the Takkan boy felt, he always pasted that smile on his face, broken by the gap between his two front teeth. The feral eyes above it made it disconcerting, but Gehrin was used to it now.

"Nin."

The smaller boy blinked as if he was coming out of some kind of trance and pulled at a shred of skin on the edge of his fingernail. "I'm alright."

Gehrin set his own bowl on the floor. "Did you kill him?"

"Ruh... Ruh did it mostly."

Ruh swallowed a large bite of soup. "I made him do the end. I know what it feels like, but he didn't."

Gehrin wasn't sure he would ever get used to Ruh's blunt way of speaking. It was different than Kajen's jeering bravado. It was a simple acceptance of everything they did, as if stabbing a person to death was the same as eating a bowl of soup.

Nin's hands trembled, tucked against his chest behind his drawn-up knees. "I tried to tell them, Liv. I tried to tell Master Tahmujin that I wasn't going to be good at killing people and fighting. My *ami* was a cook in the king's kitchens, that's how I know about herbs. She always knew what to do if anyone had a burn or a boil, all the palace slaves came to her for healing. What would she say if she had seen me kill that man today?"

He tucked his head in and sobbed quietly, hiding his face from the courtyard. Ruh continued to eat his soup, his sharp eyes darting around as he ate. He slurped the last bit and tipped the bowl against his lips to drink the dark, meaty broth.

"He wasn't going to do it, but I made him. Made it so the *aqqa* couldn't crawl away from him. It's not easy to kill a man that big, but he did it when I made him," Ruh said, his words running together like a soothing rhythm.

*Aqqa.*

Master Tahmujin hadn't given the criminals that name. They were not traitors. They were common thieves, murderers, and debtors. They were worth less than the grains of sand in the court-yard. Gehrin did not want to remember the face of the woman staring up at him from the snow. "Better to do it now," Gehrin said, pushing a quavering confidence into his voice for Nin's sake. "We are *bruhai*. Your *ami* would be proud that you are serving the king. It is better than being a cook in a kitchen."

Nin lifted his tear-stained face and rubbed the snot away from his nose with a grimy forearm. "I want to go back. I want to be a cook instead. I want to feed people, I don't want to kill them."

"Hush up before you get a beating," said Ruh. "If it wasn't him, it would've been you lying out there in the trees." He stood up and walked briskly away, holding his spoon with the same grip he'd held the knife in the woods.

Fresh tears leaked down Nin's cheeks. He blinked hard and tried to wipe them away with his hand. Gehrin picked up his bowl and scooped out a spoonful of broth, rice, and a sliver of radish. He held it up to Nin's mouth the way he had when Eiri was little and didn't want to eat.

At first, he thought Nin would refuse it, but finally he opened his mouth and ate, chewing the food slowly as if he were afraid that it might come back up onto the stones. When it didn't, Gehrin patiently offered him another small bite. Soon, Nin was holding the bowl himself and eating the last of Gehrin's soup. He still had a peaked hue to his cheeks, but the tears had stopped. He gazed out over the courtyard with a glazed numbness that Gehrin recognized.

Sometimes it was easier to let your mind go quiet, to let the sound of voices, the cold air, and the ache of the bruises overpower the feelings within. To eat a bowl of rice and leave the bodies of the dead where they lay. If there was a way to forget them completely, Gehrin had not found it. There was a small room in his mind, shut tightly behind a panel door, where his mother and the *aqqa* on the Blood Stones haunted the walls. The prisoner woman would join them there. Sometimes the door would slide open of its own accord. But he could always close it up again. Once he hadn't known how. But he was learning. Nin would learn how to close the door someday too.

"Come. Get up," Gehrin said, taking the bowl back. "Master Tahmujin is bringing out the staves. If you don't pull yourself together, you're going to get your head cracked like an egg. I don't think any of us want to clean you up off the sand."

He reached down his hand, and Nin's calloused palm appeared against his own. He pulled the smaller boy up to his feet and clapped him on the shoulder, the way Xario had so often done when Gehrin had sprawled in the dirt while sparring. Nin rubbed at his eyes one last time, and the only traces of the tears he'd shed was the slight puffiness around them. He drew in a shuddering breath and tried to square his slim shoulders.

"Thanks."

Gehrin shrugged. "Kirte gave me too much soup."

A cautious smile crept over Nin's mouth. "That's because you're her favorite."

"Fool. I'm not any such thing."

"Are so."

Gehrin shoved Nin just enough to totter him off balance, and the two of them rejoined the others in line, waiting for Master Tahmujin to bellow a command. Gehrin accepted the wooden staff, the familiar weight in his hand bringing a sudden chill despite the calm he forced onto his face. The thought of the woman's dead eyes watching him from the forest made the hairs on the back of his neck prickle and sent a chill down his spine.

*The staff. There is nothing else.* Gehrin settled his breathing into a steadier rhythm as Master Tahmujin roared at them.

"FORM ONE!"

# CHAPTER SEVENTEEN

*To the revered Master Lohi,*

*Our noble king carries a heavy burden as he decides the fate of our great nation and upon whose shoulders that burden will next come to rest. There are many who would seek to use this hour of reflection for their own gain. Of course you must know that I am, forever, the king's most humble servant and vassal. In that humility, I beg only a small favor from you, for I know that the king rightly gives your Council great value. My son, Itaki, has been raised with the utmost care and education, overseen by your own self. If a recommendation of him would come from your own mouth, I am sure that the king would find it helpful in his decision.*

*You may be assured of my continued prayers for your good health and prosperity. Sharai's blessings upon your head, heart, and feet.*

*- High Counsellor Bari Ujo*

**H**igh Counsellor Bari Ujo was a snake, fanged with schemes and a lust for power. Xario did not need his father's opinion of the man to arrive at the conclusion himself. Even now, as he sat on his cushion at Counsellor Ujo's long table, sipping his rice wine, he felt ill at ease. A beautiful servant girl in sky blue skirts played soft, soothing chords on her three-stringed *yan bhei* on a pillowed step in the corner. Her fingers plucked at the strings while a boy played a small flute next to her.

At the head of the table sat Counsellor Ujo, his white silk *seri* and domed black counsellor's hat giving him a strangely simple visage amongst the lavish apartments of his house. He sucked at a quail's egg from the plate in front of him. At the opposite end sat Xario's father, calmly eating as if sitting at his enemy's table gave him no reason for discomfort.

The smooth wood of the table was glossy with fresh wax, the swirling grains frozen like ripples in a stream. The spoons, bowls and trays were all made of hand-crafted silver, presenting a feast of the finest fare in Katesh and the surrounding regions. A bowl of deep purple Da'hamian grapes rose from the center of the offerings, spilling over the sides of the silver.

The simple clothing worn by their host was a thinly veiled façade of humility. However, where the father had chosen modesty, the son had chosen extravagance. Itaki lounged on his cushions in a black *seri* with red clouds embroidered onto the silk. White silk lined the sleeves and neckline that crossed over his chest and tucked into a wide black sash. He wore most of his hair down, the front pulled back into a small silver clip at the top of his head. A carved pin held it in place, a string of tiny golden beads dangling from the circular end. Several rings glittered on his fingers, one of them holding a blue stone as large as a fingernail. Dark kohl lined his eyes, accentuating the foxlike disdain with which he viewed the room.

Xario reached for another decadent spoonful of yoghurt, the red stain of berries swirling through smooth, milky white cream. Eating gave him something to do, but he had to pace himself. He would not lose his composure in front of Itaki.

"I hear you are to be commended for your promotion to Tenth Leader, young Xario," Ujo's voice rasped from the far end of the table as he bit into a plump tomato.

"I am fortunate to have the honor." Xario made a show of

selecting a piece of smoked fish from the tray nearest to him. "I serve where my skills are most useful."

There was a soft snap as Itaki opened a painted fan, looking bored. "Katesh is fortunate that there are men whose skills are useful out in the fields. Who better to protect us while greater minds look to the demands of governing?"

I'll not rise to your bait, fox. Xario let the tender flesh of the fish morsel flake apart in his mouth, citrus and pepper flaring against his tongue.

"A worthy occupation," added Counsellor Ujo. "And far more likely to grant you favor with the people. Heroes of battle have often become much beloved kings. King Kinhariian was a warlord unmatched in his day."

"And still remains so." Counsellor Hallix raised his cup. "May Sharai's Oathsworn strike down any who would say otherwise."

Xario hid his smirk behind his own cup as he lifted it in response. Itaki was the last to do so, pulling his silken sleeve past his wrist to reach over his food. They all drank to the king's health. The servant girl played her gentle melody, the notes shivering from the strings into the air.

Xario waited, knowing that soon his father would make the first move on the game board. It was a match played between two men whose influence shaped the future of Katesh, and the sons they hoped to see on a throne. Xario tried to imagine Itaki taking up the mantle of warlord, riding into battle robed in his flowing finery. It was a comical thought. It was far different to learn weaponry and forms as a child than it was to prove yourself among warriors.

Counsellor Hallix set his cup down on the table. "It was an unexpected honor, Counsellor Ujo, to receive your invitation. Although I must admit my curiosity. Surely there was some matter of business you wished to discuss this evening?"

One peg moved forward on the game board. Counsellor Ujo feigned surprise. "Is it business if it is between friends?"

"Let's not waste time with false niceties," replied Counsellor Hallix easily. "We may be allies from time to time for the sake of our nation, but we are not friends. That would require a greater trust than the one that exists between us."

Counsellor Ujo laughed and snapped his fingers in the air. Immediately, the musician stopped and left the room, shutting the door behind them. Xario refilled his cup, eager to let the alcohol relieve the tension in his shoulders. He would ask his father's servant Sychu to work the knots from his back when they returned home. The Maleki man's strong hands were worth their weight in silver when it came to sore muscles.

Once the servants had disappeared, Counsellor Ujo clapped his hands together. "Your honesty cuts deeper than a blade. But you are right. Pleasantries between friends are of little use to us here. Though I do not know if we are allies today, time will reveal the answer."

"Or perhaps time will prove that alliance," replied Counsellor Hallix. "Queen Xhen has reason to regret her ancestor's oath to Katesh. She is restless, but not careless. And she also has cautious advisors both here and in Ruk. It is difficult for you, I think, to be so divided in your loyalties."

The knife blade slid into Counsellor Ujo's pride and twisted. His expression darkened for the briefest moment with disgust... or was it fear? Xario could not read him as well as his father did. His own arena was on the sparring field, but Counsellor Hallix wielded subtle blades of a different kind. Ujo settled his hand on the table, his smile more courtesy than genuine.

"A few advisors in caution may be of help to you, Counsellor Hallix." Ujo's tone had lost much of its earlier levity. "My loyalty will not be questioned in my own house."

"I was not questioning it in the slightest. Only confirming it."

Counsellor Ujo's face flushed red, and his thin lips pressed inward behind his carefully groomed mustache. "Tread carefully, my lord Hallix. You hide behind the king's favor, but your power is less than you believe."

The hilts of Xario's two hidden knives pressed against his chest beneath the inner fold of his *seri*. He had left his spear behind but did not trust their host enough to enter his house completely unarmed. It would be madness to make an attempt on the life of the king's most trusted counsellor, but Xario did not put Ujo's schemes beyond such absurdity. And although Itaki lounged on his cushions with the posture of a sleeping panther, Xario knew the danger there as well.

Itaki reached out for the wine pitcher, and the sound of the liquid pouring into his cup broke the deadly silence. "You would not have agreed to come tonight if you did not also see some benefit in an alliance with my father's house. I am curious what benefit you have in mind."

Shocked, Xario could do nothing but blink at the open subversion of authority. But Counsellor Hallix took it in stride, and even accepted another refill of his wine when Itaki offered it.

"Your affection for your mother's native land is well known, Ujo," replied Hallix. He held up a hand to placate his host. "And I do not believe there is any harm in it. The tribute offered to Katesh is a long-standing oath between our two nations, and we must not forget that our ancestors helped establish the foundation of Ruk. The tribute is warranted. But perhaps it could be adjusted."

"You have already adjusted the tribute with your whispers in the king's ear. And now he discusses raising it again, and our relations with Ruk will strain until they break, and the wealth of Katesh will collapse!" Ujo smacked his palm against the table. "Despite the warnings of the rest of the counsel, which may as well be the chittering of birds for the credit you give them."

"I do not disagree that our relationship with Queen Xhen is more strained than necessary." Counsellor Hallix appeared to consider, tapping his fingers against his knee. "The king carries the burdens of a nation. I worry for his health above all things. The Council exists to help him carry those burdens, but it is weak."

"It is weak because its power has been drained into nothing."

"Perhaps that can change."

Bari Ujo's eyes narrowed. "If you are trying to trap me with treason, you will dishonor yourself first."

"I did not come here to trap you. I came to discuss how the Council might be empowered to better serve this nation."

It was an intricate game that his father played with Ujo. The king's counsellors were all bloated with their power, only a handful of truly good men and women among them. Counsellor Hallix had expected Xario to learn the history of each of them, their family lineages and holdings, their vices, and their weaknesses. It had been drudgery for a young boy who cared only for the strength in his arms when he held a spear. Xario was far more comfortable on a battle-field outside the palace walls, not the one within. And now, watching his father once again carefully maneuver Ujo where he wanted him, Xario felt painfully inadequate, wishing he had taken those lessons more seriously.

"Let us say Ruk did gain independence, as Queen Xhen wishes. What would she offer Katesh in return for such a bounty? Would she keep peace between us? She seems to turn her attention to Malek more and more as the seasons pass. One might even imagine she was scheming against us with the Nars of Malek."

Another short, barking laugh erupted from Counsellor Ujo. "A lost cause. The tribes are a lot of bickering children. They're too busy killing each other to take any notice of Katesh. And surely the splendid warriors of the Black Legion would put any insurrection to rest with ease if they are as capable as your son."

"Of course. But even children can be dangerous when knives are put in their hands."

Itaki smiled behind his fan. "It is easy to see why the king places so much trust in you, Counsellor Hallix."

The silk-swathed princeling spoke to the two older men in the room as if they were his equals, as if the table they sat beside were not his inheritance, but his possession. An ache grew behind Xario's temples. It was little wonder that the king was short tempered when-ever he sat in counsel.

Counsellor Hallix turned his cup upside down. "I believe the time has come for the Council to ask itself how we may best serve Katesh and our people. The king has placed a measure of trust in us, and we are little different than those *bickering children*, as you call them. The Council was formed long ago by our great king's forefathers to carry out the will of the kings and protect this nation. But we have grown soft and lazy in our luxury," he said, giving a pointed look in Itaki's direction. "We have left the king to shoulder the weight of his crown alone. And I would see that burden eased."

"Eased?" Ujo leaned forward. "Or removed?"

"That would be treason, my lord Ujo."

"You are no stranger to treason, despite your worthy platitudes," replied Ujo. "You simply make sure your hands are clean, and this is no different. You want me to put my neck in a noose while you reap the rewards."

"If your neck is in a noose, it is one of your own making," Counsellor Hallix said easily, "for continuing to treat your allies as enemies. Come, put aside whatever grudge you hold against me."

Counsellor Ujo sat quietly, weighing the scales in his mind. Trust between men of power was a fickle thing. But Xario could feel the shift, see the wealthy man greedy enough to recognize what Counsellor Hallix was suggesting, to imagine a future in which the Council of the king might have more power than the pittance it held now. It was a tempting thought to a man who did not have the benefit of the king's particular favor. Had he been in Counsellor Ujo's position, Xario himself might have even given in to such a prize. A Council with equal power to the king. A throne that cradled a figurehead, not a true king.

Xario could not abide the thought of becoming the counsel's puppet, but when he had declared this to his father, Counsellor Hallix had chided him for being short-sighted. There was more than one game being played, and his father's hands were on both boards. Counsellor Hallix did not intend for him to become a puppet king. Ujo's rigid posture relaxed, and he leaned back with the same jovial mood he had donned when his guests had first arrived.

"Very well. You arouse my curiosity. If such a thing can be achieved, I will hear more of it."

Xario reached for the grapes. Counsellor Ujo did not know it yet, but his father had already won. The players moved across the board, and Counsellor Ilba Hallix was the gamemaster. He crushed a grape between his molars, the sweet juice tempering the lingering taste of the fish. He felt Itaki's eyes on him before he looked up. The younger Ujo's smile was cold as ice.

Perhaps it was not Bari Ujo that needed to be played.

The warm water of the bathhouse soothed Xario's tired muscles, his shoulders still aching from Sychu's thorough fingers. The old man had even used hot stones to loosen the painful knots and had remarked that Xario was far too young for such heavy burdens of the mind to be carried in the body. Yrit had brought him a foul-tasting mixture of herbs and wine to restore his spirit. She had drawn the *illi* rune on his hand with her finger, her crone's nails digging into his skin, and told him that dark spirits would surely be drawn to his melancholy if he did not restore himself.

Finally, they had left him be when he had escaped to the bath-house to wash. The amount of wine he had drunk at Counsellor Ujo's house had left him with a throbbing in his temples. He closed his eyes and let himself sink beneath the water. As it closed over his head, he lay back, suspended, weightless and carried by the pool's warmth. The world above him disappeared, the quiet of the water wrapping him in comforting arms. He let short bursts of air out through his nostrils, each exhale constricting his lungs a little further. He wondered what it would feel like to let the water in, to sink into eternal weightlessness.

He broke the surface, shaking his head with a gasp. He rubbed a hand over his eyes to clear them and blinked. A servant stood at the edge of the pool with her head bowed, hands folded modestly in front of her.

"Forgive me for intruding, young master, apologies. There is a messenger here for you who bears the seal of the king."

"Tell him I will speak with him as soon as I have dressed."

She bowed lower and disappeared from the room. His father's servants were like wraiths. Quiet, slipping from room to room to fulfill their duties, obedient without question. His father rewarded his servants when they served well, but they knew to fear punishment sharply dealt by his hand. Xario pulled himself from the water, reaching for his clothing. He tied his simple Legion tunic at his right side, the wide white sash wrapping around his stomach. He tucked his long knife into the sash and wound his hair into a bun at the top of his head, holding it firmly with a copper pin.

When he stepped out of the bathhouse, he slid his sandals onto his feet and approached the cloaked messenger who waited for him in the courtyard. His father was there and eyed him with a small measure of disapproval.

"You will appear before the king in such simple clothes? Go back to your room and put on your ceremonial *seri*."

Xario inclined his head slightly. "Please accept my apologies, my lord. Our great king is also our warlord, and I am a soldier of his Legion. I prefer to approach him as a loyal soldier than as a perfumed noble."

Counsellor Hallix's brow furrowed in displeasure, but he said nothing more. The messenger bowed deeply. "I am Yi Jo, first messenger for the king. His majesty requests your presence immediately. May I send for a palanquin to bear you to the palace, my lord?"

"Thank you, no. I will walk."

"Very good, my lord," replied Yi Jo. He was a man older than Counsellor Hallix, his grayed beard giving a respectable nobility to his weathered face. A gold ring glowed on his right hand, and several small rings threaded through his long earlobes. His eyes glittered with intelligence beneath the hood of his cloak. He turned and led Xario away, and Counsellor Hallix walked back into the house, his shoulders rigid. Xario was surprised that his father had not insisted on accompanying him.

Lanterns lit the streets of Keld at night, their warm glow casting shadows against the walls of the closed shops. The worn gravel of the streets was packed down into a dusty powder, smooth from hundreds of feet, hooves, and wheels coming and going through the city. Yi Jo led them on the most direct route, through the merchant district and into the grand sprawling palace grounds. The massive gates opened the stone walls that surrounded the many buildings inside. The main palace hall, housing the rooms of the king's family and the Council chamber, rose above the rest, the golden peak of the central roof curving up into the black sky. The expanse of the Outer Court led Xario's eyes to the carved arches of the central palace building, statues of the wolf and fox spaced alternatingly across the massive terrace, silent guardians of the king. Looming on either side of the wide path were statues of Sharai's oathsworn, warriors from the stars, their spears and swords drawn to protect the great lords of Katesh. Their stone faces glared down at Xario fiercely as he passed them, feeling small beneath their gaze. They were three times the height of any man, sandaled feet set squarely on massive stone pedestals.

And in front of the wide arched expanse of the palace's inner wall, his great stone arm drawn back to throw a spear to the heavens, stood Sharai's statue, his simple robe flaring around his body as if it were real cloth, the noble eyes set toward the stars.

Instead of leading Xario into the Council Hall, Yi Jo continued his brisk pace around the side of the central palace building, entering a small door on the left side near the king's rooms. Xario felt that his footsteps defiled such a sacred space. Even with his father, he had never come this far into the king's private rooms. Only King Kinhariian's closest advisors, guards and servants were allowed inside. They continued down several long hallways, weaving through what seemed like a maze until they reached an open terrace that led into a garden, hidden within the outer walls of the palace.

It was a small paradise, wide stones meandering alongside a clear pool of dark water. Flashes of orange and white fish flickered beneath the surface. Brightly colored purple bushes and small green trees spilled up to the path but did not cross it. They had the appearance of a wild forest of bright colors, yet each branch and leaf was carefully trimmed into place. White stones covered the ground to either side of the path, disappearing beneath the lowest branches of the flora. Xario followed Yi Jo across a bright red bridge over the stream that emptied into the pool. A small pavilion rose from the green up ahead, the red roof tapering to upward points above a little platform. The stone path and stairs leading up to the carved railings were lined on either side by small round bushes with star-shaped leaves. Benches lined the outer circle of the pavilion, and on one of those benches sat the king of Katesh.

As soon as Xario came to the edge of the pavilion's lowest step, he stopped short and dropped to his knees, touching his forehead to the ground. He heard a soft step as the king approached him.

"You are well received, young Hallix. Rise, I did not request your presence here to speak to the back of your head."

Xario stood, keeping his head sufficiently lowered. "*Nyheli garhai.* I am honored beyond measure by your summons, my king."

"Yi Jo, leave us."

The elderly servant bowed and walked away with the same brisk pace he had kept the entire journey from Counsellor Hallix's estate. The garden was blissfully quiet, and the rich aroma of flowers and green leaves enveloped them. Xario stood silent and still, fully aware that he was standing alone in the garden with the most powerful man in the world. He did not know why the king had called for him, but it was not his place to ask any questions.

"Come. Sit in the pavilion with me."

The king returned to his place on one of the benches, and Xario slipped his sandals off on the step and chose a bench across from him. He placed his sweating hands carefully on his knees, trying to seem relaxed but attentive. The king was looking at him with great scrutiny, and the silence that passed between them tested Xario's composure. Finally, the king released him.

"You are dressed as a soldier, not as a lord."

"Forgive me if I have offended you. I will return at once..."

"Nonsense. I respect your devotion to your brothers in the Legion. And if you had come to see me dressed in finery, I would have trusted you less," the king replied, a smile twitching beneath his dark mustache. "Tell me how things are with the Legion. How are the men? Are my commanders competent?"

Xario chose his words carefully. "The commanders are competent leaders, Warlord. I serve under Third Hand Jaakar, and he has the respect of the soldiers. He is a strict taskmaster, but he is fair. The men do their duties well. I think they are sometimes restless training for battles when there are none to fight."

The king laughed, a jovial, almost fatherly sound. "As they should be. They are soldiers. As are you. I have watched you grow up from a small boy, and you were a soldier from the first moment your father put a wooden spear in your hand."

Pride washed over Xario, and he bowed his head. "Thank you, great one."

"You are the kind of man who would be happiest as a soldier for his whole life, I think." King Kinhariian nodded thoughtfully. "I recognize much of myself in you."

"I will serve wherever you need me, Warlord."

The king stood, his silken nightrobes spilling down around his feet in a smooth river of black and red silk. Gold medallions were embroidered on the long train. He still wore his bone hilted knives in his sash, despite the presence of guards dotted throughout the garden. Kinhariian was one of the greatest warriors Katesh had ever seen, capable of defending himself against any assailant. And now, as he stood at the railing looking out over the dark pool beneath the pavilion, the fine silks seemed an ill fit for the man beneath.

"Your father said those same words to me when I took the throne. He has been a loyal friend and advisor since we were boys. But the weight of a kingdom has jaded him, as it has me. There are many voices clamoring for me to make decisions, and those same voices will whisper foul things of me when I do. A king must let go of the man he was to shepherd a people who worship him for their prosperity and damn him for their trials."

Xario stood, rising to his feet as soon as the king had done the same. The king's words made his stomach roil. More than anything, he wished that he was someone else, that he wasn't the son of Counsellor Hallix, and that the king would choose another. He wished he could go back to his room in Mizak, the simple life of a soldier. He didn't realize that the king had turned and was watching him, lost in his thoughts. He quickly softened the expression on his face. But the king had seen the truth in his face.

"Tell me, Xario Hallix. Do you want to be a king?"

Lie. His father's voice in his head whispered, a threatening promise if he should fail to answer for his family's honor. Sweat gathered beneath his palms.

"It is my honor to serve you wherever you see fit, great one."

"A loyal answer, but an empty one," replied the king. "I have no use for subjects who tell me what they think I want to hear."

Xario curled his fists. "Forgive me, my lord, that was not my intent. I do wish to be of service to you. And I will do as you command. But I do not want to be a king."

Something in the king's countenance relaxed, as if a great weight had been lifted from him. He smiled. "Your honesty is a great service to me. Come." He put his hand on Xario's shoulder, his grip strong. "Someday I will ask a great service of you. I must know that I have your loyalty, not to your father, but to me. There are many people who would see our country fall to its knees. I cannot let that happen, but I cannot do it alone. There is a strength in you that Katesh will need."

Xario knew he should bow, should touch his forehead to the ground at the king's feet. He should thank the king profusely for the honor of his trust, his summons, his generosity. When he looked into Kinhariian's eyes, he saw a man that he might become, a man who was worshipped nearly as a god. But beneath the crown was a man who still needed to know who he could trust.

He met the king's eyes and pulled the sheathed knife from his belt. "I swear to you on my life that my sword and my spirit are yours. How ever I may serve, speak the words and I will do it. And may Sharai and his Oathsworn strike me dead into the dust if I betray you."

The grip on his shoulder loosened. "I will hold you to that oath. Leave me now, the night is growing long, and I will not keep you from your bed."

Xario bowed low, arms at his side. "Your eternal health, my king."

As he descended the stairs from the pavilion, Yi Jo materialized out of the darkness to walk beside him, the man's slippered footsteps silent against the smooth stone path. Xario's heart was still racing as they backtracked through the maze of corridors to the vast Outer Court at the front of the palace grounds.

# CHAPTER EIGHTEEN

*The Maleki tribes have no written language. Their stories and legends are passed down from the elders to the young, their culture and history held close to the heart. The names of their greatest warriors are spoken with utmost reverence, for those are now among the Sky Clans, the ancestors they look to as gods.*

*- Emissary Otai, "Observations on the Tribes of Malek"*

The stone was firmly lodged against the frog of the gray mare's hoof. Syndri coaxed it gently away from the tender tissue with a small knife and tucked it away into a pouch at her waist. She would toss it back into the river later. She set the hoof back down on the ground and clicked her tongue, urging the mare to take a few cautious steps forward. The limp was less noticeable now that the culprit had been removed. Syndri ran a hand down the foreleg again and smiled when the mare's shoulder quivered.

"*Aich*, what a baby you are. Such a little stone!" she chided, patting the mare and running her palms over the light sway in the horse's back. The mare's belly was not nearly as large as it would be when spring warmed the frozen ground, but already the foal within was changing her shape. The mare carried her fifth foal, and it would be her last. She let out a low *whoof* as Syndri found her favorite scratching place at the base of her withers, her tongue slobbering in and out of her mouth. She yawned up at the sky.

Syndri gave her one last pat. She would check the mare again the next morning, but already she was standing stronger on the leg. The bruising left behind by the stone would fade soon. Straightening, Syndri placed her hands at the small of her back and stretched backwards, releasing the stiffness from her shoulders. The herd was in good condition despite the winter. The rounded storehouses were packed with threshed hay, and the heavy hides layered over her tunic kept out the chill.

Finally finished checking over the herd, Syndri made the trek back to her *gat*. The lone building was small against the treeline by the river. She had not stepped one foot inside the village in at least two months, and the only face she had seen of her family was Senna's. Snow covered the circle of ash where Baya's pyre had been. Syndri gave it a wide berth whenever she walked to the herds, sealing it away in a place deep within, just as seared as the earth beneath the snow.

She lifted the flap of her *gat* and tossed off the top layer of hides from her shoulders. The little room was simply furnished, a small cooking pit in the center, a bed, and one small stump to sit on, which she rarely used. She ran her thumb over the faint calluses on her palms. Her swords were safely stored in Senna's *gat* inside the village, and her sister had promised to look after them until Syndri's return to favor.

The only weapon she had at her side was the slim hunting knife, the same one she had used to pry the stone from the mare's hoof. She kept it honed to a razor-sharp edge, pouring all the care into the smaller weapon that she once had for her warrior's blades.

She should hunt, and she needed to check her traps farther along the riverbank. But hunger was nothing more than a dull echo in the pit of her stomach. Syndri forced herself to eat a handful of dried berries and nuts from the pouch that Senna had brought her yesterday. Her sister had given her a scolding, poking at Syndri's arms and saying she was going to get thin and weak without feeding herself.

Resigned, Syndri sat down on her bed and took another handful, crunching the smooth almonds between her molars. She caught a glint of silver out of the corner of her eye, and pointedly ignored the curved silver dagger tucked behind her bed. Emissary Otai had given it to her before he returned to Ruk, a full moon past. He had ridden out to say goodbye to her after paying his respects to his hosts. Syndri had ignored him until he had pulled the dagger from his belt and pressed it into her hands.

"This is not a Garhis blade, so it does not go against your father's order. I will see you again, daughter of Malek," he had said, giving her a light bow before mounting his horse and riding off to join his caravan leaving for the north.

Syndri had considered throwing the dagger into the river, but it was a fine blade, and the gesture pleased her more than she cared to admit. She had not drawn it from its tooled sheath since. Despite the truth of Otai's words, she dared not draw a killing blade while she was Bladeless. She had taunted the Sky Clans enough.

After eating as much of the fruit and nuts as she could manage, she returned to the task of surviving the winter, armed with her hunting knife and a leather bag to carry whatever game she might find. It was scarce and would become even more so as the cold season continued. The first few crudely constructed traps were empty. She'd never been as deft at them as Senna, she had always insisted that her hands were built for holding swords, not tying delicate knots.

She plodded through the snow, listening to the comforting babble of the river as it flowed over the rocks and ice chunks gathered at the banks. She'd walked a long distance from the village by the time she reached her final snare, and it too was empty, but something had tripped it. She grumbled and tried to reset it, her fingers numb and unhelpful. After two unsuccessful tries, she threw the string down in the snow.

The bright call of a war horn broke the stillness. One sharp blast from the village. A war horn in the dead of winter. Then another blast. Syndri spun on her heel. One horn blast would've signaled a raid at the border. But two was a warning.

Her snares forgotten, Syndri ran along the riverbank back toward the village. When she came within sight of it, she saw nothing out of the ordinary. Nothing that would've caused an alarm. A figure hurried toward her *gat*, bundled in furs and hides.

Ettlan.

Syndri dropped her bag at the doorway of the *gat* and ran to meet her mother. Ettlan reached out and gripped her arm. "The Tladr have amassed near the border. They are riding toward us now."

A simple raiding party would not cause the trembling in her mother's hands. "How many?"

"Sochi said he believed they were five or six hundred."

The full might of the Tladr tribe. It was the boldest show of force any of the tribes had dared in decades. Yet if the Garhis tribe met them horse for horse, they would be outnumbered. Nar Garhis commanded eight hundred blooded warriors when they were all mounted and armed. And another seventy young warriors who had just come of age. The Tladr would be crushed. But many would die. Only a few would stay behind to guard the village. Syndri searched her mother's face.

"Father?"

"Will not lift your exile for this. I came to tell you so that when you heard the horns, you would know what comes. Yugha will lead them. We will guard the village while the warriors fight."

Anger crept through Syndri's gut, spreading its fiery tendrils through her blood. "Mother..." she began, but the words faded into the air. *I should ride with them. Give me my blades, let me spill blood for you this day.*

She said nothing. Ettlan reached up and touched her face gently. "I know, daughter. This is your test. The Sky Clans have put a choice before you, and you must bend to your father's will. I must return to our people. Be safe."

The warmth of her fingers left Syndri's cheek, and she hurried back along the faint path through the snow. Syndri rooted herself to the ground, her spirit raging against the invisible cage she had been cursed with. Her blades would stay in their sheaths, and Yugha, Senna, and the others would bring a great victory to the tribe. And she would wait and feed their warhorses when they returned. She saw the warriors running to the herds, reaching their mounts and swinging up with practiced ease. Scale armor and blade hilts gave little glints in the overcast light, but Syndri saw them, and yearned for their familiar weight. She stayed and watched until every last warrior had mounted and ridden toward the west. Among the remaining horses, a black stallion snorted and stamped, angry. His piercing whinny reached her ears, bellowing his fury at being restrained, the overwhelming desire to charge after the others. Like her swords, her warhorse was beyond her reach now. She was not a warrior, so she had no need of a warrior's mount. Her father's resolve ran deep.

Syndri stalked back to her *gat* and paced around the small room like a bear. She reached up and pulled at her braids, every muscle in her body taut. The dagger beside her bed whispered to her. *Go to Brig. Ride. Fight.*

Picking up the Rukian weapon, she slid the shining blade free of its sheath. The hilt was strange, lighter and smoother than the bone hilts of her swords. It was made of some kind of dark wood, the grain running in dancing patterns down to where it met the blade at the hilt. A red stone was set into the pommel. The blade was curved, masterfully forged and deadly.

And yet its deadly edge was no use to her. She slid the blade home and tossed it to the side. Closing her eyes, she let her mind drift across the grasslands to follow her sister. She saw Senna bent low over Rho's red roan neck, the mare's ears pinned flat against her head as they galloped to meet the Tladr. Senna's sword raised high with the others, her teeth bared as she screamed their bone-chilling war cry. Syndri wondered if her sister had chosen that Clan-forsaken shield instead of a second sword. She was stubborn enough.

The might of the Garhis tribe was far beyond that of the Tladr.

They were fools for coming en masse to threaten the mighty Garhis. Yugha would lead the warriors, and the only enemy left alive would crawl home like dogs over the bloodied snow, their horses and their blades left behind in disgrace. It was the largest battle between Tladr and Garhis that had been fought in Syndri's lifetime. And she was sitting in a *gat*, pulling at her braids like a child. The adrenaline that accompanied a good fight was surging through her, building and climbing with nowhere to go. She slammed her fist against the side of the cot.

*Sky Clans be damned.* Syndri reached for the dagger.

She lunged out of the *gat*, telling herself that she would only be running to the hill to see if the battle was visible. Anything was better than simmering like a pot of her mother's poultice herbs and waiting for the news. The dagger was comforting, pressed against her side beneath the outer cloak she hastily threw over her shoulders.

She was halfway to the herd when she heard them. To her left, the sound of hooves. Many hooves pounding against the earth, approaching fast from the south. The Garhis tribe was far to the west with the Tladr. Syndri slowed her rush toward the hill and turned, shading her eyes against the blinding white of the snow sweeping away across the grasslands.

Mounted riders, hundreds of them. The glint of spearheads and swords flashing in the sun over galloping horses rushing headlong for the village. The first war cry split the air, a wild shriek that chilled Syndri down to her bones as she caught a glimpse of tribal color. Dark blue foreheads bobbed above the warhorses' necks. Uratar.

*There is no one left to fight them.*

A war horn blew from the village. One of the herdsmen had seen them too and raised the alarm. But there were only a handful of warriors in the village. Syndri didn't have time to think. In moments the Uratar warriors would descend on them. It would be a slaughter. She ran for Brig.

The black stallion saw her coming. He'd been tied to an iron stake in the ground to keep him from running after the warriors, but his jerking and pulling at it had loosened it from the earth. The moment he caught sight of Syndri, he reared, pulling the stake free from the dirt and trotting toward her.

She reached up as he approached her, grabbing a fistful of his mane and pulling herself onto his broad back with ease. Behind her, Uhuri found a mount, as did the other few warriors left behind to guard the herds. There were only nine of them. Nine against the horde of Uratar descending on the village. Syndri felt naked without her swords, but there was no time. If she went back for them the Uratar would be among the villagers before she could do anything to stop them.

She slowed Brig once they were about one hundred lengths from the village gate. The others spread out to either side of her, forming a line against the coming tide. Uhuri offered her one of his swords, and she gratefully accepted, the familiar weight comforting.

*Sky, gift me your breath for strength. Gift me your cold wind to sharpen my blade. Gift your speed to my mount, let his hooves fly over the ground like a falcon among crows.* Syndri's chest tightened. *Let my death settle the balance, let my people free from the curse I have brought upon them.*

The Uratar were close now, she could see their faces, the dark blue of their foreheads, the lather on their horses' necks. She looked to the left and right and marked the faces of the warriors beside her. Uhuri, stoic Maj-jaken, the twins Tzenri and Rnuri, old Jenshai with his wrinkled face, totem unbroken after forty years of battles. Kesrit, the youngest of them at seventeen, her face pale beneath the tribal forehead tattoo, brighter red than the others. Malon, a veteran warrior who had lost her right arm in a raid against the Uratar years ago. She rode without reins, her warhorse responding to the pressure of her knees and thighs. And finally, Durz'ekai, his handsome face the delight of every unwed girl in the village, his black hair looped through with silver beads. The dark cloud of death hovered over them all.

A great bellow shattered the monotony of thundering hooves. Syndri glanced back and saw the hulking figure of Hyshir, his dark hide covered by leather armor, the massive bone club raised high above his horns. He bellowed again, standing in the gap of the village gate.

"We will make them bleed a river for every life they take!" Syndri shouted. She lifted her sword and roared her own war cry, her voice high and sharp against the earthy tone of the Ke'ral warrior at her back. The others lifted their weapons, and as one, they screamed their challenge to the Uratar.

Syndri steadied her sword hand, leaned over Brig's neck, and breathed one final prayer.

*Senna, live.*

She touched her heels to Brig's side, and he leapt forward, five lunging strides sending them crashing into the front line of the Uratar.

The impact of Brig's shoulder against the gray mare that crashed into them nearly sent Syndri flying from his back. Her grip on his mane and years of practice balancing on his broad back with her thighs was the only thing that saved her from being thrown beneath the hooves of the warband. A sharp line of fire cut across her arm. The tip of the sword glanced over the side of her neck, inches away from cutting into her throat. She swung wildly, and her blade connected with a rider passing by on her right side, slicing across his chest and arm. The tide of horses split around Brig, who was holding his own, biting and snapping, digging his hooves into the ground.

The Uratar slowed as they reached the village wall, but Hyshir could not keep them all back. His bone club swung in great arcs, breaking the bones of horses and riders alike. Syndri whirled Brig, charging into the back line of the Uratar warband. Brig leapt over a body. It was Kesrit, her wide eyes staring up at the sky, bones crushed. Two sections of the Uratar warband had broken off to circle around the village, headed for the other gate.

There was no way to stop them. Screaming in anger, Syndri pulled her feet up to Brig's back and threw herself at one of the Uratar riders, grabbing around his waist as they both tumbled over his horse and onto the ground. Her fingers were slick with the blood running from the cut on her left arm, but she drove her blade through the Uratar's skull and wrenched it free. Charging for the gate, she reached up for the next warrior closest to her and wrapped her hands around his knee, pulling with all her might. The spear in his hand was too unwieldy in such close quarters, and he only managed to catch her on the side of her head with the wooden haft. Her ear rang with the blow, but she dragged him down off the horse, pulling the Rukian dagger from her belt and stabbing up under his chin. Blood sprayed, and the man gurgled as he went limp.

A pained scream reached her, and she whirled to see Durz'ekai pinned against the wall by two mounted Uratar. His horse was gone, and blood poured from a wound in his side, running down over the leg of his trousers. One of the Uratar raised her spear for the killing blow. Syndri threw her dagger.

The blade struck the Uratar in the back, and she jerked, the spear falling from her grasp as she tumbled to the side. Her companion turned his horse in time to block Syndri's first sword strike, but she ducked beneath the Uratar's arm and punched hard against the back of his ribs. Grabbing for the man's belt as he gasped, Syndri unseated him. The man slashed wildly with his sword as he fell, nicking Syndri's chin.

Wrapping her fists in the front of the man's tunic, Syndri pulled him up off the ground and headbutted him. His nose crunched beneath her forehead. She wiped his blood away from her eyes and turned to see Durz'ekai sliding down the stacked stones to the dirt, his face already cast with death's approaching shadow. He pressed weak fingers against the fatal wound in his side.

"The gate!" he rasped.

Syndri left him. Her left arm was growing numb. The wound was clearly worse than she had thought, but she could not let it stop her now. The sounds of screaming and the clash of blades from within the village called her through the haze of her own bloodlust. She could taste the blood against her lips, and the feral fury that writhed within her gut was no longer bound to the little *gat* beside the river.

The space where Hyshir had stood to defend the gate was gruesomely blocked by a pile of broken Uratar, two horses among them.

He had disappeared, no doubt to rush to the aid of the villagers fighting for their lives within the walls. The sound of screams from within and the wild war cries of the Uratar clashed, discordant and deafening.

Syndri stumbled across the bodies and reached down for a second sword. She'd managed to retrieve the dagger she'd thrown and hastily wiped the grime off on the thigh of her trousers. Smoke began to rise above the tops of the *gats* beyond the wall, and Syndri felt a stab of fear through the haze of fury that enveloped her. They were setting fire to the village. This was no raid. This was meant to be a massacre.

Gripping the stones was difficult with her swords, but Syndri managed to pull herself up and over the wall. The Uratar at the gate made no move to follow. One more warrior inside the wall surely would not stop their destruction. She heard scrabbling against the rocks behind her and turned just in time to bring her sword up, ready to hack a head from its shoulders. But the head that appeared above the wall was Malon's, her blade gripped in her teeth as she climbed. Next to her was Uhuri, his youthful face splattered with blood. Whether it was his own or another's, Syndri did not know.

"Go, go!" urged Malon, straddling the wall and returning her sword to her hand. "The others are dead. Go!"

Syndri bolted into the first path between the *gats*. Fires had begun spreading, the flames licking across the flattened hides and devouring the long kehroxen hair. Garhis men, women and children ran from them through the walking paths. Several *gats* had already become round infernos, the wooden frames inside engulfed. Bodies lay on the ground, some half-burned, others lying in pools of blood. A young child crawled across the ground, dying. Smoke and ash and the acrid smell of burning hides filled Syndri's nose. Her eyes watered and stung as she headed for a *gat* where a pair of Uratar soldiers were dragging a woman out onto the beaten path. By the time they heard her and turned, Syndri's swords had cut the hamstring of one and cut through the neck of the other. They both dropped, and the scream of the man clutching his leg was swiftly silenced by Syndri's second stroke.

Dragging the woman up by one arm, Syndri recognized her face. Irah, younger sister of Tilis. She also realized she did not know where to send the woman for safety. The Uratar were everywhere.

"Come!" Syndri yelled over the din, dragging the young woman behind her as she ran for the center of the village. The woman picked up a sword from one of the fallen Uratar. There were no cowards among the Garhis people. Warrior or no, every man, woman, and child would fight.

Horse hooves thundered ahead of them, and Syndri pushed herself and Irah into the side of a *gat* as a group of Uratar thundered past them, chasing a group of fleeing Garhis. A child ran screaming behind them, and Irah ran out into the path after him. Syndri screamed after her, but her voice was hoarse. A rider appeared from a thick swirl of smoke along the path, and his spear caught Irah in the chest, lifting her from the ground and dropping her again two horse lengths later as her body slid to the ground. Ignoring the fleeing child, the rider turned his horse in a tight circle and came back for Syndri.

*Come then, you rootless dog. Bring me your spear.* More Uratar were running amongst the *gats*, leaving the Garhis inhabitants dead or dying. Syndri forced her attention back to the horse trotting back toward her. Despite the reach of the spear, she could see that the Uratar was not yet comfortable with the Northern weapon. She curled her lip in a feral grin. He would die holding a coward's weapon.

She shifted the hilts of the swords in her blood-slicked hands and heard a step behind her. Dropping to her knee and spinning to the left, a blade whistled past her ear. Stabbing up and back behind her offhand arm, she felt the blade bite into skin. Regaining her feet, she stumbled back several steps to give herself space from this new opponent, the horse and spear trotted away down the path, no doubt leaving her to her fate.

The mountain of a warrior who faced her held no spear. His twin swords mirrored hers, and yet he bested her in height by at least a head, his broad shoulders hulking forward as if he were going to fall on her and crush her to death. Scars laced his forearms. Syndri's blind stab had caught the side of his knee, but it was not a deep enough wound to cause real harm. He spat in the dirt, his face marred by ugly features and uglier hate, leering at her with the assurance of his victory. Blood and dirt clung to the black bristles along his thick jaw.

Without giving her a chance to settle herself into any stable footing, the big warrior dropped his shoulder and barreled into her like a warhorse. He drove the breath from her as she folded around his shoulder, giving no resistance. If she had, he would have broken ribs. He drove her backwards against the wall of a smoking *gat*, only just beginning to catch fire from the one beside it.

If he pinned her, she was dead.

As he wrestled her to the dirt, Syndri managed to flip the sword in her wound-weakened left hand. She plunged the blade into his side, but the power she'd had hours earlier was gone. The wound was shallow, and barely pierced through his armor. He growled and grabbed the hilt of the sword, ripping it from her hands and tossing it to the side. Somewhere beyond the wall, an Uratar war horn blasted once. Twice.

"Die with the rest of your forsaken kin." The Uratar's voice was half-stolen by the thick smoke, but for the first time, Syndri felt death brush against her throat. The man lifted his sword for the killing blow. For the briefest heartbeat, fear consumed her. She struggled against him and snaked her hand down to her belt for the Rukian blade, her fingers sticky with her own blood. This time, her strength did not fail her, driven by the half-mad panic launching her away from death's grasp. She found the gap in his scale armor where it tied beneath his arm, and the blade drove deep.

New warmth slicked her fingers, and the Uratar roared in pain and pulled away, hand pressing against his armpit to staunch the flow. Syndri scrambled away, her breath still labored. From the haze behind, a figure appeared and drove a sword deep into the back of the Uratar's neck. The man fell forward, dead.

Malon tucked her sword beneath her arm and reached out to pull

Syndri to her feet. The woman was covered in blood, a gash seeping red above one of her eyebrows. Her eyes were hard, empty, as if she were a walking corpse. Horses galloped past them. The Uratar war horn blasted twice again, calling the warriors away. The cowards were leaving. They weren't even going to stay to finish their killing. Syndri hated them for it.

Malon dragged her through the smoke. The heat from the burning *gats* was suffocating, crackling through the air and sharpening its fiery blades against Syndri's skin. It was impossible to see through the smoke, and Syndri headed for the center of the village by sense more than sight. She tripped and fell, sprawling over a body. A familiar face stared up at her, spiritless. Ganzakh-ba's leathery wrinkles framed wide eyes that were glazed over in death. The old man's fingers still clutched a tanning knife, blood coating the blade. Stains covered the front of his tunic from stab wounds.

A muffled wailing reached Syndri's ears. She crawled forward, barely regaining her feet on shaking legs. Everything was bathed in a wash of smoke, flickers of fire jumping through everywhere she looked. She was close now. Garhis bodies lay everywhere, strangely empty in death.

The smoke was clearer up ahead to her right. One *gat* stood against the wall, untouched. It was Yugha's. A pile of Uratar bodies lay strewn on the ground like broken dolls. A great dark figure knelt in their midst, guarding the *gat* behind. Hyshir's massive shoulders were hunched forward, his four-fingered hands gripping the hilt of his bone club to keep himself upright. Blood ran from dozens of wounds in his massive arms, sides, and thighs, glistening in the thick brown hair. His wide nostrils flared with the effort of breathing. And yet he did not move from his place in front of the door.

The last steps to her parents' *gat* held the weight of miles. The Garhis tribe had rushed to the defense of their Fist and Hand, even amid the chaos. Everywhere, villagers lay broken, bleeding, dying and long dead like a carpet over the same ground they had danced upon for the winter songs. Syndri's eyes burned, and she dragged her sleeve across her eyes and blinked dumbly at the carnage at her feet.

A few feet away, a child lay over his mother's breast, both lifeless. The warriors who had remained behind to protect the village had been too few. Only one or two of them had been wearing armor, and some of them had fought with wooden staves and tanning knives. One lay facedown in a pool of blood, fingers chilling around the haft of a wood axe.

The great black kehrox hide covered much of her father's body. Nar Garhis lay on his side, his face a great ruin of blood and bone as if he'd been struck with a club. One of his eyes was gone. His body had been opened with a great blade, and the broken shaft of a long spear lay beside him, its head buried deep in his chest. His carved totem was crushed into the dirt beside his head. A few feet away from him lay Ettlan, her arms outstretched over the ground, dark hair splayed around her shoulders. Even in death, her palms were open, a plea for peace.

The crackling of flames, the groans of the dying, and the far away thunder of hooves were not enough to drown the silence of the dead. Syndri's legs gave way, and she sank down to the blood-soaked earth as her fingers loosened around the hilt of the sword in her hand. The blade dropped.

A soft sound passed through Syndri's lips, a moan that broke from somewhere deep in her chest like the crack of ice on the river. Reaching out, her fingers trembled as she touched her father's face, his blood coating her hands. She drew her hands over her cheeks, and then tore the leather ties free from her braids.

There was no space for anything in her chest but grief, a vast emptiness of self, as if her spirit had been cast from her body into the air. All that remained was the sight of her father's face and her mother's outstretched hands. The smoking husk of Nar Garhis' *gat* rose blackened behind them, as if the hellish dark of the Nameless Lands had clawed its way through the earth to hover over their bodies like a charred skull.

"The warriors are returning," Malon said dully, standing guard behind Syndri.

The world was too thick and slow for Syndri to hear the sound.

She felt the rumble in the ground, but it was deafened by the roaring in her ears. And the blood on her hands. The horn of the approaching warband sounded like a faint cry across the plains. Her left arm was completely numb and useless.

"Syndri!"

Her sister's scream cut through the fog, and Syndri turned just as Senna fell to her knees, nearly crushing Syndri. The warband flooded into the central square, warriors running to find their families. There were so few... so few of them left. Syndri saw Hyshir struggle up from his place in front of the untouched *gat*, and Tilis appeared in the doorway, clutching her newborn son to her breast, her other children gathered around her skirts. Several other faces peered out around her.

Syndri touched her sister's face. "They're dead. Senna... they're all dead."

Ettlan's fingers fluttered near their knees.

# CHAPTER NINETEEN

*The Closed Fist protects. The Open Hand guides. Without one, the other cannot lead. Without one, the strength of the other is broken.*

*- Maleki Proverb*

The Tladr and the Uratar would destroy the Garhis in five days' time, and Ettlan still slept. The village lay in smoking ruins, the bodies of the dead arranged on pyres outside the walls. Yugha had assumed the mantle of the Closed Fist, gathering the people together to mourn their dead. But in five days, there would be no one left to mourn. The messenger that the Uratar and Tladr tribes had sent had told them that there would be no slaves taken. Not one child would be left alive. It would be as if the Garhis people had never walked the earth. They would give the Garhis tribe five days to mourn and do the proper rituals for the dead Nar Garhis. But the time of mourning would be followed by a time of death.

Syndri had strapped her swords to her back again, and Yugha had said nothing to stop her from doing so. She was ready to meet her end and take a host of nameless dogs with her when she drew her final breath. Her father lay on his pyre, wrapped in the black kehrox hide, his skin strangely pale in death, his spirit long fled. Without Ettlan there to lead the songs, Tilis had stepped forward at the pyre, her voice raspy from the smoke and tears shed. Syndri and the other warriors had cut lines across their palms and pressed bloody handprints against the pyre to show the Sky Clans how many names would speak for the worthiness of the man who was standing in judgment before them now. Their voices sang of his life, repeating his name over and over to the wind, so that he would not be Nameless in the dark.

And above it all, Tilis cried out the song of the fallen.

*This warrior's name rides through the sky*
*You will hear him and call  him*
*Garhis*
*He is not nameless, he has many warriors*
*He rides with the worthy ancestors*
*And brings the names of those below*

The tattered remnants of the tribe had watched the flames engulf the body of their Closed Fist, their great protector swept away in ashes on the wind. And with those ashes, the promise of uniting the tribes, the vision of Nar Garhis ruling as Great Lord of the Maleki. Now, the survival of the tribe hung on a sword's edge. They had one hundred and eighty warriors left after the battle out on the plains, and a handful of others who had survived the attack on the village. All in all, there were two hundred blades left to fight the combined forces of the other tribes.

They were outnumbered nearly three to one. But the Garhis warriors were worth three of any other tribe. Syndri knew the blades were sharp, and the need for vengeance would be running hot in the blood of every warrior left standing in the village. Her own hands itched with the need to spill blood. She would not rest until the Tladr and Uratar were destroyed.

Walking back into the village, she returned to her *gat*, where Senna kept watch over their mother. Her sister was sitting next to the cot where Ettlan lay encased in furs and hides. Syndri approached, clutching her numb and bandaged arm to her chest, hoping to see her mother's deep brown eyes open and the familiar smile on her lips. But still Ettlan lay like the dead. The slight rise and fall of her chest was the only sign of life. A poultice of herbs was held to the bruised side of her face by a cloth bandage. The bruising was far from the worst of the damage. Tilis had told them that some blunt weapon had struck Ettlan's head, and that the lack of blood they could see on the outside deceived the great river that flowed within.

Only time would tell if she would return to them from the edge of death. And how much of her would return. Tilis could not give them an answer. They could only wait, placing tiny chips of ice to melt in her cheek to try and keep her alive.

"Yugha has called the first swords to his *gat*," said Syndri. "They must choose a new Closed Fist before we can defeat the Uratar and Tladr. We do not have much time."

Senna sat hunched on her stool, her face smudged with ash and dirt, dried blood still crusted on her armor. She had not even removed it since returning from the battle. Dark circles ringed her eyes, and her hair hung free in wisps from its usually sleek braid. Syndri knelt beside her.

"*Teitei*," she said softly. "Tonight you will sleep. I will watch over her."

"I cannot lose her," whispered Senna. "Baya and our father have gone, and if she leaves us too... I will not stay here, I cannot..."

"You will. Because I cannot live if you are not by my side."

Senna's eyes were as red as the tattoo on her forehead. She looked at Syndri, searching her face. "What is left for us to do but die?"

"Close our fists, as our father would have done," said Syndri, reaching forward to pull the front of Senna's armor close. "Now we must protect those who still draw breath. We cannot leave them to the dogs."

"We cannot kill them all, Syndri."

"The days ahead are not written. We can still write the names of those who will live with our swords. You and I will be among those names. We will carve the name of Garhis into the throats of every one of their fallen, so when they go to the Nameless lands, the darkness will see our father's name written on their corpses."

Senna pushed her away. "Those are not the corpses that haunt me." She rose and walked out of the *gat*, leaving Syndri alone to watch the slow rise and fall of Ettlan's chest. The air inside the *gat* was thin, as if it was drawing all the breath away from Syndri's lungs, suffocating her in the whispers of death.

She shivered and stood up, pushing herself up to her feet and ignoring the ache of her bruised limbs. She touched her fingers to her mother's cool forehead.

"Come back to us," she said quietly.

"She will come back in her own time," said a husky voice behind Syndri. Tilis had entered the *gat*, a bundle of herbs and a bowl of water in her hands. "Go. Let me tend her in peace."

Sweeping a hand across her eyes, Syndri gave way to the older woman and left the *gat*, heading toward one of the few structures left standing in the village. The house that Hyshir had protected stood alone amidst the ruin of the others. The great beast was lying on the other side of the village, his wounds tended by those he had saved. He still breathed despite the myriad of wounds that decorated his body.

Outside Yugha's *gat*, Ikaio stood with his arms crossed in front of the door flap, and his face darkened as Syndri approached. His chest was bandaged beneath his fur cloak. Syndri stopped as he held up a hand.

"Nar Yugha has forbidden you."

Syndri curled her lip. "I am a first sword."

"You are Bladeless."

Fury curled its familiar fingers around Syndri's stomach. "I have killed in defense of our people, and I am the daughter of Nar Garhis."

Ikaio did not move, his eyes set as hard as iron. "You are still

Bladeless until Nar Yugha names you." He spat at the ground. "You are ill fortune."

Spurred on by her exhaustion and rage, Syndri stepped closer to him, looking him directly in the eyes. "Nar Yugha?" she spat. "My father's ashes still ride the wind, and you dare dishonor him by giving your loyalty so easily to another? The next Closed Fist has not been decided."

"Enough!"

Yugha stepped out from behind Ikaio, pushing aside the flap. He jerked his thumb toward the *gat*, sending Ikaio inside before facing Syndri. The warrior's face was still set like stone, as if he felt nothing in the face of his warlord's death and the destruction of their tribe. Syndri did not move back, forcing Yugha to stand close to her to speak.

"You speak truth. The Closed Fist has not been decided. And I may not be chosen. But if I am not, it still cannot be you."

Shocked, Syndri stared at him. "You think I wish to be Closed Fist? You think that is why I have come?"

"It matters not. You are still Bladeless, and you will remain that way until the new Nar has been chosen by the warriors."

"I fought beside my brothers and sisters when the Uratar attacked the village," replied Syndri, her voice low. "I watched them die as the village was overrun. You did not see it because you were not there. But I saw. And yet you would still deny me entrance to this gathering?"

Yugha rested his hand lightly on his belt near his knife. "I deny you because it is our law. When the new Nar is chosen, you will be named in honor of the blood you have shed. But I will not dishonor my Closed Fist by ignoring the exile he placed on you before his death. I will not ask you to lay down your swords. But you must remain Bladeless until the new Nar is chosen."

Syndri gritted her teeth. "And as Bladeless, I may not draw my blades as a warrior until I am named by this new Nar." She leaned forward. "I will pray to the Sky Clans that you decide quickly."

She stalked away from Yugha, the call of the hilts at her back rising to a scream in her blood. *Not yet,* she told herself. *You need your name, and the rights you claim with it.* Tomorrow she would have a name.

Yugha was chosen unanimously as the new Closed Fist by the warriors that night. Senna came back to the *gat* quietly and told Syndri everything that had happened. Not even one of the blooded warriors had spoken against Yugha.

"You spoke for him, then?" asked Syndri, gently running an oilcloth down the length of one of her blades. She watched the sword gleam in the light from the fire's final embers. Senna sat down across from her.

"Yes, I did. Our father would have."

"Our father is dead."

Senna rubbed a hand across her forehead. "He trusted Yugha enough to name him War Sword. That was enough for me. Don't be angry at me."

"I am not angry."

"No? And yet you oil and sharpen your blades as if you are going to battle in the morning."

Syndri laid the oilcloth aside. "If there is a need for it."

There was terse silence between them, and Syndri watched her sister stare at the glowing firepit. There was restlessness in Senna, and it shone in her eyes and the way she twisted her hands together. Syndri let her simmer for a few more heartbeats before speaking up.

"What else?"

Senna met her gaze. "Yugha will not meet them in battle. He means for us to join forces with Queen Xhen, as she promised. We will leave Malek."

Rising to her feet, Syndri gripped the hilt of her sword so tightly that her fingers ached and the wound in her arm flared into sharp pain. She searched for the words, but none came to her lips.

"If we stay," Senna spoke into the tense silence. "Our village will be gone for good, and then there will be no Garhis tribe. They mean to destroy us to the last child. We cannot protect the village and meet both tribes out on the plains. But together with the Northern queen, we can save the living and avenge our dead."

Syndri's mind whirled like a winter storm. There were no words for this kind of cowardice. Her father would never have left his land behind to beg help from a Northern queen in her halls of stone. The Garhis tribe was the most powerful tribe in Malek, and they did not run.

"He would let the bloodshed of our people go unanswered?"

"No. He sees that we can grow stronger and end their tribes with the help of the Rukian queen. He knows that our father would have done the same."

Syndri carefully sheathed the blade in her hand. "So, you and Yugha know what our father would have done?"

Angry now, Senna kicked at a stool, knocking it over. "Keep your tongue caged. There are many within our tribe who look to you as the reason for all this. They say your ill fortune has brought a punishment down on our tribe. If you push against Yugha now, they will tell him to kill you."

Laying her blades next to her cot, Syndri looked over her mother once more. There was no change, just the slow in and out of her breath. Tilis had washed her, braided her hair, and dressed her in a light tunic. She looked beautiful, even steps away from death.

Syndri sat down on the edge of the hides. "Perhaps they are right."

The silence that followed from Senna made Syndri's heart ache. She knew that her sister would fight to the death to protect her if the tribe tried to have her killed. But the Uratar and the Tladr tribes were responding to the actions of one warrior. A warrior who had killed a sacred messenger.

"Syndri, I do not think the other tribes put aside their differences just because of what you did. I think they saw it as a reason to attack. Their alliance formed too quickly. The Uratar and the Tladr have been enemies for generations."

"Even so."

"Do not act rashly tomorrow. Whatever Yugha does, he is trying to help you."

Syndri rested her head against the woven pillow, gingerly testing the bandage wrapped around her wounded arm. No matter what punishment the Sky Clans had dealt for her sins, she would not let her people be slaughtered.

As soon as the first light of morning woke the sky, Syndri went out to the village square and sat down in the center of it, her blades sheathed at her back. Soon Yugha would come out to begin the rituals of the Nar.

She breathed deep through the cold and closed her eyes, letting herself wander inwardly. In her mind's eye she rode the wind like a great hawk, looking down over the ruin of her village, letting the ashes and the darkened bloodstains feed the energy surging through her. She returned to the vivid memories of Durz'ekai dying against the wall, of old Ganzakh-ba lying in the dirt path, of her father and mother lying motionless in front of their *gat*, her father's face ruined by some great blade.

*Come out, Yugha.*

She remembered sitting in the darkness of her own *gat*, gripping Senna's shoulders as they both shook with silent tears, no words able to give voice to the deep cleaving of grief tearing them in two. She remembered lifting her brother's limp body up to his filly's back, the way his blood had smeared against her arms and face. She saw her mother, who was lying as still as the bodies they had burned, only shallow breaths separating her from them.

*Come out, Yugha. Give me my name.*

The morning sun warmed Syndri's chilled body as she waited. The ritual would start as soon as Yugha left his *gat*. Already some of the warriors had come out to wait for him, their faces streaked with the ash from Nar Garhis' death pyre, blades bare and ready. Only Syndri's blades were sheathed.

She watched as the flap of Yugha's *gat* opened and he walked out, bare-chested and holding his swords in his hands. The waiting warriors began their war cries, shrieking and screaming until the din was deafening. After so much death and destruction, the ritual was necessary. A promise of life continuing and returning to the balance it had left. Syndri would not hinder it. Her people needed a Closed Fist. But the man approaching her now was not the one she had chosen. She had not spoken his name last night in the gathering. Senna had spoken it, and Syndri did not fault her for it. Each of them had done what they thought was right.

The warriors brought the flats of their blades down on Yugha's shoulders, back, and chest so that he would be protected against unfriendly weapons. He walked without faltering through the barrage of their strikes until he reached the village center, standing on the very spot where Nar Garhis had met his death only three days before. The warriors put away their blades and raised their fists high above their heads.

Tilis approached her husband, dressed in black hides. She opened both of her hands, palms facing Yugha. Syndri sat still as a stone, watching Tilis stand in her mother's place. Yugha lifted his closed fists and placed them against his wife's palms.

"As the Sky Clans did before us, so we find our balance in the earth. An Open Hand must balance the Closed Fists, and through them we find strength in war and peace in plenty," said Tilis, her voice clear and loud. "Are you a blooded warrior of the Garhis tribe?"

Yugha lifted his chin. "I have shed the blood of our enemies."

"Have you been chosen by these warriors?"

The warriors cried out Yugha's name, shaking their fists in the air. Tilis placed a larger carved totem around Yugha's neck, the face of a bear growling on the end of a braided leather necklace. She had chosen him a symbol of great strength.

Syndri brushed her fingers against her own wolf totem. Her father had carved it for her when she was still toddling around the ground at her mother's feet. She still remembered how he had placed it around her neck when she had earned her warrior's blades. She remembered the tight squeeze he had given her shoulder before moving on to the next young warrior.

*Name me.*

Yugha stood tall before the warriors and the remaining clansmen and women standing beyond them, watching as their new Nar told them what their future held. Yugha lifted his hands into the air, one open and one closed into a fist.

"Nar Garhis believed that our tribe could rule all of Malek," he said loudly. "That was the vision he was given as a young boy. We will go to the land of Ruk and accept the hand of the Northern queen. We will grow strong again, and then we will return to our land with the great vengeance of the Sky Clans."

The warriors cheered, but Syndri noticed that some of the tribesmen and women did not share their enthusiasm. Several even looked away or whispered to the person next to them. Syndri saw Malon standing with Uhuri, both watching Yugha with dark expressions.

"Bladeless!"

Yugha was calling for her. Syndri rose, her swords still safely in their sheaths as she approached the new Closed Fist. She stood before him; her shoulders straight as she met his eyes without fear.

"You shed the blood of a messenger who was under the protection of the Sky Clans. For this, you have been exiled from this tribe and your warrior's blades taken from you. And yet, you have fought with honor." Yugha looked around at the people gathered. "If there is anyone who would speak against this Bladeless, speak now."

There was a low rumble of discontent from some of the gathered warriors. Several of them spat on the ground near her feet. Finally, Ikaio's voice spoke from the crowd.

"She will bring ill fortune to us. The blood of the tribe is on her hands!"

Another joined him. "If we name her, the Sky Clans will be displeased with us, and we will all die at the hands of the Uratar and Tladr tribes!"

"They would not have attacked us without the messenger's death!"

"They will kill us all!"

The voices all began to intertwine into a fearful, angry cacophony, like a flock of crows. Syndri waited, letting them wash over her. She heard some voices raised in her defense, and others calling for her permanent exile or her immediate death to appease the Sky Clans.

Yugha watched her, clearly deciding what to do. If he allowed her to live, the tribe would not trust him, and he needed their loyalty if they were to survive what was to come. But if he killed her, others in the tribe would not be pleased with more Nar Garhis blood feeding the earth. Either way, he could not keep the tribe together.

*Do not do anything rash.*

"Name me, and let me challenge for my honor," she said quietly to Yugha. "It is the only way. Let the Sky Clans decide."

He waited, thick arms crossed, his skin still red from the warrior's blades. Then he nodded. "I name you, Syndri, daughter of Nar Garhis of the Garhis tribe. You are Bladed."

"Closed Fist!" exploded Ikaio. "You cannot..."

Yugha turned on him. "You wish to challenge me and take my place?"

Ikaio spluttered. "No! But she is going to be the death of us all if you allow her to stay. It is known! Her honor is lost!"

Syndri reached behind her shoulder, grasping the hilt of her right sword. The blade slid free of the sheath, and she stabbed it into the dirt beside Ikaio's feet. "I, Syndri, daughter of Nar Garhis of the Garhis tribe, challenge you for the honor of my blades."

Ikaio pulled his own swords free. "You are a stain on this tribe."

It had not been long since Syndri had danced on this same

ground, and now she was fighting to the death. Challenging for honor and a warrior's name was rare. During all her father's years as the Closed Fist, it had happened only twice.

Either Syndri would prove her honor as one of their warriors, or she would die. Ettlan's voice echoed in her mind. *You are more than a blade.*

A young warrior named Hefiar stepped up to witness for Ikaio's honor. Syndri looked around at the others, but no one stood forward. Senna could not witness, because she was family. An unrelated warrior had to stand beside her, or she could not follow through with the challenge. Yugha could not show partiality to either side.

A quiet step to her right, and then Malon was there, her black hair newly braided and twisted in a line down the center of her head. The one-armed warrior gave her a brisk nod, her lips pursed in a tight line. "I'll stand for you."

Yugha raised his fists. "The Sky Clans witness! The surviving warrior claims honor and will keep full blade rights."

Ikaio shed his cloak and tunic, stripping down to the waist. There was no armor allowed in an honor fight, for it was a cowardly thing to seek protection from the Sky Clans' justice. Malon helped Syndri untie the leather straps of her armor and the scales fell away, leaving her feeling light as a feather. Her loose shirt and trousers did little to keep out the cold, but soon the fight would warm her blood. Her biggest concern was her heavily bandaged left arm. She could grip a sword, but her strength was gone. She would be able to block and thrust if he left her an opening, but if he threw his full weight against her, the arm would not hold.

The thin bandage across Ikaio's chest covered little more than a shallow cut. He had survived the battle on the plains against the Tladr tribe but had come away with much less to show for his trouble than Syndri. The Sky Clans had seen fit to spare her life despite facing an onslaught of Uratar with odds of dozens to one. Syndri thought perhaps that ought to speak for her honor, but Ikaio was looking for someone to blame. She saw the anger in his eyes as he shook his arms and tilted his head from side to side to loosen his neck and shoulders.

And perhaps the ancestors were simply waiting for her to be killed by a member of her own tribe. Syndri turned to Malon and smiled.

"Thank you for standing with me," she said. "If I fall, my blades are yours."

Malon pressed her fist to her chest. "You honor me, First Sword."

Ignoring the sudden burn behind her eyes, Syndri caught sight of Senna standing nearby amidst a small knot of other warriors who had not spoken for Syndri's death. Her sister was worrying her lower lip, the way she did whenever she was holding herself back.

Ikaio let out a screeching war cry and raised his sword to Yugha. Syndri pulled her swords from their sheaths, the familiar whistle of air past her ear calming her racing heart. She crossed her blades and turned to face the place outside the village walls where her father's pyre had burned.

"NAR GARHIS!" she cried.

"NAR GARHIS!" replied the crowd. Whether they blamed her or not, they would not stay silent for her tribute to their fallen Fist.

*Ikaio leads heavily with his left side. He is slower, but his strikes will break me if they land. He looks where he is about to step, so I can predict where he will go.* Syndri knew she was more agile, but with her left arm nearly useless, she could not let him get a moment's upper hand. She drew in a deep breath to steady herself as Ikaio stepped toward her, his swords held one high, one low.

He swung high overhead, taking advantage of her weak arm. She met him with her right sword, and blocked his lower jab, spinning it to the side with a flip of her left.

A heavy kick landed against her tender ribs, and she fell back, rolling to her left side as soon as she hit the ground and avoiding a killing strike that sent dirt flying into the air. She stabbed forward and sliced across the thick meat of his calf. He stumbled but made no sound.

Wincing as the wound in her arm reopened from the pressure of landing against it, Syndri flipped her stronger sword so that it ran along the length of her arm, blocking another strike and dropping to one knee under the weight. Using the blunt force of her shoulder, she shoved upwards, launching herself from the ground and pushing him back a few steps.

Before Ikaio could recover, she pressed in toward him, her blades swinging hard and meeting in the middle at his neck. He managed to block one of them, but the other bit into the fatty tissue above his shoulder. But her left arm could not swing hard enough to cut deeply, and the blow glanced away, leaving only a shallow wound. Blood trickled down his chest.

He knocked her blades aside and sent the tip of his forward sword slicing into her collarbone a finger's breadth before pulling away. The sting cleared Syndri's head. She had to end this fight, or she would lose what little strength she had left. She ducked his next swing, dropped one sword, and drove upwards with both hands gripping the hilt of the other.

The blade ripped past his throat and up into his skull. She pulled it free, and he fell to the side. Blood poured from his head. Syndri staggered to her feet and retrieved her second sword. She looked around at the faces of her people, watching her, staring at the body of Ikaio. Tears poured down Syndri's face unhindered, exhaustion and grief ripping away the final barriers holding them at bay.

She thrust her swords into the ground, facing Yugha.

"Nar Yugha," she said. "My swords are yours."

# TWENTY

*My esteemed friend Sairi,*
*I am in need of your peerless craftsmanship for a set of masks that I intend to*
*give as a gift to our great warlord the king. They must be the finest work you*
*have done for me... you must make the faces of the Ancient Oathsworn with*
*your wood and paints. They must be fearsome to look upon, so that those who*
*see them in the Council Hall guarding the king may tremble. Do not press*
*yourself, they need not be finished for some time. I will visit you after a full*
*moon's cycle to see the progress of your work.*
*Your servant and friend, Lohi*

High above the red walls of the palace, the angry light of Aqatar streamed over the city like the afterglow of a forge fire, bathing the softly sloping roofs in gold, glittering on the dusting of snow they had received that morning. The air held a biting chill as the afternoon bled into evening.

Master Lohi had finished attending to the king for the day. His time seemed so precious now that it was split between Blackvale and the royal halls of Keld. And there would never be enough of it.

As he tapped along the paved road out of the palace gates with his staff, Lohi scoffed at his younger self, a man who had once believed himself invincible with more years to his name than the Firstborn. And yet as the king drew closer to the day when he would be forced to choose his successor, Lohi's advancing age was a bigger threat than the scheming rats in the Counsel. Reaching up with his right hand, Lohi massaged the deep lines of worry carved into his forehead by the past decade. He leaned heavier on his staff and drew his outer robe closer to his thin frame. It was far too easy to feel cold even on warm days. These winter months brought out the brittleness of his bones, the shortness of his breath.

One of the king's attendants had offered to escort him to his destination, but he had refused. Best let his enemies see him walking on his own two feet, no matter how slow the journey.

Counsellor Hallix had sent him an invitation, which had been expected. Master Lohi would visit him later that night and once again play the wearisome game of saying one thing and meaning another. It was an old game, as old as the earth.

Shuffling beneath the shadow of the massive palace gates, Master Lohi saw the respectful nods that each of the guards gave him as he passed. Beyond the gate, the road sloped gently down into the first district of the noble estates and the shops of the finest craftsmen in the city. The craftsmen and women who worked magic with their hands in silk, precious metals, wood, and stone with the highest skills had no need to ply their wares in the city markets. People traveled to them, even a revered old scholar. Thankfully, it was not a long walk to the craft master that Lohi intended to visit.

He passed by the house of the king's inkmaster, a Da'hmian man nearly as old as Lohi, but twice the size, who went by the name of Bir. That was not his real name. Da'hamian names were far too long and lyrical for the simple tongues of Katesh. Inside the house, perfectly rectangular blocks of dark black ink hung in knotted rope lines from the ceiling beams, drying and aging for years before they were deemed ready for use.

There was no finer ink in the world. Each glistening brushstroke was made with the dedication and skill of generations. Just as each statue made by the stonemason family of Je Tal was a monument to their Sharai-blessed hands, working the rock into likenesses that seemed to draw breath.

The Street of the Craftsmen was a place Lohi knew well. Many of his friends resided within the walls of these houses, good people whose spirits were grounded in the earth, not wafting about in the smoky air of the Council chamber.

Master Lohi shuffled to a house that sat up on a low terrace, a little way back from the street. Several of the wall screens were slid to the side, opening sections of the walls to the soft breeze of the afternoon. The earthy smell of wood shavings reached Lohi's nose as he removed his slippers and stepped up onto the polished floor. There was no inner courtyard, just a large square room with work mats and small stacks of wood. A small pile of *sabba* wood blocks sat in one corner, the dark grain bold against the rush mats.

Reaching up to the small chime above the door, Lohi tugged on the knotted string. A soft tinkling of bells sang out through the room. A small black cat turned owlish green eyes at him from its bed on a small cushion sitting on a shelf in the wall. Lohi reached out and let the creature sniff his fingers, and it did so, before gazing at him in judgment one last time and then curling back up to sleep.

A bird squawked somewhere in the rooms beyond the partitions at the back of the entrance. Lohi smiled and shuffled his way to the wide panels, sliding one of them back just enough to step through. The room was packed floor to ceiling with wood, crates of dyes and paints, chisels, mallets, grit for sanding, and plaques with an assortment of runes and their meanings written in neat brushstrokes.

Masks in various stages of completion lay in stacks around the center mat, some of them already carved into laughing, crying, or rage-filled expressions. Some still wore their natural color, while others boasted deep colors of black, red, blues, greens, and whites.

The woman kneeling on the mat wore a simple green *sati*, the long jacket rolled up to her elbows at the sleeves. Her trousers were stained with daubs of color and textured with fine wood shavings. Her long silvering hair hung in braids on either side of her neck, framing a weathered, wise face. She ran one hand over the smooth wooden mask she held and blew a tiny storm of shavings into the air.

"If you want tea, you'll need to wait," she said, squinting at the mask in her hand before laying it back on the block at her knees and picking up a small chisel. The bird tied to a small perch in the corner let out another squawk. It was a raven, black feathers gleaming, an intricate wooden brace clipped to its left wing and tied with a leather thong around the body.

"Some say it is ill fortune to cross paths with a raven," Master Lohi said. The bird tilted its head and glared at him. "Much less keep one in your house."

The chisel slid across the mask's jaw with a soft scraping sound, each gentle movement deepening the hollow of the lower cheek. "Hm. And the same fools screech at their tea leaves and call down Sharai's protection when they step around horse dung in the streets. *Tcha*! Fools."

Master Lohi smiled. "It is good to see you, Sairi."

"Ay, I'm still alive, same as you." She laid down the chisel and gave him a cursory once-over. "You should be resting your old bones, not running errands for the king."

"These old bones are younger than yours, and yet you seem as spry as twenty years past."

She rose from the mat, brushing off her trousers and flipping her braids back out of the way. "Sitting around with books and scrolls and riding around in wagons doesn't do much for your strength." She reached for a pot of water hanging over the firepit in the back of the room and poured it carefully into a spouted pitcher. A moment later, she handed Lohi a cup, the pleasant aroma of mint and herbs reaching his nose. He drank, and the tea chased away the lingering chill.

"You'll want to see them."

Sairi bustled away to a chest, retrieving a silk-wrapped object from within. Lohi set down his cup and accepted the bundle, gently pulling away the silk. The terrifying visage that greeted Lohi sent a thrill through him. The red face had bared teeth, four protruding fangs, and a wolfish shape to the nose and jaw. This was framed by deep black tendrils snaking from the sides across to the forehead and cheeks. The eyebrows were drawn toward the eyes and arched in anger, pulled in by deep cut lines. The glimmer of gold leaf lined the shape of the eyes and curled lips. The bottom of the jaw and chin were a deep black below the protruding white teeth.

Sairi was eyeing it critically, wiping her hands on her jacket. "It's not quite perfect. The others will be better."

But Master Lohi shook his head. "No, Sairi. They must each be an identical match to this one. There must not be a single shape different. The king will be pleased. Most pleased."

Master Lohi accepted the use of a palanquin to carry him to the granaries, which was where Counsellor Hallix had suggested they meet. The huge stone buildings sat like eggs in a walled off section of Keld, not far from the counsellor's estate. Armed guards opened the gates for Lohi and the four burly men carrying the ornate red box he sat in. Master Lohi slid the screened window open to peer through the lattice. The small compound was buzzing with workers, wagons, and overseers. Several scribes and record keepers walked between the large buildings with clay tablets, making records of the wagons coming in and going out and the weight and quality of baskets being filled from each granary.

The bearers set down the palanquin in front of the counting house, and Master Lohi emerged into the earthy smell of grain. A nearby scribe bowed at the sight of him, the black hat tipping precariously on the top of his head.

"Where is your master?" asked Lohi.

"I will take you to him at once, my lord." The man gestured and padded away toward one of the granaries. Lohi shuffled after and followed him into one of the large domed buildings through a little door in the side. The rich smell became thicker, wafting from the massive pile of grain within.

Counsellor Hallix stood beside another pair of scribes, who were speaking with him quietly and showing him marks on their clay tablets. When he caught sight of Lohi, Counsellor Hallix waved them away and gave a slight bow.

"Master Lohi. I trust the palanquin I sent was comfortable for you."

"A welcome change from wooden wagons, and you have my thanks for that," Lohi replied. There were no stools or chairs in the granary, and it was by design that Hallix had invited him here rather than to a formal dinner at his estate. The days of comfortable conversations between them had long since passed. The servants and scribes left the granary, and the domed walls grew quiet.

"I apologize for asking you to come here, but as you are leaving us again in the morning, I did not have time to finish my duties here. I hope it is not an inconvenience," said Counsellor Hallix.

"The smell of good grain is a balm to weary bones. Your storehouses are filled with the promise of a future," replied Lohi, waving his hand at the kernel mountains. "I have just come from duties of my own. The king is in good health and spirits today."

"A blessing."

"Indeed. Although he did express his displeasure once again at the Counsel's impatience. I do what I can to turn them to more appropriate occupations, but I am one man, and my travels take me from the city far too often these days."

Counsellor Hallix interlaced his fingers. "Far too often, as you say. A king's counsellor should be at his master's side. It concerns me that you are so permanently detained outside the city. If you desire retirement in the stale walls of that ruined fortress, your place here can be filled by another."

"And it will be, in time. But as you have your duties, Counsellor Hallix, so I have mine. My loyalty has always been to follow the desires and command of our great king."

Hallix nodded. "Of course. You have been secretive these past years. But I have grown to distrust secrets. Katesh was founded on our people working together to create a strong nation. And yet it seems that it has lately been at the mercy of secretive old men."

Gripping his staff with both hands, Lohi tried to take a little weight off his aching hip. He was surprised it had taken this long for Hallix to confront him. "If you have questions, you have only to ask."

"And you will have prepared words that answer nothing. But I am curious anyway, these boys you train in Blackvale, do they serve the king's purpose or yours?"

Lohi smiled. "The king has reason to distrust those within his palace walls. His own son was murdered in his bedroom by a *garatelhai* who had sworn loyalty. And it is not a difficult thing to reason that there may be others plotting against our king's family, or even his own life. No, not a difficult thing at all to reason."

Reaching out into the mountain of golden grain next to him, Counsellor Hallix scooped out a handful and ran his fingers over the kernels. "A single kernel of grain seems an insignificant thing. It can be grown in a field and trampled underfoot and never reach the storehouses. And yet, in such vast quantities as this, it becomes invaluable. How many mouths does it feed? How many of our country's most valuable resources are made from these grains? It is a source of great power." He let the grain fall through his fingers back into the pile. "You have my son."

Master Lohi pursed his lips and stroked a hand down the front of his white beard. There were many secrets that each kept from the other, but this was not among them. "Whatever names they had before are gone now, and they are the sons of Katesh. They exist only to protect and serve our great king."

"The king may have given you the command, but it was you who chose them. Do you deny it?"

"I do not."

Counsellor Hallix cracked the last grain between his fingernails before dropping it to the floor. "You have always wielded the king's power as if it were your own. But in taking my son, you have considered me too insignificant, Lohi. And I will see that you live to regret it."

Stiffly, Master Lohi bent down to pick up a small black kernel on the ground at his feet. He held it up, examining it. "One rotten kernel can spoil the rest. I have never found you to be insignificant, Counsellor Hallix, not once since the days when I was your teacher. My duty is to keep the king safe." He met Hallix's gaze. "And I will do so, at any cost."

"I do not wish to see the day when our people fear a good king because of the actions you have taken. Tread carefully, Lohi. This land and its people belong to Kinhariian. Not to you."

"The people belong to the king," said Lohi quietly. "Yes. So, they do."

Counsellor Hallix offered a curt bow. "Your good health. The palanquin will return you to the palace." The man's eyes glittered darkly as he passed by Lohi in a swish of his robes, stepping out of the granary. Lohi sighed and reached out for a handful of grain, feeling the tiny kernels warm against his palm, the slight weight of them comforting. He let them sift through his fingers.

"The people belong to the king," he murmured. "From the mightiest... to the least."

Master Lohi smiled and sighed. Counsellor Hallix was like an iron rod, unyielding. But even iron breaks when the right amount of pressure is applied. Someday Counsellor Hallix would break.

# CHAPTER TWENTY-ONE

*I speak this true name to the four corners of the good earth*
*I speak it with earth, wind, water, and fire*
*I send it forth under the sky and stars to be spoken*
*In the light and in the darkness*
*So that all things I create with my hands and love with my heart*
*Will be known.*

*- Da'hamian Name Song*

When Gehrin awoke to find Sabba's hand on his shoulder, he swallowed down the startled exclamation that made it to the edge of his mouth. The Da'hamian boy held a finger to his own lips and gestured calmly toward the door at the end of the barracks room.

Reaching the courtyard, Gehrin saw Nin and Kajen already standing outside, still in their sleeping trousers. Ruh was next to them, dressed for the night watch. Nin was rubbing the sleep from his eyes, Kajen looked irritated at having been woken up in the middle of the night, and Ruh stood with his arms crossed, his usual unnerving smile still curving his lips.

"Sabba, what is this?" asked Gehrin softly. He knew that Sabba and Ruh had been on watch together that night. "Is something wrong?"

The giant shook his head somberly and addressed his next words to the four of them. "I must ask of you one time this great favor," he said slowly, choosing each word with care. "In my land we have..." he hesitated. "You have only one word for this, I think."

"Ritual," said Ruh.

"Yes, only one word when there should be many." Sabba folded his hands. "Today I was born under a great sky of stars and my mother named me. But I am living for many summers, enough to be a man. There must be this... ritual."

Gehrin frowned, a strange worry nibbling at his gut. The guards could come upon them at any time and see five boys when there should be only two. They had been expressly forbidden from even speaking about their families before, how would they be punished if Sabba was found doing a ritual from his homeland? Tahmujin would have them stripped of their skin and thrown to the forest wolves.

"Why do you need us? Just do the ritual and let us sleep, *kefe*," grumbled Kajen, scratching at his rear end.

Sabba held out his hands and smoothed them in a circle through the air. "Four ends of earth, and the name must be carried to all..." he paused again and glanced at Ruh, his forehead wrinkled in frustration. "You have words for friends who watch and carry names, yes?"

The other three boys stared at him in confusion. Ruh shrugged. Sabba reached up and tugged on his short-cropped hair, dark eyes focused on his hands as he drew the circle in the air again to try and make them understand. It was the most words Gehrin had ever heard Sabba speak at once. When they had first come to Blackvale, the Da'hamian boy had only known a scattered sampling of Kateshi, but he had learned quickly enough to communicate and to understand the commands from Tahmujin.

He had excelled in the lessons with Master Lohi, his brush-strokes finer than even Gehrin's and Tirrim's practiced hands. The Da'hamian people were artists, poets, and scholars, so it was no surprise that Sabba's skill with writing surpassed the rest, even coming from a lowly merchant family.

Sabba sighed. "I think you have one word, *witness*? It is something like this."

"You want us to witness a ritual?" asked Nin in surprise.

"Yes. It is the most important of all things in my life," said Sabba. "And we are brothers, so I will ask this great favor of you."

"I will do it," said Nin. The smallest boy looked resolute, still shivering a bit but clenching his fists to hold it in. "It would be an honor."

"*Tcha!*" exclaimed Kajen. "You gonna get us all beat to death. Alright, I will do your ritual. Quick, so I can go back to sleep."

Ruh nodded in agreement, and then Sabba turned to Gehrin, who quickly looked around the courtyard, expecting a *telhai* guard to appear at any moment and raise the alarm. "Master Tahmujin will punish us if he finds out. It isn't safe."

"Always follow the rules, eh, *icha?*" chuckled Kajen. "You just scared."

Gehrin glared at him. "Yes, maybe. But I don't want any of us to spend another night tied to that post. Sabba, we are only warriors for the king now. Who we were before..."

"Is gone, yes. But this I must do. I must take my name so it can be written in the god halls."

If he refused, Gehrin knew that Sabba would never hold it against him. But he could not bear the thought of them being caught while he was safe in his bed. He tightened the drawstring of his trousers. "Come on then. But we should go to the old well so we cannot be seen."

Sabba's white teeth appeared as he smiled and retrieved a small bundle from the ground. He led the small group toward the back of the courtyard and the crumbling stone well. There they were hidden by a partial wall, but the empty courtyard behind them could give them away as well.

The old well disappeared into the ground like a black, gaping mouth yawning out of the broken stone. Near the edge, Sabba opened the bundle and set several objects on the ground. He faced the four corners of the courtyard and bowed to each one. Then he began to sing in a deep, warm voice in his own language. Though it was hardly more than a whisper, the song was beautiful, rising and falling like waves, his mother tongue flowing out in a gentle rhythm. It was not like the songs of the Kateshi, but mellow and somber. The final note disappeared into the air, and gooseflesh rose on Gehrin's arms.

Sabba lifted the first object, a small pouch from which he drew a handful of dirt. He rubbed it over his face and neck and on the palms of his hands. Then he moved his hands in wide, sweeping motions, as if he were drawing the wind to him. He lifted the third object, a small cup of water, and tipped it over his face, washing away the dirt. Then he struck two flint pieces together against a small stick wrapped with dry grass. A tiny spark caught and leapt into flame.

Holding the flame close to his chest, Sabba passed his hand over it and pressed his palm against his face. Then he blew it out, leaving a thin wisp of smoke.

Once again, he faced each of the four corners of the courtyard, and spoke a single word to each of them, his hands held palms out. "Sabba."

Gehrin glanced to his side and saw the other boys watching the ritual with rapt attention. Even Kajen looked interested despite his earlier indifference. Ruh's white hair stood out in the darkness, and Gehrin noticed that the Takkan boy's smile had faded as he watched.

Then Sabba turned to face the other boys. He bowed to each of them and said their names. They all awkwardly bowed back, feeling the reverence of the ritual. Then Sabba smiled and lifted his big hands to the sky, tear trails running down his cheeks.

"To all four ends of the good earth, these brothers... these *daieshek'iayejos* hear my true name, my one name, and carry this name. To all ends. *Daieshek malteogarhas'a.* True name is heard."

*True name.* Gehrin's chest tightened. *Am I Gehrin? Or am I Liv?* Two names pulled at him, both trying to drag him into different worlds. Sabba had chosen his name. It had been given to him by Master Tahmujin, but then he had chosen it for himself. And Gehrin supposed that gave him a way to know who he was. *Liv.* He turned the name around in his mind, imagining the simple brushstroke to write the word. It was a word he had said to himself every time he had counted to calm himself after his mother died, while he lay trapped in the wooden box when they had brought him to Blackvale, and when he had been tied to the post in the courtyard. A simple number, and now it was his name.

*But my mother named me Gehrin.* Sabba had spoken about the name his mother had given him at the beginning of the ritual. He would remember it forever. It was still inside his thoughts in a place that Master Tahmujin could not reach.

Sabba came to them after he had gathered the objects. "I never forget this great favor, my brothers. You are *daieshek'iayejos* for all time."

Kajen slapped Sabba's thick bicep. "Yah, right now all I want to be is asleep, *kefe.*" But even as he complained, he looked pleased. The little group started back to the courtyard and stopped short when they saw a figure standing at the edge, watching them. Hajja's black mask hid all but his eyes, and his hands twisted in front of him as he looked away, turning to run back to the barracks.

In a heartbeat, Kajen was on him, wrapping an arm around Hajja's neck. Hajja's eyes flared wildly and he struggled to pull away from the stronger boy. Gehrin jumped forward.

"Kajen, let him go!"

The Wildcat's lips pulled back from his feral teeth as he held his prisoner. "*Yah*, you ten kinds of fool, *icha*! This one gonna tell on us. He spend all his time with that old graybeard. Probably a spy."

Gehrin gripped Kajen's arm so tightly his knuckles went white. His eyes locked with Hajja's as the boy twisted and squirmed. Gehrin lowered his voice. "Kajen, let him go. I trust him."

With a disapproving growl, Kajen released the masked boy and stalked away back to the barracks and his waiting bed. Hajja grabbed his own throat with both hands and dropped to his knees in the sand. Gehrin knelt beside him.

"I'm sorry."

Hajja looked away and gave a slight shake of his head. Gehrin offered his hand, and Hajja took it, allowing Gehrin to pull them both up to their feet. "Come on, Nin. We need to get back to bed before the guards patrol again."

Ruh and Sabba returned to their watch post in the center of the courtyard, and the magic of the ritual faded as Gehrin led the other two boys into the barracks, each of them treading as lightly as the rats Jai hunted in the storerooms.

Sparring sessions found Gehrin and the other boys who had taken part in the nighttime ritual dark eyed and sluggish from lack of sleep. Ruh's ghostly pale face looked even more skeletal after spending a night on watch, his eyes sunken above his sharp cheekbones.

Gehrin held his first form across from Nin, whose hair was so disheveled that it looked like a thorn bush. He'd sparred against Haveth earlier, and the tall, thin boy had nearly knocked him sense-less because his reflexes were still asleep. Tahmujin was especially short-tempered, stalking the edge of the courtyard like a panther, his staff knocking against knuckles, shoulders, and heads of anyone who was too slow or holding a messy form. He did not seem to know about the ritual that had taken place the previous night.

Only Sabba seemed unaffected by the previous night's activities. He almost seemed refreshed, moving with an agility that was unlike his usual heavy movements. He even received a curt "good" from Tahmujin after delivering a particularly well-timed blow to his oppo-nent, Yul.

Nin stepped too far forward, and his swing went to the side as he nearly lost his balance. Gehrin easily stepped away and tapped the younger boy on the neck with his own staff. Nin reddened and scowled, frustrated with himself. He'd been falling behind the others lately, and had the bruises to show for it, looking like they all had back in the days when they had first arrived in Blackvale.

"Nin!" barked Tahmujin. "Take a log and start running. Liv, you run with him. You're both moving like old women."

Gehrin jogged over to the pile of logs and hefted one atop his shoulder. Nin struggled a bit more with his, but when he met Gehrin's gaze, he offered a grin. "Kirte moves pretty fast when there's a rat in her kitchens."

They both chuckled as they started their slow run across the length of the courtyard. The logs were about the length of Gehrin's leg, just bulky enough to require a careful sense of balance. By the end, Gehrin would feel the pull in his abdomen. Nin had chosen the smallest log but had still broken a good sweat by the time they had run back to the pile the first time.

They passed Jai, who was leaving the barracks room after having cleaned it. The servant boy walked briskly with the dirty water bucket and rags in one hand, and a brush broom in the other. He smiled at them as they passed. Gehrin wondered if Jai had ever been jealous of them training to be warriors, or if he was glad, he didn't have to spend his days following Tahmujin's orders. He had grown alongside the rest of them, his scrawny body slowly morphing into the shape of a man. And yet he was still a servant, less than the others, and somehow more because of the freedom he was given. He was Kirte's grandson, so the rumor went, both parents dead and gone. He had never spoken of them. The only family he ever referred to was the other boys. *My brothers*, he would always call them affectionately, as if they had grown up as playmates in some Kateshi village.

Gehrin slowed his pace a bit to let Nin stay in stride with him. His legs were longer than Nin's, the younger boy still missing the growth spurt that had sent the others stretching up like trees. And yet, despite the obvious disadvantages, Nin continued to run and spar and try his best. He was stubborn. But it was true that Kirte had a soft spot for the boy, and often kept him with her in the kitchens in the short time they were free from the courtyard or barracks. She had taught him more about herbs and healing potions, and Nin had told them that she had even shown him the basics of poison craft.

As the two boys reached the log pile for the third time, Gehrin heard a series of loud, angry screams and yells. He stopped and tipped the log forward, letting it fall. At the far end of the sparring pairs, he saw Ruh trapped on the ground under his opponent, the boy's white hair dirty with sand and mud. The boy on top of him was Niveth, trying to push him further into the sand, pinning his arms. The screams that Ruh let out left chills in Gehrin's bones.

The Takkan boy bucked his hips hard and threw Niveth off, scrambling on top of him so their position was reversed. Then he began to rain blows on Niveth's face and shoulders with his fists, still screaming incoherent curses at the boy beneath him. Tahmujin reached them first, grabbing the back of Ruh's tunic and throwing him bodily across the sand. Regaining his feet, Ruh tried to run back to Niveth, but Sabba managed to grab him around the shoulders.

Storming over to the struggling boy, Tahmujin hit Ruh across the face with a heavy fist. Ruh went limp, the rage flying out of him as he spat blood in the sand. Tahmujin pulled him away from Sabba and shoved him toward the log pile.

"Go run! And you will run until you drop!"

Ruh lifted a log to his shoulder, his eyes burning with bright fire as he began jogging across the courtyard. Tahmujin cracked his staff against the ground, shouting at the other boys to quit gawking in surprise and continue forms. Niveth stood up, his face a bloody mess, nose crooked. Gehrin winced. It wasn't the first broken nose that Kirte would have set since the boys had arrived.

He picked his log back up, slowly returning to the monotonous path alongside Ruh. Nin followed, still wide-eyed. Ruh ran as if Aqatar himself was breathing down his neck, his slim legs keeping a pace that neither Gehrin nor Nin could match.

By the time the other boys had finished their sparring sessions and Master Tahmujin sent them off to their chores, Gehrin and Nin were walking the log path, sweat pouring down their backs. But Ruh still jogged, stumbling as he doggedly pushed his body back and forth along the length of the courtyard. There was silence between the three boys, neither of the two Kateshi willing to risk breaking into the self-imposed mental prison that Ruh had clearly locked himself in.

Nin dropped his log in exhaustion when evening finally fell. He collapsed onto the sand, arms flung out to the sides as his chest heaved with every breath. Gehrin trudged back to the pile and dropped the log with a thunk against the others.

Kirte appeared in the gateway to Blackvale's kitchen and store-room wing. "You three come in here and wash up now. You're a sorry sight."

Throwing his log back against the others, Ruh leaned over with his hands braced against his knees, blowing out sharp breaths. His sweat-soaked hair hung in strings around his face. Gehrin approached him cautiously with a bucket of drinking water, holding out the wooden ladle.

"Here. Drink something."

Ruh shook his head but offered Gehrin a smile. It was half-hearted and did not reach his eyes. Gehrin knew that the three of them were a pitiful sight walking into the stone bath house, but the pool of water was a welcome comfort to his sore muscles. He couldn't get in fast enough, shedding his clothes and letting the water close over his head as he sank under. Sound disappeared, leaving him floating in a muffled world. He pushed back up, breaking the surface and wiping the water from his face.

Nin was leaning against one side of the bath, eyes closed. Gehrin wondered if he might fall asleep. Ruh stood at the far end, scrubbing his chest and arms with the soap and oils that Kirte had left out for them.

Gehrin reached for his own soap, and side-eyed Nin every now and then to make sure the younger boy didn't slip beneath the water.

But after a few heartbeats, Nin shook himself more awake and washed, slipped out of the bath, and left to help Kirte in the kitchen.

Reluctantly, Gehrin climbed up the steps and retrieved his clothing, shaking his wet hair like a dog and tying it up on the top of his head. He was about to leave when he realized that Ruh was still scrubbing at his arms and chest with the soap. The boy's skin was rubbed raw and red from the scratchy woven cloth.

"Ruh?"

The Takkan boy avoided his gaze. "Need more soap," he muttered. Gehrin padded over to the side of the pool and crouched down.

"You used all your soap," Gehrin replied. Ruh was not himself, and Gehrin wondered if the long hours of log running had addled his brain. He tapped his fingers against the empty dish on the edge. The small chunk of soap was long gone, and the woven cloth was doing nothing but leaving angry red patches on Ruh's pale skin.

"You're gonna have no skin left," observed Gehrin, pointing at the red marks. "Come on, Kirte will have food for us. I'm starving."

Ruh's hands slowed their incessant scrubbing, and then stopped. "Can I have the rest of your soap?"

The dish on the far side of the pool still had a small lump of the stuff, but Gehrin frowned. "Ruh, we should go to Kirte. I think Niveth hit you too hard."

The smile slipped from Ruh's face at the mention of the other boy. His eyes were glazed, looking at the water but seeing something much farther away. "I would've killed him too, Liv. Killed him so he never could do it again."

Gehrin glanced at the door, wondering if he should call in a guard. "Tahmujin would strip your skin faster than that cloth if you did. Come on, let's go eat. You're talking like a crazy fool."

"It wasn't my mother," Ruh said. "They thought I killed that man because he took her when she didn't want him to, but she wasn't there. He took me instead, told me he'd paid his coppers. And then I killed him, and I watched his blood seep out until the house master found me."

Nausea curled in Gehrin's stomach. "What?"

"In Mijaro, Master Lohi found me in a pit. They were going to kill me for killing him. But I would do it again, even if I died."

Gehrin said nothing. The lives that each of them had led before Blackvale were forbidden. He felt strange, unsure what words to say. He was sick to his stomach and didn't want to think about what Ruh had said.

"You didn't die. You came here and now you're one of us," Gehrin said awkwardly. He fiddled with the hem of his trousers. "If that happened to you, why do you smile all the time?"

Ruh set the cloth up on the side of the pool. "My mother told me to. She said that every time a man walked through the door she smiled, that way they wouldn't think she was afraid."

The faint memory of his own mother's smile whispered through Gehrin's thoughts, the way she had always rubbed a small bit of red rouge over her cheeks before his father returned home from the palace, sweeping out to greet her husband and pulling Gehrin along beside her. He remembered how she had smiled at him when he had shown her the paper where he had tried to copy Xario's runes for the first time. He wondered if she had ever smiled to hide something.

"I won't tell anyone... what you said," he promised quietly. "Will you come out and get some food? You'll shrivel up like Master Lohi if you stay in that water any longer."

Ruh nodded and pulled himself up onto the stone edge, suddenly looking more like the small boy he had been years ago when Gehrin had first met him. Gehrin handed him his clothes. The bruise on Ruh's cheek from Tahmujin's fist was darkening, swelling around the cut on his jaw. The Takkan boy pulled on his trousers and tunic with trembling fingers.

Then, his hair dripping dark splotches onto his shoulders, Ruh smiled. "Food sounds good."

# CHAPTER TWENTY-TWO

*The Maleki rite of passage from child to adult is comprised of a series of ritu-als. First, they take a young horse that they have chosen from the herd and break it to ride. For four years horse and rider become as one, until the day when the child turns sixteen years old. Then their name is spoken by the Closed Fist and they are given their first swords. They are cut on both arms with the blades so that they will never forget that they are flesh and blood, and must not fall to an enemy sword. Then a tribal elder tattoos dye into their forehead from hairline to the lower eyelid, covering all the skin with the color of their tribe. The Garhis color is a deep red, like blood.*

*- Emissary Otai, "Observations on the Tribes of Malek"*

The ashes from Nar Garhis' pyre were cold to the touch. Syndri scooped another handful up and tucked it safely into a leather pouch. Her hair whipped around her face, her cheeks red and raw from the cold and the salty tears dried on her skin. She filled the pouch and pulled the leather strings tightly shut, tying it to her belt and pulling her thick cloak over it.

Touching her wolf totem, she rose to her feet, looking down at the gray and black stain that was all that remained of her father's great life.

"I will protect the tribe, Father. I will not let them die." She crossed her fists and pressed them to her chest. "Nar Garhis. May the Sky Clans honor your strength above, as we do below."

She turned her back on her father's pyre and mounted Brig, swinging up to his back with ease despite the extra weight of the layers she wore. Brig's warmth was a welcome comfort as Syndri urged him up the first rise outside the village. She turned him in a tight circle at the top and he snorted, pawing at the frozen ground. The long train of Garhis villagers moved slowly up the incline, their possessions carried on their backs, on sleds made of long poles and latticed rope and leather, and on the backs of the horses who carried no riders.

It was a death sentence, these people walking into the winter plains away from the village that had been their home for more than five generations. The grasslands would offer little protection from the enemy tribes. They had two days to reach the border of Da'ham. Emissary Otai had promised them safe passage to Ruk once they reached the other side. The Da'hamian people were not aggressive like the Malek tribes, Otai had told them. Their warlord was called The Artisan, and he had agreed to keep peace.

But the old, young, sick, and injured Garhis moved slowly. Far too slowly. The two days they had until the Tladr and Uratar returned to finish the killing they had started were not enough to reach the border. It would take them at least five days, four if they pressed hard. The warband could have traveled the distance easily, only stopping to rest their mounts for a few hours. But the pitiful survivors in the caravan were like wounded prey. The warriors would be spread thin, driving the kehroxen herd and riding the perimeter of the caravan to scout and guard the vulnerable tribe.

Near the ashes of the pyres that had been hastily burned for the dead, one still flickered hot flames into the air. Ikaio. He had died by the hand of his own tribeswoman, and his totem had not been broken. The Sky Clans would know his name. Syndri frowned. He deserved less honor than her brother had been afforded. She glanced up at the sky, feeling the light snowflakes dot her cheeks. She did not believe the Sky Clans listened to her prayers anymore. But a storm could be deadlier than the Uratar to her people now.

"Hah!" she urged Brig forward toward the caravan, momentarily leaving her place in the protective circle of mounted warriors to check on the wagon carrying her mother. The shallow wagon bed was lined with hay and hides, as warm as it could be made. Several other women sat around Ettlan, Tilis at the front. She looked up as Syndri approached, adjusting the small babe suckling beneath the furs. One small hand reached up toward her neck, the fingers gently splayed across her collarbone.

"She is warm enough?" asked Syndri.

Tilis reached down and laid her palm against Ettlan's cheek. "Warmer than many who walk outside the wagon. She is as safe as we can make her, Syndri. But if she does not wake soon, the little water I have been able to return to her body will not be enough."

"How long?"

Tilis hesitated. "One day. Maybe a little more."

Clenching her fists around the reins, Syndri turned Brig away from the wagon and he leapt into a gallop, eager to have his head. His nostrils flared as he settled into a comfortable pace, hooves kicking up dirt and snow. They returned to their position, one hundred horse lengths from the caravan on the left side. It was going to be a long, slow ride. Syndri could see the herd of kehroxen moving as one through the snow, guided and driven by small figures on horseback.

The kehroxen would clothe and feed them when they reached Ruk, and part of the herd would be sold or traded. Emissary Otai had told Nar Garhis that such animals would fetch a high price in his country.

Syndri turned her gaze out to the open grasslands, the softly rising hills, and the taller bluffs far beyond. She did not want to leave it for a world of rock and stone. The ashes they left behind would disappear, and the village walls would be overgrown with grass and young tree shoots. The thought of the Uratar and Tladr riding across their tribal home, desecrating the Garhis land and fouling the air with their breath nearly drove her mad with hate.

*I will pay for my sins.*

Hoofbeats approached, and Senna rode Rho alongside Brig, the roan mare stepping briskly next to the bigger stallion. The two horses flicked their ears forward and touched noses, whickering softly to each other. Senna wore her wooden shield strapped to her back like a turtle shell, the hilt of her single sword protruding from behind the rim.

"They will come for us when their scouts see that we have left the village," Senna said. "They will know that we mean to escape them."

Syndri cursed under her breath. "Say the word and I will turn back. Running from our land like this makes me feel like a whipped dog."

"Ettlan would be proud of you."

"What?"

Senna smiled and pulled her furs tighter around her neck. "You could have challenged Yugha, but you did not. You could have pushed harder for us to stay in the village, but you did not. You are beginning to balance your closed fist."

"It's what Father would have wanted. He trusted the Northern queen. I do not trust her, but I trust Father," replied Syndri. The intricate Rukian dagger pressed against her hip. It had been a good gift, after all. She remembered the comfortable weight of it in her hand, the way it had flown so easily to its target. It was a good blade.

"We will still have to fight them before we reach the border. We cannot reach it in time," Senna said, giving voice to the thoughts that must have been in every Garhis mind.

"Then we fight. Uhuri is scouting ahead to find a good place for us to protect the tribe."

"He looks at you as if you are the Closed Fist."

Syndri frowned. "I am not."

"But he does, and so does Malon. You fought at the village

together, and you have grown a closeness. Just be careful. I believe they and others would follow you if you challenged Yugha."

Leaning back slightly, Syndri pulled Brig to a halt. "I have not said that I will challenge Yugha. I gave him my swords and my honor as a warrior."

Senna stopped Rho, her braid fluttering over her shoulder as she looked out over the tribe. The white rabbit furs drawn around her neck made her ochre skin and red forehead stand out against the gray landscape.

"Our father's blood runs hot in you, Syndri. And even he believed you and I might rule the Garhis tribe someday. Yugha is no fool. Right now, there are still Garhis who distrust you, but you will fight and shed blood for them, and they will love you again."

The thought of walking through the warriors the way Yugha had, feeling the flat of their blades against her shoulders, the tribe shouting her name to the Sky Clans... Syndri had imagined it before. She had played at it in childhood when her forehead was still bare. But she shook her head.

"Yugha is Closed Fist."

Senna touched her heels to Rho's sides. "Don't be a fool, *teitei*. Even Yugha challenged Father. Do not let yourself be a threat to him. The tribe needs one Fist to follow. Not two."

The roan mare trotted briskly onward, leaving Syndri and Brig behind. The snow was falling a little heavier, but Syndri could still see a fair way out over the sweeping hills and grasslands turning gray-green with the light frost. She watched until Senna was a small speck in the distance, returning to her own place in the protective line. Uhuri and Malon had appeared at her side many times the past few days, but she had thought they only felt kinship with her because of their stand against the Uratar. But in her heart, Syndri knew it was something deeper than that. Malon and Uhuri had chosen to follow her that day, to stand against the tide of Uratar warriors and face death. And only the three of them remained, leaving the bones of dead warriors behind them, sinking slowly back into the earth with the ashes of her father's pyre.

Senna was right. And if Yugha could see it, there was a threat to the balance of the tribe. The warriors needed to all face the grasslands, as Ettlan would have said. If they were turned inward toward each other, they would be blind to the dangers outside. And even if they reached the border of Da'ham, there were still more dangers beyond. No, there was no good reason to challenge Yugha. Not yet. The Northern queen had promised them an alliance, and now it would be time to put her words to the test.

Brig's earlier energy had faded, and he was calmer as they settled into a steady pace. He still wanted to run, his ears flicking back and forth to catch every small sound. Syndri looked back toward the caravan, straining her eyes to catch sight of Ettlan's wagon. She saw it, barely visible from this distance. A massive dark shape walked beside it now. How the great Ke'ral warrior was still standing, much less walking after the wounds he had sustained was nothing less than a deep magic keeping him on his feet. He had torn off the bandages before they left and strapped his bone club to his back. He wore no furs, his heavy brown hide nearly impervious to the cold winter.

Tilis had told how the Hyshir had run to defend her *gat*, pushing women and children inside to protect them from the Uratar. He had slain great numbers of the Uratar, breaking them with his fists and club. Yugha had offered the Ke'ral his own swords in gratitude for saving his family from certain death. Without Hyshir, his wife and children would be among the ashes.

Syndri turned back to the swirling snow.

Temporary shelters were hastily erected each night for a few precious hours of sleep. On the third night, Syndri was nearly falling asleep atop Brig's broad back when the caravan stopped. Yugha would have them moving again early, not willing to risk more than a little rest before pushing the caravan onwards. Syndri helped hold the long structure poles as hides were thrown over the top and lashed down with rope. Only the oldest and youngest would sleep inside, and a few of the injured. The rest of the tribe would have small tents, barely large enough to crawl inside.

Senna, riding back along the path the caravan had already traveled, had come back shortly before evening to tell Yugha that the enemy raiders were approaching swiftly and would be upon them by the next morning. The shallow valley where the caravan had stopped was not the worst place they could be caught, but the wide-open grasslands to the south would make it difficult for the Garhis tribe to stop the Tladr and Uratar from reaching the caravan.

So, they devised a way to build a different kind of wall. The warband tethered their horses, and every able-bodied warrior and villager began to lay hides and brush along the mouth of the valley. The hides would burn with excessive smoke, clouding the vision of the enemy warband.

Women and older Garhis walked alongside warriors, packing the ground with any dry roots and old rags and hides. Anything that could be spared. Syndri carried a stack of hides behind a pair of elderly women, sweat running down her arms and face despite the cold. Behind her, Malon and Uhuri carried their own stacks, their outer layer of furs and hide clothing thrown to the side.

The younger warrior followed Malon around like a puppy, his fresh face still somehow innocent despite the death and devastation he had survived. Uhuri was nineteen, old enough to have seen several years of raids and be a blooded warrior, but young enough to still see the world with bright eyes. Though she was only older than Uhuri by two summers, Syndri felt as old as an elder as she bent beneath the stack of hides, and he jogged past her with his own.

When it was over, the walk from the prepared fire wall to the caravan might as well have been a mountain climb. Some of the warriors went to sleep amongst the villagers in small tents. But Syndri and most of the others were headed back to their posts. They would sleep beside their horses, taking warmth from the large beasts through the night when they were not on watch.

Malon and Syndri were paired for the watch that night. One would sleep while the other sat mounted and watching the darkness for any sign of their pursuers. The border was close now, and if they pushed hard the next day, they might reach it in one more night. They had moved faster than Syndri had thought possible, but the constant looming danger behind them had lent wings to the slowest feet.

"Sleep," Malon said abruptly when they reached their post a fair way off from the caravan. "I will watch first."

"I can watch," murmured Syndri stubbornly.

Malon snorted. "If you keep watch, the whole tribe of Uratar could ride in and kill us all, and you would still sleep like Tilis' babe."

Nodding, Syndri dismounted, too tired to argue further. Her arm itched and pulled uncomfortably at its mending skin as she moved. She pulled Brig's reins back alongside his shoulder and tapped the inside of his leg. He buckled, lowering slowly to the ground with a deep snort. Her sword sheaths came off her shoulders, but only to be tucked in against her chest for easy reach if the Uratar came upon them in the night. Pulling the heavy hide blanket from his back, Syndri wrapped it around herself, tucking her body in alongside Brig's round shaggy barrel. He lipped at her hair, pulling a few mouthfuls of frozen grass blades from the ground. His deep whoofing breaths soothed her to sleep instantly.

And she awoke to the war horns.

Malon was dragging her from her hide blanket, pushing her toward Brig as he heaved his big body off the ground. The first light of dawn was warming the plains, and as Syndri pulled her swords onto her back, she saw the tribe milling about in confusion in the little valley below, hastily pulling apart their shelters and forming back into a line.

Jumping up to Brig's back, Syndri sent him into a full gallop. To the south, she saw a mass of figures approaching, and many of the Garhis warband had already gathered, standing between the tribe and the approaching strength of the Uratar and Tladr.

Malon followed close behind until they reached the warband and heard Yugha shouting commands. The Garhis warriors were not used to this kind of fighting, standing and waiting for the enemy to approach while the caravan behind them ran for safety across the border. Brig pawed at the dirt, the scent of the approaching battle in his nostrils, and he fought against Syndri's tight hold on his reins. The warband spread out into a shallow spearhead shape, pointed toward the south and ready to punch through the line of enemy warriors. Behind the first line was a second, a smaller defense to stop the Uratar and Tladr from breaking through to the caravan in case the ditch failed.

Yugha rode along the line to the point of the warband, his swords held high as he pulled his great bay mare to a halt. "They do not pass this warband!" he roared, his face red and mottled. "They do not reach the tribe!"

"GARHIS!"

The cry went up from nearly two hundred throats in response, and as the Uratar and Tladr tribes rode closer, the Garhis warband began to move forward to meet them. Syndri caught glimpses of long spear shafts bobbing up and down alongside the enemy mounts. The familiar battle rage kindled in her belly as she cursed the Uratar and the Tladr and the Kateshi in one breath. *Nameless, rootless, they are not Malek.* There was no honor in a spear, no contest of strength and skill. It was a coward's weapon, to pierce an enemy before you could see his face.

Brig's long strides were smooth like water, and Syndri let go of the reins and drew her swords. The impact of the three tribes was crushing, the spear point of the Garhis warband thrusting through the front lines of Uratar and Tladr. Spears snapped and pierced through scale armor with the momentum, swords cleaved into necks and limbs. Horses screamed, reared, and bit at each other, driven half-mad along with their riders at the smell of blood and the deafening roar. Syndri's body moved as if it were possessed by a spirit of fire, her swords carving into man and beast alike. Brig carried her into the midst of the enemy warriors, where the mad charge stopped as the tribes tightened together like a knotted rope.

Then the grasslands bled.

Brig screamed as a spear lodged in his right flank and he stumbled, dipping to the side as he pulled away. Syndri swung with him, her legs gripping his sides. She gripped the spear shaft as it stabbed toward her a second time and yanked it from the warrior's hand, pulling him forward over his horse's neck. Her sword cut halfway through the side of his neck and bit deep into his mount's black mane. He fell beneath the stamping hooves.

There was no sound except the ringing in Syndri's ears. It was as if the whole world had gone silent to watch the slaughter, the Sky peering down in jealousy as the earth drank its fill. She killed with a reckless abandon, the faces of her brother and her father spurring her forward to live, to cut vengeance from the Uratar and Tladr like the heart from a chest. Despite his weak right hind leg, Brig carried her onwards, his muscles quivering, a dark wraith weaving through the carnage. *Sky Clans give him strength.*

Syndri pulled one of her swords free from the gut of a Tladr warrior, his spear falling limply to the side with a hollow thud. She swung Brig around on his strong side, taking heaving breaths in the small space she had created around her. The initial clot of fighting had spread out over the plains, wide swaths cleared between smaller groups still gripped in combat both on horseback and on the ground. She caught sight of Malon not far away, smashing the totem of a fallen warrior beneath the heel of her boot. The one-armed warrior was splattered in gore, her face indistinguishable between the red of her forehead and the red smeared across her cheeks and nose. Kicking the body of her fallen foe aside, Malon screamed "GARHIS" to the skies, her teeth bloody as she spat something out of her mouth.

*My father's wolves.* Brig trembled beneath Syndri, the big stallion limping with each step. She slid from his back, a hard jolt punching through her legs as they hit the ground. She ran to Malon, dispatching an Uratar warrior who came to challenge her, his sword raised just a little too high. Syndri's blades took him through his collarbone as his own swing feebly died against her armor scales.

Malon saw her and strode forward, pointing toward the thickest knot of fighting back where the Garhis warriors had formed the center of their crescent shape. A wall of fire as tall as a man had leapt up behind the tangle of tribes, cutting off the mouth of the small valley as the flames hungrily devoured the kindling and gnawed on the wine-soaked hides and rags. Beyond it, the caravan pushed onward.

Both Brig and Malon's horse were wounded, their sides heaving as they stood nearby with blood and lather on their flanks. The fighting was thickest back toward the caravan, the Garhis warband straining against the pressing current of warriors attempting to push through and attack the vulnerable men, women, and children beyond.

A flash in Syndri's peripheral vision sent her reeling back to dodge the thrust of a long spear shaft that snaked through the air two handspans from her face. She reached up and grabbed hold of the weapon, kicking out against the Tladr's chest. He stumbled back, and she stabbed her right sword into the ground, getting a good grasp on the spear haft. As the man looked up, righting himself, the spear cracked across his face, blood pouring from his mouth and nose as he fell.

Syndri stepped one booted foot on his neck as he struggled to push her away, and she leered down at him. Raising the spear, she punched it down into his chest with all her strength. The scale armor cracked, but the spearhead only made a shallow wound as it drove past the layers beneath. The man screamed and pushed against Syndri as she raised the spear again, leaning harder into the foot against his neck. The spear drove down a second time, and this time it opened a gaping hole in the man's lower chest. He went rigid and gasped his final breaths with a wet gurgling sound. Syndri left him to die, retrieving her sword and running for Brig, who was still standing where she had left him, his eyes rolling white as he stamped restlessly. The small clearing around him was littered with bodies.

Both Malon and Uhuri were locked against their enemies nearby, but Uhuri was still mounted on his roan, the horse snapping at the two Uratar who were circling them. Syndri reached Brig and pulled herself up onto his back, wincing at the way the stallion's weight shifted to stay balanced against his weaker wounded side.

Letting a burst of the charged adrenaline rushing through her out with a wild scream, Syndri pointed Brig at one of the warriors circling Uhuri, and the black stallion collided with the smaller horse, his big shoulder crashing against the Uratar mount's chest and knocking the horse from his feet, pinning the warrior beneath. Syndri raised her sword to Uhuri and urged Brig onwards toward the thick of the fighting. The noise was disorienting, screams, war cries, the sound of the horses shrieking or neighing, the clash of swords and spears, and the faint cries of the crows that were already circling above filled Syndri's head with the discordant chaos of battle.

In the distance, the caravan continued to crawl its way toward the border, leaving most of the death and violence behind. The fire wall had died down a little, still roaring in the small ditch, but the flames were not as high as they had been before. A veil of heavy gray smoke made it nearly impossible to see beyond the ditch. Soon, the wall of smoke and flame would die down too much to keep the Uratar and Tladr at bay, and there were still too many for the Garhis warband to handle at once. Syndri needed to get behind the wall.

Brig's stride was not as strong, but he carried Syndri through the carnage toward the thick line where the Garhis warriors had stopped most of the enemy mounts from crossing toward the caravan. But some of the enemy had broken through. Too many. Syndri watched as an Uratar woman dug her heels into her horse's sides and sent him hurtling over the flames.

Leaning over Brig's neck, Syndri settled into his smooth gallop as he charged for the caravan, each thrust of his powerful hind legs accented by a faint limp. Brig faltered as they approached the ditch, his ancient inborn fear of fire awakening and challenging Syndri's command for him to fling himself at the flames. The smoke wall broke around Syndri as Brig bunched his muscles and leapt over the ditch, his belly clearing the top of the fire. The valley was already littered with bodies scattered around where the small group of

Garhis warriors in the second wing had waited for their enemies to breach the ditch.

Among the warriors still locked in combat or chasing enemies across the valley floor, Syndri caught sight of Hyshir at the far end, his bone club swinging just in time to knock a Tladr warrior clear off the back of her mount. She crumpled against a boulder as if she were boneless.

A Garhis warrior was backed up against the left slope, pressed by three Uratar. Syndri slid off Brig's back and sprinted for them, driving a sword into the back of the first man's head. He dropped, taking Syndri's blade with him. She sucked in a breath and ducked to miss the swing of the woman who turned to face her.

Finally, a warrior with real weapons was facing her. The woman bared her teeth and came at Syndri like a cornered wildcat, her swords slicing through the air with blinding speed. Syndri fell back, narrowly missing having her face cleaved in two as a blade slid along the right side of her face, opening a wound from hairline to jaw. Blood trickled into Syndri's eye, and she tried to blink it away, blocking the Uratar's heavy blows with her single remaining sword.

Rolling to the side, Syndri heard the woman's blade cut into the ground behind her. Her hand closed over a fist sized rock. She shoved at the Uratar's leg, knocking her off balance and scrambling up and over the woman as she fell, knocking the sword away and smashing the rock down against her enemy's face again and again. Finally, she rose to her feet, shaky, and wiped her arm across her face.

She heard a war horn. Garhis.

On the other side of the ditch, she could make out the sight of the Uratar and Tladr retreating, the scattered remains of their warriors galloping away to the South as the Garhis held their ground. Shouts of victory began to cut through the rest of the noise, and Syndri sank to her knees.

A soft wind blew strands of her matted hair around her face. She tilted her chin up toward the Sky and raised a fist in defiance.

*You cannot turn a blind eye to us now. We have proved the honor of our blades.* Syndri reached down and yanked the dead Uratar's totem from her neck and threw it down to the ground. With her sword, she swung and cut the crude owl visage in two.

Garhis warriors began riding over the fire wall's dying flames, whooping and lifting their blades high in the air as they rode back through the valley. Others led horses through a gap at the far end where the flames had completely dissipated, carrying wounded Garhis on the backs of their mounts. Syndri stayed on the ground as the horses thundered around her. Brig limped over to her and blew hot air against her face. Syndri reached up and pulled his head down to her, pressing their foreheads together. He lipped at her tunic.

"Come," she whispered to him. "You have carried me far enough."

Pulling herself up against his shoulder, she ran her hands over his hide, the dried lather and blood caking his shaggy winter coat into a crusted sheet. His right flank quivered as her fingers reached his wound. The spear had cut deep enough to leave a jagged hole, but it would heal. She would pack it with herbs when they reached the caravan.

Hoofbeats stopped beside her, and Rho's familiar roan head bobbed into view. The mare's nostrils flared, and she stamped, still restless from the battle, but she looked unscathed. Senna was perched on the mare's back, blood-soaked, with the rim of her shield visible behind her shoulders.

"They are retreating," Senna said. "Yugha wants us to press forward to the border before they regroup. They may still come back."

Syndri looked out to the battlefield, where the crows were beginning to settle among the dead and dying. The warband gathering in the valley was much smaller than the one that had formed that morning. Perhaps one hundred swords left, if her swift perusal was accurate.

"No pyres?" asked Syndri.

"No pyres," replied Senna quietly.

Syndri knew there was no time for pyres. The bodies of the Garhis and their enemies would lie together under the Sky and wait for the vultures already beginning to circle above. It was just one more thing the Uratar and Tladr had taken from them. One more thing they would pay for in blood. Syndri gathered Brig's reins and turned to lead him toward the caravan. Senna rode alongside her in silence. There was nothing more to say beneath the weight of so much death.

As they drew close enough to see the caravan beyond the end of the valley, a gray horse galloped toward them with a small boy bumping along behind his withers. It was Tilis and Yugha's second son, waving his hands at them.

"Syndri! Senna! Come quickly, your mother has woken!"

# CHAPTER TWENTY-THREE

*When I was a boy, there was a window in my room.*
*The sky outside was bluer than lapis lazuli, the way I remember my mother's*
*eyes.*
*In a world of gray stone, when I closed my eyes, sometimes I could remember*
*the blue.*

*- Sonho*

Xario crouched in the sand of the training yard, the wide sleeves of his simple house tunic rolled up past his elbows. He pressed his hand gently against Eiri's back, straightening her posture. Her little eyebrows were pulled together in concentration, lips pressed in a thin line. She was so tiny that she barely met Xario's height when he was crouched next to her, but she held the small wooden staff tightly in her little fist, determined.

"When you let go, follow the spear with your hand," Xario whispered at her shoulder. "Don't tense your arm."

Eiri drew back and hurled the staff forward. It landed sideways about a man's height away from them. Xario laughed. "A mighty warrior we'll make of you yet."

The little girl frowned at him, her dark eyes serious. For a moment, she looked so much like Gehrin that Xario's smile faltered. She had the same brooding intensity as Gehrin when she was focused on learning something new, but in moments of play, her spirit was light and joyful like her mother's.

"I did not throw as far as you, *yabo*."

Xario pulled her up to sit on his knee. "No, but when I was young, I did not throw as far as I do now. You will grow strong and then your spear will fly over the wall like a bird."

Eiri giggled and reached up to touch his face. She inspected the light scratchy stubble on his jaw that had grown after two days without shaving. It was the first time Xario had spent a morning with her since the day he had arrived back at Counsellor Hallix's house. She had followed him around whenever he was inside, her little slippered footsteps pattering away behind him as she begged for him to play with her dolls or to teach her how to throw a spear.

"I see you are still hoping our little sister will follow in your footsteps, Xario."

Xario stood and turned to see his brother Kurin striding toward them from the stables, his green robe dusty from riding. Kurin's smile crinkled the corners of his eyes, the same mischievous gleam in them that he had always had.

"Kurin, welcome back." Xario reached out and clasped arms with his brother, still holding Eiri. The little girl squealed in delight and held out her hands, letting Kurin pull her away from their oldest brother. She immediately began pulling at the strap of his satchel.

"Have you brought me something?" she asked, eyes shining in anticipation. Kurin frowned, pretending to think.

"Was I meant to?"

Eiri pouted, and Kurin laughed at her, setting her down on the ground and opening his satchel. He withdrew a small paper package tied with a blue ribbon and handed it to her. She untied the ribbon and gasped at the fresh *kiji* cakes inside the package. The smell wafted toward Xario and he smiled at the thought of the sweetshop baker carefully wrapping his wares for yet another Hallix child.

Stuffing one of the cakes into her mouth, Eiri ran toward the house, excited to show her mother the prize.

"I am sorry I could not return sooner. Father told me to finish taking stock of the harvests before I came back," said Kurin. He wiped a hand across his forehead to clear it of the road dust and sweat and scrutinized Xario. "The Legion has treated you well, it seems."

"Well enough," replied Xario. The air seemed thin and strained, a constant reminder of the tension between them. The years had not done anything to heal the rift, and if anything, the time they had spent away from each other had only deepened it further. Kurin had set himself to the task of learning to be the overseer of their father's farmlands, proving his skill for increasing the production of each harvest and the management of his father's workers. He had left the use of spears behind, turning as far away from Xario's path as he could. His face was still fresh and youthful, but there was a hard set to his eyes, a stiff posture in his shoulders. He looked far too old for his seventeen years.

The silence stretched between them, attempting and failing to bridge the rift. Kurin brushed his hands over his clothing. "I can hardly appear at dinner in front of Thiri looking like this," he said. "The bathhouse summons me. Perhaps after dinner you would join me for drinks at the Stone Lily House?"

Kurin's casual mention of the lavish courtesan house surprised Xario, but he gave a curt nod. "If Father allows it."

"Ah yes, I often forget that Father takes a closer interest in your daily life," Kurin gave a tight smile. "Your filial loyalty is inspiring."

"Go take your sharp tongue to the bathhouse. Wash it with the rest of you," replied Xario. He watched, fists clenched at his sides, as Kurin laughed and made his way toward the small building near the house, pulling his dust-shrouded cloak off his shoulders.

Xario felt as though he were doing nothing but taking up space, casting his shadow wherever his father told him to. Master Lohi had once said that it was often the fate of sons to squabble over the affections of their father. Kurin envied him because he was the firstborn, the heir to all their father's hopes of casting more than a shadow over the great throne of Katesh. There was nothing for Kurin to lose, he would inherit the vast lands of their father's house and live wealthy, married to a daughter of one of the noble houses in the peace of his own house.

If the king chose him, Xario's future would be far bleaker, chained like a prisoner to a throne in the palace, a house of schemes and knives in the night. A future in which his own sons would tear each other to pieces to follow in his footsteps. King Kinhariian's two brothers were long dead, executed on the Blood Stones for attempting to assassinate their own flesh and blood. And yet, the King had asked him of his desire to rule. Whether or not he would free Xario from the succession was still unknown.

And even with a promising inheritance, Kurin still held contempt, still looked at Xario with the veiled face of a man trying to prove himself a stranger. Xario shielded his eyes against the light in the open sky, watching a kestrel wing high above the walls, a piercing scream against the wind. The bird wheeled in a wide bank over Lord Hallix's house, wingtips fluttering against the current. Xario thought ruefully of the golden fox and wolf carving guarding the king's throne. The fox had his cunning and the wolf his fierce bravery, but both beasts so revered by Katesh were bound to the earth, locked in an eternal battle. The kestrel rose above them both, free to soar and watch the carnage below.

The bird disappeared with a final cry, something inside Xario followed it, reaching after it beyond the walls of his father's house, far into the Northern mountains and the great sea.

The low table had nearly disappeared beneath the bowls and platters, the aroma of spiced Maleki beef, sweet rice, and steamed vegetables matching the visual delights of gem-like fruits, golden breads, and smooth mint cakes. Xario sat across from his brother, holding his back and shoulders straight with a noble rigidity that would have had no place in the camps of the Legion. Kurin seemed to have left his ire behind in the soapy water of the bathhouse. He was quiet, all his bravado dissipated in front of their father. They all held an uncomfortable silence. Counsellor Hallix had not given his permission to begin the meal, as Thiri was not present yet.

Xario almost wished he were sitting at Bari Ujo's table again, playing the dutiful son as Counsellor Hallix threw his verbal spears across the table over candied plums. There, father and son lowered blades at a common enemy. Here in the assumed sanctuary of the Hallix estate, the blades were turned on each other, held just close enough to the throat to be felt.

A panel slid open, and Thiri walked through, her gentle, tiny steps silent against the floor as she ushered in a guest. Kasaii appeared close behind Thiri, leaning on an elegantly carved staff, her wide blue skirt and white jacket hauntingly familiar. Xario's blood ran cold. Glancing across the table, he saw Kurin's jaw tighten with the same sudden emotion. The embroidered white swans spread wings over the expanse of blue silk, a striking fabric made by one of the most skilled silk artisans in Keld. A dress made for Xario's mother as a gift from Counsellor Hallix on her twentieth birthday.

Xario crushed a handful of fabric from his own *seri* in his fist, his stomach tight. It was as if a ghost had stepped through the doorway in the footsteps of his childhood friend, his mother's form carried in Kasaii's youthful beauty. Lost in confusion, Xario turned to his father and saw Counsellor Hallix reclined against his cushions, a faint smile touching the corners of his mouth.

"Kasaii, welcome. It pleases me to see you wearing my gift."

*Gift...* the word soured in Xario's ears. His father did not give gifts without a cost. Kasaii smiled through red-tinted lips and bowed. The silver dove comb was nestled in the gleaming pitch-black coil of hair at the top of her head. The pleasure of seeing it there nearly overshadowed the shock at the sight of Lady Hallix's dress. Kurin rose from his cushion and held out his hand, leading

Kasaii to the open place at the table. He gave her a bow, courteous despite the strange circumstances. Xario inwardly berated himself for not rising first. Kasaii sank to the cushion, using the edge of the table to support herself as she sat. She inclined her head to Xario, and he returned the gesture awkwardly, waiting for his father to explain.

"It is a pleasure to have you dining with us, Kasaii. You relayed my wishes for your parents' continued good health?" asked Counsellor Hallix smoothly.

"I have, my lord." Kasaii smiled. "My father and mother are both in good health and have sent their gratitude for your generosity toward our family."

Xario wanted to rip his hair out by the roots as his father and Kasaii exchanged polite formalities. Kasaii's father had joined them at the table only twice that Xario could remember, and he was head overseer of Lord Hallix's grainfields, a man of humble beginnings who had proven invaluable in his shrewd business sense and knowledge of agriculture. But Xario could think of no reason why his father would gift Kasaii such a precious possession or invite her to sit at the table without the presence of her parents.

Counsellor Hallix reached for a skewer of spiced beef, and Thiri filled the wine cups. Kurin dug into the candied plums. He still looked as if he were simmering beneath his calm exterior, bubbling like a pot of soup in a cauldron. Xario accepted a small bowl when Thiri handed it to him, but even the sight of the perfectly cooked gold, white, and orange root vegetables did nothing to restore his appetite.

Kasaii sat perfectly composed, bringing small sips of peppered cabbage soup to her lips with the spoon, looking every inch like a poised noblewoman. The little beads hanging from the silver dove's wings in her hair shivered whenever she moved.

The table was nearly silent but for the sounds of the food being eaten, very little of it by Xario. He managed a few bites of vegetables but kept more company with his wine cup. Kurin ate as if he were a man starved, eating with just enough courtesy to mask the amount of food that was disappearing into his mouth. Eiri was not present, she'd been left with the servants in the kitchens to eat so she would not disturb the conversation at Counsellor Hallix's table. Not that there was much of that to be had until the lord of the house settled back in contentment, plucking the last grapes from the stem in his hand.

"Your father's work has been exceptional," he finally said to Kasaii. "He has a rare mind for calculations and working the land. I hear that you share much of that talent. Master Lohi always praised your intelligence when you were young and learning alongside my sons."

Kasaii set down her cup and folded her hands politely in her lap, a slight flush in her cheeks. "Thank you for your generous words, my lord. If a student shows promise, the praise must be given to the teacher. I was only fortunate to learn from such a revered master scholar, thanks to your patronage. I am indebted to you."

Waving the compliments away, Counsellor Hallix refilled his wine. "I am pleased that you accepted my request. I'm sure it did not come as a surprise to you that I have need of your talents. I need someone with a mind for business and politics. My living sons are detained elsewhere, and Gehrin's place at my side remains empty."

Xario's grip tightened on his cup. Kasaii's gaze flickered over to him so briefly he almost missed it, but he saw a soft concern in it, the shared thread of his brother's death and the void of grief in their memories pulling at them both. Kurin had slowed his ravenous consumption of food and his discomfort showed plainly on his face. Whether it was from his stomach or their brother's name, Xario could not guess.

"I believe he was fond of you," said Counsellor Hallix. "A sentiment shared by all my sons in youthful years. But you are not children anymore, and duty to family and liege lord must outweigh the frivolity of youth. Can I trust you with those responsibilities?"

Though the question was directed at Kasaii, the barbs of his father's words sank into Xario like claws. He filled his third cup of wine, flinging propriety to the wind.

"If your sons thought so fondly of her, surely we can trust their judgment of her excellent character," Thiri spoke quietly, touching Kasaii's hand. "Your devotion to your family is commendable, my dear."

Kasaii smiled at her. "I look forward to serving my family and the noble house of Counsellor Hallix. If my humble talents are of use, may Sharai bless them to their purpose."

The earnestness of her words and the pure goodness that radiated from her as she sat, unmoved by Counsellor Hallix's sharply edged words, sent a knife blade twisting into Xario's chest. His father would use her to whatever end he saw to benefit his ambitions, and it would please him that one of Master Lohi's most praised students was under his employ.

Counsellor Hallix raised his wine cup. "To your family's good health." He paused, considering her for a moment. "The silver comb you wear is a fine piece. A gift from your father?"

Warmth spread through Xario's face. It had been a mistake, gifting the comb to Kasaii. It was far too expensive to be meaningless, inappropriate for the son of the king's counsellor to give to an overseer's daughter. Yet the thought of it gracing any head but hers filled Xario with a strange resentment.

Kasaii reached up and touched delicate fingers to the silver. "No, my lord. A friend."

"A generous friend, indeed. Xario?"

Shaking out of his thoughts, Xario felt as if he were being held at the point of a spear when his father's gaze shifted toward him. Counsellor Hallix left no question in his son's mind whether he knew of the comb's origin.

"Please escort our guest to her palanquin. We have kept her from her family long enough."

Xario rose to his feet and bowed to Kasaii as she carefully pulled herself to her feet with her staff and smoothed the vibrant blue silk of her skirt. He did not look at his father or Kurin as the servant opened the paneled door for them, and he led Kasaii out into the inner courtyard. She walked behind him, her skirts swishing gently over the floor, masking her uneven steps. Xario tried to think of what he could say after the uncomfortable undercurrent of the dinner conversation, but every word sounded insufficient and frivolous when he tried saying them to himself. His father had seen enough to consider Kasaii an asset, and a threat. He would not easily let her slip away now, not while he believed Xario had some attachment to her.

Xario refused to look back. He did not want to admit that there was some merit to his father's suspicion. The fondness he had once held for Kasaii as a friend in childhood was giving way to something that could threaten his father's carefully laid ambitions. Something that could stand in the way of him gaining the throne. Xario grimaced and reached out to open the door that would lead to the outer courtyard and the waiting palanquin.

"Xario?"

His name sounded far too gentle coming from her voice. The skirt swishes had stopped, and she held her hands politely folded, watching him with far too discerning a gaze. He turned back to her, trying to mask his discomfort. By her expression, he had failed utterly. She stayed an appropriate distance from him.

"Have I upset you?"

"No."

His short answer hurt her, he could tell. He looked away toward the *sabba* tree in the inner courtyard, fixing his gaze on its dim outline and calling himself every curse he'd collected in the ranks of the Legion. She smoothed the pained expression away from her face and replaced it with the bright-eyed calm that had been there before. Xario suddenly wished he could chase the hurt, soothe it away with a soft touch to her cheek.

He was the son of one of the most powerful men in Katesh, and he did not deserve her. It had twisted something primal and protective in him when his father had brought her into that room, parading her in his mother's dress like a spoil of war. He meant to leave Xario no path but the one that led to the throne, to bind him to a singular purpose until it was done.

"Thank your father again for inviting me to your home," said Kasaii softly, stepping around him toward the door. Her fingertips found the seam and pulled the panel across. "I will pray for your safe return to the Legion."

"Kasaii." He reached out and touched the soft silk of her jacket sleeve. "Are you doing this to please my father?"

"He has been generous to my family."

"You say that because it is the proper response but is it what *you* want?" replied Xario sharply. He imagined Kasaii accompanying his father to a dinner with Bari Ujo and his son, their snake's eyes marking her as prey.

Kasaii stepped through the door, slipping her feet into the small, embroidered shoes outside on the step. "What I want?" she smiled, but it was sad, drawing the sparkle away from her eyes. "We are small birds caught in a great wind, and if we do not find a perch, we will be blown away. In your father's house, I have security and the chance to use my lessons for more than a beautiful brushstroke. I could not ask to be connected to a greater house than your father's."

"He will use you."

The truth was painful as it slipped past his teeth, but Xario could not hide it in lesser words anymore. Kasaii fixed him with a hard stare.

"Do you fear him that greatly?" she asked. "Or do you think so little of me?"

Swallowing past the desire to change her mind, Xario saw the strong-willed young girl who had stood in front of Master Lohi's class and proudly recited her knowledge of history, economics, and the courts, the runes, and their meanings. She had grown, just as he had, but she had lost none of her strength. He had hidden behind the armor of the Legion, believing that it would shield him from the robes of a king. And as he stood on his father's doorstep, looking down at the silver comb crowning Kasaii's moonlit face, he realized the depths of his own fear.

"I would not see you come to harm."

The wide white sleeve of Kasaii's jacket brushed past Xario's green one as she touched his hand, the softest brush of skin against skin. "It is not just for me. If you are the king's choice, then I will be close enough to be of help to you."

Xario looked down to where her fingers were curled gently around the edge of his palm. The thought of leaving Keld and returning to the Legion lost its inviting glow, and he imagined taking her into his arms, pressing her close against his chest and smelling the soft scent of her hair. Instead, he closed his hand, enveloping hers in their shared warmth. Words were clumsy things on his thick tongue, so he said none of them.

He led her to the waiting palanquin across the little pond, helping her step up into the soft cushions, and letting go of her hand with regret. When she disappeared through the front gates, he stood in the same spot until Kurin came to find him, his thumbs tucked into his wide belt.

"Another thing you cannot have. Even a future king must make sacrifices."

The last of the warmth from the memory of Kasaii's soft hand drained away from Xario at the sound of his brother's voice. He curled his lip. "Take your jealousy somewhere else."

"Jealous? No. I pity you."

"I want neither your jealousy nor your pity."

Kurin shrugged. "You are the sum of all of Father's ambitions, and for that, I will pity you. Perhaps Gehrin might have married Kasaii, but not you. She is more likely to become Father's third wife."

Xario spun on his heel and grabbed the front of Kurin's *seri*, dragging him close. "You will not speak of her again if you cannot control your tongue."

Teeth flashed in the dark as a satisfied smile appeared on Kurin's lips. "Careful, brother. You show too much of your heart. It seems Father was right to suspect you." He yanked his *seri* out of Xario's hands. "I pity you because I am free, and you will spend your life chained to Father's will."

Kurin stalked away into the dark and called for a palanquin, his shoulders rigid. Xario stood silent, fists still clenched and shaking with his anger. The walls of the courtyard closed in around him, and he hated himself.

The black mare was skittish, and Xario had already tightened the cinch of her saddle twice. He scolded her softly, thumping a hand against her belly and pulling her a step forward. She blew out through her nose, and he pulled the cinch tighter again, finally secure now that she had stopped holding in her breath. Xario pulled himself up onto her back, once again strapped into the black armor he had worn months ago when he first rode into Keld. He had grown distant from its weight, the scales clattering quietly as he walked. He reached down for the spear that the stable servant handed to him reverently, the weapon's familiar grip returning some of the inner strength he felt he had lost during the days in Counsellor Hallix's house.

"You look like one of Sharai's Oathsworn, brother." Kurin stood near the edge of the stable yard; arms folded across his chest as he scrutinized Xario. "Armor suits you better than fine silks."

Kurin's words held none of the sharp bite of the previous night. Darkened by the remnants of his wine drinking at the courtesan house, he looked worn and far older than seventeen. Xario wished for the hundred thousandth time that Gehrin had never died, that both of his brothers stood in the yard to send him on his way. He wished that perhaps they had all been born sons of some humble farmer whose only ambitions were to tend his field and produce a harvest that provided for his family. He wished that the king's son had never been murdered, and that he had never watched the *aqqa* die on the Blood Stones. He wished for a great many things, and he knew that behind the contempt and indifference that Kurin wore like his own set of armor, that his brother wished the same.

He raised his spear in salute, and Kurin bowed. Riding past the front gates, Xario pulled the mare to a restless halt once again to bid one more farewell. Thiri held Eiri in her arms, the little girl's lower lip protruding in a pout. Xario settled the end of the spear haft into the side of his stirrup.

"Ah, this won't do," he said. Eiri looked up at him from underneath her long black eyelashes. The lip quivered. "I will have only the memory of your sad face to bring with me to the Legion. How can I be happy if I only remember your sadness?"

Eiri took a shuddering breath and offered a valiant attempt at a smile. She held something up to him, one of her small dolls.

"Take it so you remember me," she said. Xario held the small toy in his hand, the smiling face and black hair mimicking the little girl who was watching him from below. He tucked it safely into his tunic.

"I'll bring her back safely," he promised. He turned and nodded his head respectfully to Thiri.

"Thank you," she said. "We will miss you, Xario. May Sharai and his warriors protect you until you can return safely to us. And Xario? I believe he is proud of you."

Xario did not turn back to look at the house, toward the room where his father still sat at his low table, incense curling into smoke above his head, bent to some task that required his full attention. He had not said farewell, only given a curt command to continue observing his fellow commanders and to expect another summons at any moment, should his presence be required.

"Your good health. I will return when I can," Xario replied, giving Eiri one last wink. She waved at him, still holding onto her smile for him until he turned away to join the other Legion warriors waiting for him outside the gates.

# CHAPTER TWENTY-FOUR

*The runes are tethers to the deep wells of magic within the earth's heart. Those few who can feel the pulse of that power must strike a delicate balance, for if the tether is pulled too hard, it will fray and break. If it is pulled too weakly, the magic will respond in kind. I have seen many who were able to feel the presence of the earth's power, but in all my years, I have found only one for whom this balance came as naturally as breathing.*

*- Master Lohi's writings*

Hajja trembled on the stone floor in front of Master Lohi, dark circles under his eyes, his fingers gripping the carved piece of iron. Black strings of hair hung sweat-soaked over his face, and the scarred rip on the side of his mouth showed teeth with the effort of hours pulling the tethers of magic from somewhere beneath their feet. He swayed like a man drunk, the muscles of his thin arms straining. Master Lohi sighed and snapped the end of his staff against the side of Hajja's head.

"Enough."

The iron clattered to the floor, and Hajja's hands sank limply to his lap. The two boys sitting next to him were silent, waiting for

Master Lohi's instruction. Master Lohi watched the side of Liv's jaw tighten and relax. Once, Liv had attempted to plead for Hajja to be given a moment of rest, but Master Lohi had simply kept them in the small stone room longer. There was no room for such sympathies, not with the powers at Hajja's fingertips within his reach. They were still young, plagued by their own softness despite the years of training beneath Tahmujin's iron fist.

The other boy, Yan, was stocky and looked like a boulder sitting on the stone floor for how little he moved. Tahmujin said he had great promise in hand-to-hand combat and would often rely on his fists when a weapon was knocked from his grasp. Master Lohi turned back to Hajja.

"For years you have sat in this room, learning to draw on the magic like water from a well, and yet you strain and grunt like a mason trying to break stone. You cannot force the earth to give up its power. You must become one with it."

Hajja's empty eyes stared into nothing, as they often did, and Master Lohi clicked his teeth together, annoyed. The boy was plagued by too many dark spirits to be truly useful, but what was done was done.

"Perhaps we need to return to the foundation, since you seem to have lost the progress we have been making. Liv, what are the runes?"

"Master, the runes are gateways into the power within the earth," the boy responded. His voice was carefully groomed into an emotionless timbre, devoid of any true passion or interest. Master Lohi felt a pang of regret for that, at least, remembering the days when Liv had once been so attentive to his lessons on the history of the runes. But better that he understand them and be able to utilize them than feel temporary passions.

"And the rune Hajja is attempting to command?"

"*Terha*, Master. The hand defends the weak, it is a rune of protection."

"And what does the *terha* rune represent within the body?"

Liv's eyes did not flicker from the wall. "Strength, Master. It is observed to add strength beyond a man's common abilities."

"And the limitations?"

"It is difficult to maintain, Master, and leaves the body weaker when the power withdraws."

Master Lohi nodded, tapping his staff against the floor. "If you had been blessed with the abilities that Hajja was, perhaps we would be farther along in our studies. If you are to be *bruhai*, you must be greater than mortal men. Do you truly believe that your skills with a spear or a knife will keep you alive? Many great warriors have been slain more easily than a goat kid by weaker men in a moment of apathy. The power of the runes at your fingertips gives you strength like the Firstborn, taught by Sharai's Oathsworn themselves. That is the gift you give to your king."

"Yes Master." Yan and Liv spoke in tandem over Hajja's sullen silence. Master Lohi retreated to the chair at the opposite side of the room and lowered himself down into it with a groan. He had stood on the stone of Blackvale for too many days, and already he longed to return to the cushioned comforts of his home in Keld. He let his tired eyes wander skeptically over the three boys kneeling on the floor. Worthless, years of planning and training culminating in these gormless cretins, these thick-wits... he sighed, collecting himself. They would be ready. And soon there would be fewer of them to divide his attention.

"Stand, all of you. We will leave *terha* alone for today. We return to *tohl*. Yan, put on the bracers. Liv, your knife."

Hajja barely managed to regain his feet. Yan collected the leather bracers from the shelf in the corner and strapped them around his thick forearms, the small iron square engraved with *tohl* facing out. Liv pulled his small belt knife free and stood facing the stockier boy. Despite his exhaustion, Hajja closed his eyes and Master Lohi saw him take a cleansing breath to ground himself, reaching for the well of magic.

It was an ancient story, written in hieroglyphic letters on clay tablets discovered in caves dotted along the shores of the farthest north, the mad ramblings of men who believed that the sea storms were the wrath of Aqatar beating against the world of mortals. But within those mad ramblings had been the tales of great men who had commanded the earth's magic, protected themselves during battle. And protected others with that same magic. It had opened Lohi's mind decades ago to the possibility that the power of the runes could be used on oneself, and projected outward to others in the living realm. But he had never had the tools with which to prove those stories.

Yan was the seventh boy they had attempted this with, and the others had been utter failures. Each of them wore thin scars across their cheeks from the knives of their brothers, and Master Lohi's frustration grew with each new wound. True power had waned into sparse threads since the days of the Firstborn, and now he felt like a dog scrambling after the crumbs.

Hajja reached his hands toward Yan, the forceful strain gone from his body as the familiar connection to *tohl* touched him. He nodded tersely.

"Liv."

With a slow movement, Liv lifted his knife and slipped the edge of the blade across Yan's cheek. The same thin line of blood appeared on the boy's dirt smudged skin, and Master Lohi scowled. Seven. If it took every single boy in Blackvale to be covered in scars for Hajja to succeed, so be it.

"Again."

Once more Liv drew the knife, and Hajja's hands wavered uncertainly in the air, and another red cut opened on Yan's cheek.

"AGAIN!"

Yan pressed a hand to his cheek, wincing. Liv held his knife at his side. Hajja's hands lowered in defeat. Master Lohi dragged himself up from his chair, tapping toward the boys much faster than his usual slow, shuffling walk. He grasped Hajja's chin in his withered hand. Fear flickered in the boy's eyes and his breath quickened as he tried to pull away.

"You have shown great promise, and that is why I kept you alive,"

Master Lohi said, his voice as calm as the quiet stillness before a storm. "But I will send you back to that stone cell if you prove worthless to me here."

"Master," a quiet voice broke in. "May I wear the bracers?"

Liv was bowing respectfully to him, holding the bracers in his hands. Master Lohi let go of Hajja and waved his hand dismissively. "Continue. Tahmujin will find some use for you afterwards."

The boys repeated the ritual, this time with Yan holding his knife, Liv with the bracers strapped around his forearms. Yan slowly thrust the blade toward Liv's face. Hajja held his hands tentatively out in front of him like a blind man feeling his way through an unfamiliar house.

Yan's blade cut a thin line across Liv's cheek. Master Lohi wrinkled his nose in displeasure and threw his hand up. "*Aisht!*" he muttered. "Worthless. Again."

*CRACK.*

As Yan's blade moved again, there was a faint sound like breaking platters and the stone beneath Liv's foot fractured in the center, a hairline crack ripping through the rock. Liv's eyes went wide, and the blade in Yan's hands slipped away from his face as if pulled by some puppeteer's threads. Hajja's eyes were unfocused, mouth gasping as if trying to breathe underwater. The boy's hands shook, and the stones around him trembled. Yan swung the blade again, but the knife skimmed past its target, leaving Liv's skin untouched.

"Stab him," ordered Master Lohi, transfixed, and delighted.

Yan hesitated, but then jabbed the blade toward Liv's belly. His hand jumped back as if the knife had stabbed into iron. Energy thrummed through the room, ancient and wild. The hairs on the back of Master Lohi's neck stood.

"It is true, then..." he whispered, awed. He imagined great warriors of the ancient days, larger than two men, their hands pulling power from the earth, untouchable and immortal. He had discovered the truth of the runes after they had lain dormant, the nations oblivious to their true power. Not only could Hajja turn a blade away from his own skin, but he could protect those around him. He could save a king from an assassin's blade.

The energy withdrew, disappearing back into the ground as Hajja fell in a crumpled pile on the floor, passed out. Blood dripped from his nose. Liv rushed to him and shook him by the shoulder while Yan stood dumbfounded, still staring at the knife in his hand. Master Lohi leaned on his staff, his strength seemed drained along with the retreating power and his anger at Hajja's previous failures. He needed to return to his study. He needed to record it all, every detail.

"Take him to Kirte," Master Lohi said, dimly aware of the other two boys lifting Hajja's limp form from the stone. "And Liv?"

"Yes, Master?"

"You will bring the rest of the boys here with you tomorrow."

Once Kirte allowed Hajja to rise from his bed, Master Lohi summoned him back to the stone room. He brought in every one of the other boys to recreate the phenomenon that he had seen with Liv, but each one of them left with cuts. Kajen had come the closest, and his cheek wound was barely a scratch, but Hajja failed with each of the others. And then he had tried once more with Liv, and the ground trembled.

Now, Master Lohi sat aching on his cushions, kneading a sore left knee with the bony knuckles of his hand, and staring at the open books in front of him. Pages and pages of transcriptions, theories, and quoted knowledge from texts in every language Lohi could speak. Records of every day he had spent in the stone room with Hajja, watching the boy struggle over the engraved runes, watching the power respond slowly at first, then with more and more ferocity as Hajja grew accustomed to its presence.

The Maleki tribes had a name for those among them who claimed to feel the voice of the earth in their bones. *Asinya.* Sky

Walker. Someone who could see beyond the veil into the spiritual realm and be given visions. But they had never claimed anyone who could draw power from the earth the way Hajja did. And yet, perhaps there were other ways to access it, different magics that could be drawn from the rivers beneath. Master Lohi sighed and rubbed his temples.

Of greater importance was to understand why Hajja's *tohl* worked so much stronger on Liv. It was a strange thing, and nearly as frustrating as total failure. Liv felt the power of the earth, responded to it. But Kajen also showed signs of the gift, and Master Lohi also suspected that Ruh possessed it as well. Clearly Hajja had been able to draw something forth to protect Kajen, the knife had not truly found its mark.

Master Lohi traced a passage from an ancient Kateshi text with his finger. *Memories of the earth bound in rivers beneath, the stones cry out in pain...* the earth kept every memory since the beginning, every step of every creature, every death, every new life. *Memory binds.*

A distant memory of a young boy standing with his brothers to watch an execution took shape in his mind, grew more vivid and glaring, as if it had been waiting for him to take notice of it. Master Lohi frowned; his finger paused on the page. He had stood on the city wall, looking down over the crowd. He had watched Gehrin, Xario and Kurin as a traitor's blood spilled over the stones and into the ground. He had seen Gehrin respond to the power beneath those Stones. The ancient texts often spoke of great bloodshed and the dark memories held close to the earth's heart.

*The blood links them.*

He should have seen it. The blood of the father flowing through the veins of the son. Master Lohi leaned back, his hands falling limply to his lap. He turned to the window, letting the memories wash over him from a distant place and time, not so many years ago, for what is a span of a few years when you have lived nearly seventy?

. . .

*The boy had been imprisoned in Blackvale with his mother and sister. The mother was already dead, her ashes scattered without a shrine. The sister was fading quickly, she would die within days. And the boy... the boy still cried out for his father at the door of his cell, insistent and so sure of his father's innocence. He had not touched the meager meal left for him, but huddled at the door's edge until the cries tapered away into the occasional query asking when his father would come for him. Then he asked for his mother, and for his sister. When he arrived, the guards told Master Lohi that the boy had passed out from exhaustion, lying in a pitiful heap and finally silent.*

*The night hours had stretched long when the boy was roused from his cell and brought out to the chair to pay the price for his father's sins. The law was without mercy. They had taken his tongue, so that he would never speak the name of his father again. And amid the screams and the blood, the boy had reached into the earth's power. The blade yanked away from his mouth, ripping through the side of his face as the guard fell.*

*The room shook, gravel falling from the ceiling, the racks of weapons and instruments rattling against the walls. The guards and torturer had been pulled to their knees, chained by invisible force, their surprised shouts mingling with the rumble beneath the stone. Only once the boy had lost consciousness from the shock and loss of blood were they all released. And Master Lohi had known that magic still lived in the world, in far greater strength than he had ever supposed.*

*"Spare him," he had told the king. "He will prove his worth. Sometimes life is a greater price to pay than death."*

*"He is aqqa," Tahmujin had resisted. "His blood is tainted, and he will prove nothing. You are blind with the thought of this magic of yours."*

*"I will spare him," the king had finally said. "But your fate is tied to his."*

It had been a price Master Lohi had willingly agreed to. After decades of his fellow scholars' mockery over his devotion to the ancient magics and the patient patronage of a king who had once called him teacher, the terrifying thrill of watching a small boy awaken such power... there were no words that Master Lohi could record to express his emotions in that moment.

The tragedy of the Crown Prince's death had rocked the nation, the depth of grief that washed over the people like a great wave was palpable in the streets of Keld. The *feth* symbol had been drawn on every doorpost as the fear of dark spirits rose to a fevered intensity. But that trust was based in frivolous superstition, the pathetic echoes of a far greater power that Master Lohi had always known he would one day find.

And now he had, locked infuriatingly in the weak body of a traitor's son. Tahmujin allowed him no sympathy for his frustrations. The old warrior had, after all, fought against the decision to leave the boy alive. Nothing but an invitation for the dark spirits, he'd said. The father living on through the son. Tahmujin had no love for the ways of magic, he was a man of spear and steel. And he was growing impatient. The boys were old enough, and it was time to see what Tahmujin had made of them. Soon, very soon.

*He will not have the boy. I have come through too many years with too few left to cave to an old warrior's superstitions.*

Master Lohi left his room in a bitter mood, shutting the panel behind him and shuffling down the hallway. The pattering of smaller feet alerted him to Jai's presence, and the boy offered him a cup of water. He took it gratefully and drank, the water cooling his temper along with his tongue.

"Come, Jai."

The boy followed him like a shadow along the stone corridor until they reached Tahmujin's room. Jai paused at the paneled door and knocked softly.

"Master Tahmujin, Master Lohi has come to speak with you."

A gruff and inaudible answer came from within, muffled. Jai slid the panel open, and Master Lohi stepped inside the room, which was furnished quite sparsely compared with his own more lavish compartment. Tahmujin was a man of the Legion, after all.

The *garatelhai* master sat on the edge of his wooden cot, having always preferred it to the traditional floor mattress. Behind him, curled like a viper, was the Red Woman. Her eyes glittered as her perfect lips curved upwards in a disarming smile as she kneaded the muscles in Tahmujin's back and shoulder. Once again Master Lohi found himself wondering what had possessed him to agree to Tahmujin's demand that she be allowed in the old fortress. She was hardly a harmless diversion. Tahmujin's patronage had not kept her from whispering in other ears.

"Leave us," Master Lohi said, folding his hands over the top of his staff. Bithra glanced down at Tahmujin, waiting until he echoed the scholar's words. When he did, she unfolded herself, graceful as a sleek cat, and floated to the door in a parade of gauzy silks. She smiled at Jai as she passed him, and he offered her a boyish grin in return.

Master Lohi's mood did not improve with her departure. "Your weakness for that woman is a thorn in your side."

Tahmujin grunted. "So, you have said." He gestured to one of the cushions on the floor, but Master Lohi remained standing. Tahmujin threw up his hand.

"Suit yourself. What do you want?"

"I want to know if you think they are ready."

Folding his massive hands and leaning over his knees, Tahmujin narrowed his eyes, staring toward the window. "Some, yes."

"And the others?"

"They are not the quality you are looking for."

Master Lohi nodded. "I will have the *aqqa* boy. The rest I leave to your judgment." He turned to the boy standing silently by the door. "Jai, are you ready to join your brothers?"

The servant boy's face flushed with sudden excitement. "Truly, Master? Will you let me?"

"You will earn your place, just as they must."

Jai bowed so deeply that his face came near his knees. "Thank you, Master. I will earn it."

"Go now, Kirte will have use for you."

The boy slipped out of the room, the panel sliding with a soft scrape over the floor. Master Lohi turned back to the old warrior sitting in front of him. The two men regarded each other with the calm familiarity of years, a lifetime of shared purpose despite their differences. Tahmujin eyed him with faint disdain.

"Whose weakness is more dangerous, I wonder?" he asked wryly. "You will give a place in your *bruhai* to that traitor's spawn, place him next to a king, and you will destroy everything we have worked to build."

Lohi's fingers tightened on the staff in annoyance at Tahmujin's open accusation. He had thought his days of calming the warrior's ire over Hajja were past. "We cannot lose the power he has. He is well within my control, and later he will be controlled by the others."

Tahmujin snorted and shook his head. "And who would you name as their leader?"

"Liv."

"He is not the strongest."

"No, perhaps not. But he has the makings of a great man in him. It is why I chose him. The others will follow him," said Master Lohi. "I am certain of it."

The old *garatelhai* master would much rather have seen Xario walk through the gates of Blackvale, a strong boy with the makings of a powerful warrior. The whispers from the Legion spoke of him as an honorable young man reeking of promise and future glories. Every bit the king his father intended him to be. But he was not king yet.

"I will test them soon. And you will not interfere," Tahmujin's voice was low and stern. But he need not have worried. Master Lohi was content to leave the bloody business to those who were trained in it.

"No, I will not. But you will leave the *aqqa* boy to me."

Tahmujin's teeth ground together as he considered. "It is a mistake."

"So, you have said."

"You have no claims on the others, then. Even Liv?"

Keeping Hajja from the edge of the knife blade was already too far of a concession. It was a great risk, and if he took a place in the *bruhai*, another would fall to pay the price. No, this time Master Lohi could choose only one.

"Even Liv," he conceded.

"Very well. Soon, then."

Master Lohi tapped his staff on the floor softly. "There is another matter. One that I could not risk being overheard. Counsellor Hallix knows that his son is here in Blackvale. He told me directly when I was in Keld. There are only two people who leave this fortress who could have confirmed it to him, and I assure you it was not my doing."

The usual storm clouds residing on Tahmujin's face darkened even further. Master Lohi felt the deep satisfaction of seeing his warnings proven valid and knew that Tahmujin's true anger was rising from being proven wrong. Tahmujin began to rise from his cot, and while the thought of the old *garatelhai* strangling the woman appealed greatly, Lohi shook his head.

"Leave it. Let her spread her poison. She is doubtless keeping Hallix appraised of his son's condition here. We must sacrifice a little knowledge, let them believe they know our secrets. And while they whisper of Liv, other things may lie unseen."

The pleasure of seeing one of Hallix's spies destroyed was an enticing joy to surrender, but he could not risk Hallix taking even greater interest in his work here. And while Hallix believed he knew what lay within the walls, he was blind to many things. That alone would have to offer Lohi solace through the coming days before the *bruhai* were chosen. He had cast the dice, and it was time to see which of them rolled in his favor. If Liv could not prove himself, then so be it.

Tahmujin settled back to his cot, disgruntled, and still glaring toward the door where Bithra had disappeared. Master Lohi tapped his fingers against the top of the staff.

*Slither back to your master, then, witch.* Master Lohi filled his lungs with the stale air of the fortress, closing his eyes and letting his shoulders relax. *Let him have his illusions of power.*

# CHAPTER TWENTY-FIVE

*The Garhis tribe is, in my estimation, the strongest of those that I have encountered. The Maleki people are shrewd herdsmen and capable warriors, but the Garhis tribe possesses a ferocity of spirit that defies the rest. The leadership of Nar Garhis and Ettlan has built iron into this tribe. I have told you of their customs, of the Closed Fist and the Open Hand, and while I believe the Closed Fist is responsible for the protection of the tribe, the true foundation of their strength lies in the influence of their Open Hand. She possesses a resilience and wisdom I have only ever encountered in your own excellent majesty.*

*- Letter from Emissary Otai to Queen Xhen*

Shrouded in furs and hides, the woman's gaunt frame was hidden from view, revealing only a pale face and wide eyes staring off into a distant nothingness. The veil separating flesh and spirit had torn, and she had stepped through it into a world between, lost amidst the simple thoughts of a child she had not been for many years.

Tilis stood beside her protectively, her babe bound tightly to her breast with a woven wrap, warm beneath the furs. Between them, they held the shattered remains of an Open Hand, mothers to a tribe adrift, bleeding and dying in a land that was not their own.

The urge to reach up and pick at the healing wound along the side of her face burned through Syndri as she watched the two women stand on the gentle crest, looking back toward the south. She stood guard despite the promised safety of Da'ham. They were not in Malek now, the Uratar and Tladr would not dare follow them into the lands of their more powerful neighbors.

*Powerful.* The word curled unpleasantly in Syndri's thoughts. Once she had scoffed at the idea that the Northern peoples were powerful and able to offer them safe haven. She had once imagined them soft bellied and lazy, drinking wine from their cushioned thrones in their stone palaces. But her tribe's existence relied on their benevolence, and it drew her anger to the surface like a writhing serpent. She reached up and worried at the lower edge of the wound, the healing skin still raw and red beneath her fingers. Senna would have scolded her.

But Senna was not here. Her sister had been chosen to carry news of their impending arrival to Ruk, to seek the aid of the queen. The Garhis tribe could not stay in Da'ham; their alliance was not with the artisan king.

*We will see if this Rukian queen keeps her word.* As much as her hands burned with the desire to unsheathe her swords and slaughter every man, woman, and child of the Uratar and Tladr tribes, Syndri knew that her people were not strong enough to return to their homeland. It pained her to admit that the queen's alliance was necessary, but she would honor her father's trust in Ruk.

And Ettlan...

A choking lump rose in Syndri's throat, forcing a thickly painful swallow. The thin, weak figure beside Tilis was a pale shadow of her mother. She had awoken, but she remained trapped in dreams, recognizing not a single face among her tribe, even those of her own daughters. She had looked past Syndri, searching the group of faces surrounding her in the wagon as if she might find something to draw her back to understanding. Tilis had told them that the blow to her head had given wounds that could not be seen, and there was no way to know if her memory or her spirit would ever return to the child-like husk that remained.

*Ettlan lives on, but my mother is gone.*

Tilis had not been named Open Hand by the tribe by the proper rituals, but no one questioned the unspoken shift in authority. The Garhis tribe approached Tilis as their woman of wisdom, the mother of peace. In a matter of weeks, the Closed Fist and the Open Hand had changed faces.

The woman looking out over the softly frosted grasslands had held her open hands of blessing over her people, had held the broken body of her son in her arms, had cried the dark groans of a mother bereft of her child, had been the beating heart of the great warrior Nar Garhis.

Now she could not even remember their faces.

Syndri winced as she pulled a piece of flaking scab away from her face. The sharp sting was a bitter relief. She saw Tilis lean close to Ettlan's ear, whispering gently. The two women turned to make their slow walk back to the caravan.

Ettlan stopped when they reached Syndri, a soft tilted smile touching her cracked lips. Her eyes brought a fresh wave of nausea to Syndri's gut as she watched the woman who had been her mother look through her as if she were some sort of spirit.

"You are hurt," Ettlan said, reaching her hand up to touch the side of Syndri's face where a fresh trickle of blood seeped through the worried flesh. She looked back at Tilis. "So many of them are bleeding."

Tilis patted her shoulder. "They have fought a great battle to protect us. Do not worry for them, they still live, and that is a blessed thing."

Ettlan nodded, her lost gaze moving away from Syndri. "Yes..." her voice trailed off into the air. She clutched Tilis' arm, stepping tentatively over the uneven ground. Syndri watched them all the way back to the caravan, her heart in her throat. She wiped her sleeve across her eyes and returned to tend to Brig. The black's winter coat had lengthened to a shaggy fur, making him look more wolf than horse. Syndri had staked him to a small area where the snow was a bit thinner, revealing patches of frozen grass beneath. As they traveled north, winter released its grip on the land, the air's bite less sharp.

Brig *whoofed* at her as she reached out a hand to his rabbit-fur soft nose. Syndri ran her hands over his back and legs, feeling for warmth that would indicate an injury. He had seemed to heal from the battle with little damage other than the spear wound on his hip. Syndri took a pouch of herbs from her belt and settled a bit of it in the hollow of her palm, adding her spit and mixing with one finger. Gently she worked the herb paste into the reddish gouge marring Brig's dark skin. He flinched and shuddered but stood quietly while she worked.

Out of the corner of her eye, she saw a rider and horse approaching. Uhuri rode on his young gray mare, and she whinnied at Brig as they drew close. The black stallion jerked his head upwards and returned the loud greeting. Syndri winced.

"You'll make me deaf like that," she scolded under her breath. Uhuri jumped down from his mare, his long braid newly plaited and the sparse beginnings of a beard spattered along his jawline like mud. It was a rare sight to find him separated from Malon.

"Malon sent me," he said.

*Not so separated, then,* Syndri thought wryly. The woman fussed over her like a mother hen now that Senna was not there to do it. "You can tell her that I still possess all my limbs."

Uhuri grinned and shrugged his fur cloak down further away from his neck. He was a broad-shouldered lad, but there was nothing much to the rest of him, giving him the lanky, awkward appearance of a young man without the weight of years added to his frame.

"Do you think the Northern queen will let us into her city?" Uhuri asked quietly, watching her finish with the herb paste. Syndri glanced at him, smoothing a gentle finger over the edge of Brig's wound with the last of the green sludge in her palm.

"If anyone can convince her to honor her word, it is Senna."

"She is your mother's daughter."

Syndri frowned, and Uhuri quickly noticed her rigid posture. Concern lined his face, and Syndri gritted her teeth in frustration. He was altogether too soft. She didn't understand what Malon saw in him. She half expected him to put a comforting hand on her shoulder. But he kept his distance.

"Her life was spared. That is a great blessing from the Sky Clans."

"Do not speak to me of the Sky Clans," growled Syndri. "If you came just to grovel over the great blessings we have been given, go back to Malon's blankets. You will find warmer company there."

The young warrior's face flushed a deep red. She had angered him; she could see it in his eyes. But he did not say anything more. He turned and mounted the gray mare, looking down at Syndri a long moment before riding away toward the caravan. Syndri leaned against Brig's shoulder, steadying herself with slow breaths.

The only blessing she would accept was the one that saw her living, breathing, and awaiting her chance to bring vengeance to her tribe's enemies. Until she was drenched in the blood of Uratar and Tladr amidst their *gats* on their tribal lands, the Sky Clans could gaze down in displeasure at her heresy all they liked. Her fist tightened on Brig's mane as she fought away pale wraiths of the dead.

She pressed her forehead into her horse's warmth, only one prayer left. *If you listen to the cries of the Garhis, make me your Closed Fist. Let me ride with swords of fire and blood to destroy those who defile the memory of my father's people. And if you cannot give me what I ask, then get out of my way.*

The only answer was the gentle sound of Brig's teeth crushing the grass.

The gray, snow-dusted grasslands of Malek and southern Da'ham slowly bled into lusher green meadows flanked by gray cliffs. Rocky crags rose to the northwest along the border of Ruk, sharp gray teeth piercing the sky. Emissary Otai had once told Syndri that his homeland was a land of stone and iron, carved into the earth by a god's hands. Soon, the Garhis caravan would leave Da'ham behind and cross into Ruk, following a long valley toward Ujjak, the Northern queen's capital city. Senna had already been gone for days, and it would be days before she returned, even with Rho's swift pace. And her sister's absence drew the poison of grief lingering in Syndri's spirit to the surface.

Syndri volunteered for the farthest scouting positions around the perimeter of the caravan, often riding out of sight of the bedraggled line of villagers, the remaining warband, and the incessant lowing of the kehroxen. Brig was still healing, so she rode Sabayaar's chestnut filly. Itah was still skittish and spooked if she came across a flower in the grass, but Syndri quickly rode the wildness out of her. The filly had grown, and was only a hand shorter than Brig now, all long legs and flared nostrils. She lacked Brig's stability and slipped on the loose rock at the top of the cliffs. More than once, Syndri imagined herself and the filly toppling over the side, landing in a tangle of broken limbs at the base. There was no rush of terror at the thought. The usual fire of anger in her belly had dimmed, leaving her feeling like some hollow spirit.

She often slept beneath the stars, tying the filly to a tree nearby and only shivering in the deepest part of the night when the moon cast its pure light over the jagged shapes around her. She pulled the hides around herself, her breath nothing but smoky wisps. Over and over, she was haunted away from the deep peace of sleep, each night pulling her farther into the grasp of the Darkness. Her brother's smile twisted into a dark spirit leering at her from the boulders. Corpses crept at the outskirts of her vision, bones held at wrong angles, their totems crushed and dangling from rotten strings.

She began to wish for death. She began to wish that she had burned on the pyre with her brother, her father. She began to plead with the shadows, whispering at them to take her with them into the deep.

*"What is your name?"*

*"What is your name?"*

*"What is your name?"*

The last words she had allowed Ettlan to speak to her curled around her in the dark, throttling her, taunting her. She imagined the Sky Clans laughing on their cloud-horses, mocking her. She stumbled through the strange landscape like a blind child, wandering away from Itah as the young mare whinnied after her. She offered the chestnut filly to the spirits in the dark, asking the twisted mirage of her brother to return, but he danced away, disappearing with a bubbling laugh as black, rotten blood poured from the wound in his chest.

She grew angry with him.

"You died a coward's death!" she screamed after him. "It was you! You were the curse!" She lurched forward, tripping over a stone as she drew one of her swords from its sheath. She cut deep into the bark of a tree, and the sword lodged tightly in the wood. Syndri wrestled the blade free with a guttural cry. She sank down to the rocks, the sword clattering away as her hand met cold stone. She screamed; her throat raw with the force of it. Her head fell back, and something drank her spirit down beneath the rock.

*She saw stones on every side... a room made of rock, carved into smooth-sided shapes. A boy sat against the wall, half-naked and heaving, hands pressed to the stone. Baya... no, not Baya. A boy with a ruined face, his lips broken in a horrible scar that bared his teeth like a wolf. He looked at her... he saw her, and whatever bound them pulled at them like a great chain. The boy closed his eyes, and the power swept them away with a low roar that shook the ground beneath them. The stones of the boy's room fell away in a crumbling avalanche, and strange markings glowed around their hands.*

*Sand poured in around them from above, the deafening sounds of battle clanging and echoing around them as they fell. Syndri could smell flesh burn-*

*ing, and she could not find the seam separating their minds, it was as if she and the boy were one, falling to whatever hellish darkness lay in the center of the earth. She knew his pain, writhing and threading through her own. There were hands on her face, a searing, all-consuming pain as her tongue was cut free from her mouth, and she screamed.*

*Blinding light pierced through them, and claw-like hands spread like tree branches over their heads. A woman's voice, deep as a thousand pounding hooves, cut through the screaming cacophony roaring in their ears. She spoke a language that Syndri did not know. The world trembled. The boy screamed. Syndri held her crossed fists in front of her face, her body locked against the horrible force that was pulling her down.*

*"HAJJA!"*

*Someone's hands were on the boy's shoulders, shaking him, pulling him back-*

The world was calm. The soft yellow morning sky pulled its veil away from the sun and warmth touched Syndri's face. She gasped like a newborn taking its first breath of the world's air, eyes squinted against the light. Her furs and hides were gone, scattered a few lengths away, leaving her sprawled over the stony ground in her tunic and leather breeches, but the cold did not reach her.

The air flooded her mouth and nose as she gulped it in. She heard the faint sound of Itah whinnying. Slowly rolling onto her side, she pushed herself up to her knees. She was dizzy, and the ground lurched as she put out a hand to steady herself. She flinched as her fingertips met the stone, waiting to be dragged into another vision.

Nothing but the soft chirping of a bird invaded her mind.

She thought of the boy she had seen. He must have been a spirit. The Sky Clans had sent a vision, just as they had sent a vision to Senna long ago. A vision of the future? Syndri frowned around the ache in her head. The boy had not worn a totem, nor had he looked

Maleki. He looked Northern, more like Emissary Otai... but even then, different. His eyes were darker, his skin a strange hue, lighter than hers. He was young, far too young to have been mutilated the way he was.

What message was she meant to understand?

When the ground stopped tilting beneath her, she crawled to her hides and furs and gathered them up, strapping her swords around her shoulders. Her mind was strangely clear, each small sound of the land around her amplified. She heard the nearby babble of a stream. The soft rustle of leaves, a rock cracking beneath her boot. Her own heartbeat pounded in her ears. Far away, the scream of some bird of prey as it wheeled through the sky.

She walked back to Itah, the filly still tied to the twisted branches of a tree. Itah's chestnut ears pricked forward, and the plaintive whinny turned sharper and more urgent as Syndri came into view. The filly stamped and swung from side to side, her hooves dancing over the rocks.

Syndri murmured to her, ran her hands over the filly's sides and shoulders to calm her. When she rode Itah away from the cliff and back down into the broken valley beneath, a strange energy filled her, new strength in her arms. Itah sensed it and pulled at the reins, her slender legs extending as she impatiently waited for Syndri to let her run.

The caravan had moved on, but it was not difficult to follow the tramped-down path and the noisy lowing of the kehrox herd. They had crossed the border into Ruk, and when Syndri reached the mouth of the rocky chasm that wound through the mountains toward Ujjak, she passed a flag billowing atop a post twice the height of a man. In the center was a golden disc with rays shooting out over the black silk. The emblem of the Northern queen.

Itah's muscles tensed, and she walked with her ears pricked and head locked in the direction of the flag, letting out shallow gusts of breath as she pranced nervously away from it. In the distance, riding past the herd, Syndri could see the end of the caravan, the forms of horses and villagers walking like tiny ants in a line. She touched her heels to Itah's sides, and the filly jumped into a smooth gallop.

The villagers glanced up at her as she rode past, but she did not look at any of them. She rode straight to the wagon in the middle of the line. Brig walked slowly along behind, his halter tied to the wood, and he neighed when he saw them. Tilis looked up, and a shadow passed over her face when she locked eyes with Syndri. In the furs lining the wagon, Ettlan curled like a small child, holding Tilis' baby in her arms and cooing at him.

"There are warriors looking for you," said Tilis, reproach lacing her tone. "We did not know if you would return."

"Would you have mourned me if I had not returned?" asked Syndri.

Tilis looked down at Ettlan, wrapped around her infant son, and did not answer. Satisfied that Ettlan was still safe, Syndri urged Itah on to the front of the caravan. Yugha looked less pleased than his wife to see Syndri return, but he allowed her to ride Itah alongside his massive bay mare. Three of his most trusted warriors rode at his side. Syndri knew any one of them would have struck her down without hesitation if Yugha ordered her death. She had defeated Ikaio and restored her honor to the tribe, but Yugha still did not trust her. But she would not challenge him. The tribe was content to follow him, for now, and she would not take another Nar from them so soon.

She looked ahead toward a sharp bend in the canyon, and wished Senna would appear. But her sister was nowhere to be seen.

"You trust the Northern queen's word?" she asked Yugha.

"She will honor it."

Syndri gripped the reins tighter. "You do not believe I will honor mine. I pledged my swords to you and named you Nar before the tribe. I will not dishonor my father by turning my back on you now."

Stone-faced, Nar Yugha shook his head. "If you turn on me, it will be your blade, not your back."

"At least you do not name me a coward," Syndri answered, the words bitter between her teeth. "Do you think so little of my word? I have fought beside you since I was a child."

"You are still a child." Yugha looked at her the way a father might at his hot-blooded youth. "You are fire that cannot be contained, and I will not let you burn this tribe."

*There is no spirit of peace in you,* Ettlan had said once. Clearly the Sky Clans had given her great flaws, cursed her with the destruction of her tribe. Syndri smiled, but there was no warmth in it. "May the Sky Clans strike me dead here on this ground if all your distrust in me proves true."

She kicked Itah, and the chestnut leapt past the other warriors, thundering ahead around the curves of the canyon. The filly snorted with each stride, eyes bright and filled with wild joy at being given her head. It was not long before they were deep in the jagged ridges, far below the upper surface of the cliffs, and a good distance away from the caravan.

Up ahead, a second rider appeared around the bend. The sight of the roan mare brought such a wave of relief to Syndri that she nearly collapsed over Itah's neck. Desperation to be close to her sister drove her onward, seeking the calm stability of Senna's presence and recognizing the end of the yawning emptiness Syndri had felt at her absence.

Syndri called out, and saw Senna lift a hand in greeting.

Syndri slowed Itah, and by the time the two horses had come abreast of each other, hot tears were streaming down Syndri's cheeks, unbidden and shameful. She wiped at them with her hands, trying to rid herself of them before Senna could see. But her sister dismounted from Rho and nearly pulled Syndri down on top of her as they embraced. Syndri slid down from Itah's back into her sister's arms and buried her face in the hide cloak.

Drawing apart, Senna reached up and smoothed away a fresh tear from Syndri's cheek. "*Teitei,*" she murmured. "Are you alright?"

Syndri scowled, blinking, and avoiding Senna's gaze. *I feel like a toddling child,* she thought, the irony of Yugha's words fresh. "You were gone for too long."

"I have seen the Northern queen. She honors her word, *teitei*. She sends Emissary Otai with me to lead us to her city. I rode ahead to find you. Our people will have peace. They will be safe."

*Peace... safe...* Syndri nodded. For her people, she could wish for these things. For herself, the world was still spinning, casting her adrift. Senna glanced ahead down the canyon.

"Is mother..."

Syndri quickly shook her head. "She still walks in dreams. She does not know me."

Their shared pain crossed Senna's face, and she squeezed Syndri's arm. "I will not lose hope that one day she will know us again. Even if I must carry that hope for us both."

"I saw a vision, Senna."

Senna's eyes widened. "A vision? What did they show you?"

"I don't know," Syndri admitted, rubbing her forehead. "We will talk of it later. I do not understand it." Her thoughts were haunted by the fresh memories of that strange dream world, the primeval power flowing through her veins as if she were nothing more than a sieve. It was something beyond even the Sky Clans' power, beyond the ages when the first ancestors of the Maleki tribes had tamed the wind. The woman's voice she had heard held echoes of thousands more. The words she had spoken were foreign to Syndri's ears, but something within the power holding her captive had known their meaning.

A sharp tug at her wrist brought Syndri back to the present and the worried expression on her sister's face. Senna could see far beyond the façade of strength Syndri worked so carefully to construct, to the wounds that festered beneath.

"I was gone too long," she agreed. "Tonight, you will tell me everything. But right now, I must speak with Yugha. Otai will not be far behind me."

Syndri numbly mounted Itah and followed Senna on Rho back toward the caravan. She saw the straight-backed confidence radiating from her sister, the glitter of a new silver chain gleaming at her neck beneath the cloak. It was as if meeting the Northern queen had worn away the gritty heaviness of the past few months, infusing pride back into the future of the Garhis. Syndri felt none of her sister's confidence. Ruk upholding its promise of alliance was one step toward returning to exact vengeance from the Uratar and Tladr, but it would come at a price. It was childish to imagine that the queen would give them shelter and send her armies to fight with them out of some sentimental honor.

With the remains of the vision tingling through her limbs and expectations for the future cost this exodus would extract from her people darkening her joy at her sister's return, Syndri urged Itah forward to ride abreast of Rho as the twin daughters of Nar Garhis returned to the caravan to bring the news that Queen Xhen of Ruk was ready to welcome them.

# CHAPTER TWENTY-SIX

*It is easier to stab a friend in the dark.*

*- Kateshi saying*

Gehrin slipped the blade up between the man's protruding ribs, heard the startled gasp, and his quarry sagged against him as he pulled his knife free. The man's weight was greater than his own, and his knee buckled as he half dropped, half lowered the body to the ground. The final gasps of life were blessedly short as the wound in the man's heart did its work.

The front of Gehrin's tunic was wet with the man's blood, a sickly warmth sticking the fabric to his skin beneath. He shivered, hating the feeling despite its familiarity. He looked down at the man's face, the jut of the overly large jaw, the small eyes above thick cheekbones, and the broken teeth. The prayer Gehrin would have once said died before it left his lips.

Several strides away, he watched as another one of his brothers chased down a boy who could not have been much older than Gehrin himself. The pursuer was Nin, his legs pumping as fast as they could until he was within reach of his prey. The first knife he threw missed the runner by inches. Gehrin watched silently, refusing to take off in pursuit himself unless it was clear Nin would lose him.

The second knife did not miss. It landed with a hard thud between the prisoner's shoulder blades. His hands flew into the air as he tumbled forward onto his face with a scream. Gehrin turned away, satisfied. Nin had begun to show promise with the lesser blades. He was still weaker with a spear than most of the others, but knives were far deadlier in his small hands. After the shock of his first kill, Nin had settled into a grim determination that darkened his baby-soft face. He refused to talk about any of the dead they left behind in the forest.

Leaving the corpse, Gehrin moved back through the trees toward the point Tahmujin had set for their return. Tirrim appeared nearby and hurried to join him. The bigger boy grimaced at the sight of the wet red stain on the front of Gehrin's tunic.

"That's going to take some scrubbing."

"Mm."

Tirrim glanced behind them, back into the forest. "All these dead bodies are a signal fire for dark spirits," he muttered. "We'll need a *feth* rune on every tree just to keep from getting our souls sucked dry. No wonder Master Lohi is always muttering the runes."

"Master Tahmujin has killed more people than all of us together, and he doesn't have any dark spirits following him," replied Gehrin with a shrug. He didn't want to think about the shadowy horrors that could be lurking in the forest. It made the hair on the back of his neck stand on end.

Tirrim offered a dry laugh in response. "Don't think I don't hear you muttering the runes at night, Liv. If we're lucky, the spirits won't follow us when we leave."

Glancing sharply to each side, Gehrin satisfied himself that no one else was within earshot. Tirrim still took far too many chances talking about the future, in Gehrin's opinion. So far, the other boy had avoided being overheard by unfriendly ears, but one day he would take a step too far. He tightened his lips and pushed on through the trees, Tirrim striding behind him.

Hajja's dark spirits came to him at night. He did not scream or call out the way the other boys once had when they were younger. It was a quiet, guttural cry, a sound that did not even wake the other boys sleeping in the barracks anymore. Gehrin was the only one who was pulled from his own blissfully dreamless sleep and into the still night. He had tried to wake the other boy once, but Hajja had nearly choked him senseless, the masked boy's wild fear closing his mind to anything but flight from the evil that plagued him.

So, Gehrin tried to ignore it. He rolled away, covered his face with the thin blanket, recited the runes to himself in his head. *Runes of protection... feth, kri, kef, gera...*

Once he had said them in a whisper and noticed that Hajja's thrashing and whimpering had calmed more quickly than usual. And when he tried again a few nights later, it had the same effect. Slowly, the nightmares came less frequently, were less violent. Speaking the runes aloud seemed to drain the edge from the room and allowed Gehrin to go back to sleep faster. After several such nights, Gehrin had even gone so far as to draw the *feth* rune on the wall above Hajja's cot. Hajja had watched him with the same deeply distrustful eyes that he had never been able to lose even after years of familiarity with the other boys.

But this night, the spirits came back with a vengeance. And they did not come in dreams.

Gehrin awoke to the sound of Hajja's restless movement. The other boy's cot was the last one on the row, next to Gehrin. No one else wanted to sleep near him. Tahmujin held that he was cursed, and there were few enough of the boys who would believe otherwise.

With a groggy sigh, Gehrin pulled himself away from the comforting firmness of his cot and sat up, rubbing his eyes. Hajja was not on his cot. Gehrin frowned until he made out the other boy's huddled form crouched in the corner against the stone. Hajja's hands scrabbled against the blocks; eyes squeezed shut as he shook his head as if trying to deny entrance to the darkness within his mind. He began slamming the side of his head against the wall, and Gehrin rose to his feet, sleep losing the last of its grip on him.

Hajja's fingertips were bleeding, and he only stopped clawing at the walls to press his palms against the sides of his head, face contorted as if he were in pain. The mask was gone, and his broken lips were pulled away from his teeth in a horrible grimace.

Frozen in place at the foot of Hajja's cot, Gehrin fought against the urge to shake the boy. He was hesitant to repeat the feeling of Hajja's hands closing around his throat, but this was no dream. He had seen Hajja's eyes open briefly before the black hair fell like a veil over his face, hands clasped against his ears.

And then Gehrin felt the pull from beneath. The hair on the back of his neck stood up, and a rush like a bolt of crackling lightning raced through his body. Down on the floor, Hajja's head fell back, eyes wide and staring as his body shivered, bloody hands dropping limply to the stone tiles.

Something faint and powerful echoed through the room, and Gehrin turned, expecting the other boys to rise at the sound. But they did not stir. The floor opened beneath him, and he began to fall, but when he reached out to steady himself, he realized that the ground was still solid stone. He heard someone screaming. Gehrin tried to call out in response, his words trapped within the swirling gusts of power tearing his mind apart.

*Hajja!*

Gehrin sank to his knees, helpless. Though his lips would not move, he cried out to the other boy in his mind.

*HAJJA!*

Hajja's breath came back to him in a rushing gasp as if he were taking the first breath of air after drowning. The power discarded them with a startling swiftness, and the two boys crumpled to the floor, clutching at the wooden legs of the cot.

Whatever great and ancient well of magic Master Lohi had waited for them to open, it had taken control of them as easily as a mountain cat might play with a mouse. Gehrin had never felt so hopelessly small, so meaningless as in the clutches of that great and dreadful thing. Still catching his breath in short, shallow bursts, he reached out and touched Hajja's arm.

"Alright...?" he managed.

Hajja pulled away from him, crushing himself further into the corner of the room. Crossing his thin arms around his body, his shoulders trembled as he rocked back and forth on his heels, his slim frame wracked with silent tears. Gehrin could offer no comfort. He pulled himself over to the wall and sat as near as he dared. Drawing a shuddering breath, he began to recite.

"*Feth*... to protect against dark spirits. *Kri*... To guard the tongue against deceit..."

The pile of logs that had been pushed and carried from one end of the training yard to the other were missing. The usual racks of wooden staves and practice blades were also gone, leaving nothing but a tawny stretch of sand laid out in front of the line of silent boys. Jai had woken them and beckoned them out without washing or pulling on their tunics, hardly giving them time to blink their eyes before rushing outside.

Gehrin stood shoulder to shoulder in the line with Yan on his left and Yul on his right. Jai stood across from them near the brooding form of their master, and the servant boy seemed to be alight with some knowledge of what was to come, his bare toes digging into the sand as he fidgeted.

The boys bowed low as Master Lohi appeared, his carved staff tapping alongside his slippers as he moved in his graceful shuffle across the sand. Despite the long hours spent in the scholar's presence since arriving at Blackvale, Gehrin's stomach still clenched unpleasantly whenever the old man appeared. The joyful memories of sitting in Master Lohi's small house in Keld alongside his brothers were hidden beneath far less palatable layers. In truth, the clarity of his brothers' faces grew dimmer and dimmer each time he tried to conjure them. He rose from his bow, bringing his gaze back to the man who had taken his name.

Master Lohi stopped in the center of the courtyard. "You are not yet *bruhai*. You are simply the ore, misshapen and softened in flames, hammered into a useable ingot. But it will be years before you are truly blades wielded by our great warlord. Today you will prove yourselves worthy to remain in the forge."

A test. Gehrin felt nothing but calm acceptance. Master Lohi had tested them many times, as had Tahmujin. Their minds and bodies had been battered and pushed to the edge until each new test was simply some new pain to overcome. Numbness was a familiar friend, stripping away less welcome emotion.

"One of you has already been chosen to continue training."

Gehrin was surprised, and he glanced down the line. The most likely boys to have caught the master's notice were Tirrim and Ruh, the best fighters. Or perhaps Sabba, as he was the largest and strongest. But Master Lohi's wrinkled hand pointed elsewhere.

"Hajja, come."

Despite the expectation of silence, a shocked murmur snaked through the line of boys. It was no secret that Hajja was Master Lohi's pet, locked in the stone room for hours each day to reach the rune magic that the scholar so desperately wanted to have at his fingertips. But to most of them, it was a superstition, a clown's trick. At best, it was a useful diversion in a fight. Hajja was not incompetent with the staff, but every boy in the line had bested him. He had shown some promise with knives, but that alone would not mark him as one of the best.

Every eye followed Hajja as he stepped away from the line of his brothers and went to stand near Master Lohi. The mask obscured his face again, drawing attention away from the deep circles of exhaustion left behind from the previous night. Gehrin heard someone mutter a curse under their breath. Fourteen boys remained of the sixteen that had been brought to the fortress. Master Lohi turned to Jai and motioned him forward.

"Jai, do you wish to join your brothers now?"

The servant boy glowed and straightened his shoulders. "Yes, Master."

"They must accept you first," replied Master Lohi. He addressed the other boys. "Has Jai served you with honor since you came here?"

Gehrin spoke with the rest. "Yes, Master."

"Do any of you speak against him?"

No one did. The servant boy's presence was as familiar to all of them as any of the others. Gehrin remembered the gentle kindness Jai had shown him as he crouched terrified in a tiny stone cell years ago. It was strange that Tahmujin and Lohi would let him join the others now. He had not trained in anything except cooking, cleaning, and killing rats in the cellar. He was less of a warrior than Hajja. Master Lohi placed a hand on Jai's shoulder, and then slowly walked back to the shaded overhang at the edge of the courtyard. Tahmujin took his place.

The old warrior drew a curved knife sharply from its sheath. The blade glistened in the light. He eyed the boys with the same withering scrutiny, peeling flesh away with his gaze and weighing the spirit beneath. Gehrin had felt the piercing of that gaze many times and had never found himself in Tahmujin's approval.

"Prove yourself stronger than your brother and live. There is no place for weakness at the side of the king. I have trained you. Show me what you have learned."

The numbness gave way to a kernel of dread sinking in the pit of Gehrin's empty belly. Tahmujin flicked his wrist, and the knife buried itself in the sand a few feet away from Jai. Then the *garatelhai* pointed toward the line of boys.

"Haveth."

Walking forward with the cautious steps of a hare creeping away from its burrow, Haveth approached the center of the courtyard, still unsure what Tahmujin meant for him to do. The spearmaster sent Jai to the far-left edge of the sand, and Haveth to the right. The knife stood in the center, its hilt a dark stain against the ground. Tahmujin turned to Haveth.

"If you hesitate, you will die."

He had said the same words to them hundreds of times while they sparred under the heat of the sun, had beaten their legs and shoulders and heads until they felt the blows in their sleep. Gehrin could not bring himself to understand. He looked at Master Lohi, as if waiting for the old scholar to stop them. But he simply stood watching, hands folded on top of his staff.

*Stop them, by Sharai's blood!* Gehrin urged his teacher silently, eyes locked onto the old man's silk robes. Sharp memories of Deth's corpse bleeding out on the sand jabbed at the edges of his mind, threatening to open a floodgate of other fears. *Will Jai die today? Will Haveth? Will I?*

Tahmujin barked his command, and Jai sprang forward, his bare feet skimming over the ground in a blur. Haveth was slower, his lankier build more difficult to push to such speed. Jai slid the final few strides against the sand, his hand darting out to close around the knife's hilt. Haveth saw the blade rise toward him and checked his speed, twisting to the side to avoid the thrust. Jai moved with cold precision, recentering his weight on his inner foot and launching himself up toward Haveth, who was off balance. There was no way for Haveth to block the blade, so he threw his arms up in front of his chest and face, letting out a scream as the knife sank into his forearm. Jai twisted and pulled, and the blade came free, slicing toward Haveth's throat. A gasp of shock rose from the line of boys watching. No one had expected Jai to move with the obvious confidence of a trained killer. Suddenly, the servant boy was foreign to all of them.

Gehrin flinched and his eyes closed, bile rising to the back of his throat in an acid rush, confusion mingling with the shock of what he had seen. When he opened them, Jai was holding Haveth, easing him down to the sand as gently as a mother might lower her child into a sleeping basket. After an agonizing number of heartbeats, Haveth's hand loosened from Jai's tunic and fell lifeless to the ground. Jai placed each of Haveth's arms across his chest, guarding him for the afterlife. The servant boy rose and bowed to the body, his face solemn.

Tahmujin nodded in approval. "Well earned."

Jai went to stand beside Hajja, he left the knife in the sand, his face flushed. Gehrin swallowed down the vomit that threatened to explode from his stomach. Who would Tahmujin ask him to kill next? Sabba? Ruh? Nin? Half of them would be dead before Aqatar reached its highest point in the sky.

While his instincts told him to run, his training held him firmly rooted to the line. If he ran, he would die. If he fought, at least there was a chance to live. To prove himself worthy of the place beside Jai and Hajja.

"Niveth," Tahmujin called. Along the line of boys, shoulders were rigid, fists clenched, teeth gritted as the fear of being called next echoed through them. Niveth stalked to his place at the far end of the sand. Gehrin watched him, imagining how fast he would have to run, what direction he would turn if Niveth grasped the knife hilt before him.

"Nin."

*Dead.* Gehrin could already imagine Nin's body laid out on the sand next to Haveth, his eyes glazed over and staring for the last time at the blue sky. He is dead.

Nin stepped forward. Without his tunic, he looked even smaller. He paused a few feet away from the line, clearly not wanting to leave the safety of his brothers, not wanting to put himself truly at Niveth's mercy. Then he straightened his shoulders and walked to the end of the courtyard with the same expression that Gehrin had seen on the faces of his own victims, those who had accepted that their death was no longer something they could escape.

When they ran for the knife, Nin's closed fists pumped at his sides, giving him as much speed as he could muster. But Niveth's speed was greater, and he leaned down, pulling the knife from the sand, and grinning at Nin. Continuing his mad rush, Nin turned his body to slide on his forward foot, reaching down to the sand. He threw a handful of it up toward Niveth, but it fell too low, and the older boy only scowled in anger at the attempt.

Niveth made several feints toward Nin, taunting him with the flashing blade before giving him a savage kick to the knee. Nin's leg buckled and he went down, hands grasping at the sand. Niveth pushed him back, straddled him with the knife held poised above Nin's chest. Nin smacked the heel of his palm against Niveth's hand, and the wild flail knocked the knife free. It fell between them and disappeared from Gehrin's view. He saw Nin roll sideways, and Niveth fall on top of him, reaching forward.

A cry of pain.

Niveth went rigid and rolled away, hands pressed tightly to his side as red seeped between his fingers. Nin stood, limping over to the older boy with the knife tightly gripped in his hand, blood staining the blade. Nin's face contorted in anguish over what he still had to do. This was no condemned criminal killed for the king's justice. There was no locking it away in his mind, imagining that there was no name to the face lying on the sand in front of him. There was no love lost between Nin and Niveth, and yet the old command was still woven into hand that held the blade.

*Do not harm a brother.*

Nin knelt next to Niveth, who was trying to crawl away over the sand. Tears rolled down Nin's face, and he brought the knife down once, twice. Then he dropped the blade and heaved a wracking sob, waiting for it to be over. And then it was.

Gehrin stared at the second body, watching the sand turn dark. He imagined himself sitting in his father's study, listening to the harvest reports. He imagined running over the barley fields with Kurin and Xario, their tunics darkened with sweat and dirt and the hours of wild freedom allowed to the young sons of Counsellor Hallix. He imagined the sweet taste of the *kiji* cakes and Kasaii's bright smile. Their faces were blurry, and he strained to grasp the form of their noses, their mouths, the shape of their eyes. It was bitter that they were leaving him. He wondered if his father would be proud of him now.

"Liv. Yan."

Some force outside himself pulled Gehrin forward to the sand. He met Master Lohi's gaze, and the scholar's glittering dark eyes scrutinized him as they always had, waiting for him to show his worth. The old man had brought him here, and he had left Gehrin to the spin of a coin. One wrong step could be the end. At the other end of the courtyard stood Yan, the boy's strong forearms locked at his sides. He was looking at the center of the sand, avoiding the chance of meeting eyes with the boy he might kill. Gehrin glanced up at the sky.

*Oathsworn protect me.*

Master Tahmujin threw the knife down, the blade cleaned and gleaming as if it hadn't just tasted the blood of Gehrin's brothers. Gehrin leapt forward, setting his teeth hard and feeling the force of wind against his face.

Despite his stockier frame, Yan was fast, and they reached the blade at the same time, their bodies crashing into each other so hard that Gehrin's teeth rattled as he dropped to the ground like a sack of his father's barley. Yan tumbled over him and they flailed for the knife. Sand scraped against Gehrin's nose and chin as his face was pushed down, and he spat out the grains, rolling out from under Yan and gaining his feet.

The bigger boy had the knife. Gehrin jumped back just in time to avoid a sweep that would have opened his bowels. Arms flung out for balance, he ducked and weaved, forcing himself to keep his breathing even, not to think about how close the blade was to his skin.

*Breathe. Watch the blade, not his eyes. He steps heavy, it takes him a heartbeat to regain his balance after he stabs. Get in close, a fist to the throat or the sternum.*

Gehrin made his move, twisting aside and lunging in past Yan's reach, close enough to see where the first hint of black stubble was lining patches of the other boy's jaw. But he had misjudged Yan's momentum, and the knife flashed for his side. Gehrin knew he was dead.

The blade swerved past his bare skin, inexplicably missing him. He saw the shock and confusion in Yan's eyes before Gehrin's fist slammed against his jugular. Gehrin grabbed the knife away from Yan's weak grasp and slid the blade upwards as he had so many times before. He was still in the killing forest. Just another faceless criminal. He was serving the king's justice, and he was loyal. He was *bruhai*.

He stepped away, dropping the knife to the sand, and breathing heavily. He looked toward Tahmujin, toward Master Lohi, and then toward the masked boy standing near the scholar. Hajja's unnervingly blue eyes stared back at him, his face pale above the black leather. One of his hands was held ever so slightly forward from his side.

*Tohl. Guard the body against death.*

# CHAPTER TWENTY-SEVEN

*And King Heokaro, warlord of Katesh, overthrew the Kul Grijja, the blood-thirsty demons sacrificing their young and the offspring of the Rukian tribes to their carved gods. Many thousands died on the Barren Plains and in the canyons, outside the gates of Ujjak. King Heokaro slew the Kul Grijja and burned the city to purge the dark spirits that had gathered there. He raised up a man called Olik, who was a leader among the Rukian tribes, and gave him the crown of the city and a charge to rebuild it, to mine the great ores and gems beneath.*

*In return for overthrowing the Kul Grijja, King Heokaro would receive a great tribute. Half of all the gold and wealth that emerged from the mines of Ruk would be paid to the treasury in Katesh for every generation of kings ruling Ruk until the kingdom of Katesh was no more.*

*- The Founding of Ruk and the Great City Ujjak*

There was iron in the sky. Great swathes of gray painted the blue in gloom, heralding a coming storm. The canyon had split into many forks, carving through the ground like a dry delta. Emissary Otai led the caravan with Nar Yugha by his side and Senna riding near them. The air through the canyon was still, far too still. Ravens wheeled above the caravan as if hoping for death to bring them a feast.

Syndri sat astride Brig, the big black stallion growing far too restless to be tied to the back of her mother's wagon. His wound was healing, and his leg was sound enough for her to ride. But she did not let him go faster than a walk, despite him pulling at the reins. Itah was now tied behind the wagon, the young mare content to let Ettlan fuss over her and stroke her nose. The caravan's painfully slow pace had quickened slightly that morning when Emissary Otai had told them they were less than a day's ride of the city.

*Ujjak.* Syndri rolled the strange word around in her mouth. The Northern queen's city, built atop a thousand tunnels running deep into the earth where they mined the wealth of kingdoms. The north had great use for gold and baubles. Syndri ran her thumb over the hilt of the Rukian dagger tucked into her belt. The finely wrought silver bands circling the black grip were a master's work. But it was the blade that mattered, the sharpness and balance, the weight of it in her hand.

The tall canyon sides were growing more distinctly ridged as they approached the city. Soon, the road widened out into a large basin, and suddenly the outer walls of Ujjak appeared. A massive stone gate dominated the far end of the open canyon, kneeling stone warriors holding up the arch. Each one of the statues was four times as tall as a man, their muscled arms bent back over bowed heads. They wore chiseled scale armor, helms protecting their stone faces. Above the gate rose sharp peaks, a jagged ridge of mountains curving off to the east and west, a line of jackals' teeth piercing the gray sky. Syndri realized her mouth was open as she stared at the earthen giants, far greater in size than any hill or bluff in her homeland. Now, the distance from which she had always viewed the mountains to the north of the Garhis land had shrunk to mere horse lengths, and they were magnificent.

The sun was a blurred disc casting a dim glow behind the clouds, so the shadows lying over the mountainsides were simply darker aberrations against the rock. As Emissary Otai led them through the stone gate between the statues, a chill crept into Syndri's bones as she looked at those ancient faces bearing the weight of the mountains. Their grim expressions faced out into the canyon, immovable guardians of the people within. Up above the gate stood armored sentries with slender white bows taller than their heads. The warriors of Ruk were masters of the bow, Otai had once told Nar Garhis, and the weapons were crafted from a sacred tree. At the time, Syndri had scoffed, but up close, the soldiers of the Northern queen were impressive to look at.

Once inside the gate, a switchback path wound back and forth down into a massive crater scooped into the earth like a great footprint. The jagged peaks circled around it, far greater than any wall built by mortal hands. Syndri could not imagine how it could be attacked by an outside army. If her people had lived in such a place, the Tladr and Uratar tribes would have died in the attempt to take her village.

Down in the crater's bowl-like basin lay the city, nestled into the shallow inverse dome. The houses were a combination of mud and stone with slanted roofs made of deep gray slate tiles that looked as if someone had chiseled thin jagged shards from the sides of the mountains and laid them like kehroxen scales. The buildings were organized in circular lines spiraling in toward the center of the crater, where a massive tower rose like a spear. It was as tall as seven or eight of the houses stacked on top of each other, Syndri guessed.

At the far-right end of the crater was the façade of a building built into the rock, the towers half buried in stone. The palace of Queen Xhen looked as if it were trapped in time, the walls and towers slowly sinking back into the peak's base over millennia.

Syndri felt small, and the smallness was an unpleasant thing. It was as if everything she had ever known was a drop of rain in a river. If such places as this existed in the world, why was it her people that Queen Xhen had sought out?

People lined the streets as the caravan descended into the city, waving, and calling out in their strange language. Syndri supposed it was a greeting, but she was surprised at the excitement and joy she saw on the faces around her. The Rukian people were smaller than the Maleki, with eyes like darkened brushstrokes swept across their pale golden faces. Nearly all of them wore silver or gold beads in their hair, a testament to the wealth of the city. More and more of them appeared until the road Emissary Otai led them on was lined on both sides with cheering Rukians. Many of them pressed forward, offering baskets of food, fabrics, or glittering jewelry to the Garhis villagers.

A group of Rukian children followed Hyshir, laughing and running in circles around the great beast's hooved feet. He calmly ignored them, but Syndri could sense that he was not irritated by their presence.

Syndri kept Brig close to Ettlan's wagon, eyeing the people with suspicion. But then she caught sight of her mother, standing up in the wagon's bed, her face alight with joy as she held out both hands over the citizens of Ujjak, a glowing smile lighting her pale face. One woman got close enough to run alongside the wagon and grasp Ettlan's hand, giving her a handful of small purple flowers.

Emissary Otai led them into a section of the city that the queen had given to house the Garhis people. It was at the edge of the furthest ring of buildings, and they were not in the best of repair. But they were more than enough to shelter the exhausted refugees. Several of Emissary Otai's men stayed behind with the Garhis villagers to keep order as the caravan disassembled into their respective shelters.

But Senna rode back to find Syndri. The queen had given orders to Otai to bring her Nar Yugha, Hyshir, Syndri, and Senna as soon as they arrived. With a scowl, Syndri reluctantly left Ettlan in Tilis' care and rode Brig after her sister and the others. Emissary Otai stopped just inside the wall and dismounted from his horse. Syndri slid down from Brig's back, and hissed when a Rukian soldier came to take the stallion's reins. The man's hand drifted to the sword he wore at his belt,

"Draw it," Syndri warned. He did not understand her language, but the threat was clear.

"Peace, my friend." Emissary Otai stepped between them, and the soldier backed away sullenly. "He does not know your customs, daughter of Nar Garhis. There is a place for your horses in the queen's stable. Come, follow me."

The *stable* was square rooms built inside a long, squat building along the palace's outer wall. Syndri was confused until Emissary Otai explained that Brig could be kept by himself in one of the rooms. Straw had been spread on the floors and wooden buckets of water freshly filled. Brig entered his stable room without hesitation, his ears flicking back and forth as he inspected the floor and the bucket with interest. Then he drank deeply. Syndri relaxed. It was a strange custom to keep a horse in a room, but Brig did not seem uncomfortable. She checked his legs for any abnormal heat and his hooves for stones and did not leave until she was satisfied. Emissary Otai did not press her or the other Garhis warriors to hurry but waited patiently outside the stable for them to return. When Syndri emerged from Brig's stall, he smiled at her, his expression masked by hospitality. Syndri found herself wondering if she had ever seen the man's true face.

"Is it acceptable?"

Syndri grunted, still trying to take in the scope of the city and the peaks surrounding her. Yugha and Senna joined her, and Emissary Otai gestured for them to follow him into the palace. The ground under her feet was too smooth, and there was not a blade of grass in sight. Up close, the palace towers and sloped half-roofs were even more impressive. Carved scenes had been chiseled into the walls. Horses and warriors clashed together in an ancient battle, trampling down on grotesque, fanged creatures beneath. Spears, swords, and bows were held suspended in the rock, sharp blades piercing stone flesh.

The wide doors of the palace were banded with iron and guarded by more Rukian soldiers wearing their scale armor and belted swords. Emissary Otai led them through into a vaulted chamber supported by rock columns stretching more than a hundred horse lengths under the mountain's base. The air was dusky, lit by hundreds of oil lamps settled in gold stands banded to the columns.

Syndri's steps echoed in the chamber. She followed close behind Senna, feeling the hair on the back of her neck prickle. It was unnatural, all this stone and rock above them. They were hidden from the sky. Syndri would've been far more comfortable riding into the palace on Brig's back. Hyshir strode heavily behind them, his hooves making deeper echoes than the human feet around him.

The queen's chair was also made of stone, but far more crudely formed as if a great jagged boulder had fallen into the chamber and a seat had been simply carved out of it. The edges glittered black, reflecting the light in a thousand directions. Emissary Otai stopped them several lengths away from the chair. *Throne.* Syndri remembered the word from Otai's conversations. It was empty.

"The queen will not ask you to remove your weapons in good faith for the alliance that was made with Nar Garhis," said Emissary Otai quietly. "But if you draw blades in this chamber, you will die."

Syndri had seen the shadowy figures deep in the shadows of the chamber, holding more of the white bows. Her lip curled slightly in distaste. They were handsome weapons, but not fitting for a true warrior. It would take more than a small stick and an arrowhead to stop her blades. Yugha was also looking at the chamber with interest, no doubt noting the number of soldiers and the state of their armor and weapons.

They stood waiting for far longer than Syndri's patience held. She was considering turning to walk back out from underneath the stifling rock chamber when the queen finally appeared. A door opened behind the throne, and there she was, sweeping into the room in a whisper of black silk. The Northern queen, friend of Nar Garhis and the ruler of Ujjak, great city of Ruk.

Emissary Otai bowed so low Syndri thought he looked like he

was examining the floor tiles. She stood straight-backed, taking in every detail of the woman standing in front of the throne. The queen's black hair was hip-length, smooth and flat, the front wings tied back away from her round cheeks and pointed chin. Her eyes were dark like obsidian, glittering the same way the edges of her throne did. Her skin was flawless, her lips full and painted with red rouge, pressed into a firm line. The stiff, gold-trimmed collar of her dress rose beneath her jaw, sitting atop a tightly fitted chest piece that was scaled like the armor of her soldiers. Below the scales flowed a black silk skirt that trailed behind her and fell in rippling waves to the stone floor.

It was not until then that Syndri realized that the queen was easily a head shorter than either she or Senna. The proud strength the woman wore as easily as the black silk filled the room. It was the same kind of presence that Nar Garhis had held whenever he walked through the village. The queen looked over each of them in turn, and finally locked eyes with Syndri. A heartbeat passed, and Syndri felt as though she were on a raid, circling with an enemy warrior as they tried to gauge each other's weaknesses. The queen smiled.

"Welcome, warriors of the Garhis tribe."

Syndri's eyebrows rose in surprise. The queen's Maleki was perfect. Even the unique dialect of the Garhis was present, weighing the words down with a dark edge.

"Nar Yugha, your people are welcome in my city," the queen continued. "Ujjak is ready to stand by you and the promises I made to Nar Garhis."

*This queen uses honeyed words.* Despite her misgivings, Syndri did not sense any deception in the queen's steady gaze. She shifted uncomfortably. The stone was hard against the heels of her feet despite the boots she wore. The air was too stale, and it should have been her father standing on behalf of the Garhis tribe, not Yugha. The new Closed Fist stood face to face with the queen, his hulking form covered in furs and hides and strange in the queen's sleek stone halls.

"We are grateful," he said. There was an awkward silence that followed. Yugha had never been a man of many words, and the formality of the Northern rulers was far beyond the customs of the Maleki tribes.

"And the daughters of Nar Garhis. One I have met, and one is new to my land." The queen moved closer to Syndri, looking up at her face with a discerning eye. Whatever conclusion she had come to, she raised both her hands and held them palm open. "An open hand for the children of my friend Nar Garhis," she said gravely. "I am grieved not to have met him in this life, but it is honorable to meet you in his place."

The room grew deathly still. Syndri's clenched fists would not open, her fingertips digging painfully into her own palms. She could feel Senna's disapproval at her hesitation. Finally, she lifted her open hands to the queen. Somehow, she could not bring herself to speak her language to this foreign ruler, but she did not think the queen expected it of her now. The woman moved past her, and the tension eased from Syndri's shoulders.

Queen Xhen addressed Hyshir last. "It has been many years since one of the earth's shepherds has walked into my city. You honor us." Hyshir rumbled a response as he inclined his head to the queen, who was so tiny standing next to him, she looked like a child.

"Come to my speaking room, and we will talk more," Queen Xhen said, gesturing to an open doorway to their right. Once again, the Maleki tongue sounded strange coming from the queen's lips, her choice of words easily dismantling the confusion that might have been present had she attempted to insert her own Rukian word for the chamber she led them into.

The *speaking room* was a gathering place, a wide obsidian table dominating the center. Hyshir had to duck to enter, his single remaining horn barely clearing the stone. The queen sat in the chair at the end closest to a crackling fire warming the room from a pit built into the wall. A great circle of oil lamps hung from the ceiling, set into silver bands that grew smaller as they rose. There were five other people already in the room, who rose and quickly bowed to the queen and acknowledged the guests with interest. One of them, a balding man swathed in yellow silks, eyed them with a hungry stare that made Syndri's palms itch for her swords. When she met his gaze, his eyes flickered back to the queen as the thick fingers of his left hand worried a gold medallion that was hanging from his neck.

The queen motioned for them to sit. Syndri pulled one of the heavy chairs away from the table with a dull scraping sound and dropped into it. Senna and Yugha sat on either side of her. Hyshir remained standing in the corner. He would've been far too large for any of the chairs, and his intimidating presence looming behind the seated Garhis warriors was a welcome effect. Let the Rukians see that they were not weak, that even now, they were a threat to any who might try to take advantage of them. If the queen wanted them in her palace stinking of sweat and dirt and blood, so be it.

"These are the members of my council," the queen said. "They are not all First Swords as you have in the Maleki tribes. But they help me lead the people of Ruk. This is Rahian, my War Sword. He has been commanding my warriors for many years."

Syndri eyed the man sitting immediately to the queen's left as Emissary Otai softly translated the queen's words into his own tongue for the counsel. He wore black scale armor, but no helm, and his face was beardless but the hair a dark gray. He had the look of a warrior, a steadiness in his gaze as he nodded to them brusquely. His jaw was tight, and his expression held a fair amount of distrust. Clearly not all of the *Council* was as welcoming as the queen. Rahian's eyes lingered on Syndri's sword hilts, and she resisted the urge to grin. So, it had been the queen, and not her War Sword, who had given the order that their weapons remain with them.

*You do not like these blades so near your queen, I think,* she mused wryly. *If you cannot protect her, perhaps you are not deserving of the title of War Sword after all.*

The queen gestured to the youngest of the five. "This is Dexa. She oversees the city's mines."

The young woman was built strong, much like Syndri's own bone structure. Her black hair was short above sharp cheekbones and piercing blue eyes. She wore a simple shirt and no jewelry except three silver rings pierced through her ear, a welcome contrast to the gaudiness present in the rest of the counsel. The three remaining men all wore embroidered robes with wide sash belts. Each of them had gold rings in their ears and chains around their necks. The first had shorter cropped hair, but it was a mass of dark curls. His robes were a deep blood red, and his smile was pleasant.

"My high priest, Thego," said the queen. "He speaks for the earth gods."

*Earth gods...* Syndri eyed him curiously. *What kind of god stays trapped below the sky?* The man sitting next to the priest had the only beard, and when he smiled across the table, it was warm and crinkled the corners of his eyes.

"Mereo, the master of the merchants and trade in and out of Ujjak. If your people have need of anything while they are in my city, he will provide it to them."

"Welcome," Mereo said in stiff Maleki. "It is honorable to meet the Garhis."

The final member of the Council still fingered his gold medallion as if he were afraid that Syndri might leap across the table and rip it from his thick neck. There were other chains beneath it, and his ears were so heavy with gold rings that the lobes had stretched halfway down his neck. His eyes and mouth looked too small for his face, and his vague attempt at a smile lacked the warmth Syndri had seen in Mereo's welcome.

"Kiyab. He is coin master and sees to the enforcement of our laws."

*Such a strange choice of a man for this task.* Syndri let her eyes sweep over the Council once more, noting the expressions of each of them. *The queen desires to honor her alliance with my father, but I do not think all of you desire the same.* The War Sword and the master of coin looked less than pleased at the prospect of allowing a tribe of Maleki into their city. *Will they challenge the queen for her throne?* Syndri did not know how the customs worked in Ujjak, if the queen was in danger of such a challenge. The War Sword Rahian could fight, she did not doubt, but clearly Kiyab was not the sort of man who was used to wielding a blade. His fleshy, smooth palms were no doubt more used to counting gold coin in the queen's treasury.

The queen rested her hands on the arms of her chair. "Senna has told me of your mother's wounds. When she is settled, I will visit her. She is still Open Hand of the Garhis?"

Yugha answered, his voice rough. "She shares that place with my wife, Tilis."

*Ettlan shares no place.* Syndri clenched her fist beneath the table, grinding her teeth together. She saw the queen watching her and forced herself to relax. *If she thinks we are divided, she will find weakness and we will be no safer here than in Malek.*

"I see." The queen tapped her ringed fingers against the black stone table. "I will not keep you all here long, I know you need rest after your long journey. But our alliance is important, and I need to be sure that we all share one vision for the future of our peoples." She paused, looking around the room, and lingering longer on her own Council than the Garhis warriors.

"Nar Garhis shared with me that his vision was to rule a united Malek, that all tribes would be bound together under one Closed Fist and one Open Hand. The strength of Malek has long been divided, and your presence in Ujjak only proves this. I believe that the Garhis tribe is worthy of ruling Malek, and I wish to see Nar Garhis' vision come to life."

*Why? What possible reason does this woman have for keeping a promise to a dead Maleki Fist?* Syndri could see the future gleaming in Yugha's eyes as he listened. Nar Garhis' vision was now his own, and no doubt he was imagining himself at the head of the greatest warband that Malek had seen since the days of the first ancestors, before the tribes had separated to their own territories. He would be Closed Fist over all Malek. And he would stand in her father's place. The thought of it sent Syndri's blood into a boiling fervor. Her vision had always been of her father standing proud over the tribes, and her mother and sister and Baya standing at his side, with Syndri's own blades red with the blood of her father's enemies. This dark stone room with the Northern queen and her silk-robed Council and Yugha sitting in her father's chair... *he was right to see me as a threat. Even when I told myself that I would not challenge him, he knew that it was a lie.*

She pulled her gaze away from glaring into the back of Yugha's head, and when she caught sight of the queen watching her again, she bit the inside of her cheek. Did the woman have nothing better to do than to scrutinize Syndri's every expression? It made her feel as if she were being pried open and picked at like a dead kehrox.

"The Uratar and Tladr tribes have formed an alliance, and this is cause for concern. Emissary Otai tells me that it has been many generations since two tribes fought as one in Malek. Do you think they also intend to attack others?"

Yugha shook his head. "No. There is a blood feud between the Garhis and them. One of our warriors killed a sacred messenger from the Tladr tribe. I do not believe they will attack other tribes."

The soft touch of Senna's hand against Syndri's arm beneath the table was timely. Yugha was content to leave the rest of the tale dead in the ashes with Baya. But to Syndri's utter surprise, the queen raised a thin eyebrow and pushed back at the Closed Fist.

"I believe there is more to it than that," she replied. The compassion that had warmed the queen's expression earlier gave way to a cold sternness. The oil lamplight flickered across her smooth skin. If Yugha was surprised at her bluntness, he hid it well. "The death of a treasured son is cause enough for bloodshed. I am surprised you did not lead the warband against the Tladr yourself, Nar Yugha."

Pushing back his chair, Yugha rose to his feet. Within a heartbeat, the queen's War Sword Rahian was standing as well, his hand on the sword at his belt. The air in the room grew heavy, the walls leaning inward. Syndri watched the queen closely, expecting her to realize the mistake she had made in challenging Yugha's honor. But Queen Xhen met Yugha's glare with calm assurance, as if she had known the weight her words would carry. Yugha would not dare draw blades in the queen's palace, but there was no telling what he might do once he had left. The coin master leaned over to whisper something to Mereo, but the bearded advisor waved him away.

"I mean only that your loyalty to Nar Garhis has been spoken of to me," the queen amended. "But I see that I have offended you. Forgive me. Your people will need your guidance as they settle into their new home. I will speak with you again soon. Surely you have no need of the daughters of Nar Garhis. I would keep them here a little longer."

Nar Yugha cast one more scathing glance at the War Sword, and then nodded at the queen. He would bide his time, and Syndri saw in him the determined stride of a man who would not quickly forget the slight he had been given. Hyshir followed him out.

"Leave us," the queen told her counsel. The five of them rose and bowed, sweeping from the room. Last to leave was Kiyab, and he cast a glance over his shoulder as he left. Syndri wondered if he ever let go of the medallion, even to sleep. As soon as the heavy wooden door slid closed, the queen turned to Senna and Syndri.

"Let us speak honestly with each other now. I have moved your mother into the palace so that she can be kept safe. When she arrived ahead of the caravan, Senna told me that she believed Nar Yugha might seek to destroy the rest of your father's family. Particularly you, Syndri. You are a threat to him as Closed Fist. I have brought his wife Tilis into the palace as company for your mother, but also to ensure that Yugha does not act rashly while he is in my city."

*Senna...* opening her dry mouth was a feat of monumental proportions, but Syndri managed a raspy reply. "Why do you protect us?"

The queen's calculated gaze did not shift from Syndri's face. Her tone was not kind, but her words still offered comfort. "Because I promised an alliance to your father. Not to Yugha. And Emissary Otai often spoke of the proud daughters of Nar Garhis, how he believed the two of you would continue to lead your tribe after he was gone." She folded her hands in her lap. "Do you know that in Katesh, they say a great ruler is either a cunning fox or a fearsome wolf?"

Syndri shook her head. Senna nodded. She had always paid more attention to the stories of lore from the Northern nations.

"My people are strong, but they have borne the weight of servitude for many generations, and I would see that burden lifted. But they are not born and bred warriors like the Garhis. They need a god of war to lead them." The queen smiled, and her eyes shone cold as black stone. "I have need of a wolf."

# PART THREE

## THREE YEARS LATER

# CHAPTER TWENTY-EIGHT

*Sharai wrote the First Runes on a rock beside a river. He wrote runes in the trees, in the oceans, in the mountains, and in the forests and out of them walked the Firstborn...*

*And of Sharai's Oathsworn, there were Shaedrin, Nimaraii, and Aqatar, three brothers who held spears fashioned from the bones of the earth. They were gifts from Sharai to his greatest warriors, carved with powerful runes. And to these three Sharai gave stewardship of his Firstborn.*

*But Aqatar grew restless, discontent with the simple, honest work. He forced the Firstborn to bring him gifts and tributes. His brothers came to speak with him, but he would not listen to their wisdom. He grew angry, and cursed Sharai for leaving him to walk alongside lesser beings, bereft of his intended glory. The Firstborn were things drawn from dirt and stone, but he was the son of a star, and the runes that had formed him were drawn in the heavens.*

*- Gaja Teorhei, The Memory Chant*

The dark night was warm and thick with the scent of the forest beyond the walls. The stiffness in Gehrin's shoulders was growing past the point of annoyance and into the occasional sharp stab of pain. But he did not move even to twitch his fingers on the ridge of the wooden roof. He had crouched on the outer wall for nearly two hours now, waiting for the signal to creep further in. He was shrouded in the shadows beneath the tower that rose above him. There was no one inside. They would not have sacrificed one of their few guards for such a distant outpost, even with the vantage point over the forest. They knew what was coming for them.

The gray tails of the band tied around Gehrin's forehead fluttered against his shoulder, and he sensed a subtle movement in the shadows on the wall across from him, the darkness separating into the faint outline of a crouched figure. *Hajja.*

Somewhere beneath them in the culvert entrance to the cellars, Sabba would be moving into position. He was far too large to scale the rooftops with the same ease as the rest of them, but the giant could break trees with his bare hands. Gehrin felt a slight rush of relief that he would not be at the mercy of Sabba's inescapable grip tonight. Years of grappling with the Da'hamian had taught him how powerful it was.

Gehrin looked down over the courtyard. All they needed was the signal that Sabba had made it inside the walls. Soon, he saw a tiny flash of silver from Hajja's position. Move. He stayed crouched as he eased himself over the ridge, placing each foot with the practiced quiet of years until he reached the edge, still wrapped in the tower's protective shadow. He began to count heartbeats. *Nin, ruh, yan, liv, yul.* Everything hinged on their silence now. They had waited far too long for this moment to make a misstep. Gripping the roof's edge with his gloved fingers, Gehrin dropped onto a small pile of compost near the base of the tower, muffling his landing. The mask kept at least some of the unpleasant odor of rotten fruits and moldy straw from his nose. *Hajja, sabba, kajen, yelba, deth…*

He saw no sign of the guards; the outer courtyard was abandoned. But he knew better. The moment he left the shadows, some hidden eyes would catch sight of him. He touched the hilts of the knives strapped across his chest beneath his tunic. Slipping one from its snug leather sheath, he curled his fingers around the familiar hilt and moved soundlessly across the edge of the courtyard, using two wagons and a stone watering trough to hide his movements. *Niveth, rudeth, ahdeth, ivveth.*

Each step had been mapped and each heartbeat counted. He could not fall behind. He slipped into a stone corridor and flattened into an alcove as a pair of *telhai* guards passed by on the far end. There were still no shouts or signs that his brothers had been discovered. But sneaking past the *telhai* and *garatelhai* was a game now, almost ridiculous in its simplicity. The true test would be waiting for them closer to their quarry.

Like a shadowed wraith, Gehrin moved further into the stone corridors until he emerged from a doorway and the smooth stones beneath his feet grew grittier with sand that had been flung over them from the inner courtyard. He stepped more carefully now, feeling with his toes in the soft leather of his boots. He found a short hallway and slid a wooden panel open just far enough to slip inside and closed it again with steady fingertips. He was in a small storage room with baskets of linens, bedclothes, and stacks of clothing. The fresh scent of newly made soap wafted through the small room. Several jars of body oils sat on a shelf next to an array of smooth river stones.

Moving through each paneled wall, Gehrin made his way closer to the innermost rooms and finally stopped in one that had recently been slept in. The blanket on the floor looked perfectly laid out, as if it were still waiting to give comfort. But the telltale staleness of a room that had been empty was not present. Instead, there was a faint musk that wrinkled Gehrin's nose. Sweat. So at least one of them had slept and would be fresher than the others. It was possible that they had taken shifts, leaving two of them to watch for shadows in the night while the other slept. A risk.

The faint glow of light warmed the paper panels in the door to Gehrin's left. Not bright enough to be a fire. Candlelight. Two rooms away. Whoever had slept in the blanket at his feet had done so recently, and he had missed the chance to dispatch one of them with a mark of shame. He would have relished it, but the moment would come soon enough. He strode lightly to the window and a small square of cloth dangling from the edge of the roof outside. He reached out and gave it a tug, sending a signal up through the string that was attached to it. A heartbeat later, Nin had swung down and slipped through the window's space, landing soundlessly on the rush mats. Pulling his cloth mask down beneath his nose, he sniffed the air, noting the same sweaty scent. He nodded to Gehrin.

The others were in place. It was time to catch a king.

Opening the door would expose them to the guard that was doubtlessly positioned outside the king's room. But would there be two outside? Or one?

Hajja knew, watching the corridor from whatever vantage point he had found on the roofs. Gehrin stood against the wall as Nin crept to the door and peered through the tiny crack between the wood and the stone. He held up one finger to Gehrin.

So, the other two were inside, or lurking nearby. It was not likely that the last occupant of the room they stood in would return soon, having slept so recently. They were inside the walls, and they would need to move quickly. Hajja was waiting for them to emerge from the room. Sabba was close, he would've had plenty of time to come up from the cellars.

Nin slid the door open.

The sudden scrape of a boot on stone outside was the only sound in response, but it was enough. Nin twisted back against the wall as several darts thudded into the wood frames where he had stood. Whoever stood outside was ready for them.

Without time for even a curse of frustration, Gehrin slipped his own set of darts from his chest belt and fitted them between his fingers, leaping past Nin as he heard the heavy footfalls of another player entering the fray. Sabba had arrived, and Gehrin emerged upon the scene of the giant's arms wrapped around the guard who had been posted outside. The guard punched his palm upwards with a crack against Sabba's chin and sank two darts into the massive forearm choking off his air with the other hand. Gehrin surged past him into the candlelit room and caught sight of red silk robes and a figure kneeling at a low table before catching the flash of blades in his peripheral vision. He saw the face and frowned.

He ducked and pulled knives from his belt, knocking aside the blades approaching his chest. Nin rushed through the room behind him. The red robed figure rose from the mats and the candlelight disappeared, casting the room into nothing but shadows. Something ripped through the cowl around Gehrin's neck, and a body's weight pressed him back against the wall. He stabbed upwards with his fistful of darts. The figure launched back and caught his wrist. Gehrin made a swift circle with his hand, breaking the other man's grip. A cold blade pressed against his neck, and the hot breath of his opponent washed over his face.

"Dead."

*Curse you, Kajen.*

On the floor, he saw the man wearing the red robes kneeling over Nin, blades drawn and held to Nin's chest. Even in the darkness, Nin's frustration was visible.

Gehrin glanced beyond Kajen's leering grin to the open door and smirked, jerking his head to the side. Kajen looked to the right and saw Hajja standing in the outer corridor, bathed in the dim light of the crescent moon, and holding a blade to the throat of his prisoner, who was dressed in simple servant's garb. White hair glowed above the pale face.

Kajen growled and spat on the floor. "*Keht!*" he muttered angrily. He stepped back from Gehrin, his blade falling away. Outside the room, Sabba finally released Tirrim, who had taken the outer guard post.

Inside, the red robed "king" sheathed his own daggers and smiled at Gehrin. "Well done, brother," Jai said, sweeping the *heoja* hat from his head and setting it carefully on the table. "You saw past the decoy."

"Well, Hajja did," mused Gehrin. He pulled down his mask and raised a fist to Hajja, who nodded and released Ruh. The Takkan had been selected to play the part of the king when Tahmujin had separated them three days ago. Jai's decoy had been a smart move on their part, especially with fewer guards. Tahmujin's direction had been explicit: you must learn to protect a king who cannot fight, or you will rely on his skill to protect himself.

Tirrim slapped Sabba's broad back. "Sorry for the darts, brother," he chuckled. Sabba rubbed his forearm and shook his head to clear it. Two darts tipped in the paralytic poison Nin had concocted would hardly take the giant down the way it would any of the rest of them, but he would sleep deeply that night.

"Who is on watch?" Nin asked.

"Ivveth and Liv," replied Jai, untying the red king's robes and folding them. "Tahmujin will expect our report in the morning."

"Let's hope the old jackal can wake Kajen," said Tirrim with a grin.

Kajen stretched his arms across his chest and tilted his head from side to side. "Yah, I'm gonna hold that bed like a lover. Tahmujin been sleeping in his soft cushions for days while we stare at the walls waiting for these *kehts*."

The others slowly meandered away toward their cells to sleep, leaving Tirrim and Gehrin alone in the courtyard. Tirrim reached inside a pouch at his belt and tossed a small round object at Gehrin. It was a fig. They walked the span of the courtyard, sucking the sweet juice from the purple fruit just as they had ever since they were boys. If Kirte had ever noticed how many of the figs went missing from her storerooms, she never said a word.

"Master Lohi says we're going to leave Blackvale soon," said Tirrim. "All these years finally coming to an end seems like a dream, doesn't it?"

Gehrin stopped and looked up at the walls, the cracked stones that he had counted so many times trying to stay awake during the long night watches. Along the wall sat the rack of wooden staves that had bruised them countless times. They hadn't used wooden weapons since the day the others had died. Master Tahmujin had given them all knives and spears, and the bruises had turned into cuts. All of them were scarred beneath their robes, some less than others. Tirrim was the best fighter of all of them still, and Ruh and

Jai were fast enough to evade most of their brothers' attempts to mark them.

The little boy who had come to Blackvale trapped in a wooden box would hardly recognize him now. Gehrin often wondered if he was even still Gehrin. The name Liv clung to him like a second skin, hiding the son of Counsellor Hallix beneath. Even Tirrim had not called him by his first name in years. The two parts of himself warred still within, but he knew that the boy he had been was swiftly sinking beneath the surface.

"Yes," Gehrin said softly. "It all seems like a dream."

"What do you think it will be like, seeing our families again? Will they even recognize us?"

Gehrin frowned. "You have not spoken of it in years. Why now? Our family is here within these walls now. Our place is by the king's side. You know that."

Tirrim shook his head. "You've always been a fool, Liv. I love you like my own brothers, but you're a fool, and you're still letting Tahmujin's words speak for you. My father is the city lord of Fethet, and he visits Keld every year. But your father is a High Counsellor. You'll see him the moment you step into the palace."

*He won't know me.* It was the armor Gehrin wore. As the years wore on, he barely recognized himself anymore and hoped that the boy in the wooden box was truly gone. All that remained was the name, spoken only in the silence of his own mind, and even that was nothing more than a distant echo. And yet, some childlike inner self gripped it with an intense ferocity, refused to take on the full mantle that Tahmujin had given him.

"We don't even know who the king will be when we return," continued Tirrim. "My father used to say that the king's nobles were like a flock of vultures. That's why we're going back. Everything they've taught us is to build an impenetrable guard around the new Crown Prince."

*My father would stop at nothing to see Xario on the throne.* Gehrin looked up at the faint shimmer of stars above them. "The king is the great father of Katesh. When I was young, I was told that my life would be in service to him. Coming here has not changed that, and if my fate was always to be *bruhai*, I will gain nothing by resisting it."

"Fate is a fickle thing," replied Tirrim. "Don't let it trap you."

They separated, and Tirrim disappeared into the corridors while Gehrin climbed back to the rooftops, comfortable in the weight of his leather armor. His black gloves, cowl and mask hid nearly all of his skin, allowing him to blend into the night. He ran along one of the roof ridges until he reached the base of the same tower that had sheltered him earlier. Gripping the edges of the stones, he climbed upwards until he reached the tower's upper platform. He crouched on the wooden floor, the sky hidden by the tower's sloped roof. From here, he had a vantage point over all Blackvale, the inner courtyard and surrounding barracks and halls, the outer gate and the bridge spanning the deep chasm down into the killing forest. It had been a long time since Master Tahmujin had taken them there, and the bodies of the prisoners they had killed had disappeared into the wild, their remaining bones hidden in the overgrowth.

Now, every moment they were not training with Master Tahmujin, Master Lohi had them pouring over maps of Katesh and the surrounding lands, memorizing the history of each noble family and their wealth and influence, and reading ancient texts on the runes and the great power that their ancestors had wielded.

Gehrin could feel it, far beneath him, that gentle thrumming in the stones. Hajja still had dreams, but he no longer woke up in terror. Kajen and Ruh also claimed to feel some echo of the magic that Hajja could so easily wield, but only Gehrin could sense it with any clarity. Some nights, faint tendrils of whatever Hajja had seen in his sleep crept into Gehrin's awareness. Once, he had heard screaming, smelled something like sulfur. He did not envy the more vivid paths that Hajja walked.

In battle, the *tohl* rune was still the strongest of those Hajja could wield. He could turn blades aside with the careless flick of a finger. Added to *terha*, he had begun to pull power from the ground into their bodies, which gave them greater strength for a brief time. Channeling the earth's magic took its toll on Hajja, and although he had grown stronger, he had never lost the gauntness in his cheeks and his blue eyes still shone from dark sockets. Master Lohi was keen to see him master the *yba* rune, because the old scholar believed it could loosen any tongue to speak the truth, even against the wish of its owner. That would be a desirable skill in the king's court.

Were they ready? Gehrin did not know how any of them could train enough years to truly be ready for what lay ahead of them. Only days ago, Master Tahmujin had pitted them against a group of the *garatelhai* and *telhai* guards, and they had fought like shadows, each of them forged and honed to a deadly edge. The ease with which they had defeated the guards had shocked them all, a testament to the endless days Master Tahmujin had broken them and rebuilt them into something beyond their limitations.

*Even if the king chooses Xario, I am not truly Gehrin anymore. But am I truly Liv?*

Rolling his old name over his tongue silently, Gehrin eased himself into a cross-legged seat on the platform. It was the one piece of himself he had never truly let go. Within his own mind, he was still Gehrin. He rested his hands on his knees, breathing slowly in through his nose and out through his mouth, letting the sounds and sights of the night drift in. Exhaustion threatened him, but he was used to its insistent pull. He calmed his whirling thoughts and pulled them in close, sealing them away in the gentle rhythm of his breath.

Dawn eased over the top of the cliff, far above Blackvale. Aqatar's light was a soft glow, not the angry burning intensity of midday, and it touched the peaks of the rooftops, warming the gray stone and the cracked and faded carvings in the walls of the towers. Gehrin unfolded himself from the platform and rose, smoothly dropping down to his footholds on the tower's rocky face. It had been a long time since he had chosen to use the stairs once becoming so comfortable on the roofs. He heard the first rustlings of life as he passed the stable yard and saw Kirte milking one of the goats. She smiled when she saw him.

"I've left out food for you in the kitchen," she said.

"Thank you, Kirte," he replied, pausing near the goat pen. "You look as bright as a star, and it's not even morning yet."

She laughed, her wrinkled face creasing. "Save your flattery for the women in Keld. I'm far too old. Go eat."

Gehrin chuckled and strode through the stableyard and down into the kitchens. The smell of fresh rice made his stomach rumble, and he saw two platters on the butcher's block. He took the wooden spoon and dug into the bowl, bringing a huge bite of rice to his mouth. He sucked in his breath, cooling the hot grains, too famished to slow his eating. His next bite brought the sharp tang of fermented cabbage, the spice adding a pleasantly hot tingle to his lips. He sighed contentedly. Not even the palace cooks would be able to match Kirte's skill, he was sure of it. He was surprised that Tirrim had not come back for his breakfast yet.

Cupping the bowl of rice in one hand, he saw two sacks of tubers sitting near the stairway to the cellars. Kirte would try to carry them down when she was finished with the goats, most likely. Gehrin quickly finished the rest of the rice and cabbage and hefted the two sacks on top of one shoulder.

The cellars below the kitchen were filled with crates and sacks of rice, vegetables, and grains. Dried fruits sat in baskets atop the sacks, alongside an assortment of nuts and berries. Herbs hung from the ceiling alongside dried boar and goat meat. There were four or five storage chambers linked together by open doorways, and at the furthest end was the large iron grated drain that Sabba had entered through the previous night.

As he dropped the sacks of tubers down amongst the rest, a sharp clatter drew his attention further into the cellars. He walked through the first three rooms and into the fourth, where a fortress' worth of pottery, brooms and buckets, barrels of aged wine, and stacked stools and chairs sat collecting dust and cobwebs. In one corner, partially obscured by a barrel, sat Jai, his chin tipping forward onto his chest as he slept. A broom had fallen to the floor nearby, but the racket had clearly not woken him.

"Jai."

The chin lifted, revealing red-rimmed eyes full of confused grogginess. He looked around him, and quickly rose to his feet when he caught sight of Gehrin standing in the doorway. "Forgive me, I did not mean to sleep."

Gehrin glanced down at the floor, where three dead rats lay in a pile on the stone. Jai scratched at the roots of his hair and picked them up by the tails. "I still come here to hunt them. No one else does, and it needs to be done."

"You need sleep," replied Gehrin. "You could have hunted them after, why waste the hours sleeping with your chin hanging down to your stomach?"

Jai shrugged. "I don't mind. I used to fall asleep here many nights when I was a boy. It is good to do work that is familiar. Master Lohi used to say that I was a warrior defending the king's storerooms," he said with a laugh. "I used to sit down here for hours and hours waiting to hear one of them scratch at the walls."

Though the rest of them had long since ceased seeing Jai as a servant, he still stood apart from them. He had been training to be *bruhai* much longer than any of the others, born alone into a stone fortress at the edge of the kingdom. Master Lohi had said only that Jai's mother had died in childbirth, leaving her son an orphan, and that he had been raised by Kirte and Lohi as a servant to the king. Jai kept to himself at the edges of the bonds that had formed between the boys, but he was quick to encourage the others or help them with any task that the old masters set them to.

"I'm going back to the cells to get a little sleep before Tahmujin calls us out to the training yard," said Gehrin. "You can stay down here and sleep with your rats if you like."

"I will come."

The two of them left the cellars and returned to the prison wing of the fortress. They each had their own sleeping quarters, back to the cells they had lived in for the first weeks of their life at Black-vale. But now, no guard paced the hallway, and there were no iron locks on the trapdoors. Gehrin opened his and began to descend. Jai walked the length of the hallway, glancing down into each trapdoor briefly before heading to his own. Gehrin smiled to himself. Jai had always been nearly as much of a mother hen as Kirte herself. It was easy to tell that he had been raised by the old woman.

"You were my brothers long before you came here," Jai had once told them. "Master Lohi told me that one day my brothers would come, and I never knew when until the day he brought you through the gates."

Untying his leather armor, Gehrin hung it over the stand in the corner of his cell. The room was still small, but the space was no longer suffocating. It was a comfort now to close out the world above him. He folded his mask and cowl and laid them on the table, and then eased down onto his cot. Tahmujin would allow them at least a bit more sleep, and Gehrin intended not to waste any of the time. He was asleep a few heartbeats after his head rested against the cushion.

# CHAPTER TWENTY-NINE

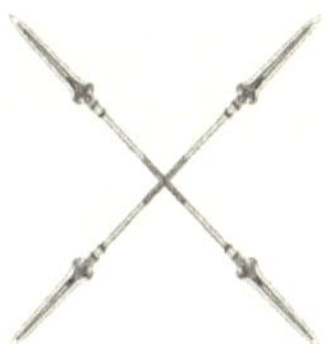

*If, by his forty-fifth year, the king has failed to produce an heir of his own body, he will choose from among the sons of his Counsel.*

*- The Chronicles of the Kings of Katesh*

The sharp end of Xario's spear punched through the edge of the wooden pell, sending a shower of wood chips flying into the air. He withdrew and jabbed again. Sweat trickled into his face despite the cloth band he had tied around his head. The heat of the summer was at its zenith, and even in his light leather armor Xario could feel the heavy weight of the air stealing his breath. He lifted his spear and squinted at the wooden stake in front of him. The sounds of blades hitting wood and other blades rose and fell in the familiar cacophony of life in the Black Legion's camp.

Drawing his arm over his face, he left a smear of grime behind as he wiped away the sweat. He went back to the sparring field. Dozens of men and women were already paired, using an array of weapons from swords to spears to knives. He passed by them at the edge of the field, marking each duel with interest until he turned into the maze of barrack houses, tents, and low wooden huts that housed the entirety of the Black Legion. The main city of Mizak was to his right, the wall half as high as the massive barrier around Keld. It was not an easily defensible city, nor had it ever been meant as one, but the presence of the five thousand mounted *garatelhai* and several squadrons of the king's foot soldiers rendered it far more impenetrable than its wall did.

The small square of tents that sheltered Xario's hundred was cloaked in a light haze from the cookfires as soldiers began to stir meats and vegetables into a thick broth in the cauldrons. Several of them nodded and held up their hands in greeting as he walked past them. He returned each gesture, making for a cookfire placed near his own tent. Two soldiers sat on stumps beside it, while a third stirred the spiced soup with a ladle. One of the seated soldiers looked up and his weathered face creased into a broad grin full of blackened teeth.

"Lord Xario, you look as if you've defeated a hundred pells!" he exclaimed jovially. "Come have a bowl of soup, Taki put in extra spices!"

Xario leaned his spear against the tent. The smaller rotund man who was stirring the cauldron's contents scooped a bowlful out and handed it to him. The two men and the seated woman all watched him expectantly as he lifted the spoon to his lips, blowing lightly on the steaming liquid. He slurped the chicken and broth in with relish, eyes widening as the full fury of the spice hit the roof of his mouth. He coughed, and the three soldiers laughed.

"Still have a noble's taste buds, eh Lord Xario?" teased the woman. Her thick hair was tied back with multiple leather strings, and her eyebrows matched the coarse black hair and crawled like two massive caterpillars above her piercing dark eyes.

"Despite Taki's best efforts," replied Xario, still chuckling around the tears in his eyes. "Don't laugh until you've had a mouthful of this, Kei."

Taki handed her a bowl and she slurped straight from the rim, then chewed thoughtfully. "It's fine. You Northerners can't handle spices." Her words were accompanied by a slight flush that rose in her cheeks, and Xario smirked.

"You're sweating a lot for someone standing in the shade, Kei."

"It's hot out here."

The jovial soldier, Nab, took his own bowl and ate with great enthusiasm, offering the occasional grunt as his appreciation to Taki's handiwork. Xario ate another spoonful slowly, sipping at it a bit more cautiously than the first. They ate together in comfortable silence.

When Kei put her bowl down, she jerked a thumb toward the larger command tent several lengths away. "The Hand was looking for you. Told him I'd send you his way as soon as you got back."

Xario glanced toward the banner posted outside the large structure, green silk fluttering softly in the breeze. Third Hand Jaakar had been summoning him more and more frequently the past few months, bringing Xario along with him as he inspected the men's armor and tents, supervising their training, leading them in drills. Xario had always been one of the commander's favorites, and despite his protestations to the contrary, even he could not deny the attention he received. Kei had told him that the men believed he would be chosen king. Xario was hard pressed to find anyone who did not believe it now.

A king must also be a warlord, it was known. And who would be better to train a warlord than the oldest and most respected commander in the Black Legion? "He's grooming you to lead the men and sit on a throne," Kei had said once. She had been Xario's second in command over their hundred for the past two years, and he trusted her completely. Nab and Taki were close thirds, and he relied heavily on all of them to help keep their squad in hand. Nab was a man who made few enemies, his big smile and words of encouragement often lifting even the darkest moods. Taki's cooking was well known throughout the Legion, even among the soldiers of the other Hands. And when soldiers were fed and happy, they talked. Taki knew the story of every man and woman in the Legion, many said.

Xario finished a few more mouthfuls of his soup and handed the bowl back to Taki, who frowned at him. The short cook shook the spoon in his face menacingly. "You gonna be a skeleton, the way you eat, guess so."

"You eat enough for both of us, Taki," replied Xario. "I'll eat more later, if there's any left once the squad is through."

He left to the sound of Taki muttering something about Xario eating his own stomach, the thick Mijaro street dialect rendering half the words unintelligible. Xario smiled to himself and headed for the Hand's tent, sucking the spices out from between his teeth. A peppercorn cracked between his molars, and he winced.

Jaakar's tent was the perfect image of a military commander's post. Inside was a large table, carefully organized with stacks of paper and tablets, several goat's-hair brushes lying on a porcelain dish. A half-used ink block sat off to the side, uncovered and wet as if it had been recently used. The crisp new map that Jaakar had commissioned lay on the flat table, edges still slightly curled and held down with stones. The deep black of the ink lines came to life on the tan parchment with the borders of Sundra, Katesh, Da'ham, and Malek curving their way into the gray seas. Xario approached the table and traced a finger over the city of Keld, across to his father's farmlands near the Keldari River, and up into the northernmost forests and mountains at the edge of Katesh.

In the center of the continent, a small triangular-shaped country sat surrounded by its larger neighbors, its massive crater-fortress city dotted near the border. Ujjak, the city of Queen Xhen.

There was a shuffling behind the curtain veiling the back of the command tent, and Jaakar appeared around it, wiping the last traces of his meal away from his gray-whiskered face. He waved his hand at the map.

"Better work than the last one. This mapmaker is from Fethet. Actually, has been past the border of Katesh," he said gruffly. High praise from the Third Hand of the Legion. Xario touched his palm to his leather breastplate and bowed.

"You summoned me, Lord?"

Jaakar picked up a cloth envelope, the red fabric embroidered with gold swans. "From the king," he said. He pulled the thin fold of paper out and handed it to Xario. "Read."

Scanning the neatly arranged letters, Xario felt as if the paper were growing heavier in his hands. He folded it carefully and placed it on top of the map. Jaakar watched him closely, his hands folded on the table. Xario drew in a deep breath.

"When do we leave?"

"Within three days. It is not a long journey, and the Third needs a change of scenery," the old man mused. "About time we came to it, I suppose."

Somehow Xario had imagined that this moment would never come, that it would remain an untouchable unknown lodged firmly in a future he would never see. But today it was written in black ink on a paper that he had held in his hand, fingers brushing over the letters written by the king himself. He wished he could set the paper in the small silver brazier in the corner, watch the ashes flicker up into the air and disappear. He faced Jaakar.

"The king expects... trouble after the ceremony?"

"It would appear so."

"The presence of the Legion should be enough to dissuade any reckless action on the part of the nobility," Xario said, as if trying to convince himself of its truth. As he said it aloud, one thousand soldiers seemed insufficient. Would the coffers of Bari Ujo buy him support if his son wasn't chosen to be the next king? Would the lesser counsellors band together to overthrow the king's decision? A military coup was nearly impossible with the Legion so firmly loyal to the king. But a coup from within the city? That seemed far more likely.

The old commander rapped his knuckle against the table. "Not even the presence of an entire army is always enough to dissuade reckless action. The king moves one Hand to the city, and only one. Why?"

"Moving multiple Hands of the Legion to Keld would make him seem afraid. One Hand is a show of strength to dissuade any who might disagree with his choice. Moving the entire Legion?" Xario shook his head. "It might be perceived as a sign of weakness."

"Mm," agreed Jaakar. "And why the Third?"

*Because he knows my own men will support me if I am chosen.* "Your influence as a senior commander of the Legion carries more weight."

"It is not my name being spoken in the marketplaces of Keld," the old man said knowingly, clearly displeased at Xario's evasion. "The king has led the Legion into battle. He knows the way of soldiers, and he knows that you have influence here."

*And perhaps he thinks I have influence over my father,* mused Xario wryly. *In that I will disappoint him. If the king names me heir, my father will expect his own influence to smother mine. I will be king in name, but the throne will be my father's.*

"Your thoughts are heavy."

Xario looked up at the Third Hand and his eyes burned when he saw the fatherly concern in the man's gaze. If only Xario had been born a different son to a different father, perhaps this wise old warrior would have also been pleased to see him rise to power, but of a far different sort. Leading soldiers would never be the kind of glory that Counsellor Hallix desired.

"Thank you," Xario said. Jaakar's eyebrows lifted slightly, and Xario clenched his fists at his sides. "Thank you for everything you have taught me."

The old man cleared his throat and slid the king's message back into its silk envelope. "You have done well." He paused, as if considering something more he might say, and then shook his head ever so slightly. "You have done well."

Xario blinked and knelt on the floor, bowing to the commander the same way he would have bowed to his father, letting his forehead touch the rush mats. He held his position until the commander reached out, gripping his shoulders and lifting him up. Jaakar let him go, patting his arms.

"We leave in three days. Get your soldiers ready. Sharpened blade, strengthened hands, focused mind."

"As you command, Lord Hand."

Excitement spread through the camp like the buzzing of bees. Everywhere he went, Xario saw the looks on the faces of his soldiers, the way they watched him as if he were a god. He hated it. He hated the way that the respect given to him as a commander had morphed into something undeserved, something he had not earned. The reality that he might not return to the Legion after the king's ceremony had begun to sink in. He grew sullen and short-tempered, moving about his tasks with a grim resignation, eating even less of the food Taki brought to him. Nab stopped trying to lift his spirits.

At the end of the second day, Kei appeared inside his tent as he sat on his cot, rubbing oil into his leather armor with a cloth. She folded her arms and watched him for a few heartbeats until he finally acknowledged her presence.

"Have you gotten your dark spirits out yet?" she asked, fixing him with a dark glare. "You're acting like a child."

He smoothed his hand over the boiled leather. "Do not test me, Kei."

"It's my job to test you, Lord Hallix," she returned curtly. "You named me your second in command. If you don't like me pointing out when you're being a *keht*, you should have chosen someone else. But you didn't."

The anger that surged hot within him was nothing but a shield to hide his shame, and Xario knew it. But the shame was still too much to uncover, even in the face of someone who knew him as well as Kei. "Don't."

She snorted. "What would Kasaii say if she could see you now?" Surprised, Xario looked up, and Kei gave him a wry smile. "Don't look at me like that. You're so besotted with that girl that you look like you've swallowed a star every time I bring you one of her letters."

*We are small birds caught in a great wind, and if we do not find a perch, we will be blown away.* Kasaii's words had haunted him since that night he had let her ride away in the palanquin, despite the encouraging letters she had sent him the past few years regarding the work she was now doing on behalf of his father's house. Xario lifted the armor cuirass from his lap and set it aside. At the sight of his face, Kei sighed and unfolded her arms.

"If you push away your friends, Xario, you will live a lonely life."

"All my life, I've only ever wanted to wear this armor," he replied, touching the ridged neckline of the cuirass. "I am a soldier, but there are others who do not believe that is enough. And now, the Legion does not believe it either."

"You don't know what your soldiers believe. They will follow you whether you are a Tenth Leader, the Commander of the Legion, or if you sit on the throne of all Katesh. They look at you the way they do because they believe you are worthy of being a king."

*I want to be worthy of a spear, not the throne.*

Kei reached out her hand. "Come. You need to eat. Taki has nearly lost half his girth worrying over you the past two days. A sour mood is never improved by a sour stomach."

Grasping her forearm, Xario pulled himself to his feet.

The road between Mizak and Keld was a familiar journey for Xario. On the second day, the Third Hand led his thousand soldiers across the Keldari River crossing, the sound of hooves against the stone bridge echoing. Xario rode behind Jaakar with the other Tenth Leaders, a front spearhead to the long line of black sleek horses that trailed them all the way back into the forest. Xario's black mare was in fine spirits. He'd brushed her to a smooth gleam the night before, and she pranced behind Jaakar's gelding, ears flickering every direction.

He was as comfortable in her saddle as he was walking on his own two feet. He held the haft of his spear, the end lodged firmly in the leather cap on his stirrup. The line of *garatelhai* spears behind him flashed and caught the light, bobbing up and down as the horses walked steadily toward the great city of Keld.

When the massive stone walls came into view, Xario tightened his grip on the spear. He could not escape his fate. Whatever the future held, he would not bring shame to his house or the Legion. The king had once been a warlord, had once ridden at the front of the Legion with his own spear. He was still a soldier.

Riding past the Blood Stones, Xario glanced down at the deep runes, the memories of that place still etched firmly in the mind of the boy who had watched the death of the Crown Prince's murderer. Something pulled at him faintly as he rode the mare past the circle of stones.

Soon the name of a new Crown Prince would be written in the royal history, the brushstroke that would immortalize the future of Katesh. Would it be his own?

Xario turned his face away from the Blood Stones and toward the massive Stone Gate on the left side of the city. There were barracks in the city that would house at least two Hands of the Legion. It was cramped quarters, but with the pleasures of the city so close at hand, none of the soldiers were likely to complain.

As they rode into the city, the people of Keld lined the streets, throwing flowers beneath the hooves of the horses and waving, screaming. Here and there a lover or parent would call out the name of a passing soldier, some with tears streaking their faces. A young woman crowded close to the horses and pressed a white stone lily into Xario's hand, her eyes shining up at him.

The lower districts were just as packed with people as the marketplace, and as they passed into the noble districts nearer to the palace, the crowds grew sparse, but dressed in their finest to welcome the Legion. They passed along the road of the Ministers, and the gilded treasury building rose to their right side, the office of the Minister of Tributes nearby. On the steps, a small crowd of green-robed scribes had gathered to watch the procession, and with them, Xario caught sight of a young woman standing out from the rest in a white and red dress. His heart leapt into his throat.

She smiled at him, and the sight warmed him down to his toes. In the perfect circle of black hair perched atop her head sat a silver comb. She raised a hand to him, and he turned his horse aside from the rest of the line and rode up to the group of scribes. They moved back respectfully, but Kasaii stood waiting for him. He reached down, offering her the stone lily. She accepted it and held it against her white jacket, pressing the green leaves to her breast.

Xario raised his hand in a salute and nudged his mare into a trot, returning to the side of the Third Hand.

*I will come back for you, Kasaii.*

# CHAPTER THIRTY

*I always believed that choice had been taken away from me. That I could either die, or exist like a spirit, wandering at the whims of the living.*

*- Sonho*

Gehrin tied the shoulder laces of his armor, and then opened the small wooden box sitting on the table, withdrawing a red robe with wide sleeves tapering to black trim. He drew it over the armor, tying it beneath his left arm. Then a belt, and the ceremonial knife, its wide leather-wrapped hilt topped with a sharp spearhead shape.

He lifted the final object in the box and held it in his hands. A mask, full-faced and made by one of the finest artisans in Keld, Master Lohi had said. The red wolf's face and eyes and drawn, snarling fangs were the sort of things that would have brought him nights of terror as a child. He stared at it, waiting for the horrific visage to illicit some kind of disgust, but instead he only marveled at the craftsmanship and the lifelike shape of the nose and teeth. Was this what he had become?

He set down the mask and drew his long hair into a tight knot at the back of his head. He hesitated, and turned the mask away from him, looking into the unpainted brown wood. It was not so fearsome now, only two holes for his eyes and two for his nostrils, simple on the inside. He set it against his face, feeling the strange weight of it as he tied the leather straps beneath his hair knot. It was comfort-able, and sat easily against his nose and ears, and the holes for his eyes were large enough that the mask did not restrict much of his vision.

The polished metal mirror sitting on the table reflected the mask and it made him look like a dark spirit's face above the blood red robes. Seven years ago, he had begged for death to find him, had wanted to disappear into the stones he stood in now, an armored killer.

"Liv."

He spoke the name quietly to the walls, and then snuffed out the oil lamp on the table and climbed the ladder out of the cell.

A fire roared in the center of the courtyard, a pyre made of logs that had once been stacked at the edge, carried the length of the sand as Master Tahmujin drove them on. Other red-robed masked figures had made their way to the sand, standing around the pyre in a circle. Gehrin joined them, and Master Lohi approached, leaning heavy on his staff.

"*Bruhai*. Bloodsworn to the king, forged in the likeness of the ancient Oathsworn. Tonight, you swear your lives in service to the king of Katesh and all those who follow his reign." Master Lohi walked around the circle of hooded masks, tapping his staff against the runes he had drawn on the floor. "You will be husband to no wife. You will be father to no children. You will have no name other than *bruhai*. You will serve no one but the king. Desertion of your post will name you as *aqqa* and you will die a traitor's death. Do you swear it?"

"I swear."

"Swear it in blood before Sharai and his Oathsworn, below the stars. If you break this oath, you will forfeit your life."

Gehrin pulled the ceremonial blade free of its sheath at his belt and held up to his left hand, placing the knife's edge against his palm. As one, the eight *bruhai* bled in front of the flames, holding their hands up above their heads toward the night sky. The masks hid their faces and any hint of who they had been, any resemblance to those who had once loved them buried beneath the gleaming fangs.

Master Tahmujin did not call them to the training yard the next morning, but Gehrin found his way there, years of waking up at the first light of dawn engrained in his body. The pyre was a pile of charred logs and ash, and a thin tendril of smoke still crept up into the air above it. Gehrin knelt beside it, holding his hand out over the warmth. Up above on the rooftop, he caught sight of Ruh crouched on top of one of the roofs, at the end of his nightlong watch. The Takkan raised a hand in greeting, and Gehrin nodded. The *garatelhai* guards rarely patrolled the fortress now, and Kajen often said that they'd grown lazy in the long months since the *bruhai* had fully taken over the watches.

Soon, they would be back in Keld. Master Lohi had told them it would be a matter of days before they returned. It had been so long since any of them had been out of the shadows of the mountains, so long since any of them had been inside a city. For Jai, it would be the first time he had ever left Blackvale in his life, the first time he had seen a marketplace or even houses. He had shown Gehrin the books that Master Lohi had brought him as a boy, full of beautiful drawings of the city and the architecture of Katesh. Seeing it with his own eyes would be a far different experience.

They would return to the palace by a secret path that would bring them into an unused house at the back of the palace compound. It had once belonged to Master Lohi himself, when he had tutored Kinhariian as a young prince. And there they would stay in hiding until the king's ceremony. It was a lot of secrecy, and Gehrin didn't understand why it was necessary now. They were *bruhai*. Surely, they were not in danger.

But Master Lohi had planned every moment long before any of them had come to Blackvale. The vision of the *bruhai* had existed since Jai's birth, or even perhaps before. But then there had been a prince. The king was approaching his forty-fifth year, and there was no more time to produce his own heir. His queen was not strong enough to bear him a child now, and the concubines had not given him any other children. The Council had been held at bay for years, and they would not rest until he had given them a name.

And when he did, the counsellors would show favor for his choice in the great halls, but their schemes would darken the corners of the palace and their supper tables, and Gehrin and his *bruhai* brothers would be standing in their way. The memory of Thiri's gentle voice echoed in his mind.

*"You are a good son, Gehrin. One day you and your brothers will honor your father and the memory of your mother in service to the king, and I will be glad to see it."*

His brothers... Gehrin could see their faces, clear and familiar. *Nin, Ruh, Hajja, Sabba, Kajen, Ivveth, Jai.* Thiri's words, spoken so long ago, accompanied soft but shadowed features. He had long since lost the clarity to see them.

A cracked old voice broke into the fog in his head. "Your thoughts have always been heavy."

The faint beginnings of blisters stung Gehrin's palm and he blinked, withdrawing his hand from the corpse of the fire. A walking staff tapped alongside the familiar footsteps of the old scholar as he approached the center of the courtyard. Gehrin rose and bowed.

"How may I serve you, Master?"

"You will prepare your brothers to leave within three days. You will see to it that they bring only what they need and nothing more. Everything else will be provided to you in Keld."

"Yes, Master." *Three days.* It would not take long to gather their few belongings. Each of them only possessed a few articles of clothing, their armor, and their weapons. Gehrin imagined with rueful amusement that Ivveth might try to bring figs.

"I have named you their leader, Liv. I know you do not wish for that title, but it is yours. I have traveled throughout the lands and seen many leaders. Warlords, kings, queens, soldiers, servants. The greatest among them are often those who possess a quieter strength. They have no need of great accolades but gain their glory in the trust of those who follow them." Master Lohi touched Gehrin's shoulder. "We must be the shadows of the glorious and take none for ourselves."

"Yes, Master."

"I believe you will be asked to prove your loyalty to the king sooner than you think. Yes, perhaps it will be soon."

"I am ready."

Master Lohi smiled. "I have never doubted it."

The scholar tapped away, leaving Gehrin alone with his thoughts once more. The day was strange, with Master Tahmujin's heavy presence removed from the courtyard. Gehrin found himself settling into his spear forms out of habit, his feet moving easily through the sand. The wooden practice spear was comforting. Each step was an instinctive movement, and his thoughts flowed away like water. A welcome peace settled over him.

It was not long before his brothers joined him, working through the forms of spear, sword, knives, and fists together while the day grew hotter above them, beating down on their skin. The night drew its cloak around them once more, and Gehrin set himself and Kajen on watch. They worked themselves to exhaustion, only pausing to eat the food Kirte brought out to them, taking turns while the other watched. Tahmujin came and hovered at the edge of the courtyard once, sheltered by the shadow of the overhang.

After eating a light meal and bathing, six of them returned to their cells. Gehrin and Kajen remained on the rooftops, perched like ravens in the shadows and watching over the quiet walls. Gehrin leaned against the smooth rock wall of the left tower, watching over the gate and the bridge. The forest and cliffs were quiet except for the occasional hooting of an owl. Gehrin imagined wide yellow eyes hidden in the branches of a tree as the great bird perched on his own midnight watch.

A footstep whispered on the tiles behind him, and Kajen appeared, settling down a few feet away. He pulled a small cloth from his tunic and unwrapped a rice ball, taking half of it in one bite.

Gehrin scoffed. "Do you ever stop eating?"

The second half of the rice ball disappeared, and Kajen shrugged, his cheeks bulging. After chewing for a few heartbeats, he turned to Gehrin with a roguish grin. "Eat while you can, *icha*. Maybe tomorrow we don't eat."

Gehrin leaned his head back against the tower. They sat quietly for a while, and Gehrin pulled his dark cowl away from his neck. The night was still warm enough to make him feel sticky beneath the fabric. Suddenly, he saw Kajen's face jerk toward the southern wall. The Wildcat held up a finger as he listened, and neither of them moved a muscle. Gehrin gestured for Kajen to stay, and rose to a crouch, creeping along the ridge. He leapt soundlessly down to the flat wall top and ran along it, feeling his way with the confidence of hundreds of trips he had made along the same stretch before, each stone familiar under the soles of his soft boots.

As he drew closer to the cliffside, he slowed, and looked down at the steep wall of rock into the forest below. Leaves rustled at the tops of the trees, and there was no sign of anyone inside the wall or clinging to the sheer drop on the outside. Still, something was wrong, sent a prickle along Gehrin's arms.

He pressed his hand to the stone and felt the soft ripple of power beneath his fingertips. A soft echo of memory filtered through his hand. *Footsteps in soft boots. There.* Pointing down the cliffside into the forest.

Unlooping the coil of rope on his belt, he knotted one end to an iron spike on the inner side of the wall, and then slowly lowered himself down until he'd reached the end of the smooth stone and his feet met rougher natural rock. He let go of the rope and continued down until he'd reached the forest floor, his arms aching from the climb. There he found what he was looking for.

The footprint off to the side in the softer earth was the same sole as his own boots. One of the *bruhai*. They never came down to the Killing Forest, even when they ventured out of the fortress walls. It was a place haunted by spirits. Gehrin looked up and saw Kajen perched on the fortress wall, watching him. Gehrin held up his hand and motioned toward the forest, and then held up a hand. Kajen raised a hand in response. He would stay and wait for Gehrin to return.

The shadows of the trees swayed as Gehrin ran through them, following in the direction the first footprint had pointed. He could not see any others in the dark, so he let his instincts guide him to the small stream near where he had killed the prisoner woman. The babble of the little brook sounded strange in the nighttime. Crouching near the edge, he looked around him, watching for any sign of one of his brothers. His hand brushed over a small clump of earth that had been torn up near the water's edge. He wanted to call out, but something told him to wait.

He followed the stream a little way further into the forest, placing each foot silently into the undergrowth. Then he caught sight of a dark figure crouched beside the water, forty or fifty lengths ahead. He knew the set of the shoulders immediately.

*Tirrim?*

Gehrin stepped out from behind the tree, letting his footsteps announce his presence. Tirrim stood up, his waterskin newly filled from the stream. He wore his armor, but not his mask, his cowl drawn up over his head like a hood.

"Ivveth," Gehrin called out.

"Where is Kajen?" asked Tirrim, looking around at the trees.

"He stayed behind. I came because he heard you when you went over the wall." Gehrin saw the pack slung over Tirrim's shoulders and pressed down the icy cold feeling that came over him. "What are you doing?"

Tirrim set down the waterskin. "I'm leaving."

"You swore an oath."

"I swore nothing," replied Tirrim. "What good is an oath that is not freely given?" He lifted his left hand, and in the dim light filtering through the branches, Gehrin saw Tirrim's palm, unscarred, and the echo of his own wound beneath the bandage stung with renewed vigor.

Tirrim lowered his hand. "Are you truly so surprised, Liv? I am my father's only son, and I did not choose this life. I waited for the day when I was strong enough to leave. I have earned my freedom."

"Freedom?" echoed Gehrin. The thought of freedom, once so desperately desired, only unsettled him now.

"Come with me."

Gehrin's hands twitched toward the hilts of his long-handled knives. Tirrim saw the movement, and his expression grew hard. He pulled the pack from his shoulders and set it down near the waterskin.

"Don't be a fool, Liv. They can't kill us now."

"If you run, who do you think Master Lohi will send after you?" Gehrin's voice came out hoarse and cracked. "How many of your brothers will you kill?"

"Brothers?" Tirrim shook his head. "They would send a knife into my back if Master Lohi commanded them to do it. I am asked to give up my name and my family, to become nothing. My father's lineage would end with me. My father told me when I was a child that a king's first duty is to his people, to protect them. He told me that our king had grown too drunk on his own power. I cannot stay here, Liv."

The memory of his own father's displeasure with the old scholar came fresh to Gehrin's mind. "You cannot leave."

"You want to protect the others," acknowledged Tirrim. "I understand it. They are far too valuable for Master Lohi and Master Tahmujin to waste them chasing after me."

Gehrin swallowed through a thick throat. "I cannot take that risk. They are my brothers, and yours. Come back, and I will say nothing of this. I will say nothing!"

Drawing his short spear from his back, Tirrim held it easily at his side. "Do you even remember your true name, Gehrin Hallix?"

Hearing it sent a dull stab through Gehrin's chest. He shook his head, calling himself a hypocrite in the same breath as he spoke the words. "We are *bruhai* now. That name means nothing."

"And your father? Your brothers?"

"The family I once had will be honored by my loyalty to my king."

Tirrim's smile was sad as he slowly flipped the spear over in his hand for a better grip. "Ever the little scholar, memorizing the words you were told to say. Come then."

"Don't do this."

Tirrim moved across the stream in a dark blur, the sharp edge of the spearhead tearing through the side of Gehrin's cloak. Jumping back, Gehrin held his hands out, palms facing Tirrim.

"Ivveth, don't do this!"

*Do not harm your brothers.*

The spear whistled past Gehrin's face as he ducked to the right, narrowly avoiding losing one of his ears. Tirrim was the best of them, and while Gehrin had defeated him in single combat before, it was rare. Gehrin pulled his knives free of his belt. Anger pushed past the surface of his emotions.

"Stop this!" he shouted. "I do not want to kill you!"

The spear whirled, a glimmer in the darkness. This time, Gehrin caught the shaft in the cross of his blades, shoulders straining against Tirrim's greater power. Tirrim yanked the spear back and made a short jab, cutting through more of Gehrin's cloak and nicking his inner arm. The spearhead was powerful enough to cut through Gehrin's leather armor if given the chance.

Backed up against a tree trunk, Gehrin dodged as the spearhead slammed into the bark, sending rough splinters flying. Gehrin's knives sliced against one of Tirrim's exposed legs, then the other. Even now, the wounds Gehrin inflicted were not deep enough to maim, only to slow Tirrim's speed.

Tirrim gave voice to no pain and showed no sign of slowing. The wooden haft of his spear slammed up into Gehrin's chin, knocking him off his feet and back into a tangle of ferns. Stars floated in Gehrin's vision, and he shook his head, scrambling backwards away from the next spear thrust toward his chest. Was it meant to be a killing blow? Gehrin crashed through the brush and slipped behind a larger tree, desperately trying to force himself to be calm. When he heard the next swing of the spear, he reached out and grabbed hold of the shaft, forcing it upward as one of his long knives made its way toward the armor gap beneath Tirrim's arm.

Tirrim pulled back far enough that the blade barely nicked his skin through the thin cloth of his tunic. They stepped away from each other, each eyeing the other with the same intensity as countless matches in the sand of the courtyard. Tirrim's face caught the dim moonlight through the trees, and Gehrin saw the cold emptiness in his eyes.

It was as if Gehrin could hear Tirrim's voice in his head, the soft lilting dialect of Fethet nearly gone from the words after so many years. *"I've made my choice."*

Gehrin ran at Tirrim with a guttural shout. Shadows curled around him, the lingering heat driving his mind into fogged fury. Tirrim's spear and his knives clattered against each other in the temple of trees. Pain bloomed in Gehrin's hip as he misjudged the speed of Tirrim's attack, and then a fist slammed into his face. He stumbled, swinging his long knives in a desperate attempt to move Tirrim away from him.

Tirrim twisted away from the knives and pressed forward, bringing the blade of his spear up against Gehrin's neck. The cold steel was like ice against Gehrin's skin. Tirrim stepped close, pressing the blade in until a thin trickle of blood opened. But he hesitated, and Gehrin could see him fighting against himself. Gehrin leaned forward into the blade's sharp sting ever so slightly, his jaw and mouth throbbing from his split lip.

"Come on then," he said. Tirrim drew the spear back, and Gehrin held his gaze, waiting for the end. The spearhead quivered.

A twig snapped behind them. "LIV!"

As soon as Tirrim glanced away, Gehrin flipped one of his knives sideways and into the gap at the side of Tirrim's armor. With a sharp cry of pain, Tirrim whirled just as a belt axe knocked the shaft of the spear away from Gehrin's neck. Kajen lunged between them, the Wildcat's eyes blazing as he fell on Tirrim in a fury. The heavy blunt end of his second axe thudded against the side of Tirrim's head before the spear could block it, and he dropped with a groan. The spear fell to the ground beside him. Kajen whirled on Gehrin, eyeing him suspiciously. Gehrin sheathed his knives.

"Ten kinds of *fools*, what is this?" Kajen spat.

Gehrin sank back against the tree, staring at Tirrim as his mind began to go numb. Kajen reached out and grabbed the front of his armor, yanking him upright.

"Start talking, *icha*."

"He's leaving."

Shock registered on Kajen's face, and the grip on Gehrin's armor loosened. He glanced down at Tirrim. "What d'you mean, leaving?"

"We have to take him back," Gehrin murmured. "We have to take him back."

Kajen let go and stepped back, still looking between the other two *bruhai* as if trying to comprehend what Gehrin was saying. Gehrin knelt beside Tirrim and pulled his cloth belt free, tying it tightly around Tirrim's wrists. A tear rolled down his cheek and he tasted the salt. He brushed it angrily away with his leatherbound forearm, ignoring the abrasion against his lip.

*If you break this oath...*

He touched the side of Tirrim's armor, feeling the torn cloth beneath and the wet gash his knife had left behind. It was an easy wound to heal, and he had intentionally stabbed too shallowly to do fatal damage.

*You will forfeit your life.*

Gehrin pulled Tirrim's arm over his shoulder, grimacing as he pushed himself up. A wave of dizziness passed over him as the wound in his hip flared. A small, boyish voice whispered from the doorway in his mind.

*He is my friend.*

"Help me carry him."

*He is my friend.*

No. Liv closed the door, shutting the small voice away for the last time. *I am bruhai.*

The boy kneeling on the sand was bound and gagged, but he did not struggle. He was naked except for the loincloth bound loosely around his hips, and the newly clotting wound at his side was red and angry.

Liv watched as it clustered into a drip, splattering against the prisoner's foot. The boy's dark hair was still smooth, unbound and falling around his shoulders. The sky above them was cast in dark clouds, the first pattering of rain against the stone echoing softly.

Seven *bruhai* stood around the prisoner in the center of the courtyard in armor and masks, the leather and steel hiding the expressions beneath. It would not have mattered, for whatever they felt looking down on the boy kneeling in their midst, it was not for them to act on it.

Master Tahmujin stood at the head of the circle, his own battle-worn armor giving him an even greater presence in the courtyard where he had forged the warriors standing around him. He looked down at the prisoner with contempt.

"*Aqqa.* His name is not worthy. He was named *bruhai* and broke the faith of his brothers, and his oath to the king."

The *bruhai* echoed his words. "His name is not worthy." As one, they withdrew their spears from the sheaths on their backs. Liv stared down at the nameless boy at his feet, saw the eyes turn to him with defiant resignation. He had not begged for his life, owning at least that small dignity as he faced his death. It was by his own choosing. He should have been standing with them, proud in his armor and the mask of the *bruhai*.

The others would wait for Liv to strike. He could feel the tension as they held their spears, the rain falling in heavy splatters against the leather. The voice within that would have held him captive in guilt had not returned. There were some spaces in his mind lost even to him. As he looked at the *aqqa*'s face, a profound numbness soothed him, strengthened his arm.

The spear plunged down.

# CHAPTER THIRTY-ONE

*The third king of Ruk was Tarxin, and he ruled during a time of great peace. When the new king of Katesh was crowned during his reign, he commanded his greatest craftsmen to smith a magnificent medallion of gold as a gift. The medallion was as tall as a man and was wrought in the image of a wolf and a fox leaping around a circle of gold. When the king of Katesh received the great gift, he was amazed by its craftsmanship and ordered the medallion to hang in the Council Hall above his throne.*

*- Annals of the Kings of Ruk*

Tilis' child chased after a small leather ball as it rolled across the floor. In his pudgy hand he clutched a doll sewn with hides and horsehair. The ball rolled to a stop near Syndri's foot where she stood in the doorway, and he paused, eyeing her with apprehension. She kicked at the ball, sending it back into the room, and he turned and ran after it again with a bright laugh.

The woman sitting on the floor watching him smiled, her eyes creasing in the corners. She'd braided her hair by herself today, one messy plait down her back with loose strands framing her face. She raised a hand to Syndri, the soft light of recognition in her expression. Time had not softened the blow for Syndri, and she still clung to the foolish hope that one day she would walk through the door of her mother's room and be recognized as a daughter. But today, she was only the warrior with a face like stone, for that was the only version of her that Ettlan knew. And each season that passed stole a little more of the hope away.

For the tribe, Ettlan's transformation had only endeared her further. She spent much of her time among them, saying simple, kind words. It seemed that despite her childlike recognition of the world, her faith remained unwavering.

Ettlan rose from the floor, steadying herself with a hand on the wall. "Tilis is not here."

Syndri watched the child play, unwilling to meet Ettlan's gaze. "I am not here for Tilis," she replied.

"Oh? You usually speak to her when you visit us."

"I am leaving. The warband is going back to our homeland to take the Tladr and Uratar tribes. After all this time we will finally have vengeance." It was strange saying the words in her mother's presence now. Ettlan remembered nothing of the village or even her husband. To her, the slaughter of their people was known only through the painful memories of the others in the tribe. Syndri carried those deaths on her shoulders for both of them.

"And vengeance... that is what you want?" Ettlan's forehead was furrowed as she tried to understand. "Will you fight?"

"Yes."

"Some of you will die."

"Yes."

Syndri looked down at her mother's face, so wide and open and innocent. Ettlan frowned, searching Syndri's expression. Then she reached up and touched Syndri's cheek. The warmth was startling, and Syndri forced herself not to pull away. Every inch of her recoiled from the feeling of desperation, wishing she could somehow reach into Ettlan's soul and retrieve the mother she had lost.

Syndri pulled away from Ettlan's hand. "The Queen will take care of you while we are gone." As she turned to leave, Ettlan spoke again.

"I am sorry that I am not what you want me to be." At Syndri's look of surprise, she continued. "I see it in your eyes when you come. You are looking for someone else when you look at me."

"You are the Open Hand of the Garhis tribe. You do not need to be anyone else." Syndri stepped away and backed out the door before Ettlan could say another word.

The queen's inner chambers were one of the few places in the palace lit by any outside light. Her rounded balcony clung to the outer stone façade of the peak, offering a view over the city. An assortment of candlestands lit the rest of the rooms, and the yellowed flames lent their small strength to Syndri's eyes as she was led through the maze of corridors up to the queen's chambers. She glanced down disapprovingly at the stone stairs as her bootsteps echoed. It was too loud and too high. There was no reason for any human to be this far from the solid earth. In three years, Syndri had never grown accustomed to it.

Ona, the queen's personal body servant, walked several steps in front of Syndri. Despite her short stature and deceptively quiet nature, Syndri was not foolish enough to dismiss the woman's presence. Beneath the ethereal black robes that floated around her, she was armed. The thin, swirling lines of her face tattoos marked her as one of the Ka'lam, mixed blood assassins that served Queen Xhen with utter loyalty. Senna had told Syndri that the Ka'lam were renowned for their venom-tipped steel *kabhara*, or small spine-like knives. One nick of the skin and death was imminent without the intervention of the spirits.

Ona opened the large door to the outer chamber where Queen Xhen received her guests, and Syndri stepped inside, her boots silenced by the massive woven rug. Sheer black curtains fell on either side of the wide stone balcony archway, the fabric pooling on the floor. Ona poured something into two silver cups from a pitcher and handed one to Syndri.

The fermented tang of mare's milk and wine wafted up from the cup, and Syndri raised her eyebrows. It was a common winter drink amongst the Maleki tribes, but it seemed out of place in the queen's ornate silver. Ona faded back into the shadows in the corner of the room, and Syndri found herself alone. She took a sip, and the warmth of the milk and the bite of the sour Maleki wine brought a familiar calm to her bones. It was a small piece of her homeland.

A door opened to Syndri's left and the queen appeared. She approached the small table and lifted the second cup to her lips. The stiffly collared dress she usually wore in the Council room was gone, and in its place was a simple black gown with gold-thread embroidery around the sleeve hems and neckline. The olive-hued skin of her neck and chest was bare, flawless, and her hands had been painted with a design of small dots that curled around the silver cup. She drank deeply and gave a contented sigh.

"I have found that I have a taste for your drink. It is called *hiffe*, yes?"

"It is."

"Come, stand on the balcony with me," the queen said, gliding over the floor toward the archway. Syndri followed. Stone pillars suspended the balcony high over the rooftops below, and Syndri stayed several steps back from the railing, annoyed by the way her knees grew weak at the sight of the ground so far below them. Soldiers, servants, and citizens moved around in the palace courtyard and stableyard like tiny black ants. Xhen glanced at Syndri with an expression of amusement.

"You believe that you will spend the afterlife in the sky, but you fear these heights."

Syndri curled her lip. "A spirit cannot fall to its death."

The queen gave a nearly imperceptible shake of her head. "No. But as you believe in the spirits of the sky, I believe that there are spirits in the earth. In the water. In the bones of the world. They hold the memories of the ages. And one day they will hold yours and mine."

Syndri said nothing. The Sky Clans held the memories of the ancestors, and the things that had happened over the lands long before she was born. Those who died in dishonor, their totems crushed, wandered the darkness, but they had no memories and no names. The beliefs of the Kateshi people had found their way into the lands of Ruk and mingled with the ancient religion there, creating a strange marriage between the two. Senna had spoken of it often as she learned from the people in Ujjak, constantly curious about their world. Syndri had little interest. There were no earth spirits. Only the Sky Clans.

*But your visions were not from the Sky Clans.*

That knowledge was seated deep within, and it gave her an uneasy pit in her stomach to admit it, even to herself. Whatever power had found her in the grove of trees on the cliff... it was far older than anything her people had ever spoken of. But now was not the time for visions.

"You did not call me here to drink *hiffe*."

"No," the queen replied. "I called you here because Rahian and Yugha believe that your people and mine are ready. I agree with them, but I wanted to hear from you before I gave the order to march. You have been training with my foot soldiers, and you know your own people well. Are they ready?"

Syndri swirled the *hiffe* around in the bottom of her cup, considering. When they had first arrived in Ujjak, she had been ready to turn Brig around and ride back. Three years had tempered her blood like the blacksmith's red-hot steel quenched in the water bucket, hardening into something cold and waiting. The queen's army was impressive, even for men who were unfamiliar with fighting on horseback. Their long pikes and bows would be deadly against the Tladr and Uratar. If the queen's men were not strong enough to face the Maleki warriors hand to hand, at least the larger numbers would prove useful. Syndri had once voiced her disapproval of their weapon choices, but Queen Xhen said they were not Maleki, so they need not fight like Maleki.

"Rahian and Yugha have given you their blessing."

"Don't be stubborn, Syndri. If you are going to be Closed Fist one day, you will have to answer these questions for yourself."

"Yugha is the Closed Fist."

Queen Xhen gave her a sideways look that suggested that Syndri was treading on dangerous ground. "There is no one here who will call you a traitor. I think your time in Ujjak has tamed you too much. Perhaps you should stay here." She smiled. "Don't look at me like that. The sooner you take your place as your father's successor, the better."

The queen was always careful with her words in Yugha's company, but the Closed Fist was no fool. He knew that she favored Syndri, and it had only widened the chasm between him and the daughters of Nar Garhis. Syndri knew it was only a matter of time before things came to a head between them. And the queen was just waiting for it to happen. Syndri knew it was unlikely that the queen held such a strong loyalty to the memory of Nar Garhis, but rather that the powerful woman had built her own vision of the future and would not be swayed from it.

"Only the Sky knows what is to come," said Syndri dismissively. If she became Closed Fist one day, it would be her own doing. "Yes, we are ready. Your soldiers are... good warriors. We will not lose."

Pleased, the queen tapped her fingers against the silver. "No," she answered quietly, her gaze sweeping out over the city. "You won't. And you will unite the tribes. We will need their warriors."

Syndri shook her head slightly. "We will serve vengeance for my father and my tribe."

The queen's head snapped around, and her voice grew deadly soft. "You do not want to challenge Yugha, yet you would so easily throw away everything your father and I built? Is this vengeance truly for him, or is it for you?"

Syndri looked down at the queen, imagining the knife stowed

away in her boot pressed tightly against that flawless neck. "I will avenge my father's death. Will you stand in my way?"

"You cannot rule over the tribes of Malek if they are all dead," the queen replied. "If you are to unify the tribes, as your father wished, there must be people still alive to rule. The Nar Tladr and Nar Uratar must be brought here, alive."

Syndri took one step forward, and she heard a soft rustle behind her as Ona moved toward them, wary, but the queen gestured her back into the shadows. Syndri towered over the queen and looked down at the woman's eyes. *A fox with the fangs of a viper...*

"I stood against the Tladr and the Uratar and watched them cut down my people like rabid dogs," Syndri growled. "I saw a child lying in the street, crawling without legs. I saw my father split open from neck to groin, bleeding in the door of his *gat*. I watched my mother come back half alive, and she does not even know that I am her daughter. You may have been my father's ally, but you are not Garhis, and you have not seen the things I have seen. I will unify the tribes, but first I will repay them in blood for what they have taken from me."

As the queen listened, a smile appeared on her face that Syndri did not like. She reached out and touched Syndri's arm. "Emissary Otai was right about you," she said. "There is great blood in your veins, Syndri, daughter of Nar Garhis. But you cannot take your vengeance without me at your side. We must not be angry with each other. It is not what your father would want. Go back to your homeland and finish what he began."

Opening her mouth again would tear away the last shreds of control Syndri held over herself, and in a matter of days she would be gone and riding back toward her homeland, away from the queen. She said nothing. Syndri turned and walked toward the door, her silver cup clanking against the platter as she returned it. Ona appeared like a ghost from the corner of the room, leading her out of the chamber and back into the corridor.

Every instinct drove Syndri to seek out her sister, but she knew that Senna would side with the queen. Not long ago they had spoken of it, and Senna had, as she called it, tried to make Syndri see reason. *Unify the tribes. When does the killing end? Baya, the Tladr's son, our village? And we will kill more of them. It is enough to leave the rest alive.*

The queen believed that someday the Tladr, the Uratar, and the Garhis would fight side by side in her war. That centuries of death and hatred could be burned away to nothing like bodies on a pyre, floating away into the air. And no matter how hard Syndri tried to imagine the Garhis tribe taking back their land on their own, she knew the truth. They needed this Northern queen, and she needed them. They were trapped by each other, spinning in a strong current toward a terrible end.

# CHAPTER THIRTY-TWO

For the first time since the faint memories of a small boy he no longer was, Liv rested his eyes on the tall stone walls of Keld, rising out of the rocky farmlands. Approaching the city from the north on a small shepherd's path that joined the wide road into Keld, the seven *bruhai* rode behind Tahmujin and a small squad of the *telhai* guards that had followed them from Blackvale. Only seven *bruhai*. They had left so many dead behind. Liv had once chased survival with clawed desperation, but the thought of death no longer left him paralyzed with fear. He had been chosen for this life, and he was resigned to it.

Liv had expected the walls of the city to illicit some emotion in him, perhaps a nostalgia or relief after all the years he had spent away. Or at the very least, he had expected some apprehension at the thought of seeing familiar faces and sights again. But as he looked out over the walls and roofs layered like scales through the city, he realized he wanted nothing more than a filling meal and a hot bath.

They'd slept on the hard ground last night, and Nin and Sabba had kept watch over the road from the little hill they'd chosen for a camp. It was strange to see them standing guard over the rolling hills instead of the stone walls of the fortress.

The fresh, clean air of the northern forests had given way to the faint musk of the city and the surrounding farmlands. The earthy stench of livestock and the press of thousands of people living in close quarters within the walls mingled with the dust and heat of the summer. Somewhere in the distance, goats and sheep bleated as they were driven into their pens for the night. Dusk was quickly falling, shielding the *bruhai* from immediate recognition. Master Lohi had left them explicit instructions to enter the city by the narrow path that wound through the grazing pastures on the northern side of the city, through the gate into the kill yards and butcher shops and on through the storehouses until they reached the palace grounds. They would be noticed but would avoid the main thoroughfares of the city. Once inside the palace, they would be brought to their quarters until the king gave further orders.

Nin, riding next to Liv, was barely hiding his emotions, even beneath the wolf mask he wore. He was the only other *bruhai* who had been born in Keld, his mother a servant in the palace kitchens. It was likely that he would see her again. But that was the road they had earned and chosen. He was no longer her son.

Liv watched Nin until the other *bruhai* noticed him. Nin clenched his fist against the reins of his blood bay gelding and shook his head. "I'm fine, Liv."

They rode down the shepherd's path after Tahmujin, and the walls grew taller and taller until they were finally under the Sheep Gate. The soldiers standing guard atop the wall and at each side of the wide gate said nothing, offering respectful nods as Master

Tahmujin rode by. The gate was the widest in the city, built for the passage of the flocks and herds of the Kateshi landowners to be driven into the holding pens just inside. The wide road between the stables, pens, and storehouses led straight toward the Temple of Sharai and the palace beyond. The herders, butchers, scribes, meat buyers, sorters, and other passersby doing their business around the large livestock square hurried out of the way of the small brigade of horses and their masked riders. Liv kept his gaze fixed forward, but he saw the expressions of confusion, curiosity, and fear mingling in the people beneath him.

The news of the *bruhai* would be spread to the farthest corners of city by the morning's first light. The king's Succession Ceremony was looming, and the arrival of these elite warriors would only add fuel to the raging fire of speculation already circulating through the city. Would it be enough to staunch the inevitable flow of discontented scheming that would follow the ceremony? Doubtful, but at least the throne and the king who sat on it would be protected by something the nobles had not anticipated.

The temple rose blood red amongst the earthen colors of the buildings surrounding it, the tall round columns supporting the slated roof trimmed with carved wooden scrolls and statues of the Oathsworn. The ancient warriors were the ancestors of the *bruhai*, Master Lohi had once said. Once, Liv knew, he had idolized them as a small boy. Now he wondered what was locked away behind their stern faces lifted to the sky.

As they rode past the temple, a small entourage following a gray-robed noble fluttered toward them down the steps. The noble stopped within range of Tahmujin's horse, and the spearmaster lifted his hand for a halt to avoid running the man over. Liv narrowed his eyes, searching the man's face. He was powdered and wore only a simple gold ring on one hand, one gold ornament hanging from his belt. But his hair was bound up with a small silver coronet and his self-assured smile spread unpleasantly over the flawless skin of his face. Counsellor Yura Okujen, the voice of the people.

"My lord Tahmujin!" Yura exclaimed loudly. "Let me be the first to welcome you and your warriors home to Keld!" He glanced over the masked riders sitting silently behind the old spearmaster. "I was told you were training new soldiers in the mountains. What fearsome warriors you have brought as a gift to our king!"

Tahmujin gathered his horse's reins, looking away from the noble and toward the palace. "Then you know that your hindrance keeps me from our warlord's side."

The man stepped back, holding his hands up in a gesture of placation. "Surely there is no *garatelhai* in Katesh with greater loyalty. Please, continue in your task!"

The man scrutinized each of them as they rode by, narrowing his eyes at their masks, hoods, and armor, the red cloaks draping over the blood bay flanks of their horses. He would not be able to recognize any of them or divine anything from their faces. They were truly nameless. Even Ruh's Takkan coloring and Sabba's Da'hamian heritage were hidden beneath the façade. Liv felt a grim satisfaction alongside the discomfort of having so many eyes turned toward him. Blackvale's calm stillness and quiet walls suddenly seemed like a luxury.

The gilded palace gates opened for them at Tahmujin's greeting, and then they were inside the entrance courtyard, which swept off to each side toward the offices of the king's government, the kitchens, the queen's house, and the great Council Hall. Behind the Council Hall were the king's private apartments, the richest, most lavish, and well-guarded rooms in the entire country. And yet, the Crown Prince had been killed in those rooms. It was no surprise that the king's trust in his household ran shallow.

Slaves from the stable ran to collect the reins of the horses, and Liv swung his leg over the mare's side and dropped to the smooth flagstones. The rush of expectations warmed his belly as he and the other *bruhai* stood in a column beneath the shadow of the great statue of Sharai.

The great Council Hall was bright, lit with the dying light of the sunset in shades of gold and orange that added a majestic glow to the gold gild on the intertwined wolf and fox medallion looming behind the king's throne and the man sitting there. Two other men stood next to the throne, one on either side. The rest of the hall was quiet and empty. Master Lohi leaned on his staff, watching the *bruhai's* entrance with a glint in his old eyes. As soon as Liv's masked eyes flickered to the man on the right side of the throne, his chest tightened.

Counsellor Hallix stood with every bit of the confident stoicism that echoed in Liv's memory. His expression betrayed nothing, and his hands were folded behind his back. There were gray streaks in the black hair around his temples that had not been there before, and the lines in his forehead and the corners of his eyes had deepened with age, adding to the stern depth of his gaze. But this man was not Liv's father.

Tahmujin lowered himself to his knees and bowed with his forehead to the floor, and the *bruhai* followed his lead, their masks hovering over the musty cedarwood planks. Liv heard the rustle of robes as the king rose from his seat and approached Tahmujin, his rich voice filling the chamber.

"Come, old friend. There's no need for such obeisance here. Let me see the fruits of your labors these many years. Rise."

Once, many years ago, Liv had seen a glimpse of the king on a visit to the palace with the man standing next to the throne. Kinhariian had looked every bit the image of the warlord who had destroyed the rebellion of the Aqatar cults plaguing Katesh, driving them into the northern mountains. The silk robes were a poor substitute for the black armor of the Legion, but somehow the king wore them with the same strength. And in all those years, the king seemed unchanged. His handsome face was nearly untouched by the inevitable ravages of age, and there was a strange familiarity to it, as if Liv had seen the king days ago rather than years.

The king stepped around Tahmujin and walked alongside the column of *bruhai*. "The rest of you, leave us."

Counsellor Hallix objected. "My lord, is that wise?"

"They have been trained by Tahmujin and Lohi. I trust every

man in this room with my life," replied the king dismissively. "I will speak to them alone."

Counsellor Hallix, Tahmujin, and Lohi walked out of the Council Hall, leaving behind an eerie silence in their wake. The king walked closer to Kajen and inspected the mask more closely. He smiled.

"Wolves... a bit theatrical, but Master Lohi knows his craft. Remove them."

The masks were pulled away, revealing each *bruhai*'s face. The king studied each of them as if he were an artist painting a portrait, seeking secrets harbored behind each set of eyes. When he reached Hajja, he lingered, the grotesque scars of the younger man's face on full display. Something painful appeared in the king's expression, as if the sight of Hajja had awoken some ancient wound. Finally, he nodded and stepped away.

"You have all been given a great burden to bear," he said. "I expect your complete loyalty, and in return for the sacrifices you have made, you will receive mine. You are under my protection, just as I am under yours. Together we will guard the throne of this nation. You have taken an oath, and I will hold you to it. When I choose the man who will succeed me, you will protect him with your lives. I will not see another son of mine destroyed by greed and evil." He met Liv's gaze and lingered there. "I know each of you. I know who you were before you became *bruhai*. But the names you have taken now will be written as sacred as Sharai's own Oathsworn."

Liv bowed deeply at the waist and was followed by his brothers. The king turned to a table with a carafe of wine and poured it into small cups, serving them with his own hands. Liv accepted the cup, feeling unworthy of the honor. The king raised his own cup, and they all saluted him, drinking the warm spiced wine to seal the oath they had taken in the courtyard. The king gestured toward Liv.

"You are Liv."

"Yes, Warlord."

"Master Lohi tells me that he believes you capable of leading these *bruhai*, and I trust his judgment. He also told me that one of your brothers broke his oath."

The still-fresh sight of the upturned face of his friend plagued Liv. But it had been necessary. One death instead of many. Liv ran his thumb over the rim of the cup.

"Yes, my king. He chose the wrong path. His name is not worthy."

The king reached out and gripped Liv's shoulder. "It steals away a part of you to put a trusted brother to death. But you showed great loyalty, and for that, I commend you." He placed his cup back on the table. "My servant Yi Jo will show you to your quarters. Please rest and send for anything you need. The servants will attend to you. Tomorrow you will stand with me, and we will see what evils you must turn aside with your spears."

The quarters that the king had given them were adjacent to his own apartments, separated only by a wide receiving hall and a corridor. Each of them was given their own room, spacious and filled with more amenities than they had seen altogether in their years at Blackvale.

Liv stood silently in the center of his own room, eyes sweeping over the items inside. A tray of fruits and cracked nuts sat beside a pitcher of wine. A chest of clothing sat near the bedding, which was a silk blanket filled with goose down. The stand for his armor was ornately carved with the faces of animals, the arms sweeping out in the shape of wings. There was a rack for his weapons. By palace standards, it was modestly lavish, but in comparison to the dark stone cells of Blackvale, Liv felt like a king himself.

That night, the room's airy lightness disturbed him. The smooth wooden headrest was too comfortable, too foreign to his body after years of sleeping on roped cots. It was as if he had forgotten the small luxuries of his youth. Without the heavy stone surrounding him, he was exposed, and the thin walls were useless against even the smallest noise. Restless, his skin crawled as if an army of tiny ants marched beneath the surface. He rose three times to pour himself a cup of wine, hoping that soothing, warm liquid might bring back the elusive calm.

Keld was a different world. It was easier to imagine the city so greatly changed and not himself. Somewhere beyond the walls lay the shrine of the woman who had been his mother. Somewhere within the noble district the man who had been his father sat in his apartments with incense burning. In the marketplace the vendors and shopkeepers repeated the day they had lived over and over again since he had left. He wondered if the old woman Yrit still lived.

He imagined the Council Hall filled with advisors, officers, and nobles as the king announced Xario as the next king. He imagined the pride on his father's face as he saw his eldest son elevated to the throne while Liv's unfamiliar face hovered in the shadows. Liv pressed his eyes tightly shut until they began to hurt, and then let out a slow breath.

Rising from the sleeping mat, he wrapped a simple robe around himself and stepped into the hallway, padding over the waxed wood floor. The other *bruhai*'s rooms were dark, except one. The faint flicker of candlelight shone from the paper panels of Jai's door. Liv paused, even his soft step enough to alert Jai to his presence.

The door panel slid to the side, and Jai motioned for him to enter. Liv stepped over the threshold and noted that Jai's bedding was also in disarray. It seemed he was not the only one spending a restless night. Liv sat cross-legged in the corner, and Jai imitated the pose on the disgruntled blanket. Jai's long hair fell to his waist, snarled by his tossing and turning. Without the mask and the armor, he looked as much like a young boy as he ever had, smooth-jawed and fine featured. He poured a cup of wine and offered it to Liv.

"Wine?"

"No."

Hesitating, Jai reluctantly drank it himself. He had rarely joined the others to drink in the past, and it was strange to see it now. He sighed and leaned forward on his knees.

"There are many people in Keld," Jai said, a quiet observation. "I never imagined so many in one place. Master Lohi always told me stories of what it looked like, but now that I am seeing it for myself, it is far beyond any picture he was able to conjure."

"We only need to concern ourselves with one man after tomorrow," replied Liv. "We will not leave the Crown Prince's side."

Jai looked down at the empty cup. "Yes. The man I've been waiting for since I was born." He paused. "The king seemed pleased with us."

"We were trained by his closest advisors."

"They are his brothers," replied Jai. He looked up and fixed Liv with a strange stare. "Do you trust me with your life, Liv?"

"Yes."

Jai smiled. "When we are all old men like Master Tahmujin and Master Lohi, they will call on us to train the next *bruhai*. Though I hope we never have to return to Blackvale. I would stay here and learn more of the world. I am tired of killing rats."

"There are more than enough rats in Keld."

"And here they wear silk and parade on temple steps," Jai replied with a quiet chuckle. After a moment, he poured himself another cup of wine and drank it much faster than the first. "Tomorrow the whole world will know our names..." he shook his head. "But they will only care about one."

"The Crown Prince?"

"The Crown Prince."

Liv shrugged. "Nothing has changed. When I was a boy, that was still the only name they cared about. The world may finally find its peace in it."

"Master Lohi says the world does not know what to do with peace. I think that is true. The *bruhai* exist because of death and the threat of war. Skills like ours are useless in times of peace. We would be as useless as a blunt plowblade. Except Nin, he would thrive in it, even after everything."

"Kajen could be a farmer," replied Liv. The thought was amusing.

Jai's eyes glinted. "Only if there was a beautiful woman walking ahead of the plow."

This time, Liv accepted the wine that Jai offered him. They sat in silence until the night had worn thin into the first hour of twilight. The candle melted down to little more than a stump on the plate, and Liv retreated to his own room. Sleep, when it finally came, was a reluctant companion.

# CHAPTER THIRTY-THREE

*Today, I will choose my son.*

*- Daily chronicle of King Kinhariian*

The purple *seri* sat untouched on the stand; the wide sleeves draped nearly to the floor. It was magnificent, embroidered with golden birds of prey and drawn with a black sash at the waist. It hung over the carved wood stand in without a single wrinkle, draping down in waves of silk. Xario touched the hem of one of the sleeves, running the fine silk between his calloused fingers. The fabric snagged against his rough skin. He let it fall back to its place. He imagined the delicate strands being pulled from the cocoons, wound into fine silk thread, dyed in the barrel vats, and hours of stitches bringing each bird to life against the purple sky. It was a masterpiece wasted on him.

Xario stood wearing only thin linen pants drawn tightly about his hips. He had been in the room for far too long, undecided. But as he took one last look at the impressive *seri*, he knew he could not bring himself to wear it. His father would be displeased, but it would not be the first time.

Drawing his hair up into a tight knot on the top of his head, he pinned it with a silver coronet, one small admission to his noble rank. He pulled on his simple layered shirt, tightening the strings at the end of its billowing sleeves. He traded the linen pants for sturdier ones that matched the shirt.

Fitting the greaves against his shins, he laced them tightly, tying ornate knots behind his calves. He tied the belt around his waist with the scaled thigh guards draped down the front of his legs. He reached for the second wooden stand, where his boiled black leather cuirass hung stiffly around the arms, unlaced on one side. The dull glitter of the iron scales sewn over the leather was a pale attempt at grandeur after the richness of the *seri*, but it was the honest garb of the Legion, and it was his. Xario slipped it over his shoulders and tied the laces up from his hip to beneath his armpit. He adjusted the shoulders, the thin pads beneath the leather protecting his skin from chafing against the cloth of his shirt. The lower flaps of the cuirass hung in tightly sewn layers below his waist. He tightened the strings of his shoulder pauldrons, the layered scales clattering softly as he moved. Scaled bracers slid over his arms and the tops of his hands, and he flexed his fingers comfortably. If he was going to be chosen by the king, he would be chosen as a soldier.

After a moment of indecision, held thrall by the sudden reminder of a long-faded pain, he went to the small jewelry box on the cupboard near the back of the room. Opening it, he withdrew a small silver chain bearing a carved medallion no bigger than his thumb. The soft lines of the *illi* rune had been tapped lovingly into the silver by a master craftsman whose true talent was far beyond such a simple piece. But it had not been too simple for his mother.

Xario clasped the chain around his neck and brought the medallion to his lips, the voice of his mother drawing close with words she had spoken to a little boy with a wooden spear.

"*My great warrior, Xario... your path is your own...never lose your courage.*"

"Master Xario?"

A soft tapping at the door announced the presence of one of the servants. Xario tucked the medallion away safely beneath his armor and slid the door open. A little house servant named Doma bowed deeply when he appeared.

"Forgive me for disturbing you, Master. May I assist you in any way?"

The servants were doubtless under strict instructions to hurry him on his way to the palace. Xario reached out for the sheathed ceremonial knife and slid it deftly into his belt.

"No, I am leaving."

"Very good, my lord." She bowed again and scurried out of his way as he strode out toward the stables. The house was quiet, even the servants were hushed as they went about their tasks. The whole city was hovering, holding its breath as it waited for news of the Crown Prince. Xario knew that his name was being whispered alongside Itaki Ujo's and others, each potential choice weighed and scrutinized until they'd been reduced to little more than caricatures of themselves, actors wearing the fixed expression of their masks. Itaki the wealthy merchant's son. Xario the soldier. Lost were the nuances that made them living, breathing men. They were simply small figures swept away in the imagination of Katesh's citizens.

Xario's black mare had been brushed to a splendid gleam, and the soft dashes of pink lining the inside of her nostrils were on full display as she whinnied loudly at his approach. The tassels on her wide collar shivered as she sidestepped away from the groom holding her bridle. Xario reached up to stroke the whorl of hairs beneath her forelock, rubbing until she lowered her head with a deep sigh. He took the reins from the servant and pulled himself up into the saddle.

The ride through the streets of Keld was an uncomfortable display. Crowds of people lined the road leading up to the palace, waiting to catch glimpses of anyone passing through the gates. A few people even threw lilies down beneath the black mare's feet, and she pranced through them with her nostrils flared. Xario kept his gaze fixed on the palace, refusing to acknowledge the premature celebration of the people who considered themselves his supporters. He had seen their faces, the vendors, the dyers, the bakers, the smiths, the scribes... endless people with names and families and hopes all hinging on this day, even though many of them would live the same life no matter who succeeded King Kinhariian. They would still knead the same bread, sell the same wares, and raise their families in the shadow of the palace. How he envied them.

Xario left his mare with a stable boy and headed for the small buildings to the left of the courtyard that housed the offices of the counsellors. His father had left instructions to join him there before going into the palace. Pushing the door open, Xario stepped in, and was immediately greeted by his father's displeasure.

"Where are your robes?"

Xario straightened from his bow. "I was called to Keld as a soldier in the Legion, my lord. I would have the Council see me as one."

Counsellor Hallix circled the tall desk and faced his son, the lines in his face drawn tight. "Do you know how much gold I have drained from our coffers to make you a king? I ask nothing of you but to come before the Council dressed for the throne you will sit on. You may as well tell them all that you wish to remain beneath the canvas roof of a Legion tent for the rest of your days!" He slammed his hand down on the desk. "The support you will be shown by the nobles today is the work of years. You know nothing of what I have sacrificed, and you dare to stand here with your delusions of chivalry? Did you imagine I would be proud of you for your obstinance?"

"Forgive me, Father."

"You always ask for my forgiveness far too late," snapped Counsellor Hallix. "Perhaps I would have been better served to raise your brother to the throne."

*He would have hated you for it.* Xario waited, his arms at his sides, letting the weight of his armor root him to the floor. His father reached for his *heoja* hat, settling it atop his head like a crown.

"It is time you stopped playing a boy's games. Your duty is to serve however your country has need of you. And if I tell you that you will be king, you will do it."

Xario bowed slightly, waiting to be dismissed. His father would not wish him to speak now, there were no words Xario could say that would improve him. Counsellor Hallix returned to his chair, picking up one of the long silk envelopes and removing the letter within.

"Master Lohi finally brought his *bruhai* to the city. They are little more than boys, but they have trained well. Lohi says they have left behind any family or previous identity. We know very little, but there are at least two noble born boys amongst them."

Xario frowned. "Do you think the king would choose one of them?"

"I believe Master Lohi is capable of convincing him, yes. The Council will be angry if he chooses you because it gives more power to our house. If he chooses Itaki, it will give more power to Ujo, and the Council is not in favor of such a shift. But they will reject an unknown with lesser claim to the throne with a vengeance. But I believe Kinhariian will do what he wishes regardless of the Counsel's whims." Counsellor Hallix fixed his son with a disapproving stare. "We are balancing on a knife's edge, and the slightest mistake will see us bleed."

*If the lack of purple robes can so easily destroy us... perhaps your plans have not been so well executed after all.* "Who are the noble-born *bruhai?*"

Counsellor Hallix slid the letter back into its sheath. "One is the son of the city lord of Fethet."

Shock stole over Xario's face. "A city lord's son?"

"Master Lohi's greed knows no bounds." The counsellor's face darkened. "But he is a fool. Queen Xhen dispatched her armies to Malek to aid one of the tribes. It is innocent enough for now, but the Rukian border must be watched in case she chooses to tempt her fate. Fethet is an invaluable city. If the city lord discovers the whereabouts of his only son, I doubt he will accept it peacefully."

"Perhaps it is Master Lohi who balances on the knife's edge."

"He has lived in Kinhariian's good graces for long enough that he has no fear. He knows his poisonous craft well."

Xario placed his hand on the hilt of his ceremonial blade. "Even trained by the greatest *garatelhai* alive, these *bruhai* cannot stand against the Legion by themselves. And the Legion obeys only the king. There is a reason why the king sent for Third Hand Jaakar. He will not let anything happen."

Counsellor Hallix looked out the window toward the palace. "You would do well to lose your youthful trust in the goodwill of other men. It will not serve you here."

Third Hand Jaakar had placed soldiers along the perimeter of the Council Hall, and the gnarled old warrior himself stood near the throne, his hands clasped easily behind his back despite the stern cast to his expression. Each *garatelhai* had polished their armor and held long spears, ceremonial swords tucked into their belt sashes. The simple masks of the Legion covered their faces. It was a show of force that left no confusion as to the severity of the occasion. The king would suffer no defiance.

The High and Lesser Counsellors were closest to the throne, and the rest of the ornate room was filled with nobles and other noteworthy persons, the wealth of the city on display beneath the carved arches above. Everywhere the glitter of gems, silver, and gold garnished the finest silks in Katesh. The counsellors had left their uniforms behind for the occasion, all except Counsellor Hallix, who stood on the right side of the king's chair in the familiar deep purple robe of the High Counsel. Counsellor Bari Ujo drew the attention of the room in vibrant blue silks embroidered with sprays of white, red, and orange flowers. Near him lurked Itaki, wearing a *seri* that was just deep enough red to avoid being mistaken for the brighter crimson of the king's robe.

Xario stood on his own, cradling a fine Da'hamian rose wine in a silver cup. He sipped at it more to avoid fidgeting than out of any desire to drink. The taste of it would have normally been a source of pleasure, but it simply slid down his throat with the same ordinary comfort as water. He avoided most of the scattered conversations by lingering toward the edges of the room, but finally he was approached by an elderly woman, her graying hair held back with ornate gold combs. Her *seri* was black, denoting her age as a respected elder. A gold medallion woven from thousands of silk threads hung from her wide sash next to a shell pendant that marked her as a physician. Two male body servants followed her closely. One of them was Takkan, his white skin and hair strikingly bold against the deep blue of his woven tunic.

"Xario Hallix. My, my, what a striking figure you make looming here in the corner," said the old woman, her intelligent eyes sweeping over him. He bowed.

"High Counsellor Euha."

She regarded him coolly. "You certainly look the part of a warrior. No doubt your father intended to frighten us into supporting you. You'll find I'm not easily frightened."

The corners of Xario's mouth tipped upwards despite himself. "I am here only as a loyal warrior of the Black Legion, honored one. The king's mind is his own, as is my father's. I am the humble servant of them both."

Her eyebrows quirked up into her wrinkled forehead. "A man with his own mind can be a dangerous thing in these walls, young Hallix."

Counsellor Euha drifted away with her servants, and Xario readjusted the cup in his hands for the eighth time. His father was talking with two of the lesser counsellors near the throne, who eventually bowed deeply and moved away to a different conversation. Counsellor Hallix returned to his place, waiting for the king, and letting himself be seen on the platform above the others. Xario was exhausted just watching the intricate display of power and influence that was being played beneath the watchful eyes of the fox and wolf. If only the king's successor was chosen through a duel with blades instead of words and favors. The thought of facing Itaki Ujo with a spear in his hand gave Xario a moment of satisfaction.

The doors behind the throne opened and the king entered, his red robes flowing behind him, his gold ceremonial crown gleaming atop his head. He swept up to the throne as the gathering turned as one to face him, bowing low and holding themselves prostrate until the king announced himself.

"Rise."

Xario straightened with the rest and set his cup of wine on a tray nearby. King Kinhariian regarded his Council with an equal measure of dignity and calm indifference, a magnificent king. Master Lohi appeared at his left side, dressed in finer robes than Xario had ever seen him wear. Gold beads had been woven into his long white beard.

"By Kateshi law written by our ancestors, I am bound to name a successor by my forty-fifth year," began the king, his voice carrying through the hall. "My son, the Crown Prince Tamarikai, was murdered by a traitor. He was the son of my body and of my queen and the throne should have been his. And yet now my son walks with Sharai in the stars."

Murmured respects hummed through the hall as the counsellors and nobles lowered their heads to honor the fallen prince. Xario had been young when he had last seen the Crown Prince, but the memory of the boy who looked like a mirror image of the king had not faded. He'd had the same sharp features and noble eyes.

"I have heard the advice of my Counsel, and I have considered each name that has been brought forward. I have meditated on this day for many years, and my final will in this may not be challenged."

The room hovered, breathless and waiting. Xario clenched his fists at his sides.

"Many years ago, I gave Master Lohi and Tahmujin of the *garatelhai* a task to prepare an elite force called the *bruhai*, warriors trained for the single purpose of protecting my son. But he is gone from my side, and they will guard a new Crown Prince, bound to him by an oath in blood. They have forsaken all claim to the names and families they held, and they will protect the son I choose today."

The doors of the Council Hall opened, and Xario turned to see the *bruhai* enter. Their black armor was shot through with red and gold, and crimson cloaks flowed down over their shoulders. Each of them wore a belt of knives across his chest, a sword in his belt, and two short spears strapped to his back. The hoods of the cloaks met the edges of lifelike wolf masks, fangs glittering at the edges of the sealed mouths. They walked with the grace of men who knew the balance of every step, their weight carried like warriors on the cusp of battle. The hall went silent as the *bruhai* elicited the awe of the spectators. The inhuman faces of the masks tricked the eye, gave them an otherworldly appearance as if they had walked out of the ancient legends, deadly servants of the king.

They were seven identical warriors, the only difference visible in their height. One of them was a giant, his massive arms straining at the sleeves of his armor, his legs as large as tree trunks. Da'hamian, Xario concluded quickly. He had never seen a man of Katesh grow to such stature. One of the *bruhai* led two columns of three and stopped a few strides away from the throne. As one, the *bruhai* bowed.

"These *bruhai* speak with my voice and carry the mark of my will. They have proven their loyalty, and I will return it in kind," continued the king. "They will be my first gift to the new prince." He looked out over the crowd and found Xario.

"Xario Hallix, come."

Bearing the weight of the hundreds of eyes locked on him, Xario walked the length of the hall and approached his king. He stood near the *bruhai*, whose masks did not move even a hair's breadth toward him. Xario knelt, pressing his forehead to the floor, and rose when he was bidden. Beneath the protective shield of his armor, his heart raced, his chest painfully constricted with the knowledge that he was giving the rest of his life to a throne he did not want. But he was Xario Hallix, and he would obey.

"Years ago, I told you that one day I might ask a great service of you. Today I will call on you to fulfill the promise you made."

Xario had never forgotten the king's words in the palace garden. *"Tell me, Xario Hallix. Do you want to be a king?"* He pressed his fist against his chest in salute, the pressure easing the thudding of his heart beneath. "I am yours to command, my king."

"You have been a Tenth Leader of the Legion, and my respected commander Jaakar speaks highly of you. He has earned an honorable retirement from his role as the Third Hand of the Legion, and I am giving his title to you. Kneel."

Xario did not remember telling his body to move, but his knees reached the wood, and his head bowed. His mind whirled with shock. He saw Third Hand Jaakar hand the ceremonial spear to the king, and Kinhariian held it over his head, the blade gleaming. The words that the king spoke over him sounded as if they came from some faraway place, muffled through the ringing in his ears.

"Will you take this oath as the Hand of my Black Legion and swear your loyalty to the throne of Katesh as long as you serve? Will you lead with honor and wield your blades to protect and defend this nation?"

Xario's voice was strong, powerful, and not his own. His thoughts whirled in a shocked and adrenaline-infused haze. "I take this oath and swear my loyalty."

"Rise, Xario Hallix, as the Third Hand of the Black Legion of Katesh."

There was a smattering of applause within the Council Hall, some in enthusiastic support, others no doubt in satisfied relief. Xario barely managed to reach his feet, hoping that his weak knees and the rush of lightheadedness that brought stars to his vision were not obvious to those around him. He saw the pride in Commander Jaakar's face, the patient smile of Master Lohi. To the side of the hall, Xario saw the pleased smile of Bari Ujo, and the snake-like anticipation of Itaki behind him. He could not bring himself to look at his father. In the span of a few heartbeats, the king had liberated Xario and brought all his father's ambitions to an end. The years of waiting and the apprehension of his name being spoken as the new Crown Prince... it was all over. Relief flooded him to the core.

The king handed the ceremonial spear back to Commander Jaakar, and Xario stepped to the side, close enough to Counsellor

Hallix to feel the weight of his father's anger bearing down on him from the platform. The Third Hand of the Legion was an honor that would have been cause for celebration, but to receive it and lose the throne of Katesh would be a disgrace that the house of Hallix would suffer for decades to come. And Xario would carry the blame alone.

For the first time, Xario began to truly wonder who the king had chosen. The Ujo family was the highest of the noble houses after Hallix to have a son who could be named. But the wealth of the Ujos behind the throne would shift the power so greatly that the Council would be forced to scramble for the crumbs they left behind, and Counsellor Hallix would be in grave danger of losing his place beside the king's throne.

The king descended from the platform onto the open floor and the whispers quieted. "By our laws, if a king possesses no natural son, he will choose a prince from among the noble families. Each of these *bruhai* have left behind the names they were born to, except one."

Xario searched the masks, each violent expression frozen in the painted wood. *He is going to choose one of them!* Across the hall, Xario saw Itaki's face tighten as he realized the same.

"Seventeen years ago, a child was born to a palace slave within the walls of the fortress Blackvale, hidden there to protect the Crown Prince and to be trained as a *bruhai*. But now he will take up the place I would have given to his brother. To name the Crown Prince, I must call upon my second son."

One of the cloaks shifted through the utter silence of the room, and a *bruhai* stepped out of the column and toward the king. He reached up with one gauntlet, and released the leather strings binding the wolf to his face and pulled it away. The hood of the cloak fell behind his back over the shafts of the short spears.

Xario stared at the profile of the young man standing in front of the king, facing each other like a mirror image. The boy's clean, youthful face could not hide the perfect resemblance to the king. It was as if the Crown Prince Tamarikai had appeared as a ghost from the stars, reborn. The king's noble visage faltered for a moment as he gazed at the face of his son.

"As my successor, I name my natural son, Crown Prince Jaharaii!"

As the boy turned to face the Council Hall and the gathering caught their first true glimpse of his face, chaos erupted. Without hesitation, the six remaining *bruhai* drew their short spears and let out a guttural shout, slamming the shafts of the weapons down against the wood with a resounding boom.

Xario pressed his fist to his chest once more and knelt before the Crown Prince. Slowly, he heard the rustle of other nobles following his lead. Even Commander Jaakar and Master Lohi managed to kneel on their ancient knees.

Xario shouted along with the *bruhai* as more voices began to join them.

"Crown Prince Jaharaii! His name is worthy!"

# EPILOGUE

Syndri let her sword fall with the body of the Tladr warrior into the mud. She caught herself just before stumbling to join them, her boots slipping in the pulpy earth and viscera. Setting her foot against the Tladr's body, her arms strained to yank the blade free of the broken scale armor as rain coursed in rivulets down her gore-slicked skin. The warrior beneath her foot gagged and clutched at the ragged wound, fingers grasping at the sharp blade as her strength drained away. The sword slid free and Syndri staggered back, lifting her face to the sky as a flash of lightning lit the rolling black clouds. The Sky Clans rode hard above them, their horses' hooves thundering over the ruined battlefield below, exulting in the blood running through the rain-carved ruts spreading out across the muddy ground.

The rain was heavy, falling in thick droplets that splattered across Syndri's cheeks. She heard the splashing step of boots behind her and spun, twisting too fast and falling atop the body of the Tladr she had just killed as she knocked aside a spear thrust. The Uratar screamed at her, his face twisted with the ugliness of all warriors locked in the beast-like rage of war. Syndri grabbed for the spear shaft, but it slipped through her hand. She rolled to the side and cold mud seeped through her sleeves and pants. The toe of her right boot found purchase against a rock, and she lunged forward, wrapping her arms around the Uratar's middle and knocking him backwards. They splashed into a puddle of thick red water, and Syndri spat as the taste of earth and metallic blood spattered against her face. She dropped one of her swords and pulled her belt knife free, slicing it quickly across the Uratar's throat.

Her arms and legs betrayed her, weakness and exhaustion pulling at her, sinking her down into a muddy grave. She shook her head and pushed away from the warm body beneath her and managed to rise, refusing to give in to the heaviness weighing her limbs.

The land was littered with the bodies of the dead. Tladr, Uratar, Garhis, and Rukian lay side by side, their final breaths wasted in the mud as the summer rain fell in a relentless torrent. The broken village of the Tladr tribe sent stubborn smoke tendrils up above the burning *gats*, the rain unable to staunch the flames completely. The screams of the dying, of terrified children, and the keening wails of those who had lost all hope echoed out over the cacophony of blades and guttural cries. The Rukian soldiers had proved their worth, fighting well against the Maleki tribes with their iron maces and archer's bows. Thin arrow shafts stuck out of the ground everywhere. It was a coward's weapon, but Syndri no longer cared. She breathed in the death and the earth and the smoke and let the memory of it wash over her with the rain.

Senna was nearby, her blade trickling a crimson stream to join the tiny rivers flowing over the ground. She caught sight of Syndri and raised her sword, her shield still strapped against her left arm with the top third broken away, leaving sharp splinters behind. Less than fifty horse lengths away, Yugha was dragging the Nar Tladr out into the middle of the field by his long braid.

A young woman followed them, crying and trying to catch the

edge of Yugha's armor. One of his First Swords kicked her away. Syndri picked up her fallen sword and flexed her fingers over the grips. She stepped over the bodies in her way and headed for Yugha. The Nar Tladr was the Closed Fist of his tribe, and his brother, the Open Hand, was lying dead in his *gat* in the ruined village. Senna had broken his skull with the shield. Yugha caught sight of Syndri as she approached and waited for her, holding his prisoner tightly. Nar Tladr was not struggling, his broken arms would have afforded him little protection from the death that awaited him. The last of the Uratar tribe had fled to his village after the Garhis and Rukian army had destroyed their village and taken the head of the Nar Uratar and her husband, the Open Hand.

Yugha shoved the older man forward toward Syndri. The wails of the young woman lying in the mud grew shrill as she begged for her father's life. Syndri looked down at the Nar Tladr in contempt, letting her hatred for him and all he had done fill her tired bones with new vigor. Yugha had promised her the man's death and totem, and he had kept his word. She squinted out over the field and watched as the Garhis warband herded the last of the warriors toward the Rukian foot soldiers, who trained their arrows on the prisoners, watching for any attempt at escape.

Looking down at the face of the Nar Tladr, Syndri memorized the angle of his eyes, the wide nostrils, the thinning hair swept away from a broad forehead, the thin lips pressed into resignation. She had gazed upon a much younger face once that had mirrored it, a face covered with white paint. He had avenged his son, and she would avenge her father and the countless bones of the Garhis who lay forever entombed in the ground beneath the ruined village. She opened her mouth and let the fresh rain quench her dry tongue. She heard Senna's step behind her, strong and reassuring.

There were a thousand words running through her mind, every one falling too short of the depth of grief she had carried. So instead, she said the only words that could ever reach those depths. She reached down and pressed her hands, still carrying the hilts of her swords, against either side of the man's face, and leaned close.

"Nar Garhis."

She let the name hover between them, lingering in the man's ears. Her grip tightened as he closed his eyes. The shadowed afterlife already pulled at his spirit.

"Sabayaar."

Her voice trembled as her brother's name passed through her lips for the first time in years. It felt strange to say it, as if the name itself had been pulled back through the veil from the darkness to haunt the breath of the living. Syndri let go of the man's face and stepped back, her swords heavy in her hands. She drank in the moment, letting the names speak for themselves in the silence.

Then she swung her sword.

The lifeless body of the Nar Tladr fell to the ground. Syndri reached down and jerked the eagle totem from around his neck, closing it inside her fist. Her brother's totem pressed against her skin beneath her armor, and she waited for the relief, for the sense of vengeance to find its completion in this moment, looking down at the body of the enemy she had sworn to kill. She felt nothing.

Yugha and his warriors left to join the Rukian commander, Rahian, up on the nearby hill. Senna reached forward and squeezed Syndri's shoulder.

"It is done."

Syndri shook her head, her throat thick. *No. This is only the beginning.* Senna moved away and followed the others. The rain had faded away, leaving the skies dark with cracks of light cutting through. Syndri sat down on a rock next to the body of the Nar Tladr and withdrew a cloth from her belt. Setting her swords over her lap, she cleaned the gore from the curved blades until they were no longer tainted with the death that lay around her. She gently slid them into the sheaths at her back.

Her hand found the leather pouch tied at her waist, and she opened it, withdrawing fingers stained with white ash. Reaching up, she rubbed the ashes into her skin until the lower half of her face was covered. The bitter taste of it hovered at the edge of her mouth.

She rose to her feet and faced the north, toward the sharp spires of Ujjak and the queen who haunted the stone halls beneath the mountain.

*I will give you your war.*

To be continued in
*The Queen's Wolf*

# GLOSSARY



## KATESHI PLACES & DEITIES

**Blackvale:** an ancient fortress in the North
**Fethet:** a city near the border of Malek
**Keld:** capital city of Katesh
**Mizak:** a small city adjacent to the Black Legion camp
**Mijaro:** a large port city

**Sharai:** the creator god of Dry'llar
**Aqatar:** a cosmic being, oathsworn of Sharai
**Shaedrin:** a cosmic being, oathsworn of Sharai
**Nimaraii:** a cosmic being, oathsworn of Sharai
**Ordrath:** patron of witches and courtesans

## KATESHI WORDS/TERMS

**Bruhai:** blood sworn warriors to the king
**Garatelhai:** *telhai* warriors of high rank
**Telhai:** warriors sworn to the army of Katesh
**Gerhai:** hired warriors brought in to the army of Katesh during times of war
**Icha:** a slang term loosely translated to "silver blood"
**Kefe:** a slang term loosely translated to "stupid"
**Uban:** a citrus flavored gelatin sweet
**Kiji:** small rice cakes made with mint and jasmine
**Seri:** a long daytime tunic/jacket reaching the knees
**Sati:** a daytime tunic typically worn for daily housework
**Yabo:** an honorific for an older brother
**Ami:** an endearment for a mother
**Abi:** an endearment for a father
**Mojar:** a healer practiced in ancient healing arts
**Heoja:** a tall black hat worn by counsellors
**Yan Bhei:** a three stringed instrument
**Nyheli garhai:** translated to "forever sworn", it is a common phrase when greeting the king
**Gaja teorhei:** the memory chant, one of the earliest texts detailing the creation of Dry'llar

## MALEKI TRIBES

"

**Garhis**
**Tladr**
**Uratar**
**Angar**
**Nazra**
**Hadi**
**Gokara**
**Bao'rin**

## MALEKI WORDS/TERMS

**Aich:** an expression of exasperation or frustration
**Gat:** a hide and wood frame house
**Hiffe:** a drink made from fermented mare's milk and fig wine
**Teitei:** a term of endearment for a sister

## RUKIAN PLACES/WORDS/TERMS

**Ujjak:** capital city of Ruk
**Ka'lam:** a sect of assassins loyal to Queen Xhen
**Kul grijja:** predecessors of the Rukian people
**Kabhara:** small venom tipped knives used by the Ka'lam

## DA'HAMIAN PHRASES

**daieshek'iayejos:** witnesses to the true name
**daieshek malteogarhas'a:** the true name has been heard and witnessed

# Acknowledgments

The overwhelming sense of gratitude I feel towards the people listed here is profound. Through the past decade, this world has grown from a few notes on lined paper in between college assignments into a real, physical book. I would never be writing this page if it were not for the village of people who supported me, encouraged me, and have given feedback on this story and its predecessors. This is going to be a long list, but it's an important one, so buckle up.

My professors - Lars Johnson, Angie Johnson, and Robert Hanna - were some of the first people to see the early scribbles of world building in Dry'llar. Their passionate guidance and support set the stage for this story to exist. Thank you all so much for believing in a college kid with an untamable love of fantasy.

To Steven Erikson, whose writing and worlds lit a fire and changed my vision of what was possible in fantasy storytelling.

My dear friend Ember was an invaluable critique partner in the early stages of this book. You can all thank her for Xario's POV chapters, which became some of my absolute favorites to write.

A big thank you to Jim Wilbourne for patiently talking to me through outlines and some of the early structure of the story. We couldn't turn me into a planner or outliner. You gave it your absolute best and most supportive effort. And to Pete Wagar, who made sure my glossary wasn't a rubbish heap.

To my fellow ginger and author K.E. Andrews, thank you so much for helping me format this book. Your stories are always presented so beautifully, and I'm grateful that you took the time to help me make mine beautiful too.

My good friend and champion of indie authors, Petrik Leo, thank you so much for using your platform to help me with the cover reveal for Blood Stones!

To my proofreader, Dom, for being the eagle eyes on the continuity and grammatical correctness of the book. Thank goodness for editors. You can all thank Dom that Kasaii and Gehrin found a street corner on which to stop and eat, instead of eating the street corner.

My beta team: Andrew Mattocks (aka Wizard), Kayla, Nuclear Katie, Ty... you guys were amazing. Writing is such a vulnerable craft, and sending it out, even to a small group of people you know and trust, can be a scary thing. Thank you for your support, encouragement, and honesty.

To the incredible alpha team of Krystle Matar, John Mauro, Thiago Abdalla... all three of you are such a gift. Your friendship and enthusiasm for this story humbles me, truly. John, your willingness to jump in and find time for my story when I needed another early reader will always be appreciated.

If readers end up with Gehrin as a favorite character, that is largely thanks to Thiago, who helped me iron out his character when I was so incredibly stuck in the beginning.

And Krystle? You saw the heart of this story so quickly and embraced it wholeheartedly, and I can't thank you enough for that. Here's a stern glower from Kinhariian, just for you. Also, the boys say hi.

To my wild and wonderful children, thank you for loving your mama even when I'm lost in another world and writing stories. The three of you are the most important story I'll ever be part of.

And finally, to the innermost circle, the people without whom this author would still be anxiously doubting herself and her ability to write this book. Andrew Meredith, a dear friend and mentor who introduced me to the indie community, has remained a tireless cheerleader through the highs and the lows of this book. I could not have written this book without your encouragement picking me back up to my feet every time I wanted to give up.

My chosen sister and creative other half, Sara Ferrari. The cover on this book speaks volumes about the artist you are, and I am so grateful to have been able to watch you build that talent. Thank you for listening to all the rants, the tears, and the excited ramblings. This finished book represents so much of the creative journey we've been on for the last twenty years together. God really delivered when I prayed for a best friend.

To the love of my life, Ben Tecken. There aren't any words I could write here to fully express my gratitude and my love for you. You've been through it all, every day, walking next to me and being my anchor. You meet every creative pursuit of mine with gentle support and love, and I am so honored to be your wife.

And last but not least, to my Lord and Savior, Jesus Christ: thank you for blessing me with this love of writing and all the people that are named above. *Soli deo gloria*.

# About the Author

When I was a little sprout my epic fantasy storytelling involved small pirate and animal figurines who invaded rival lego villages. Inspired early on by the powerful storytelling of writers like Jack London, Brian Jacques, J.R.R. Tolkien, and C.S. Lewis, I was obsessed with characters I couldn't get out of my head and the possibility of worlds undiscovered.

After writing a few books, being a self-published author starting at age 14, and teaching at Young Writers' Conferences for a few years, I went to college. I married the weirdest boy I'd ever met. We now have three small humans of our own who are just as weird as we are, but much more wonderful.

Today, I'm a wife and a stay-at-home mom, but I'm still a storyteller. I write beneath the supervision of two feline overlords in a chair that is older than I am. And I wouldn't have it any other way. Pull up a chair and join the chaos. I hope you find a world here that you can't wait to go back to.

THANK YOU.

Dear reader, it is people like you that make our stories soar. Thank you for spending time in Dry'llar, it means the world to me that you chose to read my book! Books are a beautiful connection between author and reader, and your support means that I can continue writing the stories that I love.
If you enjoyed The Blood Stones, please consider leaving a review on Amazon. Every review makes a big difference! Leaving reviews for books you love is the single most supportive thing that readers can do for their favorites.

I've been dreaming of epic fantasy stories since I was very young, and I've wanted to be an author ever since. Your support means that I can continue to write. I can't thank you enough. I hope you never lose your love of stories, and that each one you read teaches you something new.
Love always,
Tori

If you want to continue to get updates on my latest books and projects, please go to my website at: Toritecken.com and sign up for my newsletter. No spam. Just the latest information on my stories and projects that I'm involved in for my favorite people. I'll see you there!